INTERVIEW WITH A TYCOON

BY
CARA COLTER

MILLS &
BOON

Published in Great Britain 2014
by Mills & Boon, an imprint of Harlequin (UK) Limited,
Eton House, 18-24 Paradise Road, Richmond, Surrey, TW9 1SR

© 2014 Cara Colter

ISBN: 978-0-263-91313-2

23-0914

Harlequin (UK) Limited's policy is to use papers that are natural, renewable and recyclable products and made from wood grown in sustainable forests. The logging and manufacturing processes conform to the legal environmental regulations of the country of origin.

Printed and bound in Spain
by Blackprint CPI, Barcelona

Cara Colter lives in British Columbia with her partner, Rob, and eleven horses. She has three grown children and a grandson. She is a recent recipient of an *RT Book Reviews* Career Achievement Award in the Love and Laughter category. Cara loves to hear from readers, and you can contact her or learn more about her on her Facebook page through her website: www.cara-colter. com.

**To all those readers
who come to visit me on Facebook, thank you!**

CHAPTER ONE

STACY MURPHY WALKER'S heart was beating way too fast. She wondered, gripping the steering wheel of her compact car tighter, how long a heart could beat this fast before it finally calmed itself out of pure exhaustion.

Or exploded, her mind, with its tendency to be overly imaginative, filled in helpfully.

But, still, she was entirely aware the slipping of her tires on the icy mountain roads was not solely responsible for the too-fast beating of her heart.

No, it was the sheer audacity of what she was doing.

Bearding the lion in his den.

A bronze name plaque, *McAllister*—in other words, the lion—set in a high stone fence, tasteful and easy to miss, told her she had arrived. Now what? She turned into the driveway but stopped before tackling the steep upward incline.

What was she going to say? *I need an interview with Kiernan McAllister to save my career as a business writer, so let me in?*

She'd had two hours to think about this! No, more. It had been three days since a friend, Caroline, from her old job had called and told her, that amidst the rumors that his company was being sold, McAllister had slipped away to his Whistler retreat.

"This story is made for you, Stacy," her friend had whispered. "Landing it will set you up as the most desired business freelancer in all of Vancouver! And you deserve it. What happened to you here was very unfair. This is a story that needs your ability to get to the heart of things." There had been a pause, and then a sigh. "Imagine getting to the heart of *that* man."

Stacy had taken the address Caroline had provided while contemplating, not the heart of *that* man, because she was done with men after all, but the humiliating fact that what had happened to her was obviously the going topic in the coffee room.

But Caroline was right. To scoop the news of the sale of the company would be a career coup for a newly set loose freelancer. To lace that scoop with insight into the increasingly enigmatic McAllister would be icing on the cake.

But more, Stacy felt landing such an important article could be the beginning of her return, not just to professional respect, but to personal self-respect!

What had she thought? That she was just going to waltz up to millionaire Kiernan McAllister's Whistler cottage and knock at his door?

McAllister was the founder and CEO of the highly regarded and wildly successful Vancouver-based company McAllister Enterprises.

And what was her expectation? That he would open his door, personally? And why would he—who had once been the darling of the media and graced the cover of every magazine possible—grant an audience to her?

McAllister had not given a single interview since the death of his best friend and brother-in-law almost exactly a year ago in a skiing accident—in a place accessible only by helicopter—that had made worldwide headlines.

Now, Stacy hoped she could convince him that she was the best person to entrust his story to.

And here was the problem with imagination.

She could imagine the interview going so well, that at the end of it, she would tell him about her charity, and ask him...

She shook herself. "One thing at a time!"

It was a shot in the dark, after all. And speaking of dark, if she did not get her act together soon, she would be driving back down this road in the dark. The thought made her shudder. She had some vague awareness that ice got icier at night!

She inched forward. She was nearly there, and yet one obstacle remained. The driveway had not been plowed of snow, and the incline looked treacherous. It was in much worse shape than the public roads had been in, and those had been the worst roads Stacy had ever faced!

At the steepest part of the hill, just before it crested, her car hesitated. She was sure she heard it groan, or maybe that sound came from her own lips. For an alarming moment, with her car practically at a standstill, Stacy thought she was going to start sliding backward down the hill.

In a moment of pure panic, she pressed down, hard, on the gas pedal. The wheels spun, and in slow motion, her car twisted to one side. But then the tires found purchase, and as her car shot forward, she straightened the wheel. The car acted as if it had been launched from a canon and careened over that final crest of the hill.

"Oh, God," she exclaimed. "Too fast!"

She practically catapulted into the courtyard. The most beautiful house she had ever seen loomed in front of her, and she was a breath away from crashing into it!

She hammered on the brakes and yanked on her steering wheel.

She'd been on a ride at the midway once that felt just like this: the car spun like a top across the icy driveway. She bumped violently over a curb, flattened some shrubs and came to a stop so sudden her head bounced forward and smashed into the steering wheel.

Dazed, she looked up. She had come to rest against a concrete fountain. It tipped dangerously. The snow it was filled with fell with a quiet thump on the hood of her car.

She sat there in shock, the silence embracing her like that white cloud of snow on her hood that was obliterating her view. It was tempting to just sit and mull over her bad luck, but no, that was not in keeping with the "new" Stacy Walker.

"There's lots to be grateful for," she told herself sternly. "I'm warm, for one! And relatively unhurt."

Relatively, because her head ached where she had hit it.

Putting that aside, she shoved her car into Reverse, hoping no one had seen what had just transpired. She put her foot down—gently, this time—on the gas, and pressed, but aside from the wheels making an awful whining noise, nothing happened. When she applied more gas, the whining sound increased to a shriek, but the car did not move.

With an edge of franticness, she tried one more time, but her car was stuck fast and refused to budge.

With a sigh of defeat, she turned the car off, rested her aching head against the steering wheel and gave in to the temptation to mull over her bad luck.

No fiancé.

No job.

Those two events linked in a way that had become fodder for the office gossip mill. And possibly beyond. Maybe she was the laughingstock of the entire business community.

At least she still had her charity work. But the sad fact

was, though the charity was so worthwhile, it limped along, desperately needing someone prominent—*exactly like Kiernan McAllister*—to thrust it to the next level.

So engrossed was she in her mulling that she shrieked with alarm when her car door was yanked open, spilling cold air into it, stealing the one thing she had been grateful for—warmth—instantly. She reared back from the steering wheel.

"Are you all right?"

The voice was deep and masculine and might have been reassuring. Except for the man it was attached to.

No. No. NO.

This was not how she had intended to meet Kiernan McAllister!

"I seem to be stuck," Stacy said with all the dignity she could muster. After the initial glance, she grasped the steering wheel and looked straight ahead, as if she was planning on going somewhere.

She felt her attempt at dignity might have failed, because he said, his voice the calm, steady voice of someone who had found another standing at the precipice, "That's all right. Let's get you out of there, and see what the damage is."

"Mostly to your garden, I'm afraid."

"I'm not worried about my garden." Again, that calm, talking-her-down-from-the-ledge tone of voice.

"Here. Take my hand."

She needed to reclaim her dignity by insisting she was fine. But when she opened her mouth, not a single sound came out.

"Take my hand."

This time, it was a command more than a request. Weakly, it felt like something of a relief to have choice taken away from her!

As if in a dream, Stacy put her hand in his. She felt it close around hers, warm and strong, and found herself pulled, with seemingly effortless might out of the car and straight into a wall of…man.

She should have felt the cold instantly. Instead, she felt like Charlie Chaplin doing a "slipping on a banana peel" routine. Her legs seemed to be shooting out in different directions.

She yanked free of his hands and threw herself against his chest, hugging tight.

And felt the warmth of it. And the shock. Bare skin? It was snowing out. How was it possible he was bare chested?

Who cares? a little voice whispered in accompaniment to the tingle moving up her spine. Given how humiliating her circumstances, she should not be so aware of the steely firmness of silky flesh and the sensation of being intimately close to pure power. She *really* should not be proclaiming the experience *delicious*.

"Whoa." He unglued her from him and put her slightly away, his hands settled on her shoulders. "Neither you nor your car appear properly shod for this weather."

He was right. Her feet were stylishly clad in a ballet slipper style shoe by a famous designer. She had bought the red slippers—à la Dorothy in the *Wizard of Oz*—when she had been more able to afford such whims.

The shoes had no grip on the sole. Stacy was no better prepared for snow than her car had been, and she was inordinately grateful for his steadying hands on her shoulders.

"What have you got on?" he asked, his tone incredulous.

The question really should have been what did he have on—since she was peripherally aware it was not much—but she glanced down at herself, anyway.

The shoes added a light Bohemian touch to an otherwise ultraconservative, just-above-the-knee gray skirt that she had paired with dark tights and a white blouse. At the last moment she had donned a darker gray sweater, which she was glad for now, as the snow fell around her. Nothing about her outfit—not even the shoes—commanded that incredulous tone.

Then, she dared glance fully at her rescuer and realized his question about what she had on was not in the context of her very stylish outfit at all. He was referring to her tires!

"Not even all seasons," he said, squinting past her at the front tire that rested on top of what had been, no doubt, a very expensive shrub. His tone was disapproving. "Summer tires. What were you thinking?"

It was terribly difficult to drag her attention away this unexpectedly delicious encounter with *the* Kiernan McAllister and focus on the question. She felt as if her voice was coming from under water when she answered.

"I've never put winter tires on my car," she confessed. "And if I were going to, it would not occur to me to do it in October. It is the season of falling leaves and pumpkins, not this."

"You could have asked for me to send a car," he said sternly.

Stacy contemplated that. *She* could have asked *the* Kiernan McAllister to send a car? In what universe? Obviously—and sadly—he was expecting someone else.

Or, was there the possibility Caroline had done more than give her an address? Did she have some kind of in with him? Had she set something up for Stacy?

That was her imagination again, because it was not likely he would be so intent on giving an interview he would send a car!

"Were you not prepared at all for mountain driving?"

"Not at all," she admitted. "I was born and raised in Vancouver. You know how often we get snow there."

At his grunt of what she interpreted as disapproval, she felt compelled to rush on. "Though I've always dreamed of a winter holiday. Skating on a frozen pond, learning to ski. That kind of thing. Now, I'm not so sure about that. Winter seems quite a bit more pleasant in movies and pictures and snow globes. Maybe I should just fast-forward to the hot chocolate in front of the fire."

Was she chattering? Oh, God, she was chattering nervously, and it wasn't just her teeth! *Shut up,* she ordered herself, but she had to add, "Humph. Reality and imagination collide, again."

Story of her life: imagining walking down the aisle, her gorgeous white dress flowing out behind her, toward a man who looked at her with such love and such longing…

She did not want to be having those kinds of treacherous thoughts around *this* man.

"I always liked this reality," McAllister said, and he actually reached out his free hand and caught a snowflake with it. Then he yanked his hand back abruptly, and the line around his mouth tightened and Stacy saw something mercurial in his storm-gray eyes.

She realized he had recalled, after the words came out of his mouth, that it was this reality—in the form of an avalanche—that had caused the death of his brother-in-law.

Sympathy clawed at her throat, as did a sense of knowing he was holding something inside that was eating him like acid.

It was a lot to understand from a glimpse of something in his eyes, from the way his mouth had changed, but this was exactly what Caroline had meant about Stacy's ability to get to the heart of a story.

For some reason—probably from the loss of her family when she was a child—she had a superhoned sense of intuition that had left her with an ability to see people with extraordinary clarity and tell their stories deeply and profoundly.

Not that McAllister looked as if he would be willing to have his story told at all, his secrets revealed, his feelings probed.

Stacy had a sudden sense if she did get to the heart of this man, as Caroline had wistfully suggested, she would find it broken.

McAllister's face was closed now, as if he sensed he had let his guard down just for that instant and that it might have revealed too much to her.

"What did you do when you lost control?" he asked her.

Of her life? How on earth could he tell? Was he has intuitive as she herself was?

But, to her relief, his attention was focused, disapprovingly, on her tires. He was still keeping her upright on the slippery ground, his hand now firmly clamped on her elbow, but if he was feeling the same sensation of being singed that she was, it in no way showed in his face. He had the look of a man who was always composed and in control.

"What did I do? I closed my eyes, and held on for dear life, of course!"

"Imagining a good outcome?" he said drily.

She nodded sadly. The collision with reality was more than evident.

He sighed, with seeming long-suffering, though their acquaintance had been extremely brief!

"You might want to keep in mind, for next time, if you lose control on ice, to try and steer into the spin, rather than away from it."

"That doesn't seem right."

"I know, it goes against everyone's first instinct. But

really, that's what you do. You go with it, instead of fighting it."

The sense of being singed increased when Stacy became
suddenly and intensely aware that, despite the snow falling in large and chilly flakes all around them, despite the
fact the driveway was pure ice, the question really should
not have been what she had on for tires—or for clothes!
That should not have been the question at all, given what
he had on.

Which was next to nothing!

Maybe she had hit her head harder than she thought,
and this whole thing was a dream. The scene was surreal
after all.

How could it be possible McAllister was out here in
his driveway, one hand gripping her firmly, glaring at her
tires, when he was dressed in nothing more than a pair of
shove-on sandals, a towel cinched around his waist?

The shock of it made her release the arm she clutched,
and the wisps of her remaining sympathy were blown away
as if before a strong wind. All that remained was awareness of him in a very different way.

She would have staggered back—and probably slipped
again—but when she had let go, he had continued to hold
on.

His warmth and his strength were like electricity, but
not the benign kind that powered the toaster.

No, the furious, unpredictable kind. The lightning-bolt-
that-could-tear-open-the-sky kind. The kind that could
split apart trees and turn the world to fire.

Stacy realized the hammering of her heart during the
slippery trip into the mountains, and after she had bounced
over the curb into the fountain, had been but a pale prelude
to the speeds her heart could attain!

CHAPTER TWO

KIERNAN MCALLISTER WATCHED the pulse in the woman's throat. The accident had obviously affected her more than she wanted to let on. Her face was very pale and he considered the awful possibility she was going to keel over, either because she was close to fainting or because her shoes were so unsuited to this kind of ground.

As he watched, her hand, tiny and pale, fluttered to her own throat to keep tabs on the wildly beating tattoo of her pulse, and McAllister tightened his grip on her even more.

"Are you okay?" he asked again. He could feel his brow furrow as he looked in her face.

He had told his sister, Adele, not to send assistance. He had told her, in no uncertain terms, that he found it insulting that she thought he needed it. She seemed to have agreed, but he should have guessed she only pretended to acquiesce.

"I think I'm just shaken."

The girl—no, she wasn't a girl, despite her diminutive size—had a voice that was low and husky, a lovely softness to it, unconsciously sexy. She was, in fact, a lovely young woman. Dark curls sprang untamed around a delicate, pale, elfin face. Her eyes were green and huge, her nose a little button, her chin had a certain defiant set to it.

Kiernan's annoyance at his sister grew.

If she had needed to send someone—and in her mind, apparently she had—he would have hoped for someone no-nonsense and practical. Someone who arrived in a car completely outfitted for winter and in sturdy shoes. In other words someone who coped, pragmatically, as a matter of course, with every eventuality. If he was going to picture that someone he would picture someone middle-aged, dowdy and stern enough to intimidate Ivan the Terrible into instant submission.

Now, he felt as if he had two people, other than himself, to be responsible for!

"You're sure you are all right?" He cast a glance at her car. Maybe he could get it unstuck and convince her to disobey his sister's orders, whatever they were, and leave him alone here.

Alone. That was what called to him these days, the seduction of silence, of not being around people. The cabin was perfect. Hard to access, no cell service, spotty internet.

His sister didn't see his quest for solitude as a good thing. "You just go up there and mull over things that can't be changed!" his sister had accused him.

And perhaps that was true. Certainly, the presence of his little nephew did not leave much time for mulling! And perhaps that had been Adele's plan. His sister could be diabolical after all.

But the woman who had just arrived looked more like distraction than heaven-sent helper, so he was going to figure out how to get her unstuck and set her on her way no matter what Adele had to say about it.

For some reason, he did not want the curly-headed, green-eyed, red-shoed woman to make it past the first guard and into his house!

He regarded her thoughtfully, trying to figure out why he felt he did not want to let her in. And then he knew. Despite the fact the accident had left her shaken, she seemed determined to not let it affect her.

Look at the shoes! She was one of those positive, sunny, impractical people and he did not want her invading his space.

When had he come to like the dark of his own misery and loneliness so much?

"Yes, I'm fine," she said, her voice, tremulous with bravery, piercing the darkness of his own thoughts. "More embarrassed than anything."

"And well you should be." The faint sympathy he had felt for her melted. "A person with a grain of sense and so little winter driving experience should not have tackled these roads today. I told her not to send you."

She blinked at that. Opened her mouth, then closed it, looked down at her little red shoes and ineffectually tried to scrape the snow off them.

"I detest stubborn women," he muttered. "Why would you travel today?"

"Perhaps it wasn't my most sensible decision," she said, and he watched the chin that had hinted at a stubborn nature tilt upward a touch, "but I can't guarantee the result would not have been similar, even on the finest summer day."

He lifted an eyebrow at her, intrigued despite himself.

"My second name is Murphy, for my maternal grandfather, and it is very suiting. I am like a poster child for Murphy's Law."

He had the feeling she was trying to keep things light in the face of the deliberate dark judgment in his own features, so he did not respond to the lightness of her tone, just raised his eyebrow even higher at her.

"Murphy's Law?"

"You know," she clarified, trying for a careless grin and missing by a mile. "Anything that can go wrong, will."

He stared at her. For a moment, the crystal clear green of those eyes clouded, and he felt some thread of shared experience, of unspeakable sorrow, trying to bind them together.

His sense of needing to get rid of her strengthened. But then he saw the blood in her hair.

Stacy could have kicked herself! What on earth had made her say that to him? It was not at all in keeping with the new her: strong, composed, sophisticated. You didn't blurt out things like that to a perfect stranger! She had intended it to sound light; instead, it sounded like a pathetic play for sympathy!

And, damn it, sometimes when you opened that door you did not know what was going to come through.

And what came through for her was a powerful vision of the worst moment of *anything that can go wrong will* in her entire life. She was standing outside her high school gym. She closed her eyes against it, but it came anyway.

Standing outside the high school waiting anxiously, just wanting to be anywhere but there. Waiting for the car that never came. A teacher finding her long after everyone else had gone home, wrapping her in her own sweater, because Stacy was shivering. She already knew there was only one reason that her father would not have come. Her whole world gone so terribly and completely wrong in an instant...left craving the one thing she could never have again.

Her family.

She had hit her head harder than she thought! That's what was causing this. Or was it the look she had glimpsed ever so briefly in his own eyes? The look that had given her the sensation that he was a man bereft?

"You actually don't look okay," he decided.

She opened her eyes to see him studying her too intently. Just what every woman—even one newly devoted to independence—wanted to hear from Kiernan McAllister!

"I don't?"

"You're not going to faint, are you?"

"No!" Her denial was vehement, given the fact that she had been contemplating that very possibility—heart implosion—only seconds ago.

"You've gone quite pale." He was looking at her too intensely.

"It's my coloring," she said. "I always look pale."

This was, unfortunately, more than true. Though she had the dark brown hair of her father, she had not inherited his olive complexion. Her mother had been a redhead, and she had her ultrapale, sensitive skin and green eyes.

"You are an unusual combination of light and dark." She squirmed under his gaze, until he tightened his hold.

"Remember Murphy's Law," he warned her. "It's very slippery out here, and those shoes look more suited to a bowling alley than a fresh snowfall."

A bowling alley? "They're Kleinbacks," she insisted on informing him, trying to shore up her quickly disintegrating self-esteem. The shoes, after all proclaimed *arrival,* not disaster.

"Well, you'll be lyin'-on-your-backs if you aren't careful in them. You don't want to add to your injuries."

"Injuries?"

Still holding her one arm firmly, he used his other—he seemed to have his cell phone in it—and whipped off the towel he had around his waist!

Still juggling the towel and the phone, he found a dry corner of it, and pressed it, with amazing gentleness, onto the top of her head. "I didn't see it at first, amongst the chocolate curls—"

Chocolate curls? It was the nicest way her hair had ever been described! Did that mean he was noticing more about her than his sack-of-potatoes hold had indicated?

"—but there's blood in your hair."

His voice was perfection, a silk scarf caressing the sensitive area of her neck.

"There is?" She peeked at him around the edges of the towel.

He dabbed at her hair—again, she was taken with the tenderness of his touch, when he radiated such a powerful aura—and then he turned the towel to her, proof.

It looked like an extremely expensive towel, brilliant white, probably Egyptian cotton, and now it had little speckles of red from her blood. Though for some reason, maybe the knock on the head, the sight of all that blood was not nearly as alarming to her as he was.

Since he had removed the towel, Stacy forced herself not to let her gaze stray from his face. Water was sliding out of the dark silk of his hair and down the utterly and devastatingly attractive lines of his features.

"You aren't naked, are you?" she asked, her voice a squeak of pure dismay.

Something twitched around the sensual line of his mouth as McAllister contemplated Stacy's question, but she couldn't really tell if he was amused or annoyed by it.

His mouth opened, then closed, and then, his eyes never leaving her face, he said evenly, "No, I'm not."

She dared to unglue her eyes from his face. They skittered over the very naked line of his broad shoulders, down the beautiful cut of chest muscles made more beautiful by the snowflakes that melted on them and sent beads of waters sliding down to the ridged muscle of washboard abs. Riding low on his hips…her eyes flew back to the relative safety of his face.

Only that wasn't really safe, either.

"Underwear?" she squeaked.

He regarded her thoughtfully for a moment. She resisted an urge to squirm, again, under the firm hands at her elbow, and his stripping gaze.

"Kleinbacks," he said, straight-faced.

She was pretty sure the designer company did not make men's underwear, and that was confirmed when something very like a smile, however reluctant, played along the hard line of those lips. Stunned, Stacy realized she was being *teased* by Kiernan McAllister.

But the light that appeared for a moment in his eyes was gone almost instantly, making her aware he had caught himself lightening up, and not liked it. Not liked it one little bit.

"Swim trunks." His voice was gravelly, amusement stripped from it.

"Oh!" She sagged with relief, then looked, just to make sure. They were really very nice swim trunks, not the scanty kind that triathletes wore. Still, there was quite a bit more of him uncovered than covered, and she felt herself turn scarlet as she watched a another snow drop melt and slide past the taut muscles of his stomach and into the waistband of his shorts.

"It doesn't really seem like swimming weather," she offered, her voice strangled.

"I was in the hot tub in the back of the house when I heard the commotion out here."

"Oh! Of course." She tried to sound as if she was well acquainted with the kind of people who spent snowy afternoons doing business from their hot tubs—he did have his phone with him, after all—but she was fairly certain she did not pull it off.

Knowing what she did about him, it occurred to her that

perhaps, despite the presence of the phone, he wasn't doing business. One thing she knew from her life interviewing high-powered execs? They were attached to those phones as though they were lifelines!

Kiernan McAllister might be entertaining someone in his hot tub.

"Alone," he said, as if he had read her thoughts.

She didn't like the idea that he might be able to read her thoughts. But there was also something about the way he said *alone* that made her think of icy, windswept mountain peaks and a soul gone cold.

Even though he was the one with no clothes on, in the middle of a snowstorm, it was Stacy who shivered. She tried to tell herself it was from snow melting off her neck and slithering down her back, but she knew that was not the entire truth.

It was pure awareness of the man who stood before her, his complexities both unsettling her and reluctantly intriguing her. His hands resting, warm and strong—dare she consider the thought, protectively—on her. How on earth could he be so completely unselfconscious? And why wasn't he trembling with cold?

Obviously, his skin was heated from the hot tub, not that he was the kind of man who trembled! He was supremely comfortable with himself, radiating a kind of confidence that could not be manufactured.

Plus, Stacy's mind filled in helpfully, he had quite a reputation. He would not be unaccustomed to being in some state of undress in front of a lady.

Impossibly, she could feel her cheeks turning even more crimson, and he showed no inclination to put her out of her misery. He regarding her appraisingly, snow melting on his heated skin, a cloud of steam rising around him.

Finally, he seemed to realize it was very cold out here!

"Let's get in," he suggested. She heard reluctance in his voice. He did not want her in his house!

She was not sure why, though it didn't seem unreasonable. A stranger plows into your fountain. You hardly want to entertain them.

But he was expecting someone. He didn't want to entertain that person, either?

"I'll take a closer look at your head. There's not a whole lot of blood, I'm almost certain it's superficial. We'll get you into Whistler if it's not."

It occurred to her he was a man who would do the right thing even if it was not what he particularly wanted to do.

And that he would not like people who did the wrong thing. She shivered at the thought. He misinterpreted the shiver as cold and strengthened his grip on her, as if he didn't trust her not to keel over or slip badly on his driveway. He turned her away from her car and toward the warmth of his house.

Aside from her car in the garden, the driveway was empty. The household vehicles were no doubt parked in the five-car garage off to one side.

The house inspired awe. If this was a cottage, what on earth did McAllister's main residence look like?

The house was timber framed, the lower portions of it faced in river rock. Gorgeous, golden logs, so large three people holding hands would barely form a circle around them, acted as pillars for the front entryway. The entry doors were hand carved and massive, the windows huge, plentiful and French-paned, the rooflines sweeping and complicated.

Through the softly falling flakes of snow, Stacy was certain she felt exactly how Cinderella must have felt the first time she saw the castle.

Or maybe, she thought, with a small shiver of pure apprehension, more like Beauty when she found Beast's lair.

McAllister let go of her finally when he reached the front door and held it open for her. She was annoyed with herself that she missed the security of his touch instantly, and yet the house seemed to embrace her. The rush of warm air that greeted her was lovely, the house even lovelier.

Stacy's breath caught in her throat as she gaped at her surroundings.

"It's beautiful," she breathed. "Like upscale hunting lodge—very upscale—meets five-star hotel."

"It suits me," he said, and then as an afterthought, "far more than my condo in Vancouver."

Again, her intuition kicked in, and this time the reporter in her went on red alert. Was that a clue that he was going to leave his high-powered life behind him as rumors had been saying for months?

McAllister turned, stepped out of his sandals, expecting her to follow him. Stacy realized she couldn't tromp through the house in her now very wet—and probably ruined—shoes. She scraped them off her feet, dropped her wet sweater beside them, and then she was left scrambling to catch up to his long strides, as it had never even occurred to him that she was not on his heels.

As McAllister led her through his magnificent home, Stacy was further distracted from the confession she should have been formulating about why she was really here, by not just the long length of his naked back but the unexpected beauty of his space and what it said about him.

The design style was breathtaking. Old blended with new seamlessly. Modern met antique. Rustic lines met sleek clean ones and merged.

There were hand-knotted Turkish rugs and bearskins,

side by side, modern art and Western paintings, deer antler light fixtures and ones that looked to be by the famous crystal maker, Swarovski. There were ancient woven baskets beside contemporary vases.

The decor style was rugged meets sophisticated, and Stacy thought it reflected the man with startling accuracy.

"I've never seen floors like this," she murmured.

"Tigerwood. It actually gets richer as it ages."

"Like people," she said softly.

"If they invest properly," he agreed.

"That is not what I meant!"

He cast a look over his shoulder at her, and she saw he looked irritated.

"People," she said firmly, "become richer because they accumulate wisdom and life experience."

He snorted derisively. "Or," he countered, "they become harder. This floor is a hundred and seventy percent harder than oak. I chose it because I wanted something hard."

And she could see that that was also what he wanted for himself: a hard, impenetrable surface.

"This floor will last forever," he said with satisfaction.

"Unlike people?" she challenged him.

"You said it, I didn't." She heard the cynicism and yet contemplated his desire for something lasting. He was an avowed bachelor and had been even before the accident. But had the death of his brother-in-law made him even more cynical about what lasted and what didn't?

Clearly, it had.

They walked across exotic hardwood floors into a great room. The walls soared upward, at least sixteen feet high, the ceilings held up by massive timbers. A fireplace, floor to ceiling, constructed of the same river rock that was on the exterior of the house, anchored one end of the room.

A huge television was mounted above a solid old barn beam mantel. It was on, with no sound. A football game in process. A wall of glass—the kind that folded back in the summer to make indoor and outdoor space blend perfectly—led out to a vast redwood deck.

Through falling snow, Stacy could see a deep and quiet forest beyond the deck and past that, the silent, jagged walls of the mountains.

To one side of that deck, where it did not impede the sweeping views from the great room, steam escaped from the large hot tub that her arrival had pulled McAllister from.

The tub seemed as if it were made for entertaining large groups of people of the kind she had written about in her former life. She had never attended a gathering worthy of this kind of space. Or been invited to one, either. As reporter, she had been on the outside of that lifestyle looking in.

The room made Stacy uncomfortably and awkwardly aware she was way out of her league here.

What league? she asked herself, annoyed. She wasn't here to marry the man! She just wanted to talk to him.

Besides, it seemed to her that a room like this cried for that thing called family. In fact, she could feel an ache in the back of her throat as she thought of that.

"Are you coming?"

She realized she had stopped and he had kept going. Now he glanced back at her, and she sensed his impatience. She was trying to savor this unexpected glimpse into a different world, and he wanted their enforced time together over!

Given that, it would be foolish to ask him the question that had popped into her mind the moment she had entered the grandeur of this room. But ask she did!

"Do you spend Christmas here?" She could hear the wistfulness in her own voice.

He stopped, those formidable brows lowered. "I don't particularly like Christmas."

"You don't like Christmas?"

"No." He had folded his arms across his chest, and his look did not invite any more questions.

But she could not help herself! "Is it recent? Your aversion to Christmas?" she asked, wondering if his antipathy had something to do with the death of his brother-in-law. From experience, she knew that, after a loss, special occasions could be unbearably hard.

"No," he said flatly. "I have always hated Christmas."

His look was warning her not to pursue it but for a reason she couldn't quite fathom—maybe because this beautiful house begged for a beautiful Christmas, she did not leave it.

"A tree would look phenomenal over there," she said stubbornly.

His eyes narrowed on her. She was pretty sure he was not accustomed to people offering him an opinion he had not asked for!

"We—" He paused at the *we*, and she saw that look in his eyes. Then, he seemed to force himself to go on, his tone stripped of emotion. "We always go away at Christmas, preferably someplace warm. We've never spent Christmas in this house."

Her disappointment felt sharp. She ordered herself to silence, but her voice mutinied. "It's never had a Christmas tree?"

He folded his arms more firmly over his chest, his body language clearly saying *unmovable*. She repeated the order for silence, but she could not seem to stop her voice.

"Think of the size of tree you could put there! And

there's room for kids to ride trikes across the floors, and grandparents to sit by the fire."

He looked extremely annoyed.

She could picture it all. Generations of family sitting in the two huge distressed leather sofas faced each other over a priceless rug, teenagers running in wet from the hot tub, eggnog on the coffee table made out of burled wood. Toys littering the floor.

Over there, in that open-concept kitchen with its industrial-sized stainless-steel fridge, the massive granite-topped island could be full of snacks, the espresso machine pumping out coffee, or maybe you could make hot chocolate in them, she wasn't certain.

"I guess in your line of work," he said gruffly, "you're allowed a certain amount of magical thinking."

What kind of work did he think she did? And why couldn't she just leave it at that?

"It's not magical," she said through clenched teeth. "It's real. It can be real."

He looked annoyed and unconvinced.

Why had she started this? She could feel something like tears stinging the back of her eyes.

"You have that about-to-faint look again," he said, coming back to her. "I think you hit your head harder than we realize."

"I think you're right," she said. She ordered herself to stop speaking. But she didn't.

CHAPTER THREE

"IF I HAD a room like this? That is what I would want to fill it with," the woman said. "The important things. The things that really last. The things that are real. Love. Family."

Real. Kiernan could tell her a thing or two about the reality of love and family that would wipe that dreamy look off her face. But why? Let her have her illusions.

They were no threat to him.

Or maybe they were, because just for a flicker of a moment he felt a whisper of longing sneak along his spine.

He shook it off. He just wanted to have a look at the bump on her head and send her on her way. He did not want to hear about her sugarplum visions of a wonderful world!

"Nothing lasts," he told her, his voice a growl.

Stacy went very still. For a moment she looked as if she might argue, but then his words seemed to hit her, like arrows let loose that had found her heart.

To his dismay, for a moment he glimpsed in her face a sorrow he thought matched his own. He was intrigued but had enough good sense not to follow up! Not to encourage her in any way to share her vision with him.

"Follow me," he said. "I think I've got a first-aid kit in my bathroom."

His bathroom? Didn't he have a first-aid kit somewhere

else? He did, but it was outside and around the back of the house, where the staging area for outdoor excursions was, where he stored the outdoor equipment.

No, it was sensible to take her to the closest first-aid kit, to keep her out of the cold, to not take her through more snow in those ridiculous shoes.

But through his bedroom? Into his bathroom? It occurred to him that he should have sat her down in the kitchen and brought the first-aid kit to her.

He was not thinking with his normal razor-sharp processes, which was understandable. He told himself it had nothing to do with the unexpected arrival of a beautiful woman in his fountain and everything to do with Ivan.

He hesitated at the double doors to his master suite and then flung them open and watched her closely as she preceded him. He saw the room through her eyes, which were wide and awed.

The ceiling soared upward, magnificent and timber framed. But here the floors, instead of being hardwood, were carpeted with a thick, plush pile that their feet sank into. There was a huge bed, the bedding and the abundance of pillows in a dozen shades of gray.

She was blushing as she looked at the bed, which he should have found amusing as all get-out. Instead, he found it reluctantly endearing.

Who blushed anymore?

Something that heightened color in her cheeks, the way she caught her plump lower lip between her teeth, made Kiernan's mouth go dry, and so he led her hastily through to the bathroom. Again, he saw it through her eyes. A wall of windows opened to the deck and hot tub area.

There was a shower a dozen people could have gotten into, and her blush deepened when she looked at that.

He'd never shared this room with anyone, but let her

think what she wanted. It might keep him safe from this niggling awareness of her that was bugging him the way a single gnat could spoil a perfect summer day on the hammock with a book.

She stared at the deep, stand-alone tub and swallowed hard. While the shower might hold dozens, it was more than evident the tub could only comfortably fit two! Her eyes flitted wildly around the room and then stopped and widened.

Her eyes, he noticed, annoyed with himself, were green as the moss that clung to the stones of the hot spring deep in the mountains behind this cottage.

"That is not a fireplace," she whispered. "In your bathroom?"

"You want it on?" he asked innocently. "Are you cold?"

He was fairly sure it was evident to even her, with her aura of innocence, that a fireplace like that was not about cold but about romance.

And yet he did not like thinking about her in that light. It was evident to him, on a very brief acquaintance, she was not the type of woman who would share his vision of romance.

For him, it was a means to an end, the age-old game of seduction.

The remarks about his floors and the suitability of his room for a Christmas tree were little hints she was not his type. By her own admission, she was the kind of girl who believed in love and things lasting.

Romancing a girl like her would be hard work! He was willing to bet, despite her awe of the room, it would require something a little less superficial than a bathtub and a fireplace. Romancing a girl like her would require time and patience and a willingness to be a better person.

No, he would stick with his type. Because his type required nothing of him but a few baubles and some good times, no real emotional engagement.

He had always been like that, avoiding emotional attachment. He had been like that before his friend Danner had died. Kiernan had a sudden unwelcome memory of Christmas ornaments being smashed. He suspected the memory had erupted out of nowhere because Murphy here had seen Christmas in a room where it had never been. Kiernan's early life had always been threaded through with the tension of unpredictability, Christmas worse than most times of year.

For a while, having survived the minefield of his childhood, Kiernan had enjoyed the illusion of complete control. He had a sense of making not just his world safe and predictable, but that of his sister, Adele, too.

Yup, he had felt like quite the hero. And then Danner had died. Plunging him into a dark place where his real power in the world seemed horribly limited, where hope and dreams seemed like the most dangerous of things.

And none of that fit with a girl like this, who, whether she knew it or not, wore dreams on her sleeves. Who, despite—if her eyes were any indicator—having gone a round or two with life, seemed to still have that inexplicable ability to believe...

"Sure," she said after a moment, startling him out of his thoughts. "Put it on. The fireplace." She giggled. "I may never pass this way again."

"We can only hope," he muttered, and saw her flinch, the smile die, the words striking her like arrows again.

Just a reminder of how she was soft and he was hard, a reason this was never going anywhere, except him standing on the stairs seeing her off as she drove away.

"Nothing personal," he said. "It just wasn't my idea for you to come. I don't need you."

Having done quite enough damage—he really should not be allowed around these sensitive types—Kiernan turned from her and flicked a switch so that the flames within the fireplace licked to life.

"I've changed my mind," she said proudly. "I don't care to have it on."

See? In very short time his abrasive self was managing to hurt her. Not making any effort to hide his impatience, Kiernan flicked the fire back off and gestured at an upholstered chaise.

Once she was settled, he came back, towered over her and studied the top of her head. "I'm just going to clean it first. We'll see what we've got. Ironic, isn't it, that I'm rescuing you?"

"In what way?" she stammered.

"You're supposed to be rescuing me."

Stacy studied Kiernan and realized his tone was deeply sardonic. Despite the glimpses of shadows she had detected in his eyes, she was not sure she had ever seen a man who looked less like he would appreciate rescuing than Kiernan McAllister!

He was bigger in real life than photos had prepared her for, the breadth of his shoulders blocking out the view of the fireplace!

The bathroom was huge, but with him leaning over her, his real-life stature left her feeling shocked. Even though Kiernan McAllister had graced the covers of zillions of magazines, including, eight times, the one she no longer worked for, nothing could have prepared her for him in this kind of proximity.

Pictures, of course, did not have a scent clinging to them. His filled her nostrils: it was as if he had come, not from a hot tub, but from the forest around this amazing house. McAllister smelled richly of pine, as if he had absorbed the essence of the snow-laden trees through his pores!

He was considered not only Vancouver's most successful businessman, but also its most eligible bachelor, and here in the bathroom with him, his scent filling her senses, his hands gentle on her injured head, it was easy to see why!

In each of those photos that Stacy had seen of him, McAllister was breathtakingly handsome and sure of himself. Behind that engaging smile, he had oozed the confidence and self-assurance of the very successful and very wealthy. His grooming had always been perfect: smooth shaven, every dark hair in place, his custom-made clothing hinting at but not showing a perfect male body.

In those pictures, he looked like a man who could handle anything the world tossed at him, smile and toss it right back.

And that's what he had a track record for doing. From daring real estate deals to providing start-up funds for fledgling companies that no one else would take a risk on, McAllister had developed a reputation as being tough, fair and savvy. In the business world, his instincts were considered brilliant.

Not to mention that, with his amazing looks, McAllister was that most eligible bachelor that every unmarried woman dreamed—secretly or openly—of landing.

And McAllister had availed himself to every perk his considerable fortune allowed him. He had squired some of the most beautiful and famous women in the world on that arm that Stacy had just touched.

But, despite having it all, he seemed driven to more, and he had as casually sought danger as some men would sample a fine wine.

And it was that penchant for the adrenaline r[...]
had led from *that* McAllister to this one.

Being able to watch him while he tended her head[...]
could see his silver-gray eyes were mesmerizing and[...]
different in some fundamental way from how he appear[...]
in pictures.

Her mind grappled to figure out what that difference
was, but the distraction of his near nakedness, the luxury
of the bathroom and his hands on her head were proving
formidable.

"Ouch."

"Sorry."

She deliberately looked at the floor instead of up in[...]
his face to break the trance she was in. Instead, it felt [...]
intimate and totally inappropriate that Stacy coul[...]
naked length of his lower legs. His feet were t[...]

And, she thought, entirely sexy.

But she didn't find feet sexy. Did she?

Since his feet provided no mo[...]e re[...]
rible war of sensation going o[...] within[...]
her gaze away from his toe[...] and bac[...]
Despite his disheveled [...]ppearan[...]
fectly groomed for [...]agazine[...]
a cowlick at the b[...]ck of hi[...]
jut of that formidable [...][...]
kers—when Stacy look[...]
low a gulp of pure intim[...][...]

Kiernan McAllister ra[...]
not be tarnished by arr[...]
dripping wet and wi[...]
though her job at [...]
viewing dozens o[...]
was not sure sh[...]
ample of pure [...]

llister's wet hair, the color of just-brewed coffee,
rling at the tips. The stubble on his face accentu-
he hard, masculine lines of his features.

he out-of-the-storm look of his hair and being un-
aven gave him a distinctly roguish look, and despite his
tate of undress, he could have been a pirate relishing his
next conquest, like a highwayman about to draw his sword.

His eyes were a shade of silver that added to her sense
that he could be dangerous in the most tantalizing of ways.

In the pictures she had seen of him, his eyes had intrigued, a faint light at the back of them that she had interpreted as mischievous, as if all his incredible successes
in the business world were nothing more than a big game
and it was a game that he was winning.

But, of course, that was before the accident where his
brother-in-law had been killed.

There was the difference. Now McAllister's eyes had
mething in them as shattered as glass, cool, a barrier
t he did not want penetrated.

y someone looking for a story. In that moment, Stacy
Caroline had not set up anything for her. And she
ew, without asking, he would turn her down flat if
ested an interview.

pped back from her, regarded his handiwork on
"I think we're done here," he said, evidently
h his first-aid skills.

again offered his hand. She took it and he
m the chair. She relished the feeling of his
t her go as soon as she was standing. She
the mirror. It was much worse than she

s almost completely covered with
gauze.

el like the poster child

for Murphy's Law. Everything that could go wrong, *had*. Who wanted to look like this in the presence of such a devastatingly attractive man?

Even if he was sardonic. And didn't believe in Christmas. Or love.

"That's going to be murder to get off," she said, when she saw he had caught her dismayed expression.

"Isn't it?" he said, apparently pleased that his handiwork was going to be so hard to remove.

She sighed. It was definitely time to set him straight about who she really was and what she wanted. She took a deep breath.

The phone that he had set on the counter began to ring.

Only it was the oddest ring she had ever heard. It sounded exactly like a baby squawking! There was no way a man like McAllister picked a ringtone like that!

In a split second, Kiernan McAllister went from looking relaxed and at ease with himself to a warrior ready to do battle! Stacy watched his face grow cold, remote, underscoring that sense of a solider being ready for whatever came next.

"What on earth?" she whispered, taking in his stance and his hardened facial features. "What's the matter?"

"It's time," he said, his tone terse. "He's awake."

"Who's awake?"

McAllister said nothing, his gaze on the phone, his brow furrowed in consternation. If he were a general, she had the feeling he would be checking his weapons, strapping on his armor, calling out his instructions to his soldiers.

"That isn't a cell phone, is it?" Stacy asked slowly. McAllister was staring at it as if he was a tourist in some exotic place who had discovered a snake under his bed.

The squawking sound escalated, and McAllister took a deep breath, squared his shoulders.

"A phone?" he asked, his voice impatient. "What kind of person has a phone in the hot tub?"

In her career she had met dozens of men who she did not doubt took their phones everywhere with them, including into their hot tubs! Now, she could see clearly he would not be one of them.

"Cell phones don't work up here. The mountains block the signal. I think it's part of what I like about the place." He frowned as if realizing he had told her something about himself he didn't want to.

That he needed a break from the demands of his business. He was no doubt the kind of driven individual who would see some kind of failure in that.

But before she could contemplate that too long, the phone made that squawking sound again, louder.

"What is it then, if it's not your phone?"

"It's the monitor," he said.

"The monitor," she repeated.

"The baby monitor," he said, as if she had not already guessed it.

She stared at it with him, listened to the squawking noises emitting from it. The monitor was small and state-of-the-art, it looked almost exactly like a cell phone.

But if was definitely a monitor, and there was definitely a baby on the other end of it!

CHAPTER FOUR

BABY?

Stacy prided herself on the fact that she had arrived prepared! She knew everything there was to know about Kiernan McAllister.

And he did not have a baby!

McAllister folded his arms across the breadth of his naked chest and raised that dark slash of an eyebrow at her. "I told you, you were rescuing me, not the other way around."

"Excuse me?" Stacy said, dazed by this turn of events.

"Your turn to ride to the rescue, though I must say, you haven't exactly inspired confidence so far." He reached out and turned down the volume on the monitor, inspecting her anew, like a general might inspect a newly enlisted person before sending them into battle.

His voice was hard-edged, and faintly amused as he regarded her, and she was struck again that, despite his words, he was the man least likely to need a rescue of any sort. Even if he did need one, he would never ask for it!

"I'm riding to your rescue?" Stacy asked, just to clarify.

It was a good thing he seemed to be being sarcastic, because it would be terrible to break it to him that she was the least likely person to count on for a rescue, her own life being ample evidence of that.

"Just like the cavalry," he said, and cocked his head at her blank expression. "I'm stranded. The fort is under full attack. I have no bullets left. And in rides the cavalry."

"Me?" she squeaked. "I'm the cavalry?"

He eyed her with doubt that appeared to mirror her own, then sighed again. "You are the nanny Adele insisted on sending, aren't you?"

The nanny!

Stacy realized Caroline had not called and set something up for her. Far from it! *A nanny. Kiernan McAllister was expecting a nanny!* That's who he would have sent a car through the snowy day for!

Fortunately, Stacy was saved from having to answer because he turned and held open the door of the bathroom for her.

"That way," he said. "To the guest room. You can help me temporarily, until I get your car looked after."

In a daze, she turned left and went down the hall ahead of McAllister.

His voice followed her, his tone mulling. "I thought he would sleep longer. He has barely slept since he got here. Who would have thought that one small baby could be so demanding? He doesn't sleep. And he doesn't want to eat. You know what he does?"

Again, he didn't wait for an answer.

"He cries." His voice was lowered, and she thought she detected the slightest admission he might be in over his head. "Not that I couldn't handle it. But, if my sister thinks I need saving, who am I to argue?"

Stacy swallowed hard. What was it about the thought of saving a man like him that made her go almost weak with wanting? But, despite what his sister thought, the look on his face made it very apparent he did not agree!

That was the *old* her that would have liked him to *need*

her, Stacy reminded herself sternly. The old her: naive and romantic, believing in the power of love and hoping for a family gathered in a big room around a Christmas tree.

Obviously, McAllister did not need saving. She had rarely seen a man so self-assured! What man could stand outside dripping wet and barely clothed and act as if nothing was out of the ordinary?

Still, there was that look in his eyes…defiant, daring her to see need in him! Foolishly it made her want to turn toward him, run her hand over the coarse stubble of that jaw and assure him that, yes, she was there to rescue him and that everything would be all right.

Instead, she kept moving forward until she came to an open door and peered inside. There was a playpen set up in the room, and in it was a nest of messy blankets and stuffed toys.

Holding himself up on the bumper, howling with indignation and jumping up and down, was the most beautiful baby she had ever seen. He looked like he was a little over a year, chubby, dark hair every which way, completely adorable in pale blue sleepers that had the snaps done up crooked.

Was he McAllister's baby? While a secret baby would have been the story of the century, her thoughts drifted way too quickly from story potential to far more treacherous territory.

What on earth was Kiernan McAllister doing with a baby when that was what she had always wanted?

It caught her off guard and left her reeling even more than spinning her car into his front garden had!

We want such different things, her ex-boyfriend, Dylan, had said with a sad shake of his head, dismissing her dreams of reclaiming a traditional life like the one she had grown up in as a life sentence of dullness.

Their last night together, the extravagant dinner had made Stacey think he was going to offer her an engagement ring.

Instead, she had been devastated by his invitation to move in with him!

Really, his defection had been the last straw in a life where love had ripped her wide open once too often. To add to the sting of it all, they had worked in the same office, he her direct superior, and she had been let go after their breakup, which she—and everyone else at the office—knew was entirely unfair.

Still, in the wake of her life disasters, Stacy had made up her mind she would be wounded by love and life no more! But now the yearning inside her caused by seeing that Christmas-perfect great room, and now by thinking of this man before her with a baby, only made her realize how much work she had yet to do!

Though why, when she knew how much work she had to do, her eyes would go to McAllister's lips, she could not be certain. McAllister's lips were full and bold, the lower one in particular spine-tinglingly sensual.

Dangerous, she told herself. He was a dangerous kind of man. His lips should be declared the pillars of salt one should never look at for danger of being lost forever. She was stunned by both the peril and intensity of her thoughts.

She was not, after all, who he was expecting, and she was certainly not a qualified nanny.

But she felt as if she *had* to know the story of the baby.

And McAllister—despite the outward appearance of confidence—was obviously desperate for help in this particular situation.

And if she could give him that even temporarily, McAllister might be much more amenable to the real reason she had come!

Gratitude could go a long way, after all.

The baby was startled into silence by her appearance. He regarded her with deep suspicion.

As if he knew she was trying to pass herself off as something she was not.

He seemed to make up his mind about her and began to whimper again.

"Ivan, stop it!" McAllister ordered.

The baby, surprisingly, complied.

"Ivan," she said, and walked over to the baby. "Hello, Ivan."

The baby appeared to reconsider his initial assessment of her. He smiled tentatively and made a little gargling noise in his throat. Her heart was lost instantly and completely.

"You don't know my nephew's name?" McAllister asked, startled. "It's Max."

She glanced back at McAllister. His arms were folded over his chest, and he was regarding her with suspicion identical to the baby's seconds earlier.

His nephew. The blanks were filling in, but all the same it was unraveling already. Stacy was going to find herself tossed unceremoniously out into a snowbank beside her car and, really, wasn't that what she deserved?

"Aren't you his nanny?" McAllister demanded. "That's who I was expecting."

"I'm Stacy," she said, drawing in a deep breath. "Stacy Murphy Walker." Now would be the perfect time to say who she really was and why she was here.

Tell him the rest of it. But her courage was failing her. So much easier to focus on the baby!

"Uppie? Pwweee?"

And it did feel as if this baby—and maybe Kiernan, too—really needed her. And it felt as if she needed to be in this house that cried for a Christmas tree and a family to encircle it.

She reached into the playpen. The baby wound his chubby arms around her neck, and she hoisted his surprisingly heavy weight. He nestled into her and put his thumb in his mouth, slurping contentedly.

"I'm not exactly your nephew's regular nanny," she heard herself saying, "but I'm sure I can help you out. I'm very good with children."

She told herself it wasn't precisely a lie, and it must have been a measure of McAllister's desperation that he seemed willing to accept her words.

He regarded her and apparently decided she was a temp or a substitute for the regular nanny, which would also, conveniently, added to the bad roads, explain the delay in her arrival. After scrutinizing her for a moment, he rolled his broad shoulders, unfolded his arms from across his chest and looked at her with undisguised relief.

"I'm Kiernan McAllister."

"Yes, I know. Of course! Very nice to meet you." She managed to get one arm out from under the baby's rump and extended it, not certain what the protocol would be for the house staff. Did you shake the master's hand?

He crossed the room to her and took her extended hand without a second's hesitation, but she still knew extending hers had been a mistake. She had felt his hand already as he helped her from the chaise in his bathroom.

Despite the fact that his hand was not the soft hand of an office worker or of her comrades in writing, but hard and powerful, taking it felt like a homecoming.

And if she thought the mere sight of his lips had posed a danger to her, she could see his touch was even more potent. A homecoming to some secret part of herself, because something about his hand in hers sizzled and made her aware of herself as smaller than him.

And feminine. Physically weaker. Vulnerable in some way that was not at all distressing, though it should have been to a woman newly declared to total independence and a hard-nosed career as a freelancer.

She yanked her hand out of his and felt desperate not to give him the smallest hint of her reaction to him. "And just to clarify, is your nephew Ivan or Max?"

"Max. I just like to call him Ivan."

Stacy looked askance at him.

"As in Ivan the Terrible," he muttered.

She could feel disapproval scrunch her forehead—a defense against the electric attraction she felt toward him—and something like amusement crossed McAllister's features as he regarded her, as if he was not even a little fooled.

Annoyingly, the light of amusement in his eyes made him look, impossibly, even more attractive than before!

"But his name is really Max." He cocked his head. "I guess that works, too, if you think about it. He's Max everything. Max noisy. Max sleepless. Max filthy, at the moment. He's just over a year. A horrible age, if there ever was one."

"He's adorable," she declared.

"No. He's not in the least."

"Well, he is right now. Except, he might need changing—

"Never mind! If he needs *that,* you *have* arrived in the nick of time. And while you look after it I will do the manly thing, and go look after your car. You can change his nappy and then be on your way."

Well, there was no need to tell him the truth if she was leaving that quickly!

He made the declaration of assigning them duties with such abject relief that Stacy tried to bite her lip to keep from laughing.

It didn't work. It was probably, at least in part, a delayed reaction to her accident, but a little snort of laughter escaped past her clamped lips. And then another one.

McAllister glared, and more laughter slipped out of her. It seemed to her it was the first time since the disintegration of her relationship that she had had anything to laugh about.

The baby chortled, too, and it made her laugh harder.

"Sorry," she said, trying to bite it back. "Really. Sorry."

Here she was, an imposter in a complete stranger's home, so it must be nerves making the laughter bubble within her. Whatever it was, the more she tried to repress it, the more it burbled out of her, free.

"Are you laughing *at* me?" Kiernan McAllister, master of the house, asked her dangerously.

"No," she said, through giggles. "No, of course not."

"I don't believe you."

"All right," she gasped, wiping an amused tear from her eye, "it does strike me as a little funny that you would be afraid of a baby's diaper."

"*Fear* is completely the wrong word."

"Of course. Completely."

"I'm quite capable of doing whatever needs to be done."

"Yes, I can see that."

"I have been doing what needs to be done. And will continue to do so after you've gone back to Vancouver. You can report to my sister that I am more than a match for a baby."

She nodded. A giggle escaped her. The baby chortled. "So, we've settled it," she said, striving to be solemn. "It's not fear."

Kiernan McAllister glared at her, then the baby, then her again.

"*Aversion* is probably a better word. Not to Ivan himself, but to what Ivan can do."

"Do?"

"Doo."

"Oh." She caught his meaning and tried to bite her lip against the deepening of her laughter. It didn't work. A new little snicker escaped her.

"It's Murphy's Law," he said, frowning at her snicker. "In the changing-a-baby department, I learned something very quickly. I've always been a quick study."

That she did not doubt! "And what did you learn?" she asked.

"Anything that can go wrong, will."

She really did laugh then, not even trying to hold back. McAllister glared at her but could not hide his relief that the stinky baby was in her arms and not his.

Still, he squared his shoulders and said firmly, "You can help me with this one thing, and I will look after your car. Then you can leave."

And without another word, casting her one more warning look that said he was without fear, his chin tilted up at a proud angle, he turned on his heel and left the room.

"And that," she explained to Ivan, "is your uncle, the warrior."

CHAPTER FIVE

KIERNAN COULD HEAR the nanny's light laughter follow him out of the room. Despite the fact it was directed at him, the sound was as refreshing as sitting beside a cold brook on a hot afternoon.

And besides, she was right, and it probably was funny. He was a man who had a reputation for not being afraid of anything. From daring business deals to bold adventures, he had always tackled life pretty fearlessly.

At great cost, a voice told him, but he turned it off, savagely.

He went down the hall and into his bedroom to get dressed. The scent of the nanny—like lemon drop candies—tickled his nostrils. Why was he so aware of her?

When she had picked Max up, the look on her face had been completely unguarded. And she had looked radiant. It had been a Madonna-with-child moment, breathtaking in its purity. And it had moved Stacy Murphy Walker from button cute to beautiful in a stunning blink of the eye.

Kiernan had been taken by surprise by how cute the nanny was from the moment he had plucked her out of her car.

Stacy was not what he'd expected from a nanny at all. What he'd expected was someone like that famous nanny on television: stout and practical, certain of her own authority in the baby department, possibly bossy. Or perhaps, he'd expected an older woman with gray hair in a neat bun, and granny glasses.

What he had not been expecting was a young woman with dark chocolate coils of hair, skin as pale as the inside of a white rose petal and astounding green eyes, as deep and moody as the waters of a mountain pond. He had certainly not expected the nanny to show up in a toy car, whimsical red shoes and skirt that, given how conservative it was, made his mouth go dry.

Attractive women in his world were the proverbial dime a dozen. He'd dated models and actresses, as world renowned for their looks and style as he was for his business acumen.

Somehow, next to her, those women didn't seem quite *real*.

It wasn't just that the nanny was smart that set her apart, though it was more than evident she was, because he'd been around and dated plenty of very smart women, too, business associates and CEOs.

Again, in a very short time, the nanny had made them seem not quite real.

It was because of that moment in the great room, when he had watched her look around with such wistfulness, it felt as if he had seen straight to her soul. And then when she had picked up the baby…radiance.

McAllister had experienced many of the wonders of the world. He had frolicked on beaches and conquered mountain slopes, and ridden zip lines through the rain forest. He had seen lions in the jungle and ridden a camel through the desert.

He had been at the premieres of movies and plays, attended symphonies, eaten at some of the best restaurants in the world and sampled some of the most exquisite wines.

He had shared exhilarating adventure and great moments with friends.

And still for all that each of those experiences had given him that incredible feeling—the sensation of being alive tingling along his very skin—McAllister did not feel as if he had ever experienced anything quite as pure as the radiance that lit the nanny's face when she picked up the baby.

Why was he so stunned by his reaction to her? Because, he realized, he *had* reacted. It was the first time in a year that he had felt a stirring of interest in anything.

But worse, he had been totally caught off guard by the way the look in her face, even her mention of how a Christmas tree would be in his great room, had filled him with a sense of yearning.

Yearning.

He had not allowed himself to feel that since he was a child, when every single thing you hoped for just set you up for huge disappointments.

Simple yearnings back then: *normal* topping his list.

Kiernan shook himself. This was *not* him. Of course, the circumstances were no doubt to blame for the lack of discipline he was exercising over his own mind. Twenty-four hours of terror at the hands of his nephew, ending with the crashing sound of the nanny's car, and then having to rescue her from the garden had shaken his well-ordered world ever so slightly.

He had gone into rescue mode, bringing his defenses— already battered by the unexpected tribulations of caring for a baby—down yet another notch.

It seemed impossible that only yesterday, Kiernan had been in a completely different world. He'd been in his boardroom at a presentation being given by one of his top associates.

Mark had been one of his best friends, once. Now, he

could barely look at him, because he had been there that day, a witness to Kiernan's worst moment, a moment of colossal and catastrophic powerlessness.

Mark was talking about a new real estate development, a tower that combined retail outlets, offices and condos on a piece of property Kiernan's company, McAllister Enterprises, had recently acquired in a posh and trendy downtown neighborhood of Vancouver.

Kiernan had willed himself to focus on Mark. To pay attention. Kiernan was, when all the fancy titles were taken away, still the boss. He needed to care.

His attitude was probably why rumors were beginning to swirl that he had put the company up for sale.

His gaze had drifted out the window to the typical fall coastal weather. The skies were leaden, and raindrops slid, like plump drops of mercury, down the floor-to-ceiling glass of the boardroom window. Through a maze of office buildings and a haze of low cloud, he could just see the jutting outlines of the mountains.

A year.

It had been almost a year to the day.

They said time healed all wounds, and for a while, Kiernan had clung to that, like a man lost at sea clinging to a single bobbing piece of wood.

But the truth was that he'd felt the agony as sharply as the day it had happened. There was a dark place within him, contained, but it felt as if it was taking every bit of his strength to keep the lid on it.

If he ever gave up, if he let the lid off what had been in him since the day his friend died, it would ooze out, sticky and black, like melted asphalt. It felt like it would ooze out and fill him, bit by bit, until there was not a bit of light left.

"Mr. McAllister?"

He'd started. His personal assistant, the ever-competent

Miss Harris, had come into the room without him even noticing. Then she'd been at his shoulder, leaning over, whispering something about an urgent matter needing his immediate attention.

"Mr. McAllister?"

Miss Harris had *that* look on her face. It was the same look he saw on his sister's face and on the faces of his business associates, his staff, his colleagues, Mark. Concern, these days tinged with exasperation.

Kiernan interpreted it as: get with it. Wake up. *Come back to us.*

But he was not sure he could, not when it was taking everything he had to keep the lid on the box within him that contained enough darkness to completely obliterate light.

Relieved to be leaving the boardroom, and Mark, who looked at him with sadness he could not stand—he nodded his apologies, got up and followed Miss Harris out the door.

Miss Harris's voice sounded as if it was coming from underwater. *Left him here...were you expecting him...you forgot to tell me.*

They walked down the thickly carpeted hallways of his empire until they came to a smaller boardroom, across the hall from his own office.

He glimpsed inside the slightly ajar door to his domain.

Once, that room, with its priceless art, hand-scraped floors, fireplace and huge TV hidden behind a secret panel, had whispered to him smugly, *You have arrived.*

Now his victories felt hollow.

Miss Harris had opened the boardroom door and stood back to let him by. The smell that tickled his nostrils should have warned him he was not going to like what he found.

Still, his mind was struggling to categorize that smell

against the backdrop of understated posh decor of this room when he passed through the door and froze.

There was a baby in one of those carrier things, the kind with the plump padding and the handle. The carrier thing was dead center of the boardroom table. The baby's furious kicking of his stout limbs seemed to be fanning the aroma into every corner of the room.

All babies looked identical to Kiernan, but he knew exactly who this one was—Max.

His cherubic facial features had nearly disappeared behind a wall of chocolate. At least, given the stench in the air, Kiernan hoped it was chocolate.

A secretary, no doubt pressed into unwilling service, cast a nervous look at Miss Harris, and at Miss Harris's nod, which Kiernan caught out of the corner of his eye, bolted from her seat and scurried past Kiernan with a whispered "Mr. McAllister."

The young secretary had an expression on her face comparable to a peasant woman escaping the hordes of Genghis Khan.

"What the hell?" Kiernan said. "Where's Adele?"

Miss Harris stared at him. "She left him. She said she arranged it with you."

His sister, Adele, could not seriously think he was in any way suited to be a caregiver to her baby!

She had not arranged anything with him! Kiernan realized things slipped his mind these days, but he knew this was not one of those things. He would never agree to take Max, and Adele knew that, too.

But they were approaching that sad anniversary. He did remember Adele saying she needed some time to herself.

He did remember agreeing with her.

"What exactly did she say?"

"Something about you taking him to the cottage in

Whistler," Miss Harris said, consulting her ever-present notepad. "For a week. And not to worry. She's sending a nanny up to meet you there tomorrow."

He suppressed a groan and smelled a rat, as well as the other things in the room. Adele was plotting, using her child to try to get him back to the land of the living.

Her trust in him seemed entirely undeserved, especially when he reacted to the Max's screwed-up face.

"What are you doing?" Kiernan asked Max sternly. *Here,* he added silently.

But in the end, he had packed the baby into the car seat Adele had provided, texted her a stern *no nanny* while he still had cell service and driven to the cottage, because he knew how much he owed Adele and this baby.

It was his fault his sister did not have a husband, his fault the baby did not have a dad.

Still, it was hard to believe he had committed to looking after the baby only twenty-four hours ago.

It felt like a different lifetime.

And he was so exhausted it had made him vulnerable to the radiance in the surprisingly lovely nanny's face.

Now, bending over her car, already disappearing under a heap of white from the heavily falling snow, he brushed at the tires and looked at the tread, annoyed. They weren't even particularly good *summer* tires.

He was annoyed his mind was still on her, despite the fact he was out here and had things to do. He tried to figure out exactly what it was in her face that had triggered something in him.

And then he identified what that something was. When she had been able to visualize a Christmas tree in his great room, when she had lifted that baby?

He had felt hope.

Of course, she would not carry a burden of guilt the

way he did. His fault, entirely, that he and his brother-in-law had been there that day.

And when he relived that moment, which he did often, of that wall of snow sweeping down on them? He was always aware that he could or should have done something different. He was always aware that it *should* have been him instead of the man who had so much more to lose, who had left the world with a fatherless baby.

Somehow, McAllister's genuine and startling enjoyment of a pretty girl's radiant face felt like the worst threat of all.

After all, wasn't hope the most dangerous of all things?

So, here was the question. Did he walk toward the light he had seen in her face? Or did he walk in the other direction as quickly and as firmly as he could?

Away, he decided. He was, above all things, good at making decisions. He made them quickly and decisively, and he never looked back.

He was unsticking her car and sending her on her way. He frowned at the drifting snow on the driveway. It would have to be plowed before anything else happened. The plowing was contracted, and he was surprised they had not been yet.

But they might not know he was in residence, which would make his driveway a low priority. He would call them right away.

Even when it was done, what would await on the public roads?

Okay, *he* would drive the car to Whistler and grab a cab back. Stacy had already shown, in spades, she could not be trusted in these driving conditions. Except what to do with Max during all this? Was the baby seat transferable to her car? Did he want to be out on these roads with Max?

It proved to be a moot point, anyway. After spending more than an hour pitting his strength and wits against the snow and ice and the summer tires, and almost succeeding in banishing the nanny from his mind, he could not get her car unstuck.

At first his irritation was monumental, but then a light went on. No! It was a good thing. After he called the plow company, he could call a tow company and have the car towed all the way to Whistler for her, with her in the cab of the truck with the driver. He could be rid of her—and her sunshiny visions of Christmas trees in *his* great room—and he would not have to feel responsible for her safety.

Kiernan was actually whistling as he went back through the front door of his house and stomped snow off his boots.

He came through to the great room and stopped.

This was exactly what he was protecting himself against! Stacy had spread a blanket on the floor in front of the fireplace. The baby sat here, Buddha-like, his chubby face wreathed in smiles, his attention on the nanny. She was sitting across from him, on the blanket, her legs tucked underneath her, oblivious to the fact the skirt was riding up to reveal even more of those rather delectable legs.

She hadn't even noticed Kiernan's arrival.

Because she had another blanket over her head. As he watched, she lifted up a corner of it, and cried, "Peeka-boo."

Max screamed with laughter, rocked back and forth and looked like he was going to fall over. Her hand shot out from under the blanket and supported the baby.

"Aga!" he screamed at her.

Apparently it meant again, because Stacy disappeared back under the blanket. The baby held his breath in anticipation.

"Peekaboo," she cried.

Max went into paroxysms of laughter. Her laughter joined his.

For all the parties Kiernan had held here, filling this room with important people, rare wines and exquisite food prepared by an in-house chef, his house had never once felt like this.

Kiernan stared at them as if in a trance. That weakness whispered along his spine again. That longing.

For normal. For the thing he had never had. Home.

Something made her glance up, and when she saw him standing there, Stacy pulled the blanket off her head and leaped to her feet, yanking down her skirt. Her hair, crackling with static from the blanket, reminded him of dark dandelion fluff.

"Oh," she said, embarrassed, "I didn't realize you were there."

The baby was frowning at him and yelled his indignation that the game had come to an abrupt end.

Easily, as if she had been born to do it, she scooped up Max and put him on her hip. "I was just thinking of seeing what you have for him to eat," she said.

"Don't bother. You aren't staying." This came out sounding quite a bit more harsh than he intended.

"Oh," she said, looking hurt and baffled by his words, just more evidence she had to go. "You got my car unstuck, then?"

"No," he snapped. "I didn't. Not that I would let you drive if I had."

That chin went up. "That is not up to you!"

"I have to arrange for the driveway to be plowed. And then I'm calling a tow truck. He can tow you all the way to Whistler and you can ride with him."

"But—"

He held up a hand. "It's not open for discussion."

Now, as well as her chin sailing upward, her eyes were narrowed, but she had the good sense not to challenge him.

Obviously she knew her driving skills were not up to the steadily worsening conditions outside.

So, that settled, he went to the phone. And picked it up. And closed his eyes against what he heard.

Which was absolutely nothing.

The storm had taken out the phone line. There was going to be no plow. And no tow truck. Not in the foreseeable future, anyway.

In fact, Kiernan's foreseeable future held a form of torment that he was not sure how to defend himself against.

As if to prove it, Max, annoyed at the abrupt end of his game and the nanny's attention not being focused on him, curled a chubby fist in her hair and yanked hard.

"Hey," Stacy said, "don't do that!"

Max yanked harder.

"I told you he was not adorable in the least," Kiernan said, and went to untangle the baby's determined fist from Stacy's hair.

In doing so, he tangled their lives just a little more together.

CHAPTER SIX

"IVAN, LET GO."

Kiernan's voice sent a shiver up and down Stacy's spine—the man could be deliciously masterful—but the baby was not impressed.

Glaring at his uncle, Max wrapped his fist more tightly with her hair.

Kiernan strode forward, and now both their hands were in her hair.

"Don't hurt him," she said.

"I'm not going to hurt him." Kiernan snapped, insulted.

But the dilemma was obvious: without actually forcing the baby to let go of her hair, he was not going to voluntarily give her up.

"Try distracting him," she suggested.

"How?"

"Can you make a funny face?"

"No!"

"A noise?"

"Such as?"

"I don't know. Try a choo-choo train. Or a duck! Maxie, do you like ducks? Quack, quack?"

She was sure the little fist slackened marginally in her hair. Stacy wished she had a camera to catch the look on

Kiernan's face, that he, one of Canada's top CEOs, had just been asked to quack!

Instead of quacking, Kiernan reached into his pocket and took out his keys. He jingled them enticingly toward Max, who let go of her hair instantly and reached for the keys.

"Baby 101," Kiernan said. "Distraction. Do they teach you that in nanny school?"

That brought her other dilemma into sharp focus. It was, of course, the perfect opening to let him know that she was not a nanny. But now that they were snowed in together—trapped really—wouldn't it just make everything worse if she chose now as the time to let Kiernan know she wasn't exactly a nanny?

He didn't even have the option of throwing her out at this point. Nor did she have the option of volunteering to leave!

Her father had always said, *Murphy, my love, when you are given lemons, make lemonade.*

And that was exactly what she intended to do, right here and right now.

"I need to get the baby something to eat," she said. "And then he needs a bath. After that, he'll probably be ready for bed."

"Humph, he's never ready for bed. Let me show you what Adele left for food for him."

It was a turning point, because Kiernan seemed to resign himself to the idea she was staying. The fact that it was out of his control must have made it a little more palatable to him because, while she opened the baby food and prepared a bottle, he threw together some snacks for the adults.

After they had all eaten, she tackled the bath. To her surprise, Kiernan insisted on helping.

"He's bigger than you think," he said of his nephew. "And he's a slippery little character when he's dry, never mind wet."

Stacy found herself in his master bathroom again. This time, Kiernan flipped on the fireplace without being asked.

For her enjoyment, she couldn't help but wonder, or for the warmth of the baby?

Either way, the experience became wonderful. The fireplace glowing softly, Kiernan's strong hands holding the baby upright, Max gurgling and splashing while she scooped water over him with a cup.

She knew that this good working relationship wouldn't be happening if she had admitted her true identity. It would be better, she decided, for the good of the baby, if she just didn't say anything.

After the driveway was cleared, she could light out of there with no one the wiser. And she would drive her own vehicle, too!

By the time they were done, they were all soaked, but the baby was wrapped in a thick white towel and cuddled sleepily against his uncle's chest.

Stacy was not sure she had ever seen a lovelier sight than that little human being nestled so trustingly against one so much bigger and stronger.

Even the normally stern lines of Kiernan's face had softened, and in the warm glow of the fireplace the scene wrenched at her heart.

"What a beautiful father you will make someday," she said softly.

The look was gone instantly, and Kiernan glowered at her. "I do not have any intention of *ever* being a father," he snapped.

"But why?" she asked, even though it clearly fell into the "none of her business" category.

The look he gave her confirmed it was none of her business. "I'll go get your bag out of the car," he said stiffly, obviously not wanting to spend one more second than necessary with a woman who had spotted father potential in him.

Kiernan didn't just go get her bag. He went out and inspected his driveway, listened hopefully for the sound of a coming plow, but the night was silent. It was the kind of deep, deep silence that did not allow a man to escape his own thoughts.

What was going on in his house? He had just bathed a baby in front of the firelight, and enjoyed it, too.

No wonder Stacy was under the false impression he might make a good father someday.

He hated it that those words had triggered that thing in him, again.

Longing.

A yearning for something that would never be. He remembered as a kid getting the odd glance into other people's lives, a friend inviting him home for dinner, the unexpected treat of a ski trip from his best buddy's mom and dad one Christmas.

Swooping down the hill, he had felt freedom from everything. But after? Eating with that family and playing board games with them and watching them talk and tease each other on the long drive home?

He had wanted what they had as much as he had ever wanted anything. He had learned the hopelessness of such feelings at the hand of his own father, who had been furious with him for accepting the gift of the trip, an affront to his pride, and he had screamed at Kiernan.

His father was a man he tried not to think about.

A man whose brutishness he had distanced himself

from with every success, a man whose shadow he had seemed to escape when the rush of adrenaline was filling his every sense and cell.

Kiernan would never be a good father.

He was convinced it was something you learned, a lesson he had most definitely missed in life.

Though, a voice in him whispered, his sister seemed to have overcome those challenges. It could be done. There was hope.

But he hated it that he even wanted there to be hope. Hated it. And it seemed as if it was her fault, and even though they were stuck here together, he vowed to keep his guard up, find his own space, avoid her.

When he came back in the house, Stacy was sitting on his couch, legs tucked up underneath her, flipping through a book. It had gotten dark outside, and she had turned on a light and sat in its golden glow, unaware what a picture she made.

He recalled again the amazing gatherings hosted in this room, beautifully dressed people, swirls of color and motion, tinkling glasses and laughter.

Despite how much he liked it here, and the good memories he had, Kiernan was aware that, like his condo in Vancouver, his cottage lacked that little *something* that made it feel like home.

Apparently, that little something was a woman making herself comfortable on his couch! The scene was one of homecoming.

Stunned, he felt his decision to avoid her completely dissolving like sugar hitting hot water. Well, he did have her overnight bag, which he had found in the backseat of her car. What was he going to do? Drop it at her feet and bolt?

Really, it would be embarrassing for her to figure out she had rattled him.

"I brought in your bag. Are you okay sharing the guest room with Ivan the Tyrant?" At her nod, he said, "I'll put it in there. Where is Ivan the Tyrant?"

He realized it was blessedly quiet in his house. He tried to tell himself that was probably what he had appreciated at a subconscious level, as much as her presence on his sofa.

"Max is sleeping. You might want to leave the bag there for now rather than risk waking him."

He dropped the bag at his feet as though it was burning his hands. "Seriously? He's sleeping?"

"He wasn't awake very long. When I dug through his bag of things I found his soother and a stuffed toy he called Yike-Yike."

"That thing with eyes on it that looks like an overripe banana?"

"That's Yike-Yike."

Kiernan tapped himself with his fist in his forehead and groaned. "I should have figured that out. Where he goes, that thing goes!"

"Exactly! Within minutes of having both in his possession, he was out like a light. It seems early for him to go to bed, but I think he's managed to wear himself out—

"Not to mention his poor uncle!"

"—and I really think he could make it through the night. All of your problems with him crying and not sleeping and eating properly had to do with his distress over that. Bad enough, in his mind, that Mommy left. But no Yike-Yike?"

"Baby hell," Kiernan murmured.

"Exactly.'"

He said a word he was pretty sure you weren't allowed to say around babies. Or their nannies.

"Did you get enough to eat?" he asked.

"Yes, thank you."

There. No reason to stay here in this room with her. None at all. He could retreat to his bedroom. But he didn't.

"Does the fireplace in here use real wood?" she asked wistfully.

"Yeah. I didn't want to light it with Ivan on the run." *Get away from her,* Kiernan ordered himself. But the wistfulness in her face stopped him.

It was such a small thing that she wanted. Not like the things he had once wanted. He could give this to her. No one could have ever given his dreams to him.

Could a woman like this? He shook off the thought, more than annoyed with himself. Another reminder to get away from her and the spell she was casting. But now he'd offered to light the fire!

"I'll light it for you, if you want."

"Oh, no," she said, and blushed. "That's way too much trouble."

It was that blush that sealed it for him. "No, no trouble at all." And he found himself opening the damper and crumpling paper and setting kindling, striking the match.

In no time, the fire was crackling cheerfully in the hearth.

Now retreat, he ordered himself. But he didn't. He said, "I've got this contraption that supposedly you can pop corn in the fire. You want to try it?"

"Yes," she breathed with genuine enthusiasm, as if he had offered to put up a Christmas tree.

Well, what the heck? They were stuck here. Together. Entertainment was limited. Why not?

Stacy realized she should have said no to this. She should have wished him a polite good-night and retreated to her room. But she just wasn't that strong.

She joined him at his counter, and they eyed the open-fire popcorn contraption together. They took it to the fire and took turns shaking it vigorously as per the instructions.

Just when it felt as if nothing was ever going to happen,

the popcorn began to pop. First one or two kernels, and then rapidly, like a machine gun going off.

"We put too much in," she said as the hinge sprang free and popcorn began to spill into the fire. It smelled terrible. A few unpopped husks exploded into the room with the briefest whistled warning and more velocity than she could have dreamed possible.

She dropped the popcorn maker, and he took a firm hold of her elbow and shoved her behind the couch, shielding her with his own body, protection of those who were smaller and physically weaker than him coming as naturally to him as breathing.

They tried to muffle their laughter so as not to wake the baby, while the popcorn flew through the air around them.

When they were sure the fireworks had finished, they came out from behind the couch.

He surveyed his living room with shock.

She giggled. "I've heard of popcorn ceilings," she said, "but never popcorn floors."

And then the laughter died. "Thank you for protecting me," she said.

He looked at her, and suddenly it seemed very still. Almost against his will, he reached down, tilted her chin up, scanned her face, looked at her lips.

"Do unexpected things always happen around you?"

"It's the old anything-that-can-go-wrong thing," she said, but her voice was husky and neither of them was laughing.

Awareness sizzled in the air between them. He dropped his head close to hers. He was going to kiss her!

Stunned, she backed away from him. This was a lie. She was living a lie! She couldn't let it get more complicated than it already was.

She turned on her heel and ran down the hall.

"Hey, Cinderella," he called mockingly, "You are leaving your slipper."

But she had more in common with Cinderella than she ever wanted him to know. Both she and Cinderella were both pretending to be people they were not.

Kiernan watched her disappear and gave himself a shake. Had he nearly kissed her? What on earth did that have to do with the strategy of avoidance he had planned?

Crazy things were happening in this house. The popcorn all over the floor was a testament to that. Nearly quacking for her earlier was a testament to that. Crazy things were happening in his head, too, and he didn't like it one little bit.

He was strong.

Stronger than strong.

He always had been. That was why he had survived. That was why Adele had survived.

But all his strength, he reminded himself bitterly, had not been enough to save Danner.

And that's what he needed to remember, before he tangled his life with anyone's. He was not the stuff happy families were made of. And even if he was, all his strength could not do what he would most want to do.

Protect from harm.

Kiernan gave his head one more rueful shake and began to pick up scorched popcorn from his living room floor.

And the fact that he smiled when he remembered huddling behind the couch with her only reminded him he had been weak when he wanted to be strong.

And so, as one day stretched into two and they remained marooned, he made himself be strong.

He was polite. And helpful with the baby. And aloof. If watching her interact with Max and making herself at home in his house gave him pleasure—which it did—he did not let on.

And when the snow finally stopped, he practically raced outside. If he could get her car free before the plow arrived, he was one step closer to being rid of her. And her laughter. And the way she shook her curls to make the baby coo with delight.

It would be good for him to get outside and do the manly thing! But, an hour later, he was no closer to freeing her car.

Though he did have a plan!

"So, how did it go with my car?"

He had promised the manly thing, and he was not going to admit defeat.

"Still stuck, but I think we could get it out together." What did doing anything *together* have to do with avoiding her?

"Well, the baby's napping, so now would be perfect. I'll just grab the monitor."

"I'm pretty sure it's an easy fix. It just needs two people, one to drive and one to push. Despite my desire to hold you captive—"

He realized he had said that to make her blush, too, and she did.

"—because of your gift with Ivan, looking after the car before he wakes up would be good. Because once he wakes up?" McAllister wagged his eyebrows at her. "Guess what? It's all about him."

"Typical male," she muttered.

That made him frown, because he was pretty sure he heard the faint bitterness of one who had been betrayed in there. Was that the shadow he saw in her eyes sometimes?

Well, how could that be anything but a good thing, that she had no illusions about the male half of the species?

"You are so right," he said. "We are a colossally self-centered, hedonistic bunch. You'd be better not to pin your hopes to one of us."

CHAPTER SEVEN

"YOU DON'T KNOW the first thing about my hopes," Stacy said quietly. She had given him entirely the wrong impression when she had imagined a big family gathering in this very room. She had given him the wrong impression when she had told him he would make a good father. She had given him the wrong impression when she had leaned toward him that night of the popcorn and nearly accepted his kiss.

He couldn't avoid her, of course, and he hadn't. But she had felt the chilly lack of connection.

But just underneath that, something simmered between them, as if a fuse had been lit and the spark was moving its way toward the explosive.

She was so *aware* of him when he was in the same room. The same house. The same space. She was aware of loving the way he was with Max, loving the way he was willing to do what needed to be done without being asked.

Kiernan McAllister regarded her thoughtfully for a moment, his gaze so stripping she felt as if he could see her soul.

He was dressed in a beautiful down-filled parka, the fur-lined hood framing his face. Beautifully tailored slacks clung to the large muscles of his thighs, the look made less formal by the fact the slacks were tucked into snow boots.

How could a man look every bit as sexy dressed as he was now as he had when he was dressed in nothing but a towel?

But McAllister did. In the parka and the snow boots, he looked ready for anything. Very manly, indeed.

"Unfortunately, Stacy, I think I do know a bit about your hopes."

"And?" she said, bracing herself for his answer.

"Your career choice says quite a bit."

That was a relief. What he assumed was her career choice was telling him about her. Her hopes and dreams, as battered as they were at the moment, weren't really showing on her face.

"Who wants to look after other people's children?" he said. "Except someone who loves children and dreams of having their own? Probably by the bushel."

The truth was she had planned for three, someday.

It would be the perfect time to tell him she was not who he was expecting, that she was not a nanny at all. Instead, she found herself frowning at him. "Are you saying *you* don't love children?"

"I already told you, I don't plan on being a father."

"That doesn't answer my question."

"I don't even like children."

She snorted.

"Ah, indignation. As if I've announced I don't like puppies. Or Santa Claus."

"Actually, it's not indignation, Mr. McAllister—"

"It's a little late for formality."

Oh, boy. "You aren't a very good liar."

"Excuse me?"

"The baby frustrated you, and you were at rope's end, but I could tell you would have protected him with your life, if need be. Maybe that's not *like*. And over the last few days, when you see something that needs to be done, you just step up to the plate and do it. That seems suspiciously like more than that. Like love, perhaps."

He was glaring at her, and then he shrugged a big shoulder dismissively.

"Whatever, Miss Poppins," he said. "We need to look after the car before His Majesty wakes up. Have you got a winter jacket somewhere?"

"Just my sweater."

"I'll find stuff for you."

The "stuff" he found was mostly his and so, a little while later, Stacy was following him out into the darkness of a still-snowing night, dressed in a jacket that came down to her knees and that tickled her nostrils with the pine scent of him. He had found her a hat that that looked like something a turn-of-the-century trapper would wear. It was too large and kept falling over her eyes. Thankfully, his sister had left snow boots here that fit her.

Really, she should have stopped him at *Miss Poppins*.

And confessed to her true identity. For about the hundredth time in three days, she knew she should have, but she just couldn't.

Because, she had the certain knowledge, that as soon as she did it would be over. She was pretty sure she had not banked enough gratitude that he was going to grant her an interview. Especially now that she had seen him so clearly and called him a liar.

She was the liar. And revealing that to him was going to cause terrible tension and they were trapped here. It would not be good for the baby!

Even if, by some miracle, the truth came out and he did grant her an interview, *then* it would be over.

And somehow she did not want this little adventure to be done. What had he said to her earlier?

You might want to keep in mind, for next time, to try and steer into the spin, rather than away from it. It goes against everyone's first instinct. But really, that's what you do. You go with it, instead of fighting it.

So, what if she went with this? Rode the momentum of the spin instead of fighting it? Let go of her need to control, just for a little while? Isn't that what she'd been doing for the past few days?

It seemed to her that since the second she had wound up with her bumper resting against that fountain, her life held something it had not held for some time. Surprise. Spontaneity. The potential for the unexpected.

When unexpected things had happened to her before, it had been so in keeping with Murphy's Law. They were always bad.

Expecting an engagement ring and being invited to shack up being a case in point.

Dylan had guffawed when she had said that, apparently more loudly than she had thought.

Shack up, Stacy, really? What century is that from?

One where people made commitments and took vows and wanted forever things instead of temporary pleasures.

Then, she had done something totally out of character. She had dumped her wine all over his head, and yelled at him, "What century is that from?"

Unfortunately, her worst moment ever in keeping with Murphy's Law, had been recorded by someone in the restaurant with a smartphone, who had been alerted to turn it toward her by her rising tone of voice.

And then that moment had been posted on the web.

But all that was in her past. Now was now. And, as ridiculous as it seemed, Kiernan McAllister, the man who appeared to have everything, seemed to need something from her.

As did that baby. And so Stacy was going to take his advice.

You might want to keep in mind, for next time, to try and steer into the spin, rather than away from it... It goes against everyone's first instinct. But really, that's what you do. You go with it, instead of fighting it.

"Oh, Stacy," she murmured inwardly, "what kind of predicament have you gotten yourself into?"

A dangerous one, because if what she had experienced so far—his nearly naked self, fresh out of the hot tub—wasn't his idea of 100 percent manly, she was in very big trouble, indeed!

"Okay, put it in Reverse," Kiernan shouted from the front of her car.

Stacy sat in the driver's seat of her car, peering out from under her hat at Kiernan. She had the window rolled down so that she could hear instructions from him. She was already glad for the winter clothing, especially the mittens. The baby monitor was on the seat beside her as she clenched on the steering wheel. It was very sensitive. She could hear Max's soft, sleepy purring above the sound of the engine.

She contemplated the delightful if somewhat surreal quality of her life.

One of the most powerful men in the business world was getting her car unstuck from his front garden as she listened to a baby sleep.

After scowling at her summer tires, he had settled right into it.

It had been a very pleasant experience so far watching him wield a shovel, digging out the tires of her car, one by one, spreading gravel underneath.

"Give it some gas."

She did. The tires made that whining noise. Kiernan put his shoulder against the front bumper of her car and pushed.

Manly, indeed!

Kiernan did look 100 percent man. How it was even possible for him to look more manly than he had in his swim trunks baffled her, but he did and heart-stoppingly so. Of course, sharing a house with him had made her superaware of him: his scent, how his hair looked wet from the shower, the shadow of whiskers on his face late in the afternoon.

Now the winter clothes made him look rugged, tough, 100-percent Canadian male, ready for anything. He had long since dispensed with the gloves, which were lying on the ground beside him. His brute strength rocked her car, and for a moment she thought he was going to be able to push it free, but it seemed to settle back in the ruts.

She let off the gas.

"Try rocking it between Forward and Reverse."

Stacy did this, she could tell from the way his arms crossed over his chest and the expression on his face— part aggravated, part amused—that she was doing something wrong.

"Sorry," she called out the open window.

He came and leaned in the window. His breath touched her like a frosty peppermint kiss. "You really aren't great at this, are you?"

She looked at him from under the hat. Great at what? The whole man/woman thing? No, she was not.

"You're a snow virgin!" he declared. "It's a good thing it's not a full moon. We sacrifice snow virgins at the full moon."

He was teasing her.

She had never been good at this kind of banter, but she reminded herself to go with the spin.

"To what end?" she asked breathlessly.

"Appeasing the god, Murphy."

She laughed then, and the smile that she could have lived for—and that she could have told a zillion more lies to see again—tickled the sensual line of his lips.

He leaned in her window, right across her, and took her gearshift. "Put in the clutch."

He was so close his whiskers nearly scraped her cheek. She wasn't even breathing. He snapped her gearshift into Neutral and backed out of her window, leaving her feeling like a snow virgin very close to melting.

He went back around to the front of the car and showed off his manliness by shoving some more but to no avail.

"I have an idea," she called. "You drive. I'll push."

"Sure," he said cynically.

"No, really. I'm stronger than I look."

He looked skeptical, but by now he apparently had figured out she was not going to get the gas or the gears right to rock the car out of the spot it was in.

"Don't push," he instructed. "I'll see if I can get it out without you."

She could see he knew a great deal about cars. He rocked the car back and forth gently, but it would come to the same place in the ever-deepening rut her great winter driving skills had created.

She went around to the front of her car and pushed.

"Hey," he called out the window, laughter in his voice, "you are not helping. It is like an ant pushing on an elephant."

She ignored him and pushed.

"Try just putting some weight on it."

She threw her weight against the bumper, and when that didn't work, she sat on the hood. Apparently that was the ticket, because suddenly the wheels caught and the car rocketed backward.

She fell off the hood and rolled through the snow. Her hat fell off and her mouth filled up with the white stuff.

He got out of the car, raced to her and got down beside her.

"Are you okay?"

"I'm fine." She spit out some snow, and he brushed it from her lips.

"Are you always so accident-prone?"

"Murphy's Law," she reminded him.

"Ah," he said. "And we have failed to appease him." He held out his hand, and she took it—she was becoming too accustomed to this his-hand-in-hers stuff—and he helped her to sitting. He found the hat, shook the snow out of it and clamped it back on her head.

"Your car is unstuck. Let's get in out of the cold."

"I don't feel cold," she said. "You go in if you want to. I'd like to stay out here for a while. Snow virgin that I am, I want to enjoy this for just a bit longer. This might be the closest I ever get to my winter holiday."

He smiled at that.

Boldly she said, "How would you recommend losing snow virginity?"

His smile faded and he stared at her, and if she was not mistaken, his eyes went to her lips. She could feel her heart beating too fast again. She was inordinately pleased that he seemed flummoxed by her question. Then something burned through his eyes that felt too hot for her to handle.

"I will make a snow angel," she decided quickly.

He looked relieved by her choice. Obviously angels and whatever wicked thoughts he was having did not go together.

He was having wicked thoughts about her? It was dismaying…in the most wonderful way.

Still, she lay back down in the snow, splayed her hands over her head and swept the snow with her tights-clad legs.

"How does it look?" she asked.

"Angelic," he said, something dry in his tone.

"How do I get up without wrecking it?"

He seemed to ponder this and then, with a trace of reluctance—a little close to those wicked thoughts to risk touching her—he reached down. She took both his arms, and he swung her up out of the angel she had made in the snow. He let her go instantly.

"It's lovely," she declared. She stood surveying her handiwork with pleasure and leaned down to brush at the snow that clung to her legs.

"Lovely," he murmured, and she shot him a look. Had he been looking at her?

"It would be great to get Max outside tomorrow," she decided. She opened her car door and checked the monitor. The baby was still sleeping soundly. "Maybe we'll build a snowman."

What was she doing talking about tomorrow? She needed to tell McAllister the truth now. But somehow she was not so certain what truth was. Wasn't there a truth in this moment under inky skies in the way he had murmured *lovely* after watching her brush the snow from her legs?

Wasn't there truth in the way their breath was coming out of each of their mouths in little puffs that joined together to make a cloud?

Weren't these truths as profound as any other truth she had ever known?

"The snow will be gone by tomorrow," he said.

"Really?"

"It's stopped snowing, finally, and the weather has warmed. It won't take long."

He was right. When she looked up at the dark sky, wisps of clouds were moving away to reveal a bright sliver of moon and pinpricks of starlight. It was beautiful.

"It's just an early-season storm," he told her. "The snow won't stick. It'll melt by tomorrow."

Tomorrow the magic would be gone. *Then* she would tell him the truth. There would be an escape route. Max didn't have to be affected. But tonight?

"I better build a snowman now, then," she said.

"Seriously?"

"I'm a Vancouver girl. You never know when you might have another chance."

McAllister stooped, picked up a handful of snow and squeezed it. "It is perfect snow for that."

Was he going to help her? Her astonishment must have shown in her face.

"You don't have enough muscle to lift the balls on top of each other," he said, as if he needed an excuse to join her.

"Hey!" She scooped up a handful of snow and formed it into a ball. "I have muscles aplenty! I just got the car unstuck!"

"Single-handedly," he said drily. "No help from me."

"Very little," she said, and then she realized *she* was teasing *him*. In a moment of pure and bold spontaneity, she tossed her snowball at him.

He dodged her missile effortlessly and stood there looking stunned. Something twitched around the line of his mouth. Annoyance? Or amusement? Annoyance. His mouth turned down in a frown.

She thought he would tell her to knock it off or grow up or get real.

He was the CEO of one of the biggest companies in Canada. You didn't throw snowballs at him.

She held her breath, waiting to see what he would do.

Gracefully, he leaned down. She saw he had scooped up a handful of snow of his own. His gloves were still lying in the snow over by where her car had been, but that didn't seem to bother him at all. With his bare hands, not looking at her, he slowly formed the snow into a ball.

Finally, he looked at her, held her gaze.

A smile, not exactly nice, twitched around the line of that beautiful mouth.

She read his intent and, with a shriek, turned away from him and began to run through the mounds of beautiful white snow.

CHAPTER EIGHT

"Don't!" she cried. She glanced over her shoulder.

His too-large jacket flapped around Stacy's legs, making it impossible to attain the kind of speed necessary to outrun the missile he let fly.

The snowball caught her in the middle of the back. Even with the padding of the winter coat, it stung.

"I'm taking that as a declaration of war." She laughed, pushing back the sleeves of the jacket and scooping up more snow. She took careful aim, her hat slipping over her eyes, and to his shout of laughter, she pulled the hat back up just in time to see her snowball miss him by a mile.

She scooped up more snow and formed it into a hurried ball. She hurled it at him. He moved his head to one side and it whistled by his ear.

Deliberately, he walked over and retrieved his gloves. He was already tired of the silliness.

No, he wasn't. With his hands protected, it was evident he was just getting started. He stooped and grabbed a mitt full of snow. He began to shape a rather formidable looking snowball.

"There's no need to be mean about it," she told him over her shoulder, already running again.

"You're the one who declared war!"

And then he was running after her, his legs so much

longer than hers that he was gaining ground fast. She was going to have to outmaneuver him. Stacy scooted around the fountain and through the shrubs. She ducked behind her car.

Silence. She peered over the hood.

Sploosh. Right in her face.

"If you surrender now, I'll show you mercy," she shouted at him, wiping off her face and ducking behind the car to pick up more snow.

"Me surrender to you?" he asked incredulously.

"Yes!" she shouted, forming a snowball, her tongue between her teeth.

"Surrender? Lass, I'm of Scottish ancestry. That word is not in my vocabulary."

She peeked out from behind the car, aimed, let fly. She missed.

"Glad I didn't wave the white flag," he said with an evil grin.

"I'm just sucking you deeper into enemy territory."

"You're terrible at this," he told her.

"What's that called, when you play billiards badly to suck the other person in, and then place a bet and show what you can really do?"

"Hustling," he said.

"Maybe that's what I'm doing."

"I'd be more convinced if you knew the word for it."

"All part of the hustle," she assured him. She let fly a snowball that caught his shoulder and exploded with satisfactory violence. She chortled happily. "See?"

A missile flew back at her. She ducked behind her car, and it shattered harmlessly behind her. Silence. She waited. Nothing happened.

She peeked around the front fender. He had been

making ammunition and had a heap of snowballs in front of him.

She reached inside the still-open door of her car, picked up the baby monitor and held it up.

"Be careful," she said, "you don't want to get this wet."

"It's waterproof. You can take it into the bathtub." He let fly with six in a row and, as she peeked over the car, he tucked six more in the crook of his elbow.

She shoved the monitor in her pocket as he came running toward her, and burst out from behind the car at a dead run.

With a whoop he was after her. They chased each other around the circle of his driveway. As he threw snowballs, she ducked behind shrubs and the fountain and her car until they were both breathless with laughter and dripping with snow.

"Okay," she called, laughing, when he had her backed up against the fountain and his arm pulled back to heave a really good one at her, "I surrender. You win."

"What do I win?" He kept his arm up, ready, if she did not offer a good enough prize.

She licked her lips. If she was just a little bolder, she would offer him a kiss from the snow virgin.

Instead, she backed away from the intensity building between them. She pulled the monitor out of her pocket. "This! A completely waterproof baby monitor."

"Thanks, but no thanks."

"Okay, you win an opportunity to build a snowman!" she said.

"Sheesh. I was at least hoping for hot chocolate."

"Take it or leave it," she said.

"Pretty pushy for the loser." He tossed the snowball away. "I'll take it, but only because it's obvious to me you can't be trusted with making a snowman. You can barely make a snowball, and a snowman is the same principle, only multiplied."

"I'm anxious to learn whatever you want to teach me," she said.

For a moment the intensity sizzled again between them, white-hot into the frosty evening. His eyes locked on her lips and hers on his. She felt herself leaning toward him as if he were a magnet and she was steel.

He stepped back from her. "No, you aren't," he said gruffly. "I wouldn't want you to learn from me. There's something innately sweet about you. My cynicism could demolish that in a second."

Of course, he was saying that because he thought she was a nanny.

This was where lying got you.

"Maybe my sweetness could demolish your cynicism," she said.

"It's an age-old question, isn't it? Which is stronger? Light or dark?"

"Light," she said without hesitation.

He snorted but took some snow and squished it into a ball in his hands. Then he set it down, got on his knees and pushed it. Snow began to glue to the ball magically, and it got bigger and bigger.

Her skirt was not made for this kind of activity!

But what the heck? She had tights on. Following his instructions, tongue caught between her teeth, she lowered herself to her knees, too, and began to push her ever-growing snowball across his snowy driveway.

When she glanced over at him, he was straining against a huge snow boulder! It was so big he had his back against it and was pushing backward off his heels.

"That's big enough! Kiernan, it's bigger than me!"

She realized, stunned, his name coming off her lips

felt like an arrival at a place she had always dreamed of being at.

This is not truth, Stacy warned herself of the game she was playing. But she was not sure anything in her life had ever felt truer than this, playing in the snow under a night sky with Kiernan McAllister.

She was just going with the spin, instead of fighting it.

"Just a little bigger," he said. "Come help me push. It'll be just the right size by the time we get it over to the fountain."

He was far more ambitious than she was. It took them pushing together, shoulders touching, to wrestle it into place where her car had rested a few minutes before.

"You're an overachiever," she gasped, stepping back to admire their handiwork and, surreptitiously, him.

"Yes, I am," he said with complete pleasure.

He moved over to the ball of snow she had been working on. "Break is over," he told her, and side by side they pushed that one into place, too.

It took both of them to hoist the second ball on top of the first. There was much panting and laughing and struggling.

The snowman's head was the smallest of the three balls, and by now the snowman was so tall Kiernan had to lift it into place himself.

They stood back. The snowman was a good eight feet tall, but sadly blank faced.

"This is the problem with all that ambition," Stacy said. "He's so big we can't reach his face. He needs a hat. How are we going to get up there?"

"I already have it covered," Kiernan said.

"You're going to go get a ladder?" she asked.

"Ha! I'm going to be the ladder!"

She contemplated that for a moment. That sounded dangerous in the most delicious way. She saw he was moving snow to get at the rocks underneath, and she joined him.

"Do you have a carrot for his nose?" she asked.

"Oh, sure, in my back pocket. That's why I'm digging for stones."

"This one's perfect for the nose," she said, reaching down and picking up a pure black rock that he had exposed. "And these for his eyes! And these for his mouth!"

He was watching her, amused. "I think you have enough." He crouched down on his haunches.

"Here, hop up. Don't drop the rocks."

He tapped his shoulders. *As if dropping the rocks would be the most of her problems!*

She hesitated for only a moment before climbing on.

He lifted her with ease, and she found Kiernan McAllister's rather lovely neck between her legs. He grabbed her boots and held them against his chest. She had been unaware of how soggy and cold her clothing had become until she felt his warmth radiating up through her wet tights.

He pretended to stagger sideways, and she gripped his forehead and giggled when he yelped, "Hey, get your fingers out of my eyes."

She moved her hands and he staggered back in front of the snowman.

"Quick," he said. "I don't know how long I can hold you. You must weigh all of—what—a hundred pounds?"

Trembling, and not just from cold, Stacy put the face on the snowman. The nose rock was perfect, and if the smile was a little crooked, that was understandable. She snatched the hat off her own head and placed it on the snowman's.

"Okay," she called. "We're done."

But he didn't put her down. Instead he galloped around the yard, pretending he was staggering under her weight, ignoring her pounding on his shoulders and demanding to be put down at once.

Finally, he went down on one knee, but her dismount was clumsy, and she caught his shoulder, and they both went to the ground in a tangle of limbs and laughter.

Then the laughter died and the silence overtook them. They lay there in the snow, looking up at the stars.

"I haven't laughed like that for a long time," he said quietly.

"Me, either."

"Why?"

She hesitated, but from sharing the house and the baby duties there was a sense of intimacy between them. "Oh, life has taken some unexpected twists and turns. I've kind of felt just like I felt on your driveway—spinning out of control."

"A man," he guessed, with a knowing shake of his head. "Failed marriage?"

"No."

"Broken engagement?"

She winced.

"Ah."

"We never got that far," she confessed. "I just thought we were going to."

"Ah, that imagination-collides-with-reality thing again," he said, but with such gentleness she felt her heart break open wide.

Suddenly, she wanted to tell him all of it. She felt safe with him. Ironically, though she was posing as someone else, she felt more herself than she ever had. And she wanted him to know the truth about her.

"It wasn't just a man," she said quietly. "I became on orphan at sixteen."

It was terrible to feel this way: that she could trust him

with anything on the basis of a few days trapped in a house with him.

A few wondrous days, where she felt she knew more about him than she had ever known about anyone. Still, could she continue to blame that hit on the head for the removal of the filter for socially acceptable behavior? You did not unload your personal history on the most powerful man you had ever met.

Except he felt like the Kiernan she had seen bathe the baby.

And who had built a fire for her. And protected her from popcorn missiles.

And who had lent a hand whenever he saw something that needed doing. It was ironic that she could not tell him who she really was, and the more she could not tell him that the more she wanted him to know!

"They died. My grandmother, my mother, my father, my little brother. It was a car crash. My entire family," she whispered.

"I'm so sorry," he said. His voice was velvet with sincerity, and he reached out to tuck a strand of hair behind her ear. He touched her cheek for a moment before he let his hand fall away, something in his face telling her he was as surprised by that gesture as she was.

She had been dating Dylan for three months before she had told him any of this. Of course, he had never looked at her like that…

"I'm sorry," she stammered. "I don't even know why it came up."

"Thank you for telling me," he said. "I feel honored."

"And you?" she whispered, needing more from him, needing the intimate way she felt about him—the trust she felt for him to be reciprocated. Even if she did not deserve it.

The snow had stopped. By tomorrow, there was a

chance she would be gone from here. She could not stay once the snow was gone. She needed to take some piece of him with her. "Kiernan, what has kept the laughter from your life?"

He rolled a shoulder uncomfortably but said nothing.

"The death of your brother-in-law?" she asked softly.

He cranked his head and looked at her. "And what do you know about that?"

"Oh, Kiernan, you are a very public figure. The whole world knows about that."

He sighed and looked back up at the stars. "It's been a year. That's why my sister needed some time right now. People say time heals all wounds, but I am waiting for evidence of that."

"I'm so sorry," she said. "It was a terrible tragedy."

"How did you get over it?" he asked.

"I guess I hoped to have again what I once had before," she admitted, and it felt as if her heart was wide-open to him. "After my disaster with Dylan, I've given up on it."

"No, you haven't."

"I have," she said stubbornly.

"Then why can I so clearly see you surrounded by all your beautiful babies, and a man worthy of you? Someday, you'll look back on it, and be glad it happened. You'll see that he was a complete jerk and that you deserved better."

A hopeless feeling came over her. There was that imagination again. Because somehow it seemed Kiernan might be the better man she had waited for. But she knew she did not deserve him.

"As a matter of fact, I've decided to put my wildest imaginings aside," she said stiffly.

"No, you haven't," he said softly. "Because you know what is possible. You know what it is to be part of a family. You aren't imagining that part. And because you're not?

You'll never stop looking. You'll never stop seeing what could be in rooms like my great room. I need to know, step by step, how you got through the loss of your entire family."

She could hear the desperation in his voice, and she knew how vulnerable he had just made himself to her. He was asking her to help him.

Stacy took a deep breath and contemplated the stars. When she spoke, her voice was husky and hesitant.

"At first, I didn't feel as if I would even survive, not that I wanted to. I went from having this wonderful family into foster care. Thankfully, it was only for a year until I finished high school. I'm not sure you get over it. You get through it.

"Eventually, it was being around the kids in foster care that woke me up. Many of them had never had a loving family, or anyone who genuinely cared about them. At the risk of sounding corny?"

"What else would I expect from Miss Poppins?" he teased, but his tone was so gentle it was like a touch.

"Being around those troubled kids showed me what to do. Find somebody to help. That's what saved me. I started to go to university to get a degree in counseling. Unfortunately, I couldn't afford to finish the program. I became involved in starting a charity—Career and College Opportunities for Foster Kids—and I think that has pulled me through my darkest moments."

"I've never heard of that charity," he said.

"Unfortunately, neither has anyone else. We just don't have the know-how, the expertise, to get it really rolling."

"I'll give you the name of someone who will help you."

See? Despite all the evidence to the contrary, sometimes your wildest imaginings could come true.

"How did you get by?" he asked. "After you dropped out?"

"Thankfully, I had another gift that came in handy."

The other gift was writing. Was now the time to tell him? He was offering someone to help the charity under a false impression of who she was, after all.

But to lose this moment of closeness so soon after she had laughed for the first time in such a long time felt like more than she could bear.

"Your gift was with children," he said. "That's how you became a nanny."

Instead of responding to that, Stacy said, "In time, instead of focusing on the loss, I was able to feel gratitude for my family, and for the time I'd had with them. Every gift I have been given comes from the love they gave to me. Maybe you'll feel that, eventually, about your brother-in-law."

The silence was long and comfortable between them. She realized the days of being trapped together had made them friends, had created a bond between them with astonishing swiftness.

"He was more than my brother-in-law," Kiernan said, finally, softly. "We were best friends. Funny, when I first met him, I was prepared to dislike him. When my sister announced she was bringing someone home, I practically met him at the door with my saber drawn, prepared to give all kinds of dire warnings about what would happen to him if he hurt my sister.

"But Danner was just the best guy." A long silence, and then Kiernan said, "I wish it could have been me, instead of him."

CHAPTER NINE

"OH, KIERNAN," SHE said.

That *feeling* she had of experiencing truth at its deepest and finest intensified. She saw that he was a man who would see the protection of those he loved as his highest calling.

And that he had failed in it.

He gave her a look that forbade her sympathy. "He had a wife. And a baby. It would have been better if it was me."

She did not know what to say to that. She thought a deeper truth was that these things were not for mere men to decide, but she felt it would sound trite to say that in the face of the enormous pain he had trusted her with.

And so instead of saying anything, she took off her mitten and slid his glove off and took his bare hand in hers.

She held it.

And he let her. And it felt so good and so right to lie there on their backs in the snow, looking at the stars through the clouds of their own breath and feeling intensely connected by the fact they both knew the burden of intense loss.

Then he let go of her hand.

"You officially have lost your snow virginity."

She knew he was trying to change the subject, to move to lighter ground, but she felt a need to stay in this place of connection just a bit longer.

"I have built a snowman once before," she said. "With my dad. While everyone else was cursing the snow, he was out playing with us. He could make anything fun."

She could feel his hesitation, but then his hand was once again in hers, warm against the cold of the snow around them and the chill of the night.

Warm in a world that was so cold sometimes it could freeze a person's very heart.

"You're lucky for that. I wonder if that's where your dream of having a winter holiday comes from? Wanting to recapture that moment of childhood magic?"

His perception warmed her as much as his hand in hers. "Do you have moments like those, Kiernan, pure magic?"

He snorted. "Not from my childhood."

This was what being a reporter with some counseling background had taught her, that silence was a kind of question in itself. She suspected Kiernan was a man of many barriers, but for some reason, these playful moments, these few days of being snowbound, had lowered them.

"It was probably more like the kind of family kids you ended up in foster care with came from. My dad was a drunk," Kiernan said softly. "He abandoned the family when I was about twelve."

"That's terrible," she said, "and so, so sad."

"Believe me, it was a blessing. Anyway, that's why I was meeting my sister's boyfriend at the door. By default, I was the man of the house."

"Oh, Kiernan," she said softly.

"That's why my sister and I always go away at Christmas. Someplace warm and beachy and non-Christmassy. To outrun the memories of him, I guess. Adele—that's my sister—she says that's why I'm allergic to relationships."

It was a warning if Stacy had ever heard one. But it was also an admission of something deeply private.

Her hand tightened in his despite the warning. She thought he would shake her off now, but he didn't.

"You must be very proud to have accomplished all that you have," she said.

"Proud?" He was silent for a long time. "I used to be."

"And now?"

"Now I feel as if I wasted precious moments on a clock that I did not know was ticking a relentless countdown, pursuing things that did not matter."

In that moment, for the first time, Stacy realized Dylan, her ex, might have been right about her when he'd let her go from her job. It had seemed too coincidental, in light of the fact their relationship had just ended, but now his words came back to her.

Maybe Dylan had been right, Stacy thought. She just didn't have the instincts for this.

"You're a good writer," he'd told her, "but you're no kind of reporter. You don't have the guts for it. There's no daring in you. And you have to be able to be a bit ruthless in some circumstances."

A ruthless person—a true reporter—would have asked right now if the rumors of McAllister Enterprises going up for sale were true.

But Stacy could not bring herself to do anything more than be in the silence of his pain and regret with him.

"Your hands are freezing," he said, as if that was why he hung on to them instead of letting go. The warmth of his own hands was absolutely delicious on her icy flesh.

"Don't feel sorry for me," he said dangerously. "I'm sure it is also the reason I'm so driven to be such an over-achiever in everything I do, including building snowmen."

Still, holding her hand, he got up on one elbow and looked down at her, and for one breathless moment she thought he was going to kiss her.

Instead, he seemed to realize who they were—who he was and who she was, and he shook the snow off himself, let go of her hand and stood up.

"Do you always have this effect on people?" he said. "Draw their secrets from them?"

She didn't know what to say, so she said nothing at all.

The things he had told her felt sacred. Her desire to tell his story to get her career on track was leaving her like the wind leaving a sail.

He stared at her for a long time, and she was sure that he was going to recognize the danger of what was happening between them.

And perhaps he did. But instead of walking away from it, he walked right toward it.

His hand tightened on hers. He lifted it to his lips and blew the warmth of his breath into her palm. It spoke—sadly, she thought—of her past relationship with Dylan that Kiernan McAllister warming her hands with his breath was the most romantic thing that had ever happened to her.

He was right. For the first time, she felt grateful for the fact her relationship had gone sideways. In her eagerness to create a family again, she had been able to gloss over the fact her relationship had been missing a certain *something*.

It felt dangerously as if that *something* was in the air between her and Kiernan, more dazzling than the stars in the sky above them.

And then a sound split the night, deep, rumbling, jarring.

"What is that?" she asked, her eyes wide. "An earthquake?"

He pulled his hand from hers and shoved it in his pocket. "It's the snowplow," he said. "He's clearing the driveway."

It was over, she thought. As quickly as it had begun,

it was over. She could already feel the distance gathering between them, could see the distance in his eyes.

He turned quickly away from her and strode toward the house, leaving her behind.

"I bet the phone is working," he said. "I have all kinds of business to catch up on."

He was letting her know it was completely out of character for him to have been frolicking with the nanny in the snow. He knew the intimacy of the past few days was creating a grave danger between them, and he was doing the wisest thing. Backing away from it.

Returning to his world.

And she would be returning to hers.

Kiernan retreated to his master suite. He contemplated the evening: getting her car unstuck, chasing her through the snow pelting her with snowballs, the huge snowman that now graced his front yard.

He did not behave like that.

Nor did he lie on the snowy ground, the cold coming up through his jacket, telling all his secrets, telling a near stranger things he had told no one else.

Exhaustion, he excused himself. He had not slept properly since Max had arrived.

He had never abandoned his company quite so completely as he had in the past twenty-four hours.

Though he knew he had been abandoning it mentally for months. He knew about the rumors that he was selling out. Not true. He probably should contain them, but the company was not publically held, so he had no one to answer to, no stock prices plunging because of the rumors.

Still, he checked his phone. It was working, finally.

He knew Adele would be frantic and despite the fact it was late, he called her. She did not answer, so he left a message saying the phone had been out, a fact he was pretty sure Adele would have determined for herself when she could not get though.

"Everything's fine," he said in his message. He told her Max was thriving and that the nanny had arrived so all was well, despite them having been snowed in.

And then he did something he *never* did.

"Hey, sis, I love you."

He hung up the phone slowly. What did that mean, anyway, that he'd included that? His sister knew, of course, that he loved her. But he rarely said things like that.

He thought about the snowball fight, and the snowman, and lying in the snow, looking at the stars. Had the words been to reassure his sister? Or did it reflect how he really felt? Softer in some way than he had felt a few days ago. More open.

Was it possible he was happy?

Was it possible his happiness was related to the nanny?

"Don't worry," he growled, setting the phone beside his bed, stripping down and climbing between the sheets. "Life has a way of snatching those moments away."

For months—possibly even for a full year, going to sleep had been a torment for Kiernan. Those were the moments he tossed and turned and endlessly relived moments that could not be undone.

But tonight, he fell asleep instantly. In the morning, the phone rang, and it was his sister. When he hung up he knew just how right he had been.

Life *did* snatch those moments away.

CHAPTER TEN

STACY AWOKE AND stretched, luxuriating in her surroundings. Sleeping in the bed had been like sleeping on a cloud. The room was that beautiful seamless mix of elegant and rustic that she had seen in the rest of the house.

Last night, being careful not to disturb the baby, she had dug through her things until she had found the bathing suit she had brought in case she wanted to avail herself to the facilities at the Whistler hotel she had booked.

A moment of searing guilt when she had found the suit: the hotel she had booked to write a story about Kiernan McAllister.

Obviously, after he had shared so deeply last night, writing about him was out of the question now. He had trusted her.

The thought sent a shiver up and down her spine. How many opportunities had she had to set the record straight with Kiernan, to tell him she was not a nanny?

She stared at the bathing suit. It was plain and black, made for swimming, not for sharing a hot tub with the likes of Kiernan McAllister!

She looked out her bedroom window. The clouds had drifted back in, blotting out the stars. It had started to snow again, heavily. She felt Kiernan's prediction of a melt was probably incorrect.

If she put off making her confession for a little longer, she would have an opportunity to play with the baby in the snow.

She was sure she would be able to talk Kiernan into joining them. The picture of them as a happy family unit filled her with bliss.

Getting into her pajamas—no more chosen for an encounter with McAllister than her bathing suit had been, Stacy crawled between the luxurious sheets and felt herself not just looking forward to tomorrow but feeling strangely excited by it.

She slept well and deeply and woke in the morning feeling that tingle of excitement, as well as feeling rested. She rolled over and peeped at the playpen.

It was empty!

The thought that Max might be old enough to get himself over those railings and out of the playpen had not even occurred to her! Would it have occurred to a real nanny?

She scrambled out of bed.

"Max!"

No answer. And no baby under the bed or in the bathroom or hiding behind the curtains. Her door was firmly closed. Surely, he could not have gone out.

Not even taking the time to avail herself of the luxurious housecoat that hung on the back of her bedroom door, Stacy flew down the hallway to the great room of the house.

"Max!" She had to shout over something roaring.

She skidded to a halt when she came into the room. Max was sitting on a blanket on the floor, surrounded by cookies. His uncle, in a housecoat like the one hanging on the back of her bedroom door, was sitting on the couch. He was at the controls of a...

She ducked as a remote control helicopter dive-bombed her.

Max chortled and pointed and stuffed another cookie in his mouth.

It was a happy scene except for one thing. The master of the house looked far from happy.

In fact, his mouth was set in a grim line, and when his eyes rested on her, there was something in them she didn't understand.

Contempt?

She looked down at her pajamas. All right. Surely he was used to something a little sexier than oversize white flannel with cotton-candy-pink kittens in the pattern. He seemed to have things under control—literally, since his hand was on the helicopter controls. She could duck back into her room and get dressed.

But then he would know she wanted to make a good impression on him. Erase that look of scathing judgment.

Come to think of it, there was no way *that* look was being caused by a choice in night wear!

"You should have called me," she said, coming into the room hesitantly, having to speak loudly over the whir of the helicopter. Had she slept right through the baby waking up? That meant Kiernan had come into her room. Had he watched her sleep?

Of course he hadn't. That would imply far more interest than she saw in his closed features this morning.

"I would have got up with him," Stacy said. And certainly she would not have given him cookies for breakfast.

Kiernan's expression only got darker.

"Because that's what nannies do?" he asked, his tone cool.

Stacy felt something inside her flash freeze at his tone. She said nothing, but she could feel herself bracing for the worst, her heart sinking.

"The phone was working last night," he said, his voice

cool and grim. "I left my sister a message right away. Just a brief message. Don't worry. Ivan and I are fine."

Kiernan paused and stared at her so long and hard that she squirmed. "Cavalry has arrived," he finished, his voice full of menace.

Stacy held her breath. Kiernan looked away from her now, frowning at the helicopter, which had gone seriously off course while he stared at her. It was flying dangerously close to his priceless chandelier, and he corrected its flight path while the baby clapped.

"I told her the nanny was here."

Stacy wanted to flee from the look on his face, but instead she moved across the room and sank down on the couch beside him. He seemed to flinch as he moved marginally away from her.

"She never sent a nanny," he said, his voice a growl of subdued anger. "She wanted Max and I to have time together. She thought—" He stopped himself abruptly and shook his head. "Never mind. It doesn't matter what she thought."

"She thought it would be good for you," Stacy guessed.

Kiernan landed the toy helicopter on the coffee table. He put down the controls and flicked something. The whirring sound stopped, and the blades coughed to a halt. He ignored Max's shout of protest.

The silence was more unnerving than the noise had been.

"We're not talking about me right now," he said, and his tone was dangerous. "We're talking about you. So, if my sister didn't send a nanny, that begs a question, doesn't it?"

Stacy nodded, stricken.

"If you aren't the nanny," he asked quietly, his eyes dark with anger and accusation, "who are you?"

He put a very bad word in between *who* and *are*.

I'm the woman you threw snowballs at, and made a snowman for. That's what is true.

But she couldn't bring herself to say it.

"I never actually said I was a nanny," Stacy whispered.

"You implied it."

"Yes, I did," she said woefully.

"And you probably knew that I was desperate enough for help to go along without asking too many questions."

"I *did* want to help you."

He snorted.

"I'm sorry," she whispered.

"You could be arrested, you know."

She leaned her head back on the sofa and closed her eyes. She was trying very hard not to cry. The look on his face was one of utter betrayal.

"That would be just my luck," she said. "Of all the exciting things a person could get arrested for, I get arrested for impersonating a nanny." She was trying to hide the fact she was nearly crying with the attempt at humor, but she was pretty sure it was a fail.

Humor fail it would say on the internet, just as the post of her last evening with Dylan had said *proposal fail.*

"Don't try and charm me with your Murphy's Law talk," he said. "Just tell me who you are, and what you want from me."

"I'm a writer," she whispered.

He snarled, an angry sound from deep in his throat.

She shivered. "That sounds like a mountain cat, right before he attacks."

"Don't try and distract."

"All right. I'm a writer. I recently lost my job at *Icons of Business,* under very unfair circumstances."

"Lack of ethics?" he said silkily.

"No! You were right last night—"

She could tell he did not want to be reminded of last night. "I made the mistake of dating my boss. Then it ended. I lost my job over it."

"If that's a play for sympathy, it's not working."

"I just wanted you to know everything I said has been true. Except for the nanny part. Which I didn't actually *say*."

"Sure. You probably made that up about your family, just to wiggle in here. The pajamas are a nice touch. What's not to trust about pink kittens frolicking?"

She knew he was angry because she had wiggled her way not just into his home but, for a little while last night, right by his rather formidable defenses. That was what he was truly upset about—that he had trusted her and been vulnerable to her—and she did not blame him.

"That part about my family is true," she said, and felt her eyes smarting from the pain of trying to hold back tears. "Who would make up something like that? And everything I said about the charity is true. Please don't hold it against the charity."

He did not look like he believed her, and she realized her chances of him helping her were over. She could never ask him to be the honorary chair now. Even his giving her the name of somebody who would help her was gone.

Everything that could go wrong had, only she wasn't the victim. She had brought it totally on herself this time.

In a rush she said, "The only thing that isn't true is the nanny part. I was fired—"

"Unfairly," he said cuttingly.

"Yes, it was unfairly! My boyfriend was my boss, and when our relationship ended, guess what? I got fired!"

He looked totally uncaring.

She rushed on. "I'm trying to make a go of it as a free-lancer. A friend from my old office phoned and told me where you live. I thought if I could get the story about the possible sale of your company, I could save my career."

"My company is not for sale," he said grimly, then tilted his head at her and smiled tightly. "No, wait. Maybe it is."

She ignored him and continued, her voice a near whisper, "And I guess I thought maybe I could get help for CCOFK at the same time.

"But then when I wound up in your flower bed, and my head was hurt, and the baby was here, I lost that initial opportunity to be up-front with you. It did seem to me you might need me. And that you'd throw me out if you knew who I really was and what I really wanted."

"Your lies were driven by pure altruism," he said cynically. "You thought I needed help with the baby. Very nice of you. And if all kinds of details about my life that I don't want anyone to know show up in print? That's just the price I pay for being helped, right?"

"I didn't actually lie," she said again, but she knew it sounded weak. "But I did misrepresent myself, and for that I am truly sorry. I'll get dressed and leave right away."

She had spoiled everything, even CCOFK's one chance of getting a much-needed boost. Filled with self-loathing, she scrambled up off the couch, but he caught her wrist and held her fast.

She tried to pull free, but he wouldn't let her.

"You're not going anywhere until you've signed a contract saying what you heard here, from me, stays here."

"That goes without saying," she said, tilting her jaw proudly.

"Sure, it does," he said coolly. "I have your word for that."

Well, could she really expect him to trust her? On what basis? That they had built a snowman together? Chased each other with snowballs?

She thought he had *seen* her, but now she could see she had wrecked everything.

"I'll sign whatever you want," she said with stiff pride, holding back tears. "You can get it ready while I go gather up my things."

She paused at the baby.

Max was looking between them anxiously. Now he looked at her and smiled, tentatively. "Upppeee? Pweeee?"

She cast a look at Kiernan's dark features, and then she didn't care what he thought about it. She scooped up that baby and pressed her nose into the sweet curve of his neck.

"Bye, Max," she whispered. The tears she had held back came when Max pressed both sides of her face with his hands and gave her a worried look.

"No bye!" he shouted imperiously. "No bye."

She buried her teary face deeper in Max's sturdy little shoulder.

"You *are* being a little premature in saying goodbye."

She whirled, scrubbing the tears with her pajama sleeve, and looked at Kiernan McAllister.

"You aren't going anywhere." His tone was cool and dangerous.

He stood up and came over to her. His grace was leopardlike and just as lethal. She forced herself not to turn with the baby and run. Instead, she stood her ground, knowing she deserved his censure. She had to crane her neck to see him. He towered over her.

"The roads are a worse mess than they were yesterday. It's on the news. Despite my driveway being plowed, there are accidents everywhere." Then his features hardened as he realized that could be interpreted as concern for her.

"My nephew, in a very short time, seems to have become attached to you. I think he's suffered enough losses. You will stay until I find a replacement for you."

Emotion warred in her. One was relief: obviously Kiernan did not think she was as terrible a person as she herself felt she was at the moment. He would not trust her with his nephew if he felt she was really a criminal.

But the other emotion she felt was pure horror.

How could she stay here under these circumstances, with Kiernan bristling with dislike for her?

"How long will that be?" she asked, her voice barely more than a whisper.

Kiernan checked the date on his watch. "I have no idea. I've never been in the market for a nanny before."

"I can't stay here indefinitely." Under these circumstances? It was impossible. She would rather face roads with a whole winter's worth of uncleared snow on them.

"Don't even act as if you have a choice," he warned her. "You are here until I tell you you may go? Is that clear?

CHAPTER ELEVEN

STACY'S MOUTH OPENED to protest. Of course, Kiernan could not force her to stay here. Still, she recalled her premonition when she had first turned toward his house. That it was not Cinderella's castle, but Beast's lair.

Was that just a few days ago?

It seemed as if it had been a lifetime ago, as if by playing in the snow and exchanging confidences under a starry night, she had changed in some fundamental way. Kiernan McAllister couldn't keep her here against her will!

"You can't—"

She started to say it but then snapped her mouth shut. He was not the one in the wrong here, she was.

And if it was sincere interest in this baby's well-being— and okay, Kiernan's as well—that had prevented her from telling the truth, those were the very things that would keep her here. Not his order that she could not leave but her own sense of decency.

Whether he knew it or not, she had just been given a second chance to do the right thing. Do-overs were rare in life, and she was taking this one.

Kiernan came out of his home office, sniffing the air like a wolf who had caught wind of something he didn't quite understand. He'd managed to hide out in his office all day.

Finding a nanny was a little more difficult than placing a call, Miss Harris had informed him an hour ago.

You had to fill out applications. You had to provide references.

You had to have a criminal record check, for God's sake.

It was one of those rare circumstances where it did not matter how much power, influence or money you had.

Finding a real nanny took time.

Why, he asked himself, did he feel as if he needed a nanny now? He'd insisted to Adele he didn't need one before.

The truth was, for all that he was giving an appearance otherwise, he felt like an emotional wreck, unsure of himself in ways he had never felt before. He felt angry with Stacy and angrier with himself.

And it wasn't just about her *not* being the nanny.

It was about the hope that he had allowed into his life when he knew that was the most dangerous thing of all. He needed her to stay here until his disillusionment was complete. And then he needed a professional nanny to step quietly into her place and look after Max so he could lick his wounds without doing any harm to the baby.

He knew, after all, how harmful adults dealing with things could be on unsuspecting children.

Kieran was used to solving problems quickly and aggressively. He was used to knocking down obstacles that got in his way. He had found there were very few problems money could not solve.

But apparently the nanny agency was not budging from its position. No criminal record check, no nanny.

He had not even looked at the forms Miss Harris had faxed him to fill out so she could forward them to the Royal Canadian Mounted Police. Instead, he had started looking over the plans for that hotel/condo development in downtown Vancouver instead.

Stacy Murphy Walker could be the damned nanny until his sister came back.

And he wasn't hiding from her, either, as if he was scared of her.

Despite her wariness of Kiernan's scowling bad temper, Stacy seemed determined not to let that affect the baby at all.

Despite the horrible tension between them, his house was filled with happy sounds. Laughing. Lots of laughing. And singing. There was lots of baby talk.

Maxie, you are such a smart baby. And so cute. I'm falling in love with you.

Such was his aversion to hearing about Stacy falling in love that he had gone into his bathroom, ripped tissue into thin strips, which he had then rolled and stuffed in his ears.

Ears plugged, Kiernan vowed he was not going to be pulled into her world or her web. He didn't actually want to see Stacy laughing. Or singing. Or winning over that gullible little baby.

But now, just like that wolf, hunger was driving him from the safety of his den.

As soon as he opened his office door, scent smacked him in the face. His house smelled almost unbearably good, but that intensified his need to approach with extreme wariness. Good smells often laced the trap, after all.

He went down the hall stealthily, ready to retreat at the first sign of danger. He paused at his bedroom door. His bed had been stripped of bedding, and he recognized one of the smells that tickled his nostrils.

The washer and dryer, set back in an alcove in the hallway invisible behind doors, were running. Those scents were not of the kind dangerous enough for a manly man to run from, even if he was peripherally aware there was something about those scents—laundry soap and dryer sheets—that made his house a home.

Feeling even warier, he continued down the hall and came into the great room, where he stopped in the shadow of the hall and watched for a moment, undetected, to gauge the danger.

It looked very dangerous, indeed.

Again, his house looked transformed.

Wrecked but transformed. An abundance of toys were scattered hazardously over the floors.

A tent had been made—was that the goose-down duvet off his bed—between the coffee table and the couch. Max was under the shelter, babbling away happily to Yike-Yike.

Max had not entertained himself, not even once, since his arrival. They had gone through six sets of batteries on the helicopter.

Stacy was in the kitchen area of the great room. Kiernan realized how good this design was for parents—the sink faced the seating area, so a mother could be busy in the kitchen and still supervise the kids.

Not that he wanted to be thinking of Stacy as a mom.

And yet there she no denying she somehow suited for that very role. She was flitting from counter to sink, totally unaware of him. She was humming, and she had that disturbing look of radiance about her that Kiernan had first seen when she had picked up Max.

It occurred to him that instead of butting his head up against a wall looking for a new nanny, he should have been checking out her story.

Surely, someone who had experienced the kind of losses she claimed could not look like that?

Maybe what he thought was radiance was just heat. A

stove timer went off, and she put on a pair of oven gloves
and opened the oven door. As she turned back from the
oven, hot pan in hands, her face was flushed.

Her hair had been pulled back, but a few strands had
escaped captivity, and she blew one out of her eyes.

He had not made a sound or moved, but she suddenly
went very still, the doe who had realized the wolf watched
her, the prey becoming aware of predator. She looked at
him.

"Hi," she said tentatively, hopeful, no doubt, that her
flurry of activity was moving him toward forgiveness.

When he didn't say anything, she looked disappointed
but moved on quickly.

"Can you put hot pans right on this surface?" she asked,
giving a worried look to the countertop.

"What the hell are you doing?"

"I'm making things," she said, and then she beamed
at him, still foolishly hopeful of his forgiveness. "Double ovens!"

She said that in a tone that most of the women he dated
would have reserved for a diamond tennis bracelet.

"You can bake cookies and pizza at the same time," she
told him, with the kind of reverence that should be reserved
for technological wonders like putting a backup camera
in the tailgate of a truck or being able to stream live from
the International Space Station.

Now that she had identified what was cooking, his
senses insisted on separating the smells and categorizing
them in order of their deliciousness.

He could smell chocolate chips melting and cheese bubbling, bread dough crust crisping.

"Are you trying to worm into my good graces?" he asked.
Damn it. His mouth was watering. "Put those down, for
Pete's sake, before you burn a hole through the oven glove."

"I just wasn't sure if I could set them right on the—"

"Yes!" He didn't expect his voice to be such a roar of complete frustration. She set the sheet down with a startled clatter.

Cookies.

Chocolate chip, just as his nose had told him.

"I had chocolate chips?" he said.

"Actually, an incredibly well stocked pantry."

There had been many chefs and caterers in this kitchen. Someone had set it up. Still, for all the good things that had been cooked in this kitchen, Kiernan was not sure the scents had ever been quite so tantalizing.

She turned back to the other oven and came out with a pizza, and not the kind you got at the deli section of the store, prefabricated, either.

"I didn't think you'd want to eat out of cans two days in a row."

It felt necessary to let her know he was in no way reliant on her domestic diva-ishness. "I usually order takeout. There are several really good restaurants in Whistler that will deliver."

"Oh, well, this is done now, if you're hungry. I'd hate to ask anyone to tackle the roads today."

Compassion for the delivery guy was not really a sign of a devious mind, his own mind insisted on pointing out helpfully.

He hadn't been aware just how hungry he was until she put that pizza on the counter, the crust golden, the cheese brown and bubbling.

He prevented himself, just barely, from running over there and starting to gobble it up like a starving creature.

"What were you doing in my bedroom?" he demanded.

"I just grabbed your sheets. I thought—"

"I don't want you to think. I want you to stay out of my bedroom."

"I'm making amends," she said stubbornly.

"A cleaning service comes in after I leave. I don't like having staff in my houses. And my feelings about having staff are private. And I don't want you poking through my things. You have enough ammunition on me. I don't need the whole world entertaining themselves with insights into how I live."

"I wasn't poking through your things! I took your sheets."

"No snooping through my drawers looking for fascinating insights into my life?"

"What kind of fascinating insights would I find in your drawers, for heaven's sake?"

She seemed to realize that could be taken two ways and the flush in her cheeks deepened.

"I once had a reporter ask me if I wore boxers or briefs."

"Well, that was bad reporting," she said, annoyed. "Because, believe me, big man that you are, your underwear is of absolutely no interest to anyone."

But her voice sounded strangled.

"You don't care to know?" he asked, taking wicked enjoyment in her discomfort, especially after that *big man that you are* crack.

"No!"

"Neither," he said.

She took a sudden interest in the cookies. She started taking them off the cookie sheet and putting them on a rack. They were obviously way too warm to be moved, crumbling as she touched them.

And she seemed totally unaware of it!

Save the cookies or enjoy her discomfort a little more?

He could have both. He moved into the kitchen beside her and removed the utensil she was destroying the cookies with from her hand.

"There, put that in your story."

"There isn't going to be a story," she insisted. She tried to grab the utensil. "Why would I be making amends if I planned to go ahead and write about you?" she said.

He took a cookie off the sheet with his fingers, still holding the flipper out of her reach. He popped the whole thing into his mouth. "You're just trying to lure me into a false sense of security."

She looked annoyed—which was safer for him than the *radiant* look she'd been sporting as she juggled hot pans out of the oven.

But obviously, part of making her amends was biting her tongue, because she didn't voice her annoyance.

In fact, her voice seemed deliberately sweet as she responded to his just-as-deliberate nastiness.

"Well, now you can have nice clean sheets tonight, and while you're lying in them, you can think, *that Stacy is a much nicer girl than I thought. I don't think I will have her arrested for impersonating a nanny, after all. She's trying very hard to make things right. I may just forgive her.*"

In the battle of light and dark, she was not going to win! And she, he reminded himself, was the transgressor. For all that sweetness, she was the one who had behaved without integrity.

Though, he noticed uneasily, he could not bring himself to think of her as representing dark.

He knew that was his lot in life.

"I don't want to be lying in my bed thinking of you in any way," he said. "And I don't think you want me to be thinking of you, either."

She gulped. And blushed.

Which was exactly what he'd intended. No sense her thinking her *amends* were going to batter down his defenses.

Because they weren't.

He was aware he could forgive her—she'd been misguided. It was obvious to him, from the stripped beds to the tent for Max to the cookies coming out of the oven to the concern for the delivery guy trying to tackle the roads, that there was not a malicious bone in her body.

It was obvious to him that she was going to wear herself out proving that to him and that he should put her out of her misery now.

Maybe he could have forgiven her, but it seemed easier not to. It seemed to him she was the kind of girl who dreamed the kind of dreams he could not ever fulfill.

It was doubtful he could have even before the death of his friend.

After?

Not a chance.

"If I'm ever thinking of you in my bed, Stacy Walker? The last thing on my mind will be the clean sheets."

There. That should scare her right out of her annoying domestic efforts to make amends.

He went over to the counter, took a plate from where she had a stack of them and grabbed two. He filled one with pizza and the other with cookies. He had enough food to avoid her until his sister came home, since he had resigned himself to the facts he was not going to find a nanny and that he didn't really want to find one, either.

Some twisted part of him was enjoying this torment! He got in a parting shot.

"And if you are ever in my bed, the last thing you will be thinking about is clean sheets."

Her mouth opened, and closed, a fish gasping for air. But then her eyes narrowed, and she glared at him.

"You are absolutely right," she said in that same sweet tone of voice. "I wouldn't be thinking of sheets. I'd be thinking about the toilet paper in your ears."

They glared at each other. He fought back the compulsion to tell her it wasn't toilet paper and to rip the tissue paper earplugs out of his ears. He wouldn't give her the satisfaction!

CHAPTER TWELVE

KIERNAN HAD ALMOST made good his escape from Stacy when he heard the sound of a vehicle grinding its way up his hill.

Instead of turning toward his bedroom, he approached the front entry and looked out the window.

It was still snowing heavily and a cab was pulling up in front of the house. It slid in the identical spot that Stacy's car had slid in, narrowly missing where hers sat now.

"Are you expecting someone?" he called.

"Yes," she said. "My old boyfriend. I've been expecting him for months. I hoped he would realize the error of his ways, drop down on bended knee and beg me to come back to him."

Kiernan watched his sister get out of the cab.

He turned back toward the kitchen. Adele arriving meant Stacy was leaving. Since it should have been a *yahoo* moment Kiernan was taken a little aback at how he felt.

Protective.

Despite her effort to sound flippant, he realized she really had, in that wild little imagination of hers, played out her boyfriend's return to her and probably in excruciating detail, too.

Stacy Murphy Walker was leaving. What would it hurt to set her straight before she went?

"So, would you take him back?" he asked, juggling his laden plates and leaning his shoulder against the log pillar that separated the kitchen from the hallway.

"In a breath," she said.

"Why? He sounds like he was an ass."

"At least he wore underwear," she muttered.

"I never said I didn't. I just said I didn't wear boxers or briefs."

He could tell she wanted to ask what, but she didn't. She clamped her mouth in a firm line, and said, "Well, it's not as if we're interviewing you to be my boyfriend. There is going to be no boyfriend. I am going to be a dedicated career woman. I am going to devote myself to CCOFK."

"I thought you'd take him back."

"He's not coming back. It's a revenge fantasy."

"If it really was, when he got down on bended knee, you'd say no, not yes."

"Well, he's not coming back, so I have planned my life without him. Or anyone."

"Sounds lonely," he said.

"I'll get a cat."

He walked across the space that separated them. She backed up until she hit the counter with her behind and had no place to go.

"What are you doing?" she stammered.

He couldn't let her go without tasting her. He carefully set down the plates. He lowered his head to hers and took her lips in his.

In that second he knew everything that was true about her.

Every. Single. Thing.

And he knew something about himself, too. He hadn't insisted she stay here because of the roads. He hadn't insisted she stay here because of Max.

It was because of him. It was because she had succeeded, in a few short days, of doing what no one else had done. Breaking something open inside him. Something that *wanted* light instead of darkness...

The kiss deepened. Kiernan took his time exploring her lips as he felt her initial startled resistance melt. It was followed by a surrender so complete it felt as if she was dissolving into him, her slender, soft curves melding to his own harder lines.

Her hands moved from the counter where she had braced herself and twined around his neck, pulling him down to her.

There was something in her he had not expected. Sweetness gave way quickly to something more savage, more hungry.

He heard the front door open.

"Yoo-hoo? Anyone home?"

"Mama!" Max cried.

Kiernan yanked away from Stacy. They stood staring at each other, chests heaving. Her hair was mussed where his hands had tangled in it; her lips were swollen and her cheeks were flushed.

He turned from her and watched as his nephew exploded out from under his tent and headed down the hall.

"If there's a Triple Crown for babies," he said, raking a hand through his hair, trying for a casual note so that Stacy would not see how that kiss had shaken him, "he's going to win."

"What was that about?" she whispered. He shot her a glance just in time to see her touching the swollen swell of her lips with trembling fingertips. She was staring at him with wide eyes.

If his sister wasn't shaking snow off her coat in the

front hall, he was pretty sure he would finish what he started.

But then he'd known his sister was coming when he had started, a safety net, in case he fell.

And Stacy was the kind of girl who could make a guy fall: straight into the wide pools of her eyes, straight into the softness of that heart. She was the kind of woman who could make a person who had lost hope entirely think that there was a chance. Stacy Murphy Walker had stormed his world, and it felt as if there was only one defense against that. The one he should have taken the minute he found out she was an imposter but hadn't. Stacy had to go.

"It was a gift," he growled.

"A gift? Your kiss was a gift," she stammered, but her eyes were narrowing dangerously. She was incensed, and he deserved it.

"Just letting you know," he said quietly, "you'll never be satisfied with a cat."

She touched her lips again.

"Or the old beau, either," he said.

He heard his sister coming down the hall and sprang back from Stacy just as Adele came into the room, Max riding in the crook of her arm, her cheeks sparkling from the cold.

And her eyes sparkling in a way he had not seen for a long, long time.

Adele looked at him and then at Stacy and back at him. He had the horrible feeling that Stacy's mussed hair and swollen lips—not to mention the glitter in those green eyes—were a dead giveaway. Adele knew exactly what had transpired between them.

"Stacy Walker, my sister, Adele. The reason you can leave now."

"Leave?" Adele said. "No one's going anywhere in that!

The cab could barely make it from Whistler. I thought we were going to wind up in the ditch a dozen times. The roads were littered with vehicles. Your driveway was in the best shape of any road I was on today."

"I'll drive her," he said. He heard an edge of desperation in his voice. He was pretty sure, from the way Adele's head swung toward him, she heard it, too.

When he had kissed Stacy it had been because goodbye was in clear sight.

Adele had a little smile on her face he didn't like one little bit.

"Yes, that's fine," Stacy said, her voice strained. "I'd have to come back for my car, though."

"I can have it delivered."

"That seems like a great deal of trouble," Stacy said, ridiculously formal, given that he had just kissed her. And she had kissed back.

"No trouble at all."

"Quit being so silly," Adele said.

Silly? He glared at his sister just to help her remember who he was, but she wasn't even looking at him.

"You aren't going anywhere," Adele said, offering her hand to Stacy. "I've been looking forward to meeting you. And even more so now that I saw the snowman! He's adorable. I just can't wait to get to know the woman who could convince Kiernan to make a snowman."

"How do you know I made it?" Kiernan demanded.

"It's eight feet tall, for goodness' sake. Who do you think I would think made it? Max?"

Adele put her nose against her baby's and said, "Mommy missed you so much, you adorable little winky-woo. I couldn't stay away from you for another minute."

He was pretty sure it was news of the imposter nanny, whom she was now greeting with the enthusiasm of a just discovered royal relative, that had brought his sister home.

Or maybe not.

When his sister looked at Max, despite all her losses, she had the same look on her face that he had seen on Stacy's. Radiance.

Or was it all because of Max? It had never occurred to him until this very second that maybe his sister had not been alone on her getaway.

"He's not..." he told Adele, stopping just in time from saying *winky-woo,* "an adorable little anything. He's a demanding little tyrant."

"Takes after his uncle, then," Adele said with a nod.

He'd had enough of her. "Look, I'm exhausted and I need—Stacy needs to go." He felt he'd revealed way too much with that one, because Adele looked at him sympathetically.

"The morning is plenty of time to figure out who is going where. I've just been on those roads. I don't want you on them."

In her voice, he heard the thread of real fear, the understanding that life could change in an instant, in one bad decision. He had put that fear and that awareness in his sister; he had done that when he had failed to protect her husband.

"I guess we could figure things out in the morning," he conceded with ill grace, since he could clearly see an argument was going to get him nowhere.

"Good! That will give Stacy and I a chance get to know each other."

Adele and Stacy, these two ever so resilient women, getting to know each other?

He shot his sister a dark look, which didn't perturb her

in the least, retrieved his plates of pizza and cookies and headed down the hall to his room.

If he closed his door with a little more force than was strictly necessary, it was perfectly excusable.

Hours later he gave up on trying to sleep, because even with pillows over his head—he wasn't using toilet paper again—he could still hear them out there giggling away like old school chums.

A tap came on his door.

He quickly turned off his bedside light.

The door opened and Adele came in. "I saw the light from under the door."

He sat up and grudgingly turned the light back on. "What do you want?"

"You don't have to say that as if I'm some kind of traitor!"

"You knew she was an imposter! You're the one who alerted me that you hadn't sent a nanny at all. I'm surrounded by women who lie to me. What is the idea of saying you were sending a nanny when you had no intention of doing that?"

His sister made herself comfy on the edge of his bed.

"It was just hurting me so badly to see how Danner's death was affecting you, Kee. You seemed to be slipping further away every day. And there was something sharp and cynical and angry about you that I had never seen before."

"That doesn't sound like someone anyone in their right mind would leave an infant with!"

"I knew you were in there somewhere. And I thought being around Max would force you to wake up, to be *here,* instead of in that dark place you couldn't seem to come back from."

"You're saying that in past tense, as though I have come back."

"There's a snowman on the front lawn," she said.

"That is hardly the miracle you are looking for, Adele."

"I need to tell you something," she whispered.

"What?" He was not sure he liked her tone of voice.

"Mark and I started seeing each other a while back. At first, it was just comforting each other over Danner. Sometimes, we'd talk about our mutual concern for you. Anyway, that's why I needed some time this weekend. I needed to make a decision."

"About?"

"Mark has asked me to marry him."

Kiernan held his breath.

"I said yes. I love him very much."

He didn't quite know what to say. He was stunned, in a way, that life moved on. Stunned that he had missed the developing relationship between Adele and Mark. Stunned at his sister's ability to say yes to love all over again.

"Congratulations," he said gruffly. He realized he was shaken but glad for her. "I guess maybe you did get the miracle you were looking for. But don't get any ideas about me."

"I have been looking for a miracle for you," she said, "but I was looking in one direction, and it came from another."

"There have been no miracles here," he warned her. "None."

"Hmm."

"Don't say hmm, like that. If you think that lying little chit of an imposter nanny is a miracle, you need a little miracle research."

"I did some research, you know. On her. That's why I

acted as if I knew her when I got here. I kind of did. You can find out the most amazing things on the internet."

He really wanted to pretend he was not interested in this. He wanted his sister to think he was completely indifferent to what she had discovered about Stacy Walker Murphy on the internet.

Instead, in a voice he hoped was stripped of anything that could be interpreted as interest, Kiernan heard himself say, "Like?"

CHAPTER THIRTEEN

"HER WHOLE FAMILY was killed in a car accident when she was sixteen," Adele told him, her voice aching with tenderness.

"I know that already."

"Oh." Adele cocked her head at him. "Did you look her up on the internet, too?"

"No."

"So, she told you that?"

"To try and wangle her way by my defenses!"

"She *has* used her greatest tragedy as a tool, but, as shocking as this will be to you, it doesn't have anything to do with you. She started that group."

"Career and College Opportunities for Orphans."

"Foster kids," his sister corrected him mildly. She twirled some hair around her little finger. "She told you that, too?"

"She mentioned it briefly."

"Ah. You seemed to have known each other quite a short time to have shared so deeply."

He glared at Adele. "I *regret* that. I don't see it as cause for celebration. Look, the facts are the facts. She misrepresented herself on purpose. She's a writer not a nanny."

"She's a good one, too. I read some of her stuff online. She would be a great person to entrust your story to."

"What story?" he asked dangerously. "Look, sis, she needs to go. She does not need to be adopted by you."

"She's always dreamed of a winter holiday," Adele said with a frightening softness, not hearing the danger in his voice at all. "She's had so much go wrong in her life. She expects the worst."

Poster child for Murphy's Law he remembered her introducing herself.

"And I can hardly blame her. There's a video online—" She stopped.

"A video? Of Stacy?"

"I cannot believe you didn't go online yourself when you found out she wasn't a nanny!"

"Well, I didn't. What's the video of?"

"Never mind. It's not important. What's important is that she's worked really hard at giving things to others. I looked up that charity online. For a group with very little money and a low profile, they accomplish quite a bit. They've handed out two dozen scholarships in the past eight years."

"Earth-shattering," he said drily.

"That's twenty-four young people changed forever. For your information, that *is* earth shattering."

"Okay, so the company will donate some money," he said.

His sister gave him a look that said he was missing the point.

"And provide some people with know-how to get her little group off the ground."

"You're missing the point."

"Which is?"

"She expects the worst."

"It's her karma," he growled. "What do you expect with a middle name like Murphy?"

"Do not hide behind flippancy with me," his sister warned. He really hated it when she took that tone.

But then her voice softened, "What if the best thing ever happened to her? What if good came from this predicament she finds herself in, instead of bad?"

"What would she learn from that?"

"That life is good!"

"Well, it isn't!" But, he thought, though the thought was unwilling as hell, it had been good. It had been unexpectedly good for a few short days with Stacy. Not that he could ever let Adele know that!

His sister looked at him, then shook her head with disappointment. He felt her disappointment in him all the way to his toes.

He had been Adele's hero since they were kids.

Not that he deserved that title now!

"When did you become *this* person?" Adele asked.

"I'm protecting myself."

"Against what?"

"Against life, as if you should have to ask. I became *this* person the day that Danner died."

His sister suddenly looked very, very angry.

"No one," she said, her words angry, "would hate that more than him. That you would make that his legacy to the world is disgraceful. He embraced life. He treated it all like an incredible adventure, and I'm grateful for that. I'm grateful for the person I am because I got to be with him for a short time. I'm grateful for my son."

Kiernan remembered Stacy, too, had made gratitude her legacy from tragedy.

"For God's sake," his sister said, "that girl has lost everything. You are in a position to get out of your big, fat self-pitying self and do something for her."

His big, fat, self-pitying self?

"She lied to me!"

"If you couldn't tell who Stacy Walker was from the minute you laid eyes on her, there is no hope for you, Kiernan McAllister. None at all."

He remembered claiming Stacy's lips earlier.

And knowing, just as his sister had said, the absolute truth about her.

And of course, the danger she posed to him on many levels.

His sister shot him one last meaningful look and flounced off the bed, tossing her hair. She marched from his room, closing his door with a snap behind her.

One of the things that was not good about being very powerful was that people stopped telling you the truth and started telling you what you wanted to hear. One of the people he could trust not to do that was Adele.

Kiernan recognized that this brief encounter with Stacy had rocked his world, that he could not think with his normal discernment and detachment. His sister was trying to steer him in the right direction.

And his sister had never come from any place but love.

He told himself he was not going to look on his computer. He lasted about thirty seconds before he went and retrieved it from his dresser. Sometimes the internet worked up here and mostly it didn't. He was hoping it wouldn't, but he typed in her name anyway.

A video called *Proposal Fail* came up.

Stacy looked gorgeous: her hair and makeup done, in a sexy dress and high heels. He recognized the restaurant as one of Vancouver's best.

But, despite how gorgeous she looked and the fact she was in one of Vancouver's most upscale restaurants, the scene had obviously been captured after she was already angry.

"You want me to what?" she asked, her voice high and shrill.

The guy looked around nervously, twirled his wineglass and wouldn't look at her.

Kiernan found himself looking at the beau critically. She would take *him* back?

Dylan had guffawed when she had said that, apparently more loudly than she had thought.

"I thought you were going to ask me to marry you, and you're asking me to shack up with you?"

"Shack up, Stacy, really? What century is that from?"

Kiernan had the ugly feeling if he could, he would have crawled through the computer screen, picked that guy up by his throat and knocked his teeth out.

He had obviously caused Stacy intense pain…and instead of trying to make it better, he had a sneering look on his face.

She'd go back to him? Really?

Kiernan watched Stacy stand up. Pick up her wine. Take a fortifying sip and then walk over to her beau.

She dumped the whole glass over his head. It was red and it stained his pristine white shirt beyond repair.

"What century is that from?" she yelled for the entertainment of the whole world.

Only Kiernan didn't feel entertained at all. He could clearly see she was crying as she stormed from the room. The guy looked more annoyed about his shirt than the fact his girlfriend had just left him.

Good grief, what kind of bad luck was it to have a moment like that posted?

He had a moment of clarity as he shut off his computer.

What if it wasn't all about him? Adele was so right. Despite a life threaded through with the worst kind of tragedy, Stacy was struggling valiantly to make it a better place.

Even while she claimed her own dreams were in tatters, he knew she really stood on the edge.

Of going to the place where he was, a place of hopelessness and cynicism that he would not wish on anyone, or a place of being returned to faith.

He seemed like the last person who could be entrusted with an assignment like that—a return to faith—but really, it would not take much of a push to get her moving in the right direction.

What if he could, in some small way, get out of his big, fat, self-pitying self to help another human being to believe in dreams again?

His sister, he was pretty sure, was entirely correct about him. There was no hope for him. None at all.

But despite her denials, he had seen in Stacy's face she clung to hope the way a person who had survived a shipwreck clung to the lifeboat.

There was no sense crushing that thing called hope simply because he could not feel it!

What if he could do some small thing that would change her? Give her a much-needed boost? Not just protect her from the return of her boyfriend or a life as a crazy cat lady, but help her believe in the power of her dreams all over again?

He went down the hall to the room his sister preferred. She had moved Max's playpen in there and was sitting on the bed, leafing through a book.

"What would you suggest?" he asked his sister.

She looked up from the book. A light came on in her face. That light almost made the chance he was taking worth it. Of course, he thought she was going to suggest something he could *buy*. An all-expense-paid week or two to a world-class resort. Like Whistler, only that was probably too close to home to seem like a real dream.

Steamboat, Colorado, maybe.

Les Trois Vallées, in the French Alps. Why had he thought of that? Because of Brides-les-Bains, one of those three very famous resorts?

If his mind was making weird jumps in logic like that: from helping her dreams come true to thinking of her in any context with *bride* in it, then the farther away the better.

"I was thinking you should take her up to Last Chance tomorrow," his sister said.

He had to refuse. Last Chance was, in his opinion, one of the most beautiful places on the planet. And Kiernan had been to many beautiful places on the planet.

The humble little cabin named Last Chance, behind his house, way up the mountain in a grove of old, old cedar, as well as having one of the most panoramic views he had ever seen, had its own private natural hot spring.

"Can you think of a better place for the perfect winter getaway?" Adele asked.

No, he couldn't. On the other hand, did he really want to be at a place named Last Chance with Stacy Walker? Last chance to make things right? To be a better man?

Last chance to hope, to live again, to...

As well as being remote and beautiful, it was a place of romance and magic.

"I'll come, too," Adele said, as if she read each of his doubts. "We can put Max in the sled and you can pull it."

The truth? He'd always had trouble saying no to his sister. Since he had killed her husband, the father of her child, his sense of obligation to her, of somehow wanting to make up to her that which could never be made up felt like a boulder sitting on his chest, slowly crushing the life out of him.

He owed his sister big-time, a debt he had no hope of repaying. There was that word again, hope.

And so if Adele wanted to take Stacy Murphy Walker to Last Chance, that was what he would help her do. He was being given an opportunity to get out of his big, fat, self-pitying self long enough to be the better man.

Temporarily.

The words...

CHAPTER FOURTEEN

"LAST CHANCE?" STACY said, dubiously. "What is that?"

Kiernan glared at her. She was looking the proverbial gift horse in the mouth. He was doing her a favor. He was making her dreams come true, for Pete's sake. Did she have to look so reluctant? But things had been awkward between them since he had kissed her.

That kiss in the kitchen was supposed to have been *goodbye*. But she was still here, and the memory of that kiss sizzled in the air between them this morning.

"It's actually the reason I bought this property," he said, striving for patience in the face of her lack of enthusiasm. "Danner found this little cabin to rent one winter. The only way you can reach it once the snow flies is on cross-country skis. There's a natural hot spring right beside it."

He could see the war in her face.

"Perfect winter getaway," he said. "I've been at some of the best resorts in the world, and it beats all of them. And it's a two-hour ski from here."

He'd almost had her, until he'd mentioned the ski part.

"Oh, I've never skied. I'm sure I would make a complete fool of myself. No, really, now that your sister is here, I have to leave."

Her voice was firm, but unless he missed his guess, Stacy looked wistful. Besides, when he saw her fear of making a fool of herself, he thought of that internet video posting, knew she was still suffering the humiliation of it and committed even more to convincing her to go. He hated the thought of her going through life being afraid to do things.

"The roads are worse this morning than they were last night," Kiernan said. Well, since the fear was there anyway, he might as well press it to his advantage. He hoped her fear of driving on the roads would be greater than her fear of making a fool of herself.

"And I still don't think the snow will last," he continued. "This might be your only opportunity to get up there."

"Last chance?" she said, and hazarded a smile.

"Exactly."

He certainly wasn't inviting her back here, ever.

Because she did all sorts of things to him that he wasn't sure he wanted done. Like made him aware, for the first time in a long time, what it felt like to be alive.

To notice what the light looked like kissing chocolate curls and how her laughter, ringing out with the baby's laughter, made everything different.

Who was he kidding?

The moment the shift had happened was when his lips touched hers.

"I don't have any of the right stuff," she said, and now he could hear in her voice, too, that she had capitulated and was wistful to go.

"Don't worry, I have all the right stuff."

And she looked at him as if that could be taken two ways and that maybe she really thought he did have all the right stuff, despite the fact he had been a complete jerk to her.

Well, she had been frantic in her attempts to make amends. He had slept aware it was her hands that had put the sheets on his bed, with a belly satisfyingly full of really good things.

So, he would make amends, too.

Give her that winter holiday she had always wanted, then send her on her way. No more kissing. *Toodle-oo.*

Kieran McAllister frowned. He did not say *toodle-oo.* Maybe one more kiss to cement it in her mind about leaving both cats and the old boyfriend out of her plans for the future.

The thought of that kiss may have flashed through his eyes, because she looked flustered suddenly, too.

He wasn't going to kiss her again. "We're going to be chaperoned!" he recalled, a touch desperately. "Adele and Ivan are coming, too."

"Oh!" Stacy still seemed underenthused.

And he recognized he had to take a risk. He had to tell her the truth.

"And I've behaved badly toward you," he said. "I don't want our time together to end on this note."

And instantly he was aware of the most dangerous thing of all: this really wasn't about her, no matter how he tried to cloak it in altruism.

He did not want their time together to end at all.

Was that why he was really offering her the journey to Last Chance? It was. It was to see if there was any hope at all, and if there was, if he was brave enough to reach for it, to reach for the life rope that had been thrown into the quagmire he had existed in.

The truth was he needed this trip to Last Chance way more than she did.

Something softened in her face, and he knew she had heard the truth. And he knew she was remembering: snowmen and snow angels and dodging popcorn missiles and sharing ordinary moments together that had somehow become extraordinary.

"Yes, all right," Stacy said. "I'd like that."

Thank goodness for chaperones, he thought.

But Adele announced, minutes before they were set to leave, that she wasn't coming. Stacy reacted to the announcement by blushing, Kiernan smelled a rat, the same as he had when Max had been left in his office without warning.

"I think Max is getting a cold," Adele said. "It wouldn't be good for him to be outside all day. Look at his nose."

Kiernan, to his everlasting regret, looked at his nephew's nose. Even his sister could not manufacture something like that!

In light of Stacy's blush of discomfort, he debated canceling. But only for about two seconds.

Because sometime during the night he realized he was looking forward to going up there as much as he had looked forward to anything for a long, long time.

And he knew part of it was he was excited about showing it to her, the nanny imposter.

How could he think that—nanny imposter—and feel only amusement and no anger at all?

He was working at being a better man. He would show her a great day, enjoy her wonder, bring her home.

There would be absolutely no need to reinforce the cat, ex-boyfriend lesson.

With his lips!

Stacy probably needed her head examined, but here she was having a ski lesson from Kieran McAllister

She hadn't even backed out when she heard Adele and Max were not coming.

Because, really, she had played it safe her entire life. And where had that gotten her?

No, if she had learned one thing in her short time here, it was this: when things started spinning out of control, go with it rather than fight it!

And spinning out of control was a very apt description of how she had felt after Kiernan had kissed her in the kitchen.

One kiss, and she was pretty sure she was cured forever of wanting Dylan back. Or a cat.

Though as a point of pride, she could not let Kiernan know that his kiss had cured her of those desires.

What she did desire now, in a way she had never wanted it before, was to embrace it all, including the uncertainty she felt every single time she looked at Kiernan.

She was being offered an adventure. Not just any adventure. A chance to do something she had longed to do ever since she had enjoyed the snow with her beloved father.

Her dad had never called her Stacy. He had always, affectionately, teasingly called her Murphy.

Bur for once something seemed to be going right for her, and she was not saying no to that.

And it was true she was getting in way over her head with this family. Since Kiernan had kissed her, she felt as if she had the shivers, which could not be cured by anything, not even a roaring fire in the hearth in the great room.

But the thing was, she didn't mind feeling that way.

She felt alive. And so, marveling at the unexpected spin her life had taken, she watched Kiernan get ready.

His comfort with the equipment inspired confidence. She watched him waxing the skis, listened to him explaining how the waxes depended on the temperature and the snow.

"You can buy skis that don't need waxing, but I don't," he said. "I'm a purist."

There was a whole section underneath the back deck of his house devoted to outdoor equipment. He could provide skis and snowshoes and skates to about twenty people.

"We always make a skating rink at the back of the house later in the year," he told her.

And Stacy's desire shifted again: to see that. To see him on skates, to have him teach her that, too. But she knew that was taking it too far into the future, and that today was called the present, because that's what it was, a gift.

A gift that did not promise the future.

She vowed to herself she would just enjoy this day without overlaying it with anxiety about what could possibly happen next.

He'd had no trouble at all finding her size of skis and boots. Adele had lent her a jacket that fit, a hat and good mittens.

"Are we getting on a chairlift?" she asked nervously, despite her confidence in him, she had some doubts about herself. *Anything that can go wrong, will.*

He laughed. "No lifts for this. This is cross-country skiing," he said. "It's way different than downhill skiing, which is the chairlift kind."

"In what way is it different?"

"More work. Everything we do, we do under our own power." Satisfied with the wax, he led the way outside and set two pairs of skis on the ground.

"Okay, these are yours. Put your toe in there and step down."

It was difficult to hold one foot up, position it into a very small area and step down. Her foot slid uncooperatively everywhere *but* into the binding.

To her embarrassment, he had to get down in the snow

and guide her foot into the right place, snap the binding down. Then, while he was already on the ground, he did the other one, too.

She looked down at his head. That their acquaintance could be marked in days seemed impossible.

She felt as if she had known Kiernan McAllister forever. *And would know him forever.*

And there went her vow not to spoil any part of this day fretting about the future and what could happen next.

Still, it took all her will to stop herself from reaching out and sliding her hand through the silk of his hair. He glanced up at her, his long lashes over those amazing silver eyes holding speckles of frost. Her heart swooped upward, like a bird that had been freed from a cage.

Was she falling in love with him?

Of course not. She reprimanded herself. She barely knew him.

But she *had* kissed him. And made a snowman with him. And lain on her back beside him, their cold hands intertwined as they looked at the stars and exchanged confidences.

Of course she did not love him. But the air seemed to sparkle with diamond drops of possibility that outshone the diamond drops that sparkled in the pristine snow all around them.

She felt some exquisite awareness tickling along her spine as she watched him expertly step into his skis.

And then, thankfully, the time for thinking was done, because she was swept into a world of movement and laughter, pure physical activity and exertion.

"I'll show you a few basic moves." He showed her the step and glide.

Then she tried it. "Argh! You are pure power and grace. I am a penguin waddling!"

"Relax. It's all just for fun. I'll break trail, you put your skis in my tracks and follow me. Just do what I do and everything will be fine."

And then, amazingly she did relax, because he was in front of her and not witnessing her clumsy efforts to follow his ski tracks. It was fun and easier than she had anticipated.

"See? Everything is fine, isn't it?"

And it was. No, it was more than fine. Seconds from the house, they entered the trees. The silence was broken only by the occasional branch letting go of its load of snow, and her breathing, loud in her own ears.

"You doing okay?" he called.

"It is hard work. But so much fun!"

He glanced over his shoulder at her, his approving smile lit up her world.

She loved being behind him. She could drink her fill of him without him ever knowing how she gloried in his easy strength, his power, his confidence.

The woods were extraordinarily silent and beautiful. They had been making their way up a very gradual slope, and now it steepened.

"Like this," he said. He set his skis like triangles and walked his way up the hill, making a fishbone pattern in the new snow. She tried it. Now this was harder than he had made it look.

Partway up the incline, she could feel herself sliding back instead of going forward. She let out a little shriek of dismay, threw herself forward on her poles and froze leaning heavily on them.

He looked back at her and burst out laughing. He turned and skied back to her, stopping with a swish of snow.

"I'm stuck," she said.

"I can see that," he said with a smile. "I'll get you unstuck."

He regarded her predicament thoughtfully, then pulled in right behind her, his skis forming a sandwich around her own.

She could feel his breath on her neck, and his hands went to the small of her back and he shoved.

"Okay," he said, his breath still warm on her neck and tickling her ears, "pull with your poles and dig in those edges. That's it. Just one small step. Good. And another one."

A lot of things seemed to be coming unstuck, most of them within her.

"I'm sliding back on your skis." She was. She slid right back into him, and for a breathless moment they stood there, glued together, the majesty of the quiet mountains all around them.

His arms folded lightly around her. "You're doing great." And then he let her go and shoved her again.

Huffing and puffing, she managed to inch her way up the steep incline.

"You've got it." And then he left his place behind her and moved ahead of her, with a powerful skating motion that broke the trail.

Of course, what goes up must come down, and as she crested the hill, she saw it was a long downhill run.

He swooped down it, a cry of pure joy coming off his lips. She watched as he invited speed, crouched, played with the hill and the snow and gravity.

He reached the bottom, slid to a sideways stop in an incredible display of agility and spray of snow.

"Come on," he called.

The truth was she was terrified. Her heart was doing that beating-too-fast thing that it had been doing for almost two full days. She stared down the hill. It seemed a long way down. And it seemed very steep.

"You can sidestep it if you want," he called. He climbed partway back up the hill and demonstrated a way she could come down.

But suddenly she didn't want to play it safe. She let out a war whoop and shoved her poles to get going. Then she was swooshing down the hill so fast she could feel her stomach drop. Her eyes got tears in them. Her hat flew off.

She gained speed. She let out another whoop, the pure joy of letting go completely! She raced by him, screaming with laughter.

Except that beyond him, he had not broken the trail. Her skis hit the virgin snow and slowed so abruptly she thought she was going to be tossed right out of her bindings.

As soon as she started to think about what could happen, it did. She caught an edge and could feel herself cartwheeling through the snow.

Only it didn't hurt. It was like tumbling into a cold pillow. After she stopped, she lay there for a moment, staring at the sky.

He skied over and peered down at her. "Are you okay?" he asked.

"Really?" she said. "Never better."

And then they were both laughing.

And it felt as if *really* she had never had a better moment in her whole life.

CHAPTER FIFTEEN

TWO HOURS LATER, coated in generous amounts of sweat, crusted in snow and dazzled by laughter and the sun that had come out on the mountain, they burst into a small clearing.

Stacy was aware that Kiernan was watching her, and from the small smile that played across his lips, her reaction did not disappoint.

She clapped her wet, mittened hands over her mouth, but not before a gasp of pure wonder escaped it.

There was a cabin at the far edge of the clearing. It was tiny and humble, the logs long since weathered to gray. And yet, set amongst the drifts of snow, with snow sparkling on its roof and the red curtains showing through the window, it was a homey sight in the middle of the majesty of the mountains. Even the little outhouse that was behind it, a half-moon carved in the door, was adorable.

On the other side of the cabin, a stream trickled down rocks, heavy mist rising off of it.

"What is that smell?" she asked, the only thing not in keeping with the beauty of the scene.

"That stream is a natural hot spring. You're smelling minerals, mostly sulfur. Despite the smell, they are supposed to be very good for you. Tracks show us that even the animals come here. Come on. I'll show you."

He glided forward. After two hours, she felt her abilities had not improved all that much. She still waddled after him.

He skied right to the cabin, kicked off his skis and shrugged off the pack he had carried the entire way. She arrived and he showed her how to release the binding by putting the tip of the pole on it and pushing.

She stepped out of the skis and had to reach for his arm.

"My legs feel wobbly," she said, and then let go of his arm and went to the edge of the water.

"That water will have you feeling back to normal in no time." He had come to stand beside her.

"This must have taken someone hundreds of painstaking hours," she said, regarding the rock pool, complete with an underwater bench that had been built to capture the steaming water from the springs.

"I had the good fortune to get it exactly as it was. You see how the water is seeping out of the rocks on the downhill side? It acts as a natural filtration system. The water is constantly being replaced."

"The rocks are like artwork," she said. The constant flow of water over them turned colors that might have been muted if they were dry to spectacularly jewel like. There were rocks in golds and greens and grays and blues and pinks.

"Are we going to go in that?" she breathed.

"Of course. If you brought a bathing suit."

Her face crumpled. "No. You never said to. I'm not sure I would have believed you if you had. This is pure magic, Kieran, but I didn't bring a suit. I guess I can't go in."

He raised an eyebrow wickedly. "Unless…"

"No!" she said.

"Well, guess what, Murphy?"

"What?"

"Unless somebody has figured out that anything that can go wrong will, and that someone had your back."

Him?

She could feel tears pricking her eyes.

"What's the matter?" he asked softly.

"Nothing. My dad used to call me Murphy. No one has for a long time."

"Ah, Murphy," he said gruffly, put his arm around her shoulders and pulled her hard against his own shoulder. "Adele packed you a bathing suit," he said, his tone gentle as a touch.

"Oh, Adele," she said, not sure if she was disappointed or relieved. Well, maybe relieved. She certainly wouldn't want him packing her a bathing suit. Come to that, did she want to be sharing a very romantic moment with him in a bathing suit she had not even chosen herself?

"She packed us lunch, too. You want to do that first?"

She realized she was ravenous…and that lunch would give her reprieve from donning the bathing suit. It was hard enough to put on a bathing suit you had chosen yourself, after many self-critical moments in front of the mirror. What would Adele have chosen for her?

He laughed at her expression. "Lunch it is. We just burned about a million calories each." He opened the backpack and took out the contents. "Hot dogs and marshmallows. A good thing we burned so many calories."

He rummaged through the pack some more. "Look, she packed a bottle of wine to go with our hot dogs." He shook his head. "Not exactly hot dog wine. It's a rare bottle of ice wine."

"We don't have to drink it," Stacy said. In fact probably better if they did not. "You are probably saving that for a special occasion."

"I was," he said, rummaging again, and then he hesitated at something he found in that pack, "and I can't think of an occasion more special than this one."

"In what way?" she stammered.

"Part of the snow virgin ceremonies," he teased, and pulled something else out of the pack and held it up.

"I'm pretty sure I lost my snow virginity on the night of the snowball fight," she choked out. "Snowball fight. Snow angel. Snowman. Yup. Done."

"I'm pretty sure you're not done until you've been dipped in the waters of Last Chance in this."

She looked at the tiny piece of black-and-white fabric he was waving, not comprehending.

"Adele packed you a bikini!"

Well, that answered the burning question of what kind of bathing suit Adele had packed for her!

"Let's eat," she said, strangled.

"How are you at fire starting?"

"Is this still part of the whole snow virgin thing? Because I'd be about the same at that as I am at snowman building. And skiing."

"All the same," he said, and tossed a package of matches at her. "You can be in charge of the fire pit out here. I'm going to start a fire in stove in the cabin, too, so we have a warm place to get changed."

Into a black-and-white bikini that looked, at a glance, as if it didn't have enough fabric in it to make a good-size handkerchief.

She was probably going to need the wine to find the nerve to put on the bathing suit. Meanwhile, she would distract herself by trying to start a fire.

Kiernan came back outside and helped her. Soon he had turned her little pile of twigs and tiny flame into a roaring blaze and they were toasting hot dogs on sticks over it.

"Oh, my," she said an hour later. "Did I eat three hot dogs?"

"You did."

"Why did it taste like food from the gods?"

"They're pleased about the sacrificing of the snow virgin?" He laughed at her face. It was so good to hear him laugh like that, boyishly, carelessly, mischievously. He could tease her for a hundred years about being a snow virgin, if she just got to hear him laugh.

"I'm getting a little confused," she said. "Am I being sacrificed or deflowered?"

It was her turn to feel richly satisfied when a tide of brick-red worked its way up the strong column of his neck.

"The cabin is probably warm by now, if you want to go put on your suit," he said gruffly, not looking at her. Really, for the first time since she had gotten on those skies, it felt as if she had the upper hand.

The inside of the cabin was rudimentary but darling. She found the bathing suit wrapped in a towel on the bed.

It was definitely the tiniest bathing suit she had ever put on! So much for having the upper hand. Stacy felt like a nervous wreck after donning the bathing suit. There wasn't even a mirror to check how revealing it was. She wrapped herself in a towel and headed outside.

He was already in the hot pool and she gulped at the pure wonder of the moment life had delivered.

She slipped off the towel and felt a surge of fresh wonder at the look in his eyes, stormy with appreciation, on her. Rough stone steps went into the water, and she took them and then waded across to the bench on the opposite side of the pool from him.

After a moment, she closed her eyes and allowed herself to feel the full glory of it: the hot, natural water massaging her exhausted muscles and her many bruises.

"I didn't really realize I hurt all over, until I got in here," she said.

"You took some pretty good tumbles."

"The water feels great on all my aches and pains. I didn't deserve a day like this, Kiernan. Does it mean you have forgiven me?"

She opened her eyes and looked at him. She saw his answer before he said it.

"Yeah," he said, "I suppose that is what it means."

"Thank you." She took a deep breath. "Now you just have to forgive yourself."

He looked across the steam at her, raised an eyebrow. "What do you mean by that, exactly?"

"Your sister and I talked last night."

"That was my fear," he said.

"She's fallen in love."

"Yes, she told me."

"She's worried about you accepting Mark. She's worried you can't get beyond what happened that day."

"Are you giving me some free counseling?" he said.

She could hear the warning in his voice, to back off, to leave it, but she could not.

"Why are you mad at Mark?"

"I'm not mad at him."

"Adele said you seem furious with him. She thinks it's because he lived and Danner died."

Kiernan swore softly. "That's not it. That's not it at all!"

"What is it then?"

"It's that I lived and Danner died."

"And Mark?"

"He was there." The anger faded from him, and he looked dejected. She saw his heart, and it was just as she had always suspected. She saw Kiernan McAllister's heart and it was broken.

She scooted over on the bench beside him and took his hand. "He was there and…?" she whispered.

"He was there for the moment of my greatest failing," Kiernan said. "It's not his fault, but I can barely look at him. Because he knows."

"Knows what?"

Kiernan's sigh was long and followed by a shudder so massive that the water of the pool rippled.

"It was my fault. I killed him."

She was silent, but her hand tightened on his, and her eyes would not leave his face.

"Danner was different than me. I had used adrenaline all my life, like a drug. Flying down a mountain, flat out, there is nothing else. Just that moment."

"I just experienced that myself," Stacy said.

He nodded. "Danner was more like you. Willing to embrace it, but cautious. I introduced him to that world of untouched snow, but he never took leadership. He always trusted me and followed me.

"And that morning, I picked the wrong slope. And I was strong enough and experienced enough to outrun it, and he was not."

He stopped, but she had read it in his voice and his eyes and the heave of his shoulders.

"And I will feel guilty about that for the rest of my life. That I misjudged his ability to cope and it cost him his life. I will feel responsible for that for the rest of my life.

"When I close my eyes, I can still see it and feel it. I glanced back over my shoulder, could see his skies cutting a line out, setting a shelf of snow free. The sound was like a freight train. It was right on top of both of us. I was closer to Mark, and I shoved him hard, and he saw what was going on and managed to kind of squirt out to the side.

"I thought Danner was right on my shoulder. I could feel

the wind being created by that snow coming. But when I skied free of it, he wasn't there. He'd been swept away."

The silence of the mountains felt heavy and sacred.

"But what could you have done differently?" she finally whispered.

"That is what I lay awake at night asking myself. That's why I wish sometimes it would have taken me, too. So that I would not have to live with this ultimate failure, the sense of being powerless when it mattered most. The only time it really ever mattered."

"And Adele would have lost both of you, maybe even all three of you," Stacy said softly. "I don't know that she could have survived that."

"What if we'd had breakfast a little later, or decided not to go out that day, or what if I had asked to take a different trail?"

"That's why it's your fault?" she asked quietly.

"It's part of it. Wrong decisions, from the very beginning of that day." His voice was broken.

"My family dying was my fault, too," she whispered.

His head jerked up.

"I was going to my first high school dance. Oh, Kiernan, I was so excited. I had a new dress, and I'd been allowed to wear makeup, and my mom had done my hair for me. My imagination, of course," she admitted ruefully, "had gone absolutely crazy creating scenarios. I thought Bobby Brighton might notice me and ask me to dance. Or Kenny O'Connell.

"And then I got there, and it wasn't like the middle school dances, where everybody just kind of danced together, and had fun.

"All the boys were on one side of the room, and all the girls on the other, and pretty soon all the popular girls were being asked to dance, and I wasn't. By the halfway intermission, I hadn't been asked to dance, not even once, not even by the science nerds.

"And so I called my Dad. And I was crying.

"And he said my grandma was over visiting, and they had been talking about going out bowling and for iced hot chocolate after, *and Murphy, girl, we wouldn't have had any fun without you, anyway, so I'm coming to get you. And when I get there, I better not be beating off those boys with my shovel.*

"But—" Her voice had become a whisper. "They never got there. A drunk driver ran a red light and it killed them all."

"Stacy," he said, and his voice was a whisper that shared her agony.

"I didn't tell you that because I wanted you to feel sorry for me," she said. "I told you because I always felt I had killed them, too. If I hadn't have called. Was my Dad rushing to get to me? Was he so focused on the fact his little Murphy girl was in distress, he missed something, that flash of motion, or a sound that would have alerted him to the fact that car was coming? I have tormented myself with this question—what if I had called ten minutes later or earlier?"

"Stacy," he said again, and now his powerful arms were wrapped around her, and he pulled her hard against himself.

"Do you think I killed them?" she demanded.

"No! Of course not!"

"I don't think you killed Danner, either."

Beneath his skin, for a moment she thought she felt his heart stop beating. And then it started again and instead of putting her away from him, he drew her closer.

He pushed the tendrils of wet hair from her face, and he

looked down at her, and it felt as if no one had ever seen her quite so completely before.

"Thank you," he whispered.

And it was a greater gift, even, than being brought to this incredible place.

CHAPTER SIXTEEN

KIERNAN WAITED FOR it to happen. All his strength had not been enough to hold the lid on the place that contained the grief within him.

The touch of her hand, the look in her eyes, and his strength had abandoned him, and he had told her all of it: his failure and his powerlessness.

Now, sitting beside her, her hand in his, the wetness of her hair resting on his shoulder, he waited for everything to fade: the white-topped mountains that surrounded him, the feel of the hot water against his skin, the way her hand felt in his.

He waited for all that to fade, and for the darkness to take its place, to ooze through him like thick, black sludge freed from a containment pond, blotting out all else.

Instead, astounded, Kiernan became *more* aware of everything around him, as if he was soaking up life through his pores, breathing in glory through his nose, becoming drenched in light instead of darkness.

He started to laugh.

"What?" she asked, a smile playing across the lovely fullness of her lips.

"I just feel alive. For the past few days, I have felt alive. And I don't know if that's a good thing or a bad thing."

"This is what I think," she said, slowly and thoughtfully,

"we are, all of us, vulnerable to love. And when we lose someone, or something that we have cared about, we are like Samson. We think the source of our strength is gone. We have had our hair cut.

"But without our even realizing it, our hair grows back, and our strength returns, and maybe," she finished softly, "just maybe we are even better than we were before."

Her words fell on him, like raindrops hitting a desert that was too long parched.

His awareness shifted to her, and being with her seemed to fill him to overflowing.

He dropped his head over hers and took her lips. He kissed her with warmth and with welcome, a man who had thought he was dead discovering not just that he lived but, astonishingly, that he wanted to live.

Stacy returned his kiss, her lips parting under his, her hands twining around his neck, pulling him in even closer to her.

There was gentle welcome. She had seen all of him, he had bared his weakness and his darkness to her, and still he felt only acceptance from her.

But acceptance was slowly giving way to something else. There was hunger in her, and he sensed an almost savage need in her to go to the place a kiss like this took a man and a woman.

With great reluctance he broke the kiss, cupped her cheeks in his hands and looked down at her.

He felt as if he was memorizing each of her features: the green of those amazing eyes, her dark brown hair curling even more wildly from the steam of the hot spring, the swollen plumpness of her lips, the whiteness of her skin.

"It's too soon for this," he said, his voice hoarse.

"I know," she said, and her voice was raw, too.

And then, despite having said that, they were drawn

together again, into that sensual world of steam and hot water, skin like warmed-through silk touching skin. Peripherally, he was aware of snow shining with diamonds, and mountain peaks soaring to touch sky, and the insistent call of a Whiskey Jack.

He pulled away from her the second time.

It was too soon to kiss her so thoroughly. Their days together had been intense. This feeling of being cracked wide open was something that could make a man do something irrational.

And he could not do that to her. You did not kiss a woman like Stacy Murphy Walker like that unless you knew.

Unless you knew what your feelings were.

And unless you knew the future held some possibility.

He had brought her here as a gift, to help her heal her pain, not to cause her more. But he had come here for himself, too. Maybe mostly for himself. To see if there was hope, and it seemed to him that maybe there was, after all.

And it seemed to him part of hoping, part of breaking open inside was a requirement to have the events of his life to make him better.

Not bitter.

Worthy of the love of a beautiful woman like this one.

That's what Adele had tried to tell him. That's what Danner would have wanted. Danner would have wanted him to embrace *all* of what he was, darkness and light, and let them melt together.

"We need to go," he said, letting go of Stacy reluctantly, knowing he could not push the bounds of his own strength by kissing her a third time.

He stood up, put his hands on the rock edges of the pool and heaved himself out of it. "We don't want to be trying to get home in the dark."

It was an excuse. An excuse to step back from the intensity between them. Because that kind of intensity did not lend itself to rational thought and it seemed to him he owed her at least that.

To make decisions from here on out, as far as she was concerned, based on reason.

And not what he had felt there in the pool with her: the powerful release of something he had been holding on to, followed all too quickly by the ecstasy of her lips on his.

She looked disappointed.

And maybe a touch relieved, too, as if she knew things were going too fast, spinning out of their control.

He grabbed his dry clothes from the toasty warm cabin, leaving it to her to get dressed in privacy. He ducked behind the cabin, hoping the cold air on his heated skin would be sobering.

Instead, being able to feel the cold air prickle across his skin only increased his sense of being alive as totally and completely as he ever had been. He quickly packed up their things, waited for her to come out of the cabin and resisted the temptation to greet her with a kiss, as if they had been separated by weeks instead of minutes.

He schooled himself to be all business as he helped her into her skis. The sun was now warm, and the snow was melting quickly. It made it heavy and hard to ski, despite the fact he had changed waxes. Partway home, they lost the snow completely.

They took off the skis, and he shouldered them. They walked along the forest trail. Stacy slipped at one point, and he reached back and took her hand, and somehow he didn't let it go again until he noticed she was limping.

"Are you okay?"

"I think the ski boots are rubbing."

"Let's have a look."

"It's okay. I can practically see your house from here."

"I think I should have a look."

Cross-country boots were not made for walking. His were custom, so they fit him well, but hers were not.

They sat in the snow, and he took her boots off, and then her socks. She did, indeed, have terrible rubs starting on the back of both heels. One of them was bleeding.

"Why didn't you say something sooner?"

She looked sheepish. "To tell you the truth, I hardly noticed."

And so, she, like him, was in an altered state, one where maybe the best decisions were not made.

With a tenderness he had not known he was capable of, he found a little of the snow that remained in a shaded spot beside the trail and rubbed it on the frayed skin of her heels, aware of how he loved caressing her feet and the look on her face when he did it.

And then, ignoring her protests, feeling stronger than he had ever felt, feeling like Samson who once again had hair, he picked her up and cradled her against his chest.

"I can walk," she protested.

But he didn't want her to. He wanted to carry her. He wanted to protect her and care for her. Maybe he wanted to show her how strong he was.

"What about the skis?" she asked, when it was evident he did not intend to put her down.

"I'll get you there and then I'll come back for them."

She looked as if she was going to protest. But then she didn't. She snuggled deep into his chest, and he strode along the trail that led toward home.

He set her down on the front steps of his house, and still feeling strong and full of energy, he went back up the trail to retrieve their skis.

When he came back to the house, she was waiting at

the door. He could tell by the look on her face something was wrong.

"What is it?"

She passed him the note. In Adele's handwriting it said that Max had gotten worse since they left and had developed a high fever. She had taken him to the hospital in Whistler.

Kiernan stared at the note.

It seemed as if his whole world crashed in around him. While he'd been out playing in the snow, entertaining foolish notions about the nature of love and forever, of hope and of healing, his nephew had been getting sicker and sicker.

Sick enough, apparently, to require a trip to the emergency room.

It was a reminder, stark and brutal, of what was real, of how quickly everything could change and of how what you loved most could be snatched away from you. That was reality.

What was not reality was the way he felt after he had showed his soul to Stacy. It was not the laughter that had entered his life since she had been here.

It was not snowmen and snowball fights, homemade cookies, bikinis in hot springs.

Reality was a man who was not in control of any of the things he wanted to be in control of. The way he had felt, carrying her the last few yards, strong and able to protect her with his life if need be, was the biggest illusion of all.

He was not Samson.

Because he did not have the strength to say yes to any of this again. To be open to the caprice of fate and chance.

That's what love did, in the end—it made a man's life uncertain. It left his heart wide open to the unbearable pain of loss.

He took the note and shoved it in his pocket. He went

through the house and found the phone and dialed Adele's number.

"Everything okay?" he asked when she answered. He was aware he was bracing himself for the worst.

"Everything's fine," she said, and the air went out of him like a man who had dodged a bullet whistling by his ear. "The doctor says Max has an ear infection. They're keeping an eye on him for a bit, but it looks like he'll be released in about an hour."

Relief welled up in him. "That's good," he said in a calm voice that gave away nothing of the precipice he felt he had just stood on. "How did you get to the hospital?"

Better to deal with details and logistics than that uncontrollable helpless feeling that came with loving someone.

"I took a cab. I'm going to rent a car, and go home. I think Max needs to be at home. How was your day?" she asked. "Did you have fun?"

And he heard it in her. Hope for him. And the one thing he did not want to do was give anyone false hopes. Not her.

And certainly not Stacy.

"I'll come get you," he told his sister. "I'll drive you home."

"But what about Stacy?"

He said nothing.

"Oh, Kiernan," she said, her voice part annoyance and part sympathy. "Don't throw this away."

He ended the call without responding to that. Stacy was in the kitchen putting on a kettle. For a moment his resolve wavered. He could picture them sitting together having hot chocolate. Max wasn't here. He could build a fire in the hearth without concerns for the baby's safety.

It felt, for a moment, as if he could picture their whole lives together...for a moment he could see this room the way she had seen it the first time she had entered…full of laughter and family, a big Christmas tree and toys on the floor.

And he steeled himself against the yearning that vision caused in him.

"How is Max?" she asked anxiously.

"It's an ear infection. He's being released in an hour or so. I'm going to go get them."

"All right." She had heard something in his tone. He could see his coolness register on her face. "Do you want me to come with you?"

It felt like that *no* was the hardest thing he'd ever said. But no, there was something harder yet that had to be said, that had to be done.

She had to know there was no hope. Not for them. None.

"I'll go back to the city with them," he said. "I won't be coming back here."

"Oh! I'll get my things, then. And clear out, too."

"I'll need your contact information."

Hope flickered briefly until she registered how he had worded that. Not *I'll call.* Not *I'll be in touch.*

"My lawyer will contact you," he said, struggling to strip all emotion from his voice. "I'll want you to sign something saying the things we have discussed were in strictest confidence."

It did exactly as he had both hoped and dreaded it would do.

It shattered her.

She turned swiftly from him and unplugged the kettle. She went through the drawers until she found a piece of paper and a pen.

She wrote her information down, her curls falling like a curtain in front of her face. He didn't stay to watch. He went to his room and shut the door. He did not come out until he heard the front door close behind her.

He ordered himself not to look, but he went to the front window anyway and watched her drive away.

Then he went and retrieved the information from where she had left it on the counter. He unfolded the piece of paper.

Written on it was not her mailing address or her phone number or her email.

Written on it in unhesitating script, it read, *"Go to hell."*

And despite the pain he was in, he could not help but smile. Because, unlike him, Stacy Murphy Walker had long ago learned to roll with the punches.

He crumpled up the paper and threw it on the counter. He went and looked at the guest room.

There was nothing in there to show she had ever been there. The faint smell of lemons and soap would not be here by the next time he came back. The fountain she had toppled would be righted, eventually, and the shrubs replanted.

Probably all that would happen before he came back here, because he was not at all sure when that would be.

Wouldn't this place, now, be forever connected in his mind to her?

All he had left of her was a wet bathing suit in his backpack. A bathing suit Adele might want back.

And then in a moment that he recognized as utter weakness, he went back into the kitchen, picked Stacy's note up off the counter and straightened the crumples out of it with his fist. He folded it carefully and put it in his shirt pocket.

He wanted to keep something of her. Even if it was this.

Maybe especially if it was this. Something that showed him, after all, that she was strong. And spunky. She was going to be fine.

He was just not so sure about himself.

CHAPTER SEVENTEEN

STACY MURPHY WALKER would have been stunned to know that Kiernan McAllister thought she would be fine. She was not fine.

She cried for a week. She screamed into her pillow. She didn't get dressed. Or comb her hair. She didn't brush her teeth or pick up her newspapers from the front door.

She made cookies and ate them all to prove cookies tasted just as good without him in her life. She drank a bucket of hot chocolate just to reassure herself that it was still good.

But the truth was, the cookies tasted like sawdust and the hot chocolate might as well have been bathwater.

A few days with him, and she was reacting like this! With more drama and heartache and grief than the end of her six-month courtship with Dylan. It was shameful! She was lucky it had only been a few days with him! Imagine if it had been longer? Imagine if they had let that kiss get away from them? Then what would she be feeling?

Though, in truth, she wondered if she could possibly be feeling any worse!

This seemed like a preview of her future life: drab and tasteless, unexciting. The potential for it to be something else had shimmered briefly and enticingly, and now that was gone.

At the end of a full week of immersion in her misery, Stacy knew she had to pull herself together. She had bills to pay! Other people might have the luxury of wallowing in a heartbreak but she did not!

Murphy's Law once again: everything that could go wrong, had. Why should she be surprised? It was the story of her life, after all.

And there was a positive side: nothing could steal those moments from her. Nothing could take the memories of her snow angel, and their snowball fight, the snowman that might still be melting in his yard. Nothing could take the ski trip and that beautiful little cabin and those moments in the hot tub, where it had seemed, for one shining instant, as if the events of all her life had led her to *this*.

"Stop it," she ordered herself. It was her imagination, run wild again, that had got her in all this trouble.

Had she actually talked herself into believing a man like Kiernan McAllister could feel anything for her?

She snorted her self-disgust out loud.

Then, newly determined, Stacy went and gathered the newspapers from her front door and went through them, one by one, looking for the lead that would launch her new career as a freelancer.

But nothing in the business section interested her.

In fact, if she was really honest about it, business had *never* interested her. In a moment of desperation, with no funds to complete college, she had taken the first job that had been offered to her. Fallen into it, really.

And if she looked at her failed relationship with Dylan, it had the same hallmarks: the relationship had presented itself to her. She had fallen into it rather than chosen it. She had been flattered by his attention. It had been convenient. It had seemed like the easiest route to what she wanted: to feel that sense of home again.

And then she had made the same mistake with Kiernan, skidded into his life instead of choosing it for herself.

"That's done," she told herself firmly. "Falling into things is done. My life happening by accident is done."

Stacy set down the papers. She got out her laptop.

What did she want to write about? If she was going to steer into the spin instead of away from it, what story would she tell? Asking herself that question seemed to open a floodgate.

A week later she sold the piece to *Pacific Life* magazine for more money than she had ever expected. The article sparked interest in her charity the likes of which she had not seen before.

Some of the kids she worked with had seen the piece, and they wanted to write their stories.

She started a blog for them. *Pacific Life* picked up some of stories.

Speaking invitations began to roll in. Stacy began to have a life she had never dreamed possible.

And if it was missing one thing, she tried not to think about that.

It was only at night, when another hectic day had ended, and her head was on the pillow, that she would let herself think of those few days of wonder.

And the newest success story in Vancouver would cry herself to sleep.

Adele walked into Kiernan's apartment as if she owned the place. She looked around as if she was going to set Max down, but what she saw must have made her think better of it.

Kiernan glared at her. The apartment was dark, and he was sitting on the couch, remote control for the TV in his hand. He muted the sound on the television. "What are you doing here? And how did you get in?"

She wagged a key at him. "I got it from the apartment manager. I said I was conducting a well-being check."

"He fell for that?"

"Women with babies are nearly always perceived as trustworthy."

"I'm going to see that he's fired."

Adele made a sucking sound through her teeth. He never liked it when she made that sound. It never boded well for him.

"God, where's your housekeeper?"

"I fired her."

"Well, it smells in here."

"I burned the pizza."

"You tried to make your own pizza?"

She said that as if it told her a deep dark secret about him. And maybe it did. He had tried to cook pizza in an effort to prove to himself he could have the very same life without Stacy that he could have with her. The experiment had been a dismal failure, but apparently, from the look on Adele's face, she already knew that.

"Did you fire your housekeeper before or after you fired Miss Harris?" Adele asked.

"I hired her back! Where did you hear I fired Miss Harris?"

"Mark told me."

"Well, tell him he can be fired, too. What happens at the office stays at the office."

"Look, brother dear, you can fire everyone you come in contact with, but it's obviously not going to make you feel any better."

"It does make me feel better," he insisted, watching her darkly.

"You have to deal with what's at the heart of the matter, Kee."

"And I suppose you know what that is?" he snarled.

"Of course I do!"

He cocked his head at her, raised an eyebrow.

"Your heart," she said. "Your heart is at the heart of that matter."

Her eyes, unfortunately, seemed to be adjusting to the dark in here, because she picked her way through the dirty socks and shirts on the floor and stood over him. Max peeked at him and apparently didn't like what he saw— or feared being left again—because he nuzzled into his mother's shoulder and sucked feverishly on his thumb.

Adele reached down and picked up a magazine off a heap of them on the coffee table.

"What's this?"

"Don't touch that!"

"*Icons of Business.* Haven't you been featured in this?" When he didn't answer, she frowned. "Good grief, Kee, are you ego-surfing through your glory days?"

"You're saying that as if they are in the past," he said, increasingly annoyed at this invasion into his misery, wanting to deflect her from seeing why he was really surrounded by several years of issues of *Icons of Business.*

She was juggling Max, flipping through the magazine, obviously totally looking in the wrong direction, thinking she would find a story about him.

Then, to his chagrin, a light went on in her face. "Oh my God, you are reading all Stacy's stories!"

She said that as if he was being adorable.

"I'm gathering ammunition to help me prepare the lawsuit when she writes the unauthorized story about me!"

It was weak and not credible and he knew it.

"You'll be preparing your own lawsuit, I guess, since you fired Harry last week?"

He didn't even ask her where she had heard that. He hoped his glare balanced out the flimsy explanation of why he was reading Stacy's writing enough to make his sister stop talking and leave. Apparently it didn't.

"She's not going to write about you, silly."

"Silly?"

"I had coffee with her. After I saw the article she wrote in *Pacific Life*."

"You had coffee with Stacy? Last week?" He had to bite his tongue to keep from asking all the questions that wanted to tumble off it. *Was she okay? Was she happy? Did she ask about him?*

Instead he asked, "What was the article about?"

"Not you." She let that sink in, just to let him know the whole world was not about him.

"Is there a point to this visit? Oh, just a sec. Well-being check. You can clearly see I'm alive, so—"

"I brought you a copy to look at." Still juggling the baby, she put down the copy of *Icons of Business* and fished around in a purse enormous enough to hold a Volkswagen. She found what she wanted and put it on top of his mess on the coffee table.

"Why?"

"Oh, quit snarling. Because I love you, and care about you and trust that after you have read it you will still know how to do the right thing."

He decided, stubbornly, even before his sister left, that he was *never* reading the article. He made it for twenty minutes, pretending interest in the football game his sister had so rudely interrupted.

But he was once again, Samson, sans hair. He had no strength.

He picked up the magazine and flipped through it until he found the article that Stacy had written. It was called "Murphy's Law: Confessions of a Foster Child," and it started with the words, *I believed in magic until I was sixteen years old...*

When he finished it, he read it again. He was aware his face was wet with tears.

And he was aware of something else. His sister was right. He still did know how to do the right thing.

And somehow finding his checkbook in this mess he had created of his life and writing a big fatty to CCOFK was not going to cut it.

By the time he had finished reading that story, he knew what he had always known in his heart. He knew exactly who Stacy was.

But he knew something beyond that, too. And it was something that could change his life and lead him out of darkness if he had the courage to embrace it.

CHAPTER EIGHTEEN

STACY WAS BEYOND EXHAUSTED. Her life had taken off in so many unexpected directions in the past few weeks! Though she had sworn her cookie-and-hot-chocolate days were over, it did sound like an easy supper after a long, hard day. And she was putting on her pajamas to eat it, too.

Her doorbell rang and she went to it, in her pajamas, cookies in hand. She peeked out the side window and reeled away, her back against the door.

Her heart was beating too fast.

Just as if it might explode.

She was not opening that door. She was not. She had cookies melting in her hands. She was in her pajamas at seven o'clock at night. Her hair was a mess, and she had already wiped all the makeup off her face.

In her imagination, she had pictured seeing him again, down to the last detail. She had thought maybe their paths would cross at a charity function. And that she would be wearing designer clothes and Kleinback shoes. Her hair would be upswept, her makeup perfect, and she would be sipping very expensive champagne.

Nothing, she thought, a touch sourly, *ever goes the way I plan it.*

He knocked again. She was not going to open that door.

But she could not resist putting her eye to a little slit in the drapery to have one last look at him.

Kiernan McAllister did not look anything like he did in her imaginings. In fact, he looked awful! His face was whisker roughened like it had been the first day she saw him. His hair hadn't been cut recently, and it was touching his collar.

He was not dressed in one of the custom suits that he always wore when he graced the cover of a magazine.

Or in the casuals he had worn at his cottage.

He was in a thin windbreaker that wasn't warm enough for the blustery Vancouver day. His jeans had a hole in the knee.

But it was his eyes that made her fling open the door.

They had dark circles under them. The light in them was haunted.

"Hello," she said. She took a bite of her cookie to make sure he did not have a clue her heart was beating so fast it might explode at any second.

"Hello, Murphy."

Her defenses were down quite enough without him calling her that.

"How have you been?" he asked softly.

As if he really cared.

"All right," she said. She took another bite of the cookie and hoped to hell she wouldn't choke on it. "You?"

It was ludicrous, them standing there asking each other these banal questions as if they had bumped into each other on the street.

"I haven't been doing so good," he said.

She gave up all pretense of eating the cookie and really looked at him. It felt as if her heart were breaking in two.

"Can I come in?" he said. "I really need to talk to you."

Did he have to? Come in? To her space? It wasn't that

it was humble, because it was, and that did not embarrass her in the least.

It was that once he had been in here, some part of him would linger forever. She would never feel the same way about her space again.

Still, she stood back from the door.

He came by her and looked around, a little smile playing around the edge of his mouth.

"What?"

"It's just as I imagined."

"*You* imagined where *I* live?"

"I did," he confessed. He took off his coat and, seeing no place to hang it, put it on the doorknob.

She watched him go and flop down on her couch. He closed his eyes, like a man gathering himself.

Or like a man who had found his way home.

"How did you imagine it?" she asked.

"Like something I saw in a children's book a long time ago—a little rabbit warren, safe and full of color and coziness and those little touches that make a house into a home. Like this." He picked up a doily on her coffee table.

"Why are you here?" she asked, and she could hear something plaintive in her voice that begged him to put her out of her misery.

He patted the spot on the couch beside him.

She hesitated, but she could not say no. She went and sat beside him. The couch was not large enough to leave as much space between them as she would have liked. Her shoulder was nearly brushing his. She could feel the heat and energy pulsating off him. His scent tickled her nostrils, clean and tantalizingly masculine.

"I always thought I was a courageous man," he said, his voice soft. "When I was swooping down mountains where no one had ever skied before, when I was jumping out of airplanes, when I was zip-lining through the jungle, I was always congratulating myself on what a brave guy I was."

She said nothing, but she felt herself move, fractionally, closer to him.

"Of course, I wasn't at all," he said slowly. "I was just filling up all the empty spaces in my life with one adrenaline rush after another. I was outrunning something, even before Danner died."

She shifted again until their shoulders were touching lightly.

"I was outrunning the thing that took the most courage of all. I was terrified of it. I had experienced its treachery, and I couldn't trust it.

"And when Danner died, I took it as proof that I was right."

"Love," she said, her voice choked, her shoulder and his leaning against each other, supporting each other. "It's love that takes the most courage."

"Yes, love."

The way he said the word, love could be taken two ways, one of them as an endearment.

"But the thing I was running hardest from is the thing that will be brought to you again and again. It's like the universe cannot accept no as an answer to that one thing.

"And so love tracks you down. In a baby whose laughter could make a heart of stone come back to life. In a sister who is so brokenhearted and who needs you to man up.

"In a woman who crashes into your fountain, and announces to you, who already knows, that anything that can go wrong will."

"How can you love me?" Stacy whispered.

"I didn't say I loved you."

"Oh," she said, not even trying to hide how crushed that made her feel.

He turned his face to hers, put a finger under her chin and tilted it up to him. "I said I had been brought the opportunity to say yes to love. You see, Murphy, that's why I'm here."

"Why?"

"To see if you can teach me about real courage. You're right. I don't know if I love you. But I have this feeling that I could. And it terrifies me."

"I have nothing to teach you," she whispered.

"Yes, you do." His finger was still under her chin, and he was still gazing into her eyes. After a long time, he said, "I read your article."

"You did?"

"And it's all there. Everything that you are. But maybe, Stacy, writing, at its best and its highest, does not just show who the writer is. Maybe it shows the reader who they are, too. For the first time in a long time, I feel as if I know," he said. "I know exactly who I am."

Stacy looked at him.

And she knew, too. She knew exactly who Kiernan McAllister was. And for the first time in a long, long time, she began to smile, and the smile felt as brilliant and as warm as the sun coming out after a snowstorm.

CHAPTER NINETEEN

WHEN KIERNAN MCALLISTER first began to woo Stacy Murphy Walker, he did it the way he did everything else. He went flat out and over the top. He wanted this woman to know that he meant business.

And so he chartered a chopper and had a white tablecloth dinner for her on a mountaintop, complete with white-gloved, black-suited waiters.

He took her on the company's jet for a weekend of theater and shopping and exploring in New York City.

Kiernan showered Stacy with gifts and baubles and flowers.

He took her to the most select restaurants in Vancouver. He took her to his exclusive fitness club with its climbing wall, indoor pool and steam room.

Her first time downhill skiing was at Steamboat in Colorado, with him by her side.

In other words, he treated her the way he had treated all the other women he had ever dated.

And all those brand-new experiences delighted her, and he enjoyed them more than he ever had, experiencing them anew by running them through the filter of her complete wonder.

But it quickly became apparent to him that Stacy was not like anyone he had ever dated before.

Because while her enjoyment of each of the experiences was genuine, it became more and more apparent to Kiernan that it was when Stacey suggested how they would spend time together that they had the most fun.

Not only had the most fun but really started to get to know each other, on a different level, on a deeper level.

Stacy's idea of a good time was popcorn and a movie in her cozy little Kitsilano basement suite. Stacy's idea of a good time was a long walk, hand in hand along a deserted, windy stretch of beach. Stacy's idea of a good time was a game of Scrabble and a cup of hot chocolate.

One of her favorite things was babysitting Max so that Adele and Mark, who had slipped away quietly to the Bahamas and gotten married, could have some grown-up time together.

Because of that Kiernan got used to eating hamburgers under the Golden Arches and puzzling together the toy that came in the kid's meal. Because of that he got used to visiting the aquarium and going to story time at the library.

"He's not old enough for story time," he had protested when she first suggested it.

And then been proved wrong when the wriggly little Max had sat still as a stone as the librarian read a picture book.

Because of that, he got used to the park, and pushing a stroller, and visiting the pet store and fishing kids' music CDs out of the player in his car. Because of that he knew all about the elf on the shelf, and he knew who Thomas and Dora were.

Stacy's idea of a good time was serving Christmas dinner to her "kids." Her idea of a good time was being able to organize a day of skiing for those foster kids, or a picnic or a day of swimming.

More and more, Kiernan was aware that Stacy's idea

of a good time was often intrinsically intertwined with helping others.

And somehow, he had become involved in that, too. Those kids she introduced him to, the ones in foster care, were so much like his younger self.

But today, Kiernan had chosen what they were doing. He was leading the way to Last Chance. There had been no early snowstorm this year, and so they were hiking up there to what had become one of their favorite places on earth.

"So beautiful," Stacy said, shrugging off her pack.

He was already being distracted by thoughts of what bathing suit she might have brought.

She seemed distracted by food. Getting out the hot dogs, and buns and marshmallows and, as had become their tradition, a very expensive bottle of ice wine.

Later, in the hot pool, with the steam rising around them, he looked at her and thought she was the most beautiful woman he had ever seen.

She was leaning back in the water, her eyes closed, her hair floating around her, her face tranquil.

But he didn't feel tranquil. He was not sure he, who had defied death with countless feats of daring, had ever felt more nervous in his whole life.

"Stacy?"

She turned and looked at him, righted herself. Something in his face must have told her something very, very important was going on. She came over to him and wrapped her arms around him, looked up into his face.

"What is it, Kiernan? Is something wrong?"

Yes, something was wrong. He hadn't planned to do this in the hot pool. The ring was in the backpack inside the cabin.

He swallowed hard. "Do you know what day it is?" he asked her.

She looked puzzled. "October twenty-sixth?"

He nodded, and could not speak past the lump in his throat.

"Oh, no," she whispered. "It's the anniversary of Danner's death, isn't it? Oh, Kiernan."

And then she said, "Oh, gosh, we should be with Adele."

"It's not," he said. "It's not the anniversary of Danner's death."

Though that day was coming, he recognized, a little shocked, it was not the raw, open wound it had been just a year ago.

"Then what day is it?" she asked. "What is wrong with you?"

"It's a year to the day since you chugged up my driveway and slid into my fountain."

"Oh!" she said.

"It's a year to the day since my life began to change forever. For the better. In ways I could not have imagined. I have something I want to tell you."

"What?" she whispered.

"I'm going to leave McAllister Enterprises."

Did she look disappointed? Yes, she did. He could thank his lucky stars, he supposed, that he hadn't cracked open the wine yet, or he might be wearing it!

"With your blessing," he continued, watching her closely, "I want to turn running it completely over to Mark."

Had she been expecting a proposal? If she had, she seemed to be getting over her disappointment a little too quickly.

"But it's your life!" she said. "Your baby. You started that company. You took it to where it is today."

"It was only a step in the road," he said. "It was only to give me the skills I need to do something else."

"But what?"

He took a deep breath. "I feel as if my whole life has been leading me to this," he told her, the person he could tell anything to. "My whole life, every triumph, and every tragedy, too, has led me to this moment, and this decision."

He felt how right this was.

Will you marry me?

But he made himself wait.

"I want take on Career and College Opportunities for Foster Kids. Stacy, that group is getting ready to explode. It's ready to become more than a tiny charity in Vancouver. It needs to go North America wide."

He could tell she was excited, and disappointed, too. He would play her just a little while longer, the anticipation building in him.

"I want to be at the helm when that happens," he told her, having trouble concentrating on what he was saying. "I want to guide it through its infancy. I have an opportunity to do so much for those young people. Working with it has given my life meaning like nothing else, except..."

He looked at her.

She was holding her breath. She knew what was coming. She had to.

He felt his heart swell inside him. He felt the light dancing with any darkness that remained within him, dancing until they all swirled together and became one magnificent, glorious thing.

"...except you," he said quietly. "Stacy, I don't want to take it on by myself. I want you at my side."

"Of course," she whispered, tears running down her beautiful cheeks.

"I don't just want you at my side to take CCOFK to the next level. I want you at my side for everything. Stacy, I want you to marry me. I want you to be my wife."

For a full minute, she tilted back her head and stared at

up him as if she could not comprehend what he had just said, as if maybe she had not expected this after all.

And then she let out a whoop of pure joy that said everything about what she had become in this past year.

Love, he could see, had taken her to the next level.

He was not sure he had ever been in the presence of such pure joy as Stacy radiated an unbelievable enthusiasm for life, an ability to embrace each day as an adventure.

"Will you marry me?"

Kiernan had thought he would be down on one knee, with the ring extended, but he could see that now, as always, when he let go of control just a little bit, life had a better plan for him than anything he could plan for himself.

Because he knew he would remember this moment, in its absolute perfection, forever.

"Yes!" she cried.

And the mountains rang with her joy and echoed that yes back to him as he picked her up and swung her around in the warm steamy water and then kissed her face all over as if he could never, ever get enough of her.

"Yes," she whispered. "Yes, yes, yes."

EPILOGUE

THE MOUNTAIN TRAIL was beautiful in the springtime. The trees were breaking out in tender, lime-green leaves; the grass shoots were young and fragile, and the moss along the path was like velvet under Stacy Murphy Walker's feet.

Kiernan had said he would deliver her by helicopter, but she'd said no. If her life had taught her anything, it was that it was the journey that mattered, not the arrival.

This day was like nothing she had ever imagined, she thought, as she came into the clearing of the little cabin, Last Chance.

The clearing was full of people. The chairs and the pagoda and the tent for the reception festivities afterward had all been delivered by helicopter.

She was in a long white dress, and a cheer went up when people saw her come from the forest. She walked down the aisle, lifted her skirt to let everyone see her hiking boots and was rewarded with laughter.

Waiting, under that pagoda, was Kiernan, his eyes soft on her, a look in them better, so much better, than anything Stacy could have ever imagined.

Oh, everything that could go wrong had. The minister had suffered a bee sting and been airlifted out with one of the supply helicopters. A new official had been found at the last minute—Kiernan's amazing staff, especially Miss Harris, could do anything.

One of the food boxes had been dropped—from a considerable height—and naturally, it was the one that had contained the cake.

Adele had been in charge of the wedding band, and she had turned away from Max for just one second, and turned back to find the jewelry box empty, the ring nowhere to be found and Max looking innocent as could be.

All of those mishaps seemed fairly minor, even comic, to Stacy. One thing about living a life where things tended to go wrong? You developed a certain grace for dealing with it.

Now, as she walked toward the man who would be her husband, all of it faded: the little cabin and the turquoise waters of the spring that bubbled behind it, Max throwing a tantrum because his mother and Mark were at the front and he was not.

All of it faded: the tent that she passed that was as exquisitely set up as if they were having their wedding at the finest hotel instead of in the wilderness; their guests, some of them dabbing at their eyes as she passed them, doing her little heel kick with the hiking boots.

All of it faded, except him.

Her beloved. Kiernan.

She came to a stop before him, and he reached for her, and their hands joined, and their eyes remained on each other, never straying as they exchanged those age-old words:

In sickness and in health,
In good times and in bad,
In joy as well as in sorrow...

It seemed to Stacy that Kiernan's voice rose out of the

mountains themselves, it was so strong and so sure as he spoke the final vow to her.

"Stacy Murphy Walker, I will honor and respect you. I will laugh with you and I will cry with you. I will cherish you, for as long as we both shall live."

When his lips claimed hers, the world, despite the great cheer from the onlookers, went silent.

And when she stepped back and looked into his silvery eyes, Stacy felt a deep truth within herself.

It was the truth that was stated in those simple vows they had just spoken.

There would be moments like this and many of them— moments of genuine and complete bliss.

But even the wedding vows made room for Murphy! In health *and* in sickness, in good times *and* in bad, in joy *and* in sorrow...

And all lightness aside, as she looked into her new husband's eyes, this was the truth that Stacy Murphy Walker McAllister stood in.

It was not the triumphs that shaped the human race. It was not these moments of temporary bliss that were gone in a second or an hour or a day, and that left people in the everlasting pursuit of *more*.

No, these moments were the gift at the end of the long hard climb, like reaching the mountaintop after climbing the long, rocky trail. Only you didn't get to stay there, on top of the world, drinking in the glory and the magnificence forever. No, eventually, you had to eat and sleep and get some clean clothes and brush your teeth. Eventually, you went back down the mountain to the valley that was life.

To the rainy days and the kids crying, to burned cookies and a fender-bender, and maybe a career disappointment or a goal not reached. Eventually you went back down the mountain to a life that was real.

And in that life that was real, Stacy felt it was tragedies that truly shaped people.

It was the breakdown of a relationship.

It was the death of a parent.

It was watching helplessly as someone you loved struggled with an unexpected illness.

It was an able-bodied person becoming disabled.

It was the business decision gone sour.

It was the friendship betrayed.

It was a parent, for reasons real or imagined, cut from a child's life.

These were the things that shaped people forever, what made them who they really were. These were the things that asked them to be stronger, more compassionate and more forgiving than they ever thought they were capable of being.

It was in these moments of utter defeat and utter despair, these moments of absolute blackness, when a person cast their glance heavenward, toward the light.

It was in these moments, where a person found their knees and whispered that plea of one who had been humbled by life and struggled with darkness—*help me*.

And that plea, if you listened carefully and with a heart wide open, was answered with, *how will you handle this?*

How will you use this, your worst moment, your heartbreak, your disappointment, your tragedy—how will you use this in service?

And sometimes if you were very lucky, or very blessed, as Stacy Murphy Walker McAllister had been, as Kiernan had been, you were allowed to stand in the light, in a moment of complete grace, when you could see.

When you could see who you really were.

And when you could see who your beloved really was.
And then you could sigh with contentment and proclaim it all, every single bit of it, light and darkness, and especially love, to be good.

* * * * *

"I thought we'd have a drink, celebrating our new relationship," he told her in his best Southern-gentleman drawl.

"Our relationship?" Alisha echocd incredulously.

"Landlord and tenant," Brett replied, indicating first himself, then her. "Why? What did you think I was referring to?"

Still sitting on the stool, she squared her shoulders. "I didn't have a clue," she lied. "That's why I asked."

"You want something light and fruity—or something hard?" he asked her.

The words seemed disconnected as they came out of the blue like that. Confused, she could only ask, "What?" as she stared at him.

"To drink," Brett prompted. "Light and fruity—" he gestured toward the small array of bottles filled with colorful mixed drinks "—or hard?" he concluded, waving a hand toward the bottles that contained alcohol his customers downed straight.

"What did you just have?" she asked, nodding at his empty shot glass.

"Wild Turkey, 101 proof," he told her.

She pushed her glass to one side and said, "I'll have the same."

Brett looked at her uncertainly. "Are you sure?" he asked. "It's rather strong and you might get more than you bargained for."

Her eyes locked with Brett's. "I think I already have."

HER FOREVER COWBOY

BY
MARIE FERRARELLA

Published in Great Britain 2014
by Mills & Boon, an imprint of Harlequin (UK) Limited,
Eton House, 18-24 Paradise Road, Richmond, Surrey, TW9 1SR

© 2014 Marie Rydzynski-Ferrarella

ISBN: 978-0-263-91313-2

23-0914

Harlequin (UK) Limited's policy is to use papers that are natural, renewable and recyclable products and made from wood grown in sustainable forests. The logging and manufacturing processes conform to the legal environmental regulations of the country of origin.

Printed and bound in Spain
by Blackprint CPI, Barcelona

A *USA TODAY* bestselling and RITA® Award-winning author, **Marie Ferrarella** has written more than two hundred books for Mills & Boon, some under the name Marie Nicole. Her romances are beloved by fans worldwide. Visit her website, www.marieferrarella.com.

To
Pat Teal,
who, 33 years ago,
said to me,
"Have you thought about writing a romance?"
Rest in peace, Pat.
I miss you.

Prologue

No one looking at her would have suspected that her heart had just been broken, or even bruised. She made sure of that.

Dr. Alisha Cordell prided herself on being self-contained. She wasn't the type to let people in on her private hurt. Nor would she allow herself to shed tears. At least, not publicly.

Publicly, if she included the half-naked hospital administrator closeted with her fiancé as being part of the general public, the only display of emotion anyone had witnessed was when she'd thrown her three-carat diamond engagement ring at Dr. Pierce Belkin— a neurosurgeon who was much in demand, not always by his patients—and the aforementioned hospital administrator.

A flash of fury had accompanied the flying ring as well as a single seething word that wasn't part of her usual vocabulary.

It hadn't even been the sight of the ruggedly handsome *Mayflower* descendant making love to the vapid, overly endowed blonde that had made Alisha throw her ring at him. It was Pierce's complete lack of contrition coupled with the snide remark—"Oh, grow up, Alisha.

Just because we're getting married doesn't mean I'm going to be your slave"—that made her lose her composure and had her throwing the ring and then telling Pierce to take up residence in a much hotter location.

The story was *already* making the rounds by the time she'd taken the elevator from the fifth floor down to the first. Not that she cared about the gossip. She'd never been the kind to pay any attention to whispers. But what convinced Alisha that she needed a change of scenery was the fact that although the hospital was far from a small place, there was no doubt in her mind that she wouldn't be able to avoid running into Pierce *or* any of what she had come to realize were his numerous conquests.

Good at shutting out things that irritated her, Alisha still knew that she would be able to hold her head high for only so long before the situation would become intolerable to her.

There was no way around it. She needed to find somewhere else to be. Preferably somewhere far away.

As a rule, Alisha didn't make friends easily. Dedicated, driven, she'd ignored socializing to focus on becoming the best all-around general surgeon she could be. In part—a large part—to honor her father.

A giant of a man, Dr. William Cordell had been a family-practice physician. Alisha was his only child, and she had adored him. A nature enthusiast, he would go camping whenever he could get away. His wife hadn't shared his interest in the great outdoors, but Alisha had, and he had taken her with him, teaching her all the fundamentals of survival.

Cancer had abruptly ended her father's life when she was just fourteen. She'd never been close to her mother, and the two had drifted even further apart after that. Alisha closed herself off emotionally and worked on achieving her goal to the exclusion of almost everything else. It kept her father's memory alive for her.

The people she'd been thrown in with at college studied hard but partied harder. She remained on the outside fringes of that world. Looking back, she realized that the only reason Pierce had pursued her with such vigor was because she was the only female who had ever said no to him. He viewed her as a challenge as well as a budding gifted surgeon. In time, he thought of her as a worthy extension of himself, a professional asset.

Added to that, his parents liked her, and his grandmother, a very wealthy woman, was crazy about her. She'd referred to her as her grandson's *saving grace* and wholeheartedly looked forward to their wedding.

Secretly missing the comforting security of a home life, Alisha had accepted Pierce's proposal despite the uneasiness she experienced when she'd actually uttered the word *yes*. Her uneasiness refused to completely go away even as the weeks went by.

She should have gone with her gut. Alisha upbraided herself after the engagement ring—a family heirloom— had left her finger. It was her gut that had told her to turn Pierce down; her gut that told her that a so-called fairy-tale wedding and marriage were *not* in the cards for her, not with this self-centered Adonis. But loneliness was a powerful persuader, and she really had liked his family. In a moment of weakness, she'd agreed.

And now she was paying for it, Alisha thought ruefully.

The worst part was that this was *not* the first time she'd caught Pierce being unfaithful. But in each case, it had been after the fact, certainly not *during* the act, the way it had been this last time. And those other times, he'd made apologetic noises that she'd accepted. This time, there hadn't even been the pretense of regret or remorse. If there *was* any regret about the incident, it was that he had gotten caught, nothing beyond that.

Well, her engagement—and Pierce—were now part of her past, and she wanted no reminders, no chance encounters to haunt her and make her uncomfortable, even inwardly. It didn't matter how good a poker face she could maintain, she didn't want to be reminded of her near-terminal mistake.

Moving away was not a problem. But finding a destination was. Where could she go? As if some unseen force was taking matters in hand, Alisha became aware of the fact that she was pondering her fate standing next to the physicians' bulletin board, the one where almost anything could be found by those who had the patience to carefully scan the different missives tacked onto that board. There were courtside tickets to the next basketball game being offered for sale—or more accurately, resale—slightly used furniture *in reasonable shape* could be gotten for a song and so on. All in all, it was like a visual bazaar without the noise.

For a fleeting moment, looking at the bulletin board, it occurred to Alisha that she could have offered her engagement ring up for sale, but she decided that throwing it at Pierce was infinitely more satisfying than any money she could have gotten for it.

Besides, it had belonged to his grandmother, and she had liked the woman.

That was when she spotted it. A letter tacked on the upper left corner of the bulletin board. It was almost obscured by an ad for a *European cruise of a lifetime*. Moving the ad aside, she saw that the neatly typed letter was addressed to "Any budding, selfless physician reading this letter who might be willing to put in long hours for very little financial reward, reaping instead endless emotional satisfaction that he or she was making a difference in some good people's lives." There was more written after that, an entire long paragraph, describing the conditions in the area as well as summarizing the basic requirements. It was signed by a Dr. Daniel Davenport.

Alisha stared at the letter for a minute or so before she finally took it down to read more carefully.

Was this Dr. Daniel Davenport for real, sending something like this here? Alisha wondered. The recently graduated physicians at this teaching hospital were all aiming at practices that would have them working a minimum of hours for a maximum financial return. This letter sounded as if it was an appeal for a saint, or at the very least, for a doctor who was willing to travel to a third-world country on a regular basis.

Well, you wanted to get away. This certainly qualifies as getting away, a voice in her head pointed out.

Alisha stared at the address at the top of the letter. This Dr. Davenport lived somewhere called "Forever, Texas."

Alisha frowned. Okay, not a third-world country, but she still hadn't heard of the place. But then, she hadn't heard of a great many places, and this Forever certainly sounded as if it was far away enough to qualify as *getting away*.

Alisha stared at the letter, weighing her options. The

one thing she knew was that she did *not* want to remain here a second longer than she had to.

After a moment's internal debate, rather than tack the letter back up on the bulletin board, she carefully folded it and put the letter in the pocket of her white lab coat.

Forever, Alisha mused. It had an interesting ring to it.

Chapter One

"Pinch me, brother."

Brett Murphy, one-third owner of Murphy's and the older brother of the other two-thirds owners, Finn and Liam, paused wiping down the long, sleek counter of Forever's only saloon as he saw Dr. Dan Davenport, walking by the establishment's tinted bay window.

It was not the town's only physician who had caught Brett's attention but the tall, willowy young woman who was walking beside Dan. The tall, willowy young woman who was *not* Dan's wife, Tina, or Holly Rodriguez, his new nurse.

"Why?" Liam asked, only half listening to him.

Though the saloon wasn't actually open yet, and certainly not ready to go into full swing for a number of hours, Liam was doing a preliminary instrument check—for the second time. He and his budding band were playing here tonight, and Brett had raised him never to leave anything to chance or take anything for granted. Liam had his eye on someday leaving the saloon behind him and going professional.

Though he was seldom mesmerized by *anything,* Dan's companion had managed to completely captivate him, even at this distance.

Now, that is one gorgeous woman, Brett couldn't help thinking.

"Because, little brother," he said aloud, "I think I've just seen the woman of my dreams."

That managed to get Liam's attention. His guitar temporarily forgotten, Liam looked up at his oldest brother then turned to see what Brett was talking about.

At that point, the young woman who had so completely caught Brett's fancy had disappeared from view. Her presence was replaced by another female who was passing by. Mildred Haggerty.

Liam's jaw slackened and dropped as he turned back to look at his brother.

"Mrs. Haggerty is the woman of your dreams?" he asked incredulously. "Have you had your eyes checked lately? Better yet, have you had your *head* checked lately?" Liam asked.

Mildred Haggerty was as tall as she was wide, had an overbearing personality with an unabashed drive to dominate everyone she came in contact with. A woman of some independent means, in her lifetime, she had buried three husbands. Rumor had it that they had all died willingly in order to permanently get away from the source of their misery, Mildred.

Brett looked at Liam as if the latter was the one who had lost his mind. But before Brett could remark on it, the front door began to creak, announcing that someone was disregarding the hours that were posted outside and coming into Murphy's. In general, Brett was rather flexible about adhering to the hours carved into the sign, enforcing them when the whim hit him. He was not above welcoming the lone, stray customer before hours.

Thinking that Mrs. Haggerty was the one entering—

possibly trolling for husband number four—Liam took it upon himself to loudly announce, "We're not really open for business yet."

"How about pleasure?" Dr. Dan Davenport asked as he held the door open for the reason he had come to Murphy's in the first place. The young woman accompanying him walked into the saloon, squinting slightly as her eyes became accustomed to the darkened interior. "Are you open for pleasure?" Dan asked, a broad grin on his lips.

All in all, the physician looked like a man who had just caught hold of a lifeline, one he hadn't really expected to materialize, Brett thought.

His green eyes slowly traveled over the length of the woman who'd been ushered in by the town's only doctor. Brett took in her long, straight blond hair, her fair complexion and her almost hypnotically blue eyes.

If possible, the woman looked even better close-up than she did at a distance.

"Pleasure it is," Brett acknowledged, wondering who this woman was and, more important, if she was staying in town for an extended visit. Was she a friend of the doctor's, or perhaps a friend of Dan's wife, Tina, neither of whom were actual natives of the town?

Dan inclined his head, picking up Brett's answer. "Then it's my sincere pleasure to introduce you two to the lady who answered my ad—and my prayers." For his part, Dan resembled a little boy who had woken up on Christmas morning to discover that everything he had asked for was right there, beneath the Christmas tree.

"You advertised for an angel?" Brett asked, putting his own interpretation to Dan's introduction.

Alisha Cordell had always had sharp eyes that missed very little. She narrowed them now as she looked at the man behind the bar.

This dark-haired, green-eyed bartender fancied himself a charmer, a smooth talker, she thought with an accompanying degree of contempt. The contempt rose to the surface as a matter of course. After Pierce, she'd had more than her fill of good-looking men who felt they were God's gift to women. Her conclusion had been that the better-looking they were, the worse they were.

"Dr. Davenport advertised for a doctor," she informed the would-be Romeo massaging the counter in no uncertain terms.

The look she gave the man just stopped short of being contemptuous. If this two-bit cowboy thought she would instantly become smitten with him because he was clearly handsome and capable of spouting trite compliments, he was going to be very sorely disappointed, Alisha silently predicted. She hoped the rest of the men in town weren't like this.

And if she was going to be staying in this dusty little burg, even for a little while, this cowboy—and anyone else who might share the same stereotypical mind-set—needed to be put in his—and their—place, as well as on notice that she wasn't here to indulge their fantasies. The only reason she was here and would even entertain the idea of remaining here was to help Dr. Davenport heal their wounds and take care of their ills.

Nothing else.

Brett detected the flicker of fire in her eyes, and his grin widened. "Well, I think I'm getting feverish, so I just might wind up being your very first patient," he told what was hopefully Forever's newest resident.

Alisha took a certain amount of pleasure shooting the sexy bartender down.

"I'm just here to observe for the first few days, so I'm afraid that Dr. Davenport would be the one who'll have to treat your fever," she informed him crisply.

Dan cleared his throat and launched into introductions. "Brett and Liam Murphy," he said, waving a hand at first one, then the other of the brothers as he said their names for Alisha's benefit, "I'd like you both to meet Dr. Alisha Cordell. Dr. Cordell," he went on, reciprocating the introduction, "Brett and Liam. They're two-thirds of the owners of Murphy's, Forever's only saloon."

Brett inclined his head. "Pleased to have you in Forever," he told her. His voice became only a tad more serious as he said to her, "The doc here could really use the help."

"I'm sure," Alisha replied, sounding exceedingly formal.

She hadn't wanted to be impolite to the doctor, but she'd tried to tell him that this tour of the town and its residents was really unnecessary. She'd come here to practice medicine, to answer the call for a physician, not concern herself with socializing. After the fiasco with Pierce, she'd had more than enough of *socializing* to last her for a very long time.

Possibly forever. The irony of that thought was not lost on her.

But since she was here, Alisha thought with resignation, she might as well pretend she was taking the scenery—and its people—in.

Alisha scanned the saloon slowly. The place had an exceedingly rustic look to it, as if the building had been here for at least the past seven or eight decades, if not longer.

Was this the extent of the diversion that the town had to offer? she wondered in disbelief.

"And this is where people come for a *night out?*" she asked, not bothering to hide the incredulous note in her voice.

"Dr. Cordell is from New York," Dan felt obligated to tell the two men. It wasn't an apology so much as an explanation for the obvious disbelief in the young woman's voice.

He'd come from New York himself, although at this point, it felt as if that had been a hundred years ago instead of just four. At the time, it hadn't even been a sense of altruism that had brought him here. Guilt had been the emotion that was responsible for bringing him to Forever.

Guilt and a sense of obligation.

He felt he owed it to Warren. Warren had been his younger brother, and a more quietly dedicated human being hadn't ever walked the face of the earth. He'd been the one to fatefully convince Warren to come out on one last night on the town before Warren left for the godforsaken dot on the map where he intended to set up a practice. Forever hadn't had a doctor for thirty years and was in desperate need of one within its borders.

A car accident that night had claimed Warren's life while leaving him with nothing more than an outward scratch. Internally, though, was another matter. For weeks afterward, he had been all but hemorrhaging guilt. But even so, he'd initially planned to stay in Forever only until a suitable replacement for his late brother could be located.

He hadn't counted on falling in love—with the town and with Tina Blayne, a single mother and the sheriff's sister-in-law.

Life truly happened while you were making other plans, Dan thought now. And while he didn't expect this young woman who had responded to his letter to feel the same way about the town, he had to admit that he was secretly hoping that she would in time.

"New York, eh? Don't worry," Brett assured Dan, even though his eyes never left the woman. "We won't hold that against her."

Alisha raised her chin, as if she had just been challenged. Of late, she knew she had gotten extremely touchy, but knowing didn't seem to help her rein in that feeling.

"Why should you?" she asked.

Brett didn't take offense at her tone. Rather, he just rolled with it, asking, "Short on senses of humor back in New York, are they?"

Alisha never missed a beat. "Not when something's funny," she said.

"Feisty," Brett pronounced, this time directing the comment toward the senior doctor. The grin on the bartender's face seemed to grow only sexier as he observed with approval. "She might just survive out here, then."

Dan made a quick judgment call, seeing the need to usher the young woman out before barbs began being exchanged. "Let me bring you over to Miss Joan's," Dan suggested.

Alisha glanced over at him, trying to hide her uneasiness. "That's not a brothel, is it?"

Brett was the first to succumb, laughing at the idea of the vivacious septuagenarian and diner owner who was part of all their lives for longer than anyone could remember running a house of ill repute. Liam quickly followed, and Dan held out for almost a minute, biting his tongue and trying to think of other things.

But the very image of the redheaded Miss Joan as a madam proved to be too much for him, as well, and he laughed until his sides ached, all the while trying to apologize to a less-than-entertained Alisha.

"I take it the answer's no," Alisha surmised, doing her best to maintain her dignity amid this joke she felt was at her expense.

It was Brett who answered her because Dan appeared to still be struggling for control. "Miss Joan runs the local diner. She dispenses hot food and sage advice, depending on what you need most. She's been here for as long as anyone can remember. Longer, probably. The diner's also the place where everyone goes to socialize when they're not—"

"Here, drinking," Alisha said, reaching the only conclusion that she could, given the facts as she perceived them.

Brett corrected her. "When they're not here socializing." His manner remained easygoing, but he wasn't about to allow misinformation to make the rounds. Murphy's wasn't only his livelihood, a way that had allowed him to raise his brothers while keeping an eye on them; it was also his heritage. The saloon had been passed on to him after his uncle had died. Before that, his late father had run the establishment. To Brett, Murphy's was almost as much of a living entity as his brothers were.

"Don't they come here to get drunk?" Alisha pressed, recalling some of the parties that had gone on after hours while she was attending medical school. Nobody drank for the taste or to just pass away an hour; they drank to get drunk and even more uninhibited than they already were.

Out of the corner of his eye, Brett saw that his brother was taking offense at the image the young doctor was painting. He wanted to set this woman straight before something regrettable might be said. Liam was soft-spoken and he meant well, but a lasting relationship between his brain and his tongue hadn't quite been reached yet.

"Not nearly as much as you would think," Brett told her, keeping his smile firmly in place. "I'm not sure exactly how it is in New York, but out here, we do look out for each other—and that includes knowing when to cut a customer off."

"Except for Nathan McLane," Liam interjected. The youngest Murphy brother was nothing if not painfully honest—to a fault, Brett sometimes thought.

Alisha looked from Liam to Dan. "Who's Nathan McLane?"

"A man who's married to the world's most overbearing wife," Brett answered. "Nathan has a very strong reason to come here and drown his sorrows."

"So you let him get drunk?" she asked, trying to get the story straight.

Brett caught the slight note of disapproval in her voice. "It's either that, or raise the bail for his release because the poor guy's going to strangle that woman someday just to get her to stop nagging him."

Alisha frowned. The dark-haired man was making it sound as if he was doing a good thing. "How noble of you."

Brett didn't rise to the bait. He was not about to argue

with the woman. He wasn't in the business of changing people's minds, only in telling it the way he saw it. "Dunno about *noble,* but it does keep everyone alive," he informed her.

Dan lightly took hold of Alisha's arm, wanting to usher her out while the young doctor who could very well be the answer to his prayers was still willing to remain in Forever and lend him a hand.

Glancing over her head, he indicated to Brett that he had a feeling that if his new *recruit* remained here, talking to him for a few more minutes, she might be on the first flight out of the nearby airport—headed back to New York.

"Next stop, Miss Joan's *Diner,*" Dan announced.

"Hey, Lady Doc," Brett called after her. Pausing by the door, she turned to spare him a glance. "Nice meeting you."

"Yes," she replied coolly. "You, too." The door closed behind them.

"Wow, if that was any colder, we'd have to bring out the pickaxes to break up the ice around you," Liam commented.

Brett saw no reason to dispute that assessment. However, true to his ever increasingly optimistic, positive nature, he pointed out, "That means that we can only go up from here."

Liam shook his head. It was clear that wasn't what he would have come away with. "You know, Brett, when I was a kid, I never thought of you as being the optimistic type."

"When you were a kid, you never thought," Brett reminded him with an infectious, deep laugh. Then he pretended to regard his brother for a moment before saying, "Come to think of it, you haven't really changed all that much—"

"Yeah, yeah," Liam said, shaking his head as he waved away his brother's comment. Glancing toward the door, he asked Brett, "Think she'll stay? She didn't look too impressed with the place."

"Neither was Dan when he first arrived," Brett reminded his brother. "But Forever's got a lot of positive things going for it, and besides, it's got a way of growing on people."

"Yeah," Liam laughed shortly as he went back to checking out the musical instruments. "Well, so does fungus."

"And that, little brother, is one of the reasons why no one's ever going to come up to you and ask you to write the travel brochure for Forever," Brett said wryly.

Liam looked at him quizzically. "Forever's got a travel brochure?"

Brett sighed and shook his head. "Sometimes, Liam, I do despair that all that higher education you were supposed to acquire while I was here, slaving away to pay the bills, was just leaking out your ear as fast as it went in."

Liam frowned at his brother, but his mood left as quickly as it had materialized. Ever since he was a child, it was a known fact that Liam didn't have it in him to stay mad at anyone, least of all his brothers.

Finished with what he was doing, Liam went on to step two of his process. "I've got to go round up the band and make sure everything's set for tonight."

Brett nodded as he went back to cleaning an already gleaming counter. He wasn't content until there were at least two coats of polish on it, buffed and dried.

"You do that, Liam," he told his brother. "You do that—just as long as you remember to get back here by six."

Liam stopped just short of opening the front door. "I don't go on until nine," he reminded Brett.

"Right," Brett agreed, sparing his brother a glance before getting back to polishing, "but you're tending bar at six. Tonight's our busy night," he added in case Liam had lost track of the days, "and I can't manage a full house alone."

"Get Finn," Liam told him. "He doesn't have anything else to do."

Brett caught his brother's meaning. That he felt he had found his calling and wanted to be free to put all his energy toward it.

"Don't belittle your brother just because he hasn't found his heart's passion yet," Brett chided. "It doesn't come to everyone at the same time."

"How about you, Brett? What's your passion?" Liam asked.

"I like running the bar." He made no apologies for it. His running the bar had been the family's saving grace. Rather than feel restrained by it, he was grateful for it and enjoyed being the one in charge of the place.

But Liam looked at him in disbelief. "And that's it? Nothing else?"

Brett took no offense at the incredulous tone. Liam was young and couldn't understand anyone who had a different focus, or aspirations that differed from his. He'd learn, Brett thought.

Out loud he said, "I like having my brothers pitch in without having to listen to some complicated internal argument that they feel obliged to repeat for me out loud."

Liam's handsome baby face scrunched up for a moment, as if thinking took every shred of concentration he had at his disposal. "That's supposed to put me in my place, isn't it?" he asked.

Brett flashed a tolerant grin at him. "Nice to know that all my money for your higher education *wasn't* completely misplaced. Okay, go," he said, waving Liam out the door. "Get your band ready and get back here by six."

The expression on Liam's face testified that he'd thought this argument had been resolved in his favor. "But—"

Brett pretended he didn't hear his brother's protest.

"With luck, I'll get Finn to help. He doesn't whine," he added for good measure.

"Oh, he whines. You just don't hear him" were Liam's parting words.

But Brett had already tuned him out. There were still things to see to before Murphy's officially opened its doors for the evening.

Chapter Two

"It's open, but I'm not serving yet," Brett called out in response to the light knock on the saloon's front door.

He thought it rather unusual that anyone would be knocking rather than just trying the doorknob and walking in. Most everyone in town knew that the door was unlocked not just during normal business hours—hours that extended way into the night—but also during non-business hours if any one of the Murphys were down on the ground floor. The only time the doors were locked was if they were all out or if one of them was upstairs.

The upper floor housed a small apartment that had once been occupied by Patrick Murphy, their father's older brother, when he was alive and running the family establishment. Although Brett and his brothers lived in a house close to Murphy's, there were times when Brett stayed in the apartment after putting in an exceptionally long night, too tired to walk home. And there were those times when he just wanted to grab a little time away from everyone in order to recharge batteries that were almost perpetually in use.

"That's fine because I'm not drinking yet," Olivia Santiago replied as she walked into Murphy's.

Turning around to look at the tall, slender blonde,

one of Forever's two lawyers, Brett was more than a little surprised to see the woman here at this hour—and
alone. It wasn't even noon.

He stopped restocking and came to the bar closest
to the front door. "And to what do I owe the pleasure
of having the sheriff's wife grace my establishment?"

"I'm not here as Rick's wife," Olivia told him, sliding onto a bar stool.

Brett reached for a bottle of ginger ale, knowing that
was the lawyer's beverage of choice before six o'clock.
Taking a glass, he filled it and then moved it in front
of her, before pouring one for himself.

He took into account the way she was dressed. Olivia
had on a dark gray jacket and a straight matching skirt.
A soft pink shirt added a touch of warmth to her appearance. Nonetheless, she was dressed for business.

"Then this is an official visit?" he surmised.

"If you mean am I here as a lawyer, the answer's
yes," she confirmed, then paused to take a sip.

"Someone suing us?" Brett asked, unable to think
of any other reason she'd be here in her professional
capacity. Even so, he couldn't think of a single reason
anyone would be suing them.

Olivia's mouth curved. "Should they be?" she asked
after taking another long sip from her glass.

Brett paused for a moment, as if giving her question due consideration. "Can't think of anyone who'd
want to, but both my only relatives are accounted for
and alive, so I can't think of another reason for you to
be here at this hour like this."

"Maybe I decided to take a break from work," she
suggested.

"You're a workaholic. You don't take a break. I don't

think you even stopped to take a breath after you gave birth." Births and deaths were very big events in a town the size of Forever. Each were duly noted and remembered by one and all.

"Oh, no, I stopped," Olivia assured him with feeling. "Trust me, having a child is a pretty life-altering event. You have to stop whatever else you're doing in order to absorb the full impact."

"I wouldn't know firsthand, but I'm not about to dispute that," he told her. He nodded at her glass and asked, "Can I get you anything else?"

Slight confusion creased her brow. "I thought that you and Miss Joan had an agreement. She doesn't serve any alcoholic beverages, and you don't serve any food."

"We do and I don't," he confirmed. "But I've got several kinds of nuts to offer my customers." Then, by way of an explanation in case, as a lawyer, she viewed that as a deal breaker, he said, "I don't think anyone really considers nuts to be food."

"Don't tell that to the squirrels," she commented, then smiled. "I'm fine," she assured him before adding, "No nuts. Thanks."

Brett shrugged as he returned to restocking the bar. "Don't mention it. Any time I can not get you something, just let me know."

Olivia remained silent for a few minutes, as if waiting. She smiled at Brett when he turned around again to pick up another bottle of alcohol.

"You're not going to ask, are you?" she marveled. "You have an amazing lack of curiosity. Either that, or you have remarkable restraint."

"It's not that," Brett replied. "If there's one thing I've learned on the other side of this bar, it's that if someone has something to say, you give them enough time, they'll tell you—if only to get it off their chest. All I have to do is wait—and if there's one thing I've gotten really good at, it's waiting."

Olivia bided her time until he'd set down the two bottles of vodka in his hands before telling him, "That's not the only thing you're good at, apparently."

"Okay, *now* I'm curious," Brett admitted. "That comment's going to need some explaining."

Olivia leaned slightly over the bar, her body language calling for his undivided attention even though they were the only two people in the bar. "Do you remember Earl Robertson?"

He thought for a moment—not because he couldn't put a face to the name, but because he was trying to remember the last time he'd seen the man who had been a friend of his father's. It had to have been at least three years since the man left town. Maybe more.

"Sure, I remember Earl. He took off to live in Taos, New Mexico. Said he always wanted to see that part of the country."

He didn't add that he had tried to persuade the man to stay. Earl had been getting on in years, and as far as he could tell, the man had no friends or family in Taos. No one to look out for him. But to suggest that would have meant wounding the man's pride, and that was something he hadn't been willing to do. For some men, pride was all they had. That was the case with Earl.

"What's he doing these days?" he asked, keeping his tone light.

"Not much of anything," Olivia replied. "Earl Robertson died last week."

The words hit harder than he'd expected. The man

wasn't family, but at this point, Earl was the closest thing to family he and his brothers still had. He felt he owed the old man a lot.

"Oh, I'm sorry to hear that. He was a good guy," Brett said after a beat.

"Apparently," Olivia went on, "Mr. Robertson thought the same thing about you." Brett looked at her, not sure what to expect as she continued. "He was grateful that you came to look in on him when he was sick that last time."

Brett wasn't much for taking credit for things. He preferred being perceived as a laid-back, carefree man rather than the nurturing person he actually was.

He shrugged off Olivia's words, saying, "Hey, he didn't have anybody, and he'd been there to help out when my parents died in that car accident. I think Uncle Patrick would have been completely at a loss as to what to do about the funeral and—to be honest—us, if it hadn't been for Earl.

"And then when Uncle Patrick passed on," he recalled, "Earl was there to make sure that my brothers and I were okay. He told me that if there was ever anything that I needed, to be sure to come to him. I was just sixteen and determined to look after Finn and Liam. I don't have to tell you that I was pretty damn grateful that there was someone to catch me if I fell." He shrugged as if his own actions were no big deal. "I was just trying to pay him back a little."

Olivia nodded. Brett's summary was in keeping with what she knew. "Well, Mr. Robertson apparently re-membered that."

There was something in the lawyer's tone that caught his attention. "Where's this going, Olivia?"

Olivia smiled, obviously happy to be the bearer of good news. "It seems that Earl Robertson left his ranch to you."

Brett stared at her. Although Forever was surrounded by ranches, the thought of him owning one had never crossed his mind. He knew that Earl had the ranch, but he'd never wondered who it would go to if the man didn't return from New Mexico.

"You're kidding," he all but whispered, somewhat stunned by the news.

"Not during office hours," Olivia replied with an exceptionally straight face.

Numb, he asked, "Did Earl say what he wanted me to do with it?"

Olivia finished the last of her ginger ale, placed the empty glass on the bar and then said, "Anything you want would be my guess. Looks like you're finally a cowboy, Brett."

He thought about the plot of land that had belonged to Earl. As far as he knew, it hadn't been worked since the man had left. For that matter, it hadn't really been worked for a year before that, either. That was about the time when the man's health had begun to take a turn for the worse. He did recall that during the man's final days in Forever, Earl had him sell off his stock. After Earl left for Taos, the place remained abandoned.

What the hell was he supposed to do with an abandoned ranch? Brett wondered.

"You sure about this?" he asked Olivia. "I've got enough on my hands just running this place." Then, in the next breath, he asked, "Can I sell it?"

"Sure. You can do anything you want with it," she reminded him. "But if I were you, I wouldn't sell it just yet. You might want to consider doing something with the spread down the line. After all, you and your brothers take turns running the bar. Can't see why you can't do the same thing with the ranch. Maybe turn it back into a working spread again. Rick told me that's what it was before Earl got sick."

Brett laughed shortly. "What the hell do I know about running a ranch?" he asked her.

"I don't know. I do know that despite that laid-back charm of yours, you're actually a very determined man, accomplishing anything you set your mind to. Learning how to run a ranch would come easy to you. Besides, you've got friends, and they're probably more than willing to pitch in and help you out.

"And," she continued logically, "if, after a while, you decide you still don't want to be a cowboy, then I'll help you locate a buyer. I'm sure we can find someone who'll be happy to take it off your hands. The property's just outside the north border of the town. Being that close, there're endless possibilities for it if ranching doesn't appeal to you. Town needs a hotel. You could build one on the property and still have enough left to have a small spread, or anything else that presents itself to you."

She leaned back on the stool for a minute, studying him. Her smile widened.

"What?"

"Just picturing you riding around your property." She cocked her head, thinking. "I don't believe I've ever seen you on a horse, Brett."

Brett began to dust off some of the bottles that hadn't been pressed into service for a while. He believed in running a relatively pristine establishment. "There's a reason for that."

"You don't ride?" she guessed.

"I don't own a horse," he corrected. "Don't have a reason to."

Her curiosity aroused, she pressed for an answer. "But you can ride?"

"Everyone can ride in Forever," he told her. "Some of us just choose not to." He stuck the dust cloth in his back pocket while he rearranged a few of the bottles.

"Understandable." Olivia slid off her stool in a single fluid movement. "Well, I've got to be getting back. Come by the office when you get a chance so I can officially show you the will. I should have the deed transfer all squared away and notarized for you in a couple of days."

Brett nodded, still trying to come to terms with what she'd just told him. Owning Murphy's was something he'd just accepted as part of his heritage. Owning property—a ranch, no less—was something he was going to have to get used to.

"Will do," he told her. And then a thought hit him. "Oh, Olivia?"

About to cross to the front door, Olivia turned to look at him, waiting. "Yes?"

He tried to make his question sound like a casual one. "What do you know about the new doc?"

Olivia smiled. "Other than the fact that Dan's overjoyed she's here, and Tina is now hopeful that she'll see Dan sitting across from her at dinner at least a few times a week?"

Brett laughed. "Yes, other than that."

"Not much," she admitted.

The new doctor had been in town for a couple of

weeks, and no one had struck up a casual conversation with her, as far as he knew.

"Dan says her credentials are impeccable, she graduated at close to the top of her class and her letters of recommendation are glowing, although I have a feeling that he would have hired her even if the letters had been only a tad better than mediocre. Right now she's staying with Tina and Dan until she can find a place of her own, and according to Tina, she's not exactly very talkative. Why?" she asked as it suddenly dawned on her why Brett was asking. "Are you interested?"

"I'm always interested in a pretty woman," he answered. "Especially when I can't figure out what she's doing here." He saw Olivia raise an eyebrow quizzically in response to his words. "Someone who looks like that doesn't just pick up and move out to the middle of nowhere."

Olivia pretended to be insulted. "Are you telling me that I'm not attractive?"

"You didn't move out into the middle of nowhere. You came looking for your runaway sister," he reminded her. "And while you were looking, you fell in love with Rick. *Then* you decided to stay. *That's* different."

Olivia considered his narrative. "Maybe she came here looking for something, too," she suggested.

"Like what?" he asked.

"That would be something for an enterprising cowboy to find out," Olivia told him with a knowing wink, looking at him significantly. "I'll see you later."

"Later," Brett echoed.

Brett paused, thoughtfully watching Olivia leave. The last part of their conversation had intrigued him more than the first part of it had, despite the fact that he had apparently just inherited an entire ranch that he hadn't a clue what to do with.

As with everything else that challenged his problem-solving skills, he pushed the matter temporarily from his mind. He'd much rather center his thoughts on the lovely, uncommunicative lady doc.

Now, there was a challenge he would more than willingly tackle.

The word *tackle* caused his smile to widen as he went about his work.

THE NOISE LEVEL in the bar that night made it difficult to carry on a decent conversation that went beyond a few simple words. As had become the habit on Friday nights, Liam and his band were providing the entertainment at Murphy's. The band was in full swing, the music all but shaking the rafters. He could just see the few knickknacks in the apartment above slowly vibrating across the floor.

Listening, Brett had to admit, if only to himself for now, that his little brother was a damn fine performer. Liam played the guitar as if it was an extension of himself, and his voice wasn't just tolerable; it was actually good.

And getting better all the time.

As far as he knew, Liam had been at this for about a year, finally finding the courage to play in front of the people he had known all his life. Fearing that his aspirations could never reach the heights he'd wished for himself, that he was good only in his own mind, Liam had even held back from playing for his own family. It wasn't until both he and Finn had all but bullied their younger brother into giving them a demonstration that

Liam had finally played for them. What began hesitantly had gone on to be a performance worthy of a budding professional—and Brett had been the first to realize that.

After a bit of soul-searching—he'd always been protective of his brothers, although the two really weren't that aware of it—Brett had been the one to light a fire under Liam and encouraged his brother to bring his band and play at Murphy's.

For now, the weekly performances were enough to satisfy the budding artist within Liam. But Brett knew in his heart that Liam wouldn't be satisfied with this level of performing forever. Eventually, Liam would want to try his wings elsewhere. To see if he could fly.

As a rule, Brett didn't much care for change, but at the same time, he understood that nothing ever really stayed the same. But that was his problem, not Liam's. He just had to make his peace with that.

He wanted Liam to do whatever it took to make himself happy.

For a moment, Brett tuned out everything else in the bar and just listened to Liam play.

"He's better than I thought he'd be."

The comment, spoken in a normal tone of voice, still managed to cut through the din and his concentration to reach Brett. Half turning, Brett looked over to his right to see the woman who had voiced her opinion. He just wanted to verify that it was who he'd thought it was.

And he was right.

And surprised. She was the last person he would've expected to be here, given what she'd implied two weeks ago. And while he'd considered coming to Dan's clinic with some bogus health complaint just to see her in action, he'd decided to hold off and see if the woman was actually staying—or if she couldn't hack it and decided to turn tail and run.

So far, the jury was out on that decision.

"That makes two of us," he told Alisha in a vague, preoccupied voice. And then he turned on his charm. It was never far from the surface. "First drink's on the house," he told her, "although I have to say, I'm surprised to see you here."

That made two of them again, she thought. "No more surprised than I am to find myself here."

"You're sleepwalking?" Brett asked, tongue in cheek, although there was amusement in his eyes.

She didn't bother answering that since they both knew she wasn't sleepwalking, and the suggestion bordered on the absurd. She didn't know just what she was supposed to say in response to something like that. Bantering wasn't her forte and, as far as she knew, Pierce had next to no sense of humor. It probably couldn't find a place for itself with his giant libido taking up so much space.

Rather than make small talk, which she had no patience with and was not very good at in any event, Alisha went directly to the heart of the matter that had brought her here to this dim little establishment with its scent of alcohol, noisy occupants and high spirits.

"I'm told you have an apartment," she said to Brett. And with those words, Forever's new physician managed to accomplish the rare feat of surprising Brett Murphy twice in the space of a few minutes.

Chapter Three

The noise level being what it was, Brett decided that he couldn't have heard her correctly. Leaning in closer, he said, "Excuse me?"

"An apartment," Alisha repeated, raising her voice to be heard above the din. Maybe that rancher she'd treated this morning had misinformed her, and there wasn't any unoccupied living quarters to be had in this town. Doubts as well as frustration began to set in. "Do you or don't you have one?"

Had she asked that question of Finn, Brett was fairly certain that his younger brother would have thought that Forever's new lady doc was hitting on him. But Brett had a few miles on him, not so much in age—he was just thirty-two—but in what he'd experienced during that time, and he knew the look of a woman who was coming on to a man. The lady doc was most certainly not hitting on him.

To be quite honest with himself, he didn't think he could accurately describe the expression he saw on her attractive face.

From where he stood, Lady Doc was an enigma, a puzzle waiting to be solved. In a nutshell, the lady was a challenge, and it had been a while since he'd been challenged.

His interest level went up several notches.

"I do," he replied, then asked, cautiously, "Are you interested in seeing it?"

Viewing the accommodations didn't really interest Alisha. As long as the apartment—probably nothing more than an oversize closet, she guessed, given the nature of this town—didn't come with a roommate, that was all that really mattered to her.

"I'm interested in renting it," she informed him in no uncertain terms. "It is for rent, isn't it?" Alisha asked, realizing she hadn't been told that one crucial piece of information.

"I thought you were staying with Dan and Tina. Did I get that wrong?"

"No, you didn't get that wrong," she acknowledged. "For the moment, I *am* staying with Dr. Davenport and his family." There was less than enthusiasm in her voice.

"I take it that's not working out for you? Living there?" he added when she didn't answer.

Brett couldn't envision either Dan or his wife making the lady doc feel uncomfortable enough to get her looking for other living arrangements. Both Dan and Tina were warm, giving people.

Maybe it was the other way around. Alisha Cordell's looks were hot enough to melt a passing iceberg at twenty paces, but for the moment, he had to admit that the woman didn't exactly strike him as being all that warm and toasty.

Alisha frowned. She didn't like being questioned or prodded. Still, if he *did* have an apartment, she couldn't exactly just walk out now, the way she wanted to. So she answered his question—but let him know that she didn't appreciate his prying into her motives.

"Not that it's any business of yours, but I feel like I'm in the way. It's not that big a place," she added when Brett continued studying her.

Brett took a bottle from behind him on the counter and poured a glass of pinot grigio, then placed it in front of her. She looked at the glass, then at him. "I didn't order that."

"I know. It's on the house."

Another good-looking male who thought he was God's gift to women, she thought, tamping down her anger. Just because the man had a killer smile—and he knew it—did he think he could ply her with alcohol and get instant results? He was about to be surprised, she silently promised the bartender.

Taking out a five-dollar bill, she placed it on the counter. "I pay for myself."

Rather than offer her an argument, Brett merely took the money and put it into the till. "Suit yourself," he told her then got back to the business at hand. "As to the apartment, if space is what you're after, I don't think you're exactly going to be thrilled with it."

"Why?" she asked.

"To be honest, the whole thing is really just one big room," he told her.

His late uncle's apartment was predominantly meant to be just a place to sleep or to get away for a few hours, nothing more. It was not intended to suit the tastes of someone who was high-maintenance, and at the moment, that was exactly the way this woman struck him. Extremely high-maintenance.

But if that was the case, what the hell was she doing

here? He sincerely doubted that a sense of altruism was what had brought her to Forever.

She surprised him by saying, "As long as I have it to myself, that'll be fine. I don't care if it's small."

Maybe he was misjudging her. He'd been wrong before—once or twice.

Her answer led him to the only conclusion he could make. "So I guess that means that you're staying in Forever?"

"For now," she qualified guardedly. Alisha didn't believe in verbally committing herself to anything, especially not in front of someone who was the very definition of a stranger.

"How long is a *now* in your world?" he asked.

"Why?" she asked, looking at him quizzically.

As far as she could see, there was no reason for Murphy to be asking her about her plans. It wasn't as if renting the apartment to her would keep him from renting it to someone else. Obviously, the man had had no plans to rent it out to begin with. There was no sign out, advertising its availability. According to the rancher who had told her about the place, the apartment had never been rented out before to his recollection.

"That's easy," he told her. "I want to know if I'm going to be charging you by the day, the week or by the month."

"By the month will do," Alisha answered, her voice irritatingly high-handed.

He couldn't help wondering if she was that way with her patients and decided that she probably was. It looked as though this angel of mercy needed a little help getting her signals right.

"You didn't ask for my advice, but I'm going to give

it to you anyway." He saw her opening her mouth to respond, and he just kept on talking. "You might find it a whole lot easier adjusting to Forever if you stop being so formal and loosen up a little."

"You're right," she informed him stiffly. "I didn't ask for it."

Then, because he'd stirred her curiosity and because she did have to try to get along with these people at least until she decided what she was going to do with the rest of her life and where she was going to go in order to do it, she said, "Just out of idle curiosity, exactly how, by your definition, would you suggest that I go about *loosening up?*"

"Well, for one thing, people here call each other by their first names—just like I'm pretty sure they do in New York City."

She really wished he'd stop smiling at her like that. She found it annoying—and unnerving. "I don't know what you're referring to."

"Okay." Brett tried again. "For instance, you keep calling him Dr. Davenport—"

"That's his name," Alisha interrupted.

"It is," Brett agreed. "But so is Dan. Around here, people call him Dan or Dr. Dan if they aim on being extra respectful. You keep calling him Dr. Davenport, and Dan's liable to think that you're mad at him."

That was ridiculous. "Mr. Murphy—" Alisha began in an exasperated voice, ready to put this man in his place—and that place definitely did not include giving her lectures.

"Brett," he corrected, cutting in.

She didn't come here to argue, Alisha reminded herself. She came to Murphy's to try to get herself a little organized and ultimately secure a place to stay where she could have enough peace and quiet to hear herself think. The wounds from her sudden disillusionment and subsequent breakup were still very raw, and she needed to find a place where she could heal without hearing children squealing in the background.

This apparently was her only option, and she'd learned how to deal with limits before. "Okay, have it your way, *Brett*," she said, deliberately emphasizing his name. "Now, are you or aren't you going to rent out that apartment to me?"

Brett thought for a moment. The apartment was his hideaway, his home away from home. But since Olivia had informed him that Earl Robertson's place was now his, that meant he could stay at that ranch house if he felt the need to get away for a few hours.

Besides, if she lived upstairs, this would give him the opportunity to interact with this iceberg who needed thawing in order to get in touch with her human side. The possibilities began to intrigue him.

His eyes met hers. "I'll rent it to you," Brett replied.

She felt an uneasy quiver in the pit of her stomach, something warning her that she was taking a step she might regret. The next moment, she locked the thought away. What was the worst thing that could happen? If she decided she'd made a mistake—again—coming here, she could just apply to another practice, pull up stakes and move on. It wasn't as if this move couldn't be undone.

"Good," she replied, refusing to look away. "Let's talk terms, Mr. Murphy."

"First term is that you remember to call me Brett," he told her patiently.

This man just didn't give up, did he? "And the second term?" she asked him warily.

If there was a first term, there had to be a second one, Alisha reasoned, and she found herself definitely not trusting this man. He was far too good-looking and smooth to be someone she could trust.

Again, Alisha noted, her would-be landlord's grin grew unnervingly wider. "The second term is that you don't forget the first term."

She waited, but nothing more came. "And that's it?" she asked, still waiting for the other shoe to drop—hard.

"That's it," Brett told her guilelessly.

"And the monthly rent?" Alisha pressed, wondering if it was going to be prohibitive—at least by his standards, she silently amended.

The woman really did seem anxious to live by herself, Brett thought, wondering if it was that she was antisocial, or if there was more to it that she wasn't telling him. And just possibly, herself, he added.

"Why don't you come upstairs with me and take a look at the place first," he suggested. There was the chance that she really didn't know what she was getting into, and what he thought was small might be unacceptable to her. "If you find that you like it, then we'll discuss the rent."

"I said I don't have to see it. I'll take it."

Brett was not about to back off from this point. "And I said that I'd rather that you *did* see it," he countered.

If she was going to rent the apartment, he didn't want her turning around in a month and stiffing him for the rent because something about the place wasn't to her liking. Having her view the place just meant there'd be one less problem down the road.

"Okay, show me the apartment," she said, barely managing to stifle a huge sigh.

Brett nodded. "Knew you'd see things my way," he told her.

Alisha swallowed the retort that rose to her lips as she reminded herself that for the time being, while she was here, this man's apartment was her one and only option.

"Hey, Finn!" Brett called out to his brother from the far end of the bar.

Finn had just poured one of their regular customers a whiskey, neat, and glanced in his older brother's direction. Brett beckoned him over with an exaggerated hand gesture.

Crossing to Brett's end of the bar, Finn asked, "What?"

"I need you to take over the bar for a few minutes," Brett answered.

"Where'll you be?" Finn asked.

Brett nodded toward the woman on the other side of the bar. "I'm going to be showing Lady Doc here the apartment upstairs."

"Oh? Oh," Finn cried as the truth of the situation, at least as he perceived it, suddenly dawned on him. "Sure." If possible, his grin was even wider than his older brother's. "You take as long as you like," he said, looking significantly at the new physician.

"That is strictly up to Lady Doc," Brett informed him.

"Gotcha. You lucky dog," Finn murmured to his older brother in a tone low enough for only Brett to hear. When it came to securing female companionship, both he and Liam agreed that Brett was the master.

"Strictly business," Brett assured him.

Finn's grin grew wider still, all but splitting his face in half. "If you say so. When I grow up, I want to be just like you," he told Brett with a wink.

Brett's response was to playfully cuff him.

Growing up an only child with no siblings to share anything with, good or bad, this kind of a physical exchange mystified Alisha—and, in a way, made her a little envious, as well.

"What was all that about?" Alisha asked. She'd heard only a few words of the exchange between the two brothers.

"A misunderstanding" was all Brett seemed willing to say. His answer made no sense to her since his cheerful expression did not match his words. "C'mon. This way," he told her, leading the way to the rear of the saloon. There was a narrow corridor there that led to the restrooms on one side and an even narrower stairway on the other.

Alisha looked at the wooden staircase with its narrow steps in obvious dismay. Was that the only way to get to the second floor?

"There's no private access?" she asked.

"The original owner didn't think to build one," he told her. His uncle had always liked to take the simplest path available to him.

The din suddenly swelled, growing even louder. Alisha glanced over her shoulder at the people at the bar and sitting at the small, round tables scattered throughout the room. A thought suddenly hit her. "I have to walk through the bar in order to get to the apartment—and in order to leave in the morning?" she questioned.

He answered, pretending that she was objecting to the distance, not the location. "It's not that far from the front door to the back," he told her. "You should be able to cross it making good time."

Alisha glared at him. He was talking down to her, she thought. "I don't need sarcasm."

Brett inclined his head. "Duly noted." With that, he

began to retrace his steps, leaving her standing where she was.

Surprised, she called out to him, "Where are you going?"

"Back to the bar." He nodded toward it. "Since you're not interested in the apartment, I thought I'd get back to work."

"I didn't say I wasn't interested in the apartment," Alisha protested.

He made his way back to her. "You made it sound as if the lack of a private entrance killed the deal for you."

She hated when things were just assumed about her—the way Pierce had just assumed she would go along with his behavior in exchange for his family name. "Did I say that?"

"No," he allowed.

"Well, then, let's go and see it," she said, pointing up the stairs toward where she assumed the apartment was located.

Brett laughed, shaking his head as he got in front of her to lead the way up the stairs. "Lady Doc, you give out really mixed signals."

"Why do you keep calling me that?" Alisha asked as she climbed up the stairs behind him.

"Calling you what?" he asked as he continued climbing.

Almost slipping, she clutched on to the banister more tightly. "Lady Doc," she repeated unwillingly.

He spared her a glance, making note of the white-knuckle hold she had on the banister. Was she afraid of heights? he wondered.

"Well, aren't you a doctor?"

"Yes, of course I am." She was frazzled at this point, and it took effort not to snap.

"Then you object to being called a lady?" he asked, doing his best to keep a straight expression on his face.

She glared at his back. She really hoped that interaction with this man was going to be at a minimum. "No, of course not."

"Then what's the problem?" he asked mildly.

Maybe he was just dense, but she had a feeling that he wasn't. What he was was annoying. "For one thing, it's not my name."

"Not your *legal* name," he emphasized. "Like I told you, we're not uptight and formal here." Reaching the top of the stairs, he stepped aside on the landing to give her space. There was very little available. "Lady Doc suits you," he told her.

He was standing much too close to her, she thought, stepping to one side. Otherwise, if she took a breath, her chest would come in contact with his, and that was completely unacceptable.

"Dr. Cordell suits me better. What?" she asked when she saw the expression on his face.

"I think Lady Doc is a better fit, at least while you're here."

"Fine, just show me the apartment so I can write you a check and get this over with." She gestured toward the closed door. "Why don't you people have a hotel here?" she asked. All this could have been avoided if she could have just rented a room at the start of this whole venture.

He shrugged carelessly. "Haven't gotten around to building one."

"I noticed that."

He pretended not to notice that she was being sarcastic now. "You might have also noticed that Forever isn't exactly a tourist attraction. Most people who pass through here pass through here," he underscored. "Those that come for a visit usually stay with the people they're visiting. Having a hotel here wouldn't exactly make wise business sense."

Turning the knob on the door that led into the apartment, he pushed it open.

"Doesn't that have a lock?" she asked, stunned. She was accustomed to apartments that came equipped with triple locks on their doors.

"It has a lock," he replied, gesturing at it.

"With a key?" she emphasized through clenched teeth. Why did she have to spell everything out? Was he slow-witted, or did he just enjoy getting her annoyed?

"Ah, well, that's another story."

"Does it have a happy ending?" she asked.

He laughed. "There's a key around here somewhere. I just have to find it."

And most likely, make a copy of it, she thought. He'd probably think nothing of coming into the apartment—with her in it—in the middle of the night. "Better yet, once I rent this, can I get a locksmith in here?"

"Do you have a locksmith?" he asked her innocently.

"Don't you?" she asked incredulously.

Just exactly what did this town have by way of services?

"Nope." He saw her rolling her eyes and waited until she stopped. "We have a handyman, though."

Alisha searched for inner strength. "Does he change locks?"

"I'll have to ask him."

"Do that," she said pointedly.

"Then you're going to rent this?" he asked.

Did she have a choice? "Is there another apartment in this town?"

"No."

Just as she suspected, she was back to having no other options. It was this apartment, or living with Davenport and his family. She knew what her choice had to be.

Chapter Four

"Well, then, I guess you have yourself a tenant," she told Brett after a few seconds had gone by.

Saying that, Alisha took a second, longer look around the premises. The last time she'd been in living quarters of this size, she was sharing the area with another medical student.

Alisha pressed her lips together, trying to focus on the upside of the situation, such as it was. Thinking back to her medical-school existence, she supposed this meant that she had twice the room now that she had then.

However, if she compared it to the accommodations she'd had when she and Pierce had lived together after they'd gotten engaged, well, then that was a whole other story. Coming from money, he'd resided in a Park Avenue apartment that was bigger than the clinic and Murphy's put together. The walk-in closets were bigger than this apartment.

You could have still had that—if you didn't have principles—and a soul.

Ultimately, she had no regrets over her decision to break it off with Pierce. If he felt free to cheat on her while they were engaged, nothing would change once they were married—for that matter, they might have just gotten worse. She'd made the right move in that situation. She just wasn't all that sure about the move that had brought her to this backwater town.

"Having second thoughts?"

Brett's question wedged its way into her train of thought. Alisha blinked, rousing herself and pushing aside memories that she no longer wanted to have any part of.

Turning toward him, she said, "Excuse me?"

"Second thoughts," Brett repeated. "You had a strange look on your face just now, and I thought that maybe you wanted to change your mind about renting the apartment."

He certainly couldn't blame her if she did. He imagined that, coming from where she did, she was accustomed to far better accommodations. There was a manner about her that didn't strike him as belonging to a struggling former medical student.

"No, I'll take it," she told him. This was better than nothing, and she really did want to have some time to herself.

"You haven't heard the rent yet," Brett reminded her.

She shook her head. "Doesn't matter. I'll take it—although I doubt if you're going to charge me very much," she added, slanting a glance at him.

Walking into the space for the first time, she took a long, hard look around. Was it her imagination, or did the place seem smaller each time she did that?

"You weren't kidding when you said it was small," she commented.

"The last owner, my uncle Patrick, didn't spend much time up here. Just used it for sleeping, mostly. There's

a combination stove, sink and refrigerator over there."
Brett pointed to a multipurposed appliance that stood
against the opposite wall. It was a faded white, but he
knew for a fact that it was still fully functional.

Alisha walked over to it, an expression of faint disbelief on her face. "Is that what this is?" She'd never heard
of anything like that before. "And it really works?" she
asked skeptically.

"It really works," he assured her, turning on the faucet to prove his point. Shutting the faucet off, he then
switched on one of the two gas burners adjacent to the
sink. Instantly, a hypnotic blue flame leaped up as if
on cue. Lastly, he opened the door below the sink/stove
to show her the interior of the refrigerator. "What did
you think it was?" Brett asked, shutting the door again.

"I don't know," she answered honestly. "Some cre-
ative toy meant for a child playing house would have
been my best guess." Looking around, Alisha realized
that there was a very crucial piece of furniture missing. "There's no bed."

Brett's smile contradicted her. "There's a bed," he
said.

It wasn't as if they were standing in a huge loft and
she'd somehow missed it. "An invisible bed?" she countered.

Rather than answer her, Brett went over to the closet
on the opposite wall and opened it. Just as he did, she
crossed to it, thinking that perhaps he was about to lead
her into another room. The next thing she knew, Brett
was grabbing her and pulling her to one side.

"What the hell are you—"

Alisha didn't get a chance to finish voicing her in-
dignant question, as the bed that had been upright and

hidden behind the closed door came flying down. Its four feet landed with a small thud on the wooden floor, part of it taking up the space where she had been standing just a moment ago.

Stunned, she found herself staring at a bed, comforter and all.

"Just keeping you from being smashed by your Murphy bed," Brett answered as if she had just asked a perfectly logical question in a normal tone of voice.

The fact that he was still holding her didn't immediately register. Her eyes widened as she turned her head to look at the bed that hadn't been there a minute ago.

"A what?" she asked, referring to what he'd just called it.

Damn, but she felt soft and round in all the right places for such a compact woman, Brett couldn't help thinking.

"A Murphy bed—no relation," he quipped. "Some people call it a hideaway bed."

"Just how old *is* this place?" she asked.

"Old," he allowed. "The saloon downstairs has been renovated, but I didn't see a reason to do anything up here since it really wasn't being used very much."

Suddenly aware that the man was much too close to her for her comfort, Alisha turned to look up at him, blanketing her vulnerability with bravado and doing her damnedest to ignore the rising heat she felt. "Is anything else going to come flying out at me?"

"Not that I know of," he replied. A laugh punctuated his words.

"Then I guess you don't have to go on holding on to me."

Her tone was cool and authoritative, meant to cover

up the fact that just for a split second, she was reacting to this closer-than-necessary contact between them. Reacting in the very worst possible way. Her body temperature had gone up, responding to his before she could forcefully shut everything down.

She'd already been this route before and learned a valuable lesson. Men who looked like Pierce—and Brett— weren't capable of maintaining lasting relationships. They were far too enamored with themselves to spare the time for anyone else.

She didn't need to bang her head against that wall twice, she silently reminded herself.

"Oh, I can think of a whole lot of reasons to hold on to you, Lady Doc," Brett told her with a smile that was half wicked, half arousing. "Reasons that have nothing to do with falling Murphy beds."

She needed to draw her lines in the sand *now,* so no mistakes could be made. "If you value hanging on to your limbs, *Brett,* I'd forget all about those reasons if I were you."

She expected another dose of his charm and was surprised—and relieved when Brett raised his hands in an exaggerated fashion, breaking the physical contact he'd established, and took a step back.

"Whatever you say, Lady Doc. I've never forced my attentions on a woman yet, and I'm not about to start at this late date," he assured her. "I wouldn't have grabbed you now, but if I hadn't, that bed would have landed right on top of that pretty little head of yours. You're welcome, by the way."

"Thank you," she said stiffly. "I'll write you that check now." As she took out her checkbook, another question suddenly occurred to her. This time, she looked around twice before asking, "Where's the bathroom?"

Brett nodded toward the entrance of the room and the stairs just beyond. "You passed it downstairs."

He obviously didn't understand, she thought. "I mean the one that goes with this apartment."

"You passed it downstairs," Brett repeated.

Her jaw almost dropped. "There's no bathroom up here?" she cried.

"Not that I know of."

"Didn't your uncle have to relieve himself?"

"I'm sure he did," Brett replied. "When he did, he went downstairs."

That still didn't solve the problem. Just how backward were these people? "What about bathing? Didn't he bathe?"

"As a matter of fact, he did," Brett answered, taking no offense at her tone. "That's why he built a small room onto the back end of the men's room—so he could take a shower there."

Part of her couldn't believe she was actually having this conversation. "Is there one like that in the back of the women's bathroom?"

Brett shook his head. "Was no reason for it. Uncle Patrick never got married."

Alisha felt as if she'd somehow fallen through the rabbit hole without realizing it. In an odd sort of way, she wanted to see just how far this would all go. "I can't go into the men's room to shower."

"Don't see why not as long as there're no men in it. The place is pretty empty until about two in the afternoon or so, and it doesn't really get going until about five, six o'clock," he told her. "Listen, if you like, I can see about having Clarence bring a cast-iron tub up-stairs. But you've got to remember that it's going to take up most of the available space in the apartment," he warned her.

"Clarence?" Who was named Clarence these days? she couldn't help wondering.

"He took over running the hardware store after his dad retired," Brett answered. "The man's an absolute wizard with coming up with ways to get things that you need."

Alisha laughed shortly to herself and murmured, "How about a brand-new start?"

"You need a new start?" Brett asked her, interested. "Why?"

She'd said too much, Alisha thought. That wasn't like her. She waved away his question as she moved around Brett, anxious to get back downstairs to the shelter of the smoke-filled room and the anonymity provided by the wall-to-wall noise.

Turning on her heel, she started to leave. Brett caught her by the arm, anchoring her in place.

Now what? she thought.

The question he'd just put to her still hung in the air, unanswered. "I don't know how much experience you have with little bars like mine—or any bars, actually." His opening line caught her attention, and she turned around to put him in his place for whatever *knowing* thing he was about to say.

Brett continued as if he didn't notice that this new-comer was about to give him a piece of her mind.

"But when you're in a bar," he told her, "the bar-tender is like your best friend, your father and your father confessor all rolled up into one. And, also like the confessional, what is said to a bartender in confidence stays in confidence. At least that's always been my rule," Brett stressed. "People find that it helps them cope with whatever is bothering them if they know they can unburden themselves without any consequences." Brett looked at her significantly. "I don't judge."

Now, there was a new line, she thought. She could almost see how he would be successful, getting to women, having them open themselves up while they looked into those eyes that all but sparkled with some kind of mischief.

Taking a breath, she proceeded to shoot him down— or so she thought. "Number one, I don't have a best friend. Number two, my father's been dead a long time, and number three, I haven't made use of a priest since I don't know when."

Actually, she did, she silently amended. The last time was when her father had died. There'd been no solace, no consoling her grief. God had taken her father all too soon, and listening to a sympathetic-looking priest telling her that we had no way of knowing God's reasons for doing things just wasn't good enough for her.

However, she wasn't about to share any of that with this complete stranger. She had a fatalistic feeling that somehow, if she did, if she took Brett Murphy at his word, it would all wind up blowing up on her, or it would come back to haunt her when she least expected it.

Keeping her own counsel was the best way to go in this case. In every case.

But Brett, obviously, couldn't seem to take a hint, she thought in frustration. He'd taken her words of dismissal and twisted them around to indicate need.

"All the more reason to make use of me, Lady Doc. I'm here. Use me."

Desperate, her eyes flashed as she tried to make him back off one last time. "Look, I'm sure that all the women in this town would love to have you say that to them, but I am just not interested in what you're selling." She couldn't make it any clearer than that—and she didn't want to cause a scene or completely alienate him because she did want that hole-in-the-wall that he called an apartment. At least until she figured out what she wanted to do with the rest of her life.

"Not selling—offering," Brett corrected, then added, "Friendship," before she could put her own meaning to his words and light into him again. "I think you could use a friend."

So now he was clairvoyant? He was claiming to see into her heart, was that it? She was fairly certain that she had buried her loneliness better than that.

The man was probably just shooting in the dark, nothing more.

"Do you, now?" she asked, tossing her head in a studied movement of nonchalance.

He would have had to have been deaf not to pick up on her mocking tone, but he ignored it. Something told him he'd struck a nerve. Something had made her answer Dan's letter and come here, and it wasn't selfless dedication. He'd bet the saloon on that.

"I do," he acknowledged amicably. "Never knew anyone who couldn't use a friend."

"Then prepare to be astounded," she informed Brett.

He wasn't about to push himself on her in any capacity, but that didn't change the fact that he still felt he'd gotten it right. The woman needed a shoulder to lean on—and maybe to cry on once she trusted him. But that was for later, he decided.

"Have it your way," he said easily. "But the offer's still there if you ever change your mind."

Her eyes met his, and the sarcastic retort that rose to her lips died there without making it to the light of day. Maybe, in his own way, Brett was trying to make her feel welcome. For now, she gave him the benefit of the doubt.

"I won't," she told him quietly. "Now, how much do you want?"

They'd just been talking about friendship—at least he was. Her question seemed to come out of left field. Brett shook his head slightly, as if to indicate that something had been lost in translation. "For?"

"The apartment," she cried. Wasn't the man listening at all? "How much do you want in exchange for renting out the apartment to me?" she asked, carefully specifying everything so there wouldn't be any further confusion—or whatever it was that he was feigning.

"You're still interested?" Brett asked incredulously. He'd been fairly confident that not having a bathroom or shower on the same floor as the bedroom would have sent her hurrying off into the night.

"*Interested* is probably too positive a word in this situation," she granted. "But it is what it is, and I do want to have some peace and quiet and *privacy*." She underscored the last word intentionally, hoping that got the message across to her new landlord. Once she was inside the apartment, she wanted to be left alone. "There's very little of either in Dr. Daven—in Dan's house," Alisha amended, catching herself at the last moment.

Why she felt it was necessary to go along with what Murphy had cited as the *terms* of their agreement was really beyond her. After all, the man would have had to have been crazy to declare the rental agreement null and void if she referred to the doctor by his occupation coupled with his surname.

On second thought, she reconsidered, looking up into Murphy's eyes; maybe he *was* a little off-kilter. Just off-kilter enough to want her to live up to that ridiculous term he'd given her—or else. Who rented out a box of a place without a bathroom and still expected to be compensated for it?

Well, he thought, the woman definitely knew what she was getting into. There were certainly no hidden surprises to spring on her. She'd seen the place, for better or for worse.

Grinning, Brett put out his hand. "Works for me," he told her.

Alisha looked at him and then down at his hand. She shook it almost hesitantly.

"It's my hand, Lady Doc," he prompted, "not a rattlesnake. Don't be afraid to shake it."

That goaded her enough to firmly grasp his hand this time and shake it the way she would have if a sane person had offered her his hand to shake.

"Okay, now do you have papers for me to sign?" she asked.

Every rental agreement she'd ever known or heard about came with legal papers to sign—and notarize, most of the time. He hadn't said anything about that, or standard things like first and last months' rent.

An uneasiness whispered along the fringes of her mind. Just what was she getting herself into? a little voice in her head whispered.

"No," he replied guilelessly.

She stared at him, confused. "What do you mean, *no?* Don't we have a deal? Or did you suddenly just decide *not* to rent the apartment to me?"

Now that she thought about it, it would seem in keeping with the man to just jerk her around like this. There was obviously a lack of entertainment in this town, at least from what she'd witnessed so far.

"We most certainly have a deal," Brett told her, nodding at the hand that she had dropped to her side. "We just shook on it."

He *was* jerking her around, Alisha thought. "I don't understand."

Maybe she didn't, Brett decided. Glancing toward the bar, he saw that Finn seemed to be holding his own serving the customers. That cleared the way for his taking another minute or so to explain things to this beautiful tenderfoot who had been sent their way.

"Around here, we seal our deals with a handshake," he told her.

Yeah, right—sure they did. They couldn't be that naive—could they?

"And that's enough?" she mocked.

"Shouldn't it be?" he asked her seriously. He felt sorry for the world she had come from, where trust seemed to be such a rare commodity. "If a man's—or a woman's—" he amended in case she was the type to take offense at what she perceived was a slight "—word isn't good enough, then there's no point in entering into any kind of an agreement with them, because they'll break a contract just as easily as they'll break their word."

"The difference being is that lawyers can make you live up to a contract." Didn't he realize that?

Brett smiled a rather unfathomable smile. "They can

try," he corrected. "Depends on where you are. Lawyers are only as good as the respect they command—and that involves their word, and whether or not they keep it."

Another argument that wouldn't be going anywhere, Alisha thought wearily. As a last sarcastic gesture, she took out her handkerchief and waved it in the air in front of him.

Brett merely nodded, the corners of his mouth curving significantly. "I knew you'd see it my way."

"I didn't exactly have a choice," she said pointedly.

The corners of his eyes crinkled. "I guess you didn't," he acknowledged in the nicest tone she'd heard in a very long time.

Chapter Five

"There," Alisha said, ripping out the check from her checkbook and handing it to the man on the other side of the bar. "Two months' rent," she added, confirming what they had just agreed on.

Quoting a nominal amount as the rent, Brett had initially requested only one month. Since it was so low, she had insisted on paying him for two—just in case, in that amount of time, she hadn't made up her mind about remaining. It gave her some leeway.

Alisha had taken a seat at the end of the bar in order to write the check out. Finished, she put her checkbook away and started to get off the stool.

"If there's nothing else…" she said, her voice drifting off, her meaning clear. If he didn't want her to sign a lease or anything of that nature, then she was leaving.

Brett put a hand on hers to keep her seated for a moment longer. She looked at him quizzically. "Wait—you can't leave yet."

Now what? Alisha thought uneasily. Had he realized that he'd charged too little? "Change your mind about the amount?" she asked.

When he'd quoted her the amount for the rent, she thought he was giving her the weekly figure, not the monthly one. Even though the apartment was so small, he was renting the place out for way too little, in her opinion. She kept that thought to herself.

Even as she wrote out the check, Alisha had a feeling it was going to suddenly dawn on her new landlord that he could get more for it, even though it was little more than coffin-sized. Granted, she was accustomed to the astronomical rents in New York City, but she had a feeling that what he was asking for was low, even for a tiny Texas town.

"What?" Belatedly, he replayed her words in his head. "No, the amount's fine," he reassured her. Brett planned on putting whatever checks he received from her into an account earmarked for repairs and future renovations for Murphy's. It seemed like the only fair thing to do since, as far as he was concerned, this was an unexpected windfall.

"Then why's your hand on mine?" She looked down at it and then up at him, waiting for a reasonable explanation as well as a withdrawal of that same hand.

Rather than raise his hand away from hers, he lightly drew it back, his fingers ever so softly sliding along the length of hers.

The crackle of electricity that sizzled between them was hard to miss. He had a feeling she was thinking the exact same thing. Only difference, he mused, was that she wouldn't be willing to admit it. Given half a chance, he would.

"I thought we'd have a drink, celebrating your new quarters and our new relationship," he told her in his best Southern-gentleman drawl.

"Our relationship?" she echoed incredulously.

What was he talking about? There was no relationship. Had she made a mistake, renting this apartment?

A nervous restlessness began humming through her. At the very least, she needed that handyman he'd mentioned to come by and install a dead bolt—provided the man knew what that was, she added with a note of weary despair. She was beginning to think she'd set up camp at the end of civilization.

"Landlord and tenant," Brett replied, indicating first himself, then her. "Why? What did you think I was referring to?"

Still sitting on the stool, she squared her shoulders. "I didn't have a clue," she lied. "That's why I asked."

Brett nodded toward the collection of spirits behind him. "You want something light and fruity—or something hard?" he asked her.

The words seemed disconnected as they came out of the blue like that. Confused, she could only ask, "What?" as she stared at him.

"To drink," Brett prompted. "Light and fruity—" he gestured toward the small array of bottles filled with colorful mixed drinks "—or hard?" he concluded, waving a hand toward the bottles that contained alcohol his customers downed straight.

She shook her head to both choices. "Nothing, thanks. I need to get going."

"The evening's young, and so are you," he told her with a grin that insisted on corkscrewing right into the center of her chest. "One drink to toast the apartment—and your settling in Forever. Just our way of showing how very welcome you are," he added. Before she could turn him down, he said, "The town's not exactly growing by leaps and bounds, but we're still wearing Dan out. You came just in time to save him—and us." There was the underlying sound of amusement in his voice. She couldn't tell if he was being serious or not.

She still hadn't made up her mind about this town and its inhabitants. She'd come here because it was somewhere to go in order to get away. But now that she was here, she had to rethink the idea of remaining in town for any length of time, never mind about *Forever*. That wasn't even on the table at the moment.

After a beat, she realized that he'd stopped talking and was looking at her with the most soulful, knee-melting eyes she'd ever encountered—and that included Pierce's, whose eyes, until this moment, had held the record for being able to make her melt in an astonishing amount of time.

But she'd been in love with Pierce, which partially accounted for her reaction to him, Alisha silently argued. She certainly wasn't in love with Brett Murphy.

As a matter of fact, she sincerely doubted she was even *in like* with the man. As far as she was concerned, he rubbed her completely the wrong way. Lord knew, she'd had her fill of men who *knew* they were seductive, complete with bedroom eyes, and used that so-called *talent* to get whatever they wanted.

So what exactly did Brett Murphy want?

"One drink isn't going to hurt anything," Brett coaxed her.

She supposed that he had a point. A single drink *wouldn't* hurt anything.

Putting her purse on the counter, she said, "All right. I'll have a Long Island Iced Tea." When he didn't ask her what that was—as she'd half expected him to—she said, "How much?" Opening her purse, Alisha took out her wallet.

"Put your money away," he told her. "It's on the house." With that, he began mixing the drink.

Rather than do as he'd said, she took out several bills. "Oh, no, I want to pay for it. I don't like being in someone's debt."

"If anyone is in anyone's debt," he told her seriously, "the town's in yours—for coming to help Dan and making it so that he can take a vacation without feeling like he was abandoning us." Finished, he set the drink down on the bar in front of her.

Without thinking, she automatically drew the drink over to herself. Her mind was on what Brett had just told her. A cold chill ran down her spine. She'd never been the only doctor in charge before. At the hospital, there'd always been a multitude of seasoned physicians to turn to, veteran physicians to use as a sounding board if something was unusual. The thought of being strictly on her own was *not* a heartening one.

"Vacation?" she repeated. "He didn't say anything about a vacation."

Her voice had gone up slightly. It wasn't exactly panic he heard, but it wasn't the last word in confidence, either. He hadn't meant to rattle her. At least, not about her work. If he was going to set her pulse racing, it would be with a whole different goal in mind. Fear wouldn't have been part of the equation.

"Don't worry. Knowing Dan, he's not going to leave you until he thinks you can fly solo for a week…or two," he added more quietly.

"Or two?" Her eyes widened as she struggled to get her nerves under control. She'd be treating colds and hangnails and aching muscles, just like she had been these past two weeks under Dan's tutelage. How hard could it really be?

She still couldn't quite manage to get her uneasiness to subside completely.

Brett gave her his most reassuring smile. "He's not pushing you out of the plane until he knows for a fact that you can open the chute."

"Do all your pep talks involve being airborne?" she asked, redirecting her edginess to focus on Brett rather than her own uneasiness.

Brett lifted a shoulder and let it drop in a careless shrug. "Seemed to fit the occasion, seeing as how the look on your face was as white as a parachute," he commented. "And technically, even if Dan does go on vacation, you won't be alone," he assured her.

"Don't tell me you studied medicine on the side, between mixing drinks."

"I won't tell you anything that's not true."

The way he said it, with his eyes holding hers, cut through the layers of doubt, distrust and sarcasm, going straight for softer territory. She could almost believe that he was being truthful.

Almost.

"Then you'd be the first man to do that since my father," she replied quietly.

"Heady company," he commented, inclining his head. "I'll be sure to act accordingly." With that, he raised the glass he'd poured for himself, indicating that she should follow suit. When she did, he said, "To the beginning of a beautiful friendship."

Then, because the evening had settled into a comfortable rhythm, his brother doing, in his opinion, very well without him, he lingered, adding, "And to you, Lady Doc, for coming to tend to our wounds and our ills."

With that, he downed his drink. She took a sip of

hers, then regarded it thoughtfully for a moment. "What did you just have?" she asked, nodding at his empty shot glass.

"Wild Turkey, 101 proof," he told her.

She pushed her glass to one side and said, "I'll have the same."

Brett looked at her uncertainly. "Are you sure?" he asked. "It's rather strong, and you might get more than you bargained for."

Her eyes locked with Brett's. "I think I already have."

Because something told her that this man was going to be there, around her, at every turn, in spirit if not in the flesh, she needed to show him that she could go toe-to-toe with him if need be. And that she wasn't about to become one of the worshipful cluster she was certain he availed himself of from time to time, when the whim hit him. She had no wish to blend into a crowd.

"The Wild Turkey," she prompted, looking at the bottle that was back among the others on the counter behind him.

Taking a double shot glass, he put it on the bar in front of Alisha and poured a serving accordingly. "Your call—" he began.

Before the words had left his lips, the whiskey had gone past hers. She had thrown it back in one fluid movement.

The smooth liquid blazed a trail of fire all the way down her throat and into her stomach. She felt it reaching all her limbs almost simultaneously.

Returning the shot glass to the counter, she looked at him unwaveringly, silently informing him that she was up to any challenge he threw her way.

Whether or not that was true was another story entirely.

Her eyes weren't tearing up, Brett noted, relieved. That meant this wasn't her first go-round with the potent alcohol and that her bullheadedness hadn't gotten her in too deep.

He'd misjudged her. And he had to admit, he was somewhat impressed.

"Want another?" he asked, waiting to see what she'd say. If bravado had been her intention, she would have asked for another. But she didn't—which impressed him even more.

Moving the drink he'd previously poured for her back in front of her, Alisha said, "I'll pass." A touch of humor curved her mouth. "I need to stay clearheaded. After all, I might be on call if there's a three-horse pileup on Main Street."

He studied her for a long moment, trying to make up his mind about her and realizing that in order to do that accurately, he was going to need more input. Maybe a lot more input.

"Why'd you come here, Lady Doc?"

Her eyes narrowed. "I thought we just settled that. To rent the apartment you have upstairs."

"No, I mean, why did you come to Forever?" he specified.

"Daven—Dan told you that. I answered his open letter. He said he sent it to half a dozen teaching hospitals— I was the only one who answered him."

Brett knew all that. Even if Dan hadn't told him, there were hardly any secrets in a town the size of Forever. But that wasn't what he was asking her.

"Why did you *really* come?" he asked. "And don't

give me any altruistic pap," he added with another sensual smile that ultimately made it difficult for her to get angry at him.

"You don't think I'm altruistic?" she questioned.

Some of the alcohol must have gotten to her, Alisha surmised, because this was where she should be taking offense—and she wasn't. But she was surprised that she managed to be that transparent to this bartender/confessor.

"Oh, I'm willing to believe that you're altruistic enough," Brett allowed. "But that's not the reason you're here." He leaned in across the bar, dropping his voice so that only she could make out his words, which seemed only right, seeing as how they were meant for only her and no one else. "What are you running from?" he asked her quietly.

She knew she should be angry at his assumption, both that she was running from something and that he had a right to ask as well as a right to know. But she was struggling with shutting out the warm, aroused feeling that had washed over her when his breath had touched her cheek as he spoke.

Alisha did her best to block out everything, both the good and bad. "What makes you think I'm running from anything?"

The lady doc had just proved his point and didn't realize it, he thought. "Because you didn't say no, that you weren't."

"No, I'm not," she replied firmly with a toss of her head. The movement brought with it the hint of a headache, a bad one, in the making. Damn, what did he *put* in that whiskey? she wondered. She usually didn't get strong headaches after having just a single drink, even if that drink was strong enough to dislodge blasting caps a quarter of a mile away.

Brett looked unconvinced at her belated protest. "Sorry—it doesn't count when I have to prompt you," he told her.

"You're not prompting me," she denied vehemently, then stubbornly insisted, "And I am *not* running." She waited a beat before adding, "I'm walking."

"From?" he asked gently, giving every indication that he could wait until the second crack of eternity for her answer, if that was what it took.

Oh, what did it matter? Maybe saying it out loud would help purge her of all this anger. "From a rich, self-centered bastard who thought that just because he had relatives who smuggled themselves on board the *Mayflower,* that meant he could do whatever he wanted to whomever he felt like—and I would be patiently waiting in the wings for him to come back."

Brett unscrambled the rhetoric rather quickly. He'd heard it all before. Not quite in those terms, but he'd definitely heard it before.

"He cheated on you."

"Apparently with the immediate world," Alisha bit off.

He went a little further out on the limb and made a guess. "You were married to him?"

"Oh, please," Alisha protested with an exaggerated expression of disdain as she rolled her eyes. "I was engaged to him," she corrected before she realized that she was laying herself bare before this smooth bartender. She never went on like this—*ever.* She looked into her now-empty glass as if she'd find some clue at the bottom of it. "Damn, what did you lace this drink with? Sodium Pentothal?"

"Gotta plead not guilty to that one. I'm fresh out of truth serum," he told her. "All I've got at my disposal is a bartender's willingness to listen."

"Or a bartender's willingness to pump the new kid on the block for information," she corrected.

Brett laughed softly, shaking his head. "No pumping. Just a willing ear," he reminded her. "So what happened to the cheating bastard you were engaged to? I don't picture you as the type to let him get away with it."

This had gone way beyond any of his business. This was the part where she knew she should just stand up, tell the man she would be moving in tomorrow morning and then walk out.

That was what she knew she should do.

It wasn't what she did.

The reality of it was that she remained sitting on the stool. Sitting there and telling this imperfect stranger what had been festering within her and eating away at her for the past month.

"No, I didn't let him get away with it," she replied. "I threw my engagement ring at him, told him it was off and told him where he could permanently take up residence. I also," she added with relish, "told him not to pack suntan lotion because he was going to fry anyway."

Now, *that* he could see her doing. The guy deserved it, he thought. He had to have confetti for brains to go wandering off, bedding other women when he had someone like this woman waiting for him at home.

Brett laughed. "Remind me never to get on your wrong side."

"You've already come close a couple of times," she

informed him, wrapping both hands around the empty glass as if to anchor herself to something.

"I'll keep that—" *and you* "—in mind," he told her amicably.

He was smiling at her—so why did she suddenly feel as if she'd been put on notice?

"Okay, I'll be back in the morning to move in," she told him.

"I'll be here," he promised.

"I figured that," she replied.

In Brett's opinion, she didn't sound all that happy about his presence. It was going to take a bit of work, but he and the lady doc were going to find some interesting middle ground, he promised himself.

Alisha slid off the stool and slowly tested the strength of her legs—just in case. Despite having knees that felt a little wobbly, her legs were just fine.

She left the saloon without a backward glance. Even so, she could have sworn she felt Murphy's eyes on her, watching her all the way to the front door.

And even after the door had closed, even though she knew it wasn't possible.

Chapter Six

"So? What was that all about?" Finn asked. The moment the door closed behind Alisha, Brett's brother made his way over to his brother's side of the long bar. "Saw you and that new lady doctor raising your glasses and toasting something. Anything I should know about?"

Brett saw at least three regulars close to him leaning in, ready to hear anything he had to say. He deliberately moved to the side and lowered his voice before answering. "I just rented out Uncle Patrick's old room."

Finn looked at him in surprise. Following his brother's lead, he turned his back to the men at the bar. The noise level and Liam's band took care of the rest. "I didn't know we were looking to rent it out."

"We weren't," Brett replied. Taking her empty glass and the two shot glasses, he made his way over to the sink to wash them out. "It was her idea."

"I thought she was staying with Dr. Dan and his wife."

Finished, Brett picked up a dish towel to dry the glasses before putting them back near the liquor bottles. "She was."

This obviously wasn't making any sense to Finn. He

liked having things spelled out. "They get into some kind of argument or something?"

Based on what she had shared with him, Brett had his doubts about that. "She didn't mention that, just said she wanted her own space."

Finn laughed shortly. "She's not getting much more than just a *little* of it. Does she know there's no bathroom up there?"

One of the customers at the bar raised a hand to attract his or Finn's attention. No more communication was necessary than that since he knew what Max Keller drank. Clan MacGregor whiskey without fail. Picking up a bottle of the whiskey from the counter, he made his way over to the man.

"She knows," he told his brother.

Like a dog with a bone, Finn followed him around, asking questions. "And she's okay with that?"

Brett shrugged as he poured two fingers' worth into Max's glass. "I think *okay* is stretching it a little, but for now, she's willing to go along with using the facilities down here."

Moving away from Max, Brett turned and looked at his brother thoughtfully. They were all, perforce, handy when it came to small fixes and doing what needed to be done, but Finn had a real talent not just for taking things apart and repairing them, but for building things from scratch, as well.

"How long do you think it would take you to put in a small bathroom upstairs?" he asked Finn.

The question took the younger Murphy aback. "Where would you suggest I put it? That space is pretty cramped as it is."

Neither one of his brothers ever went up there any-

more and had obviously forgotten about the layout, Brett
thought. "There's the storage closet," he reminded Finn.

A light entered Finn's eyes for just a moment, then
went out again as he recalled the area. "It's full of junk."

"We can empty it," Brett said with finality, dismissing the minor problem. Leaning a hip against the bar,
he studied Finn. "So how long do you figure it would
take?"

Finn thought for a moment, then said, "Well, that depends."

Now that he'd made up his mind, Brett wanted to
nail things down as quickly as possible. "On what?"

Three new customers came in and took the last available seats at the bar. This time, Finn made his way over
to the men, and Brett followed him. "On whether or
not you've got me working shifts at the bar at the same
time," Finn answered.

"How long if that bathroom's the only thing you're
working on?" Brett specified.

Finn set out three shot glasses and deftly filled them
with an easy flick of his wrist. "I can have it done inside a week as long as I can get the supplies I need and
a little help with the demolition."

Quoting a price to the new occupants at the bar, Finn
collected the amount and rang it up at the register behind them. Finished, Finn paused, studying his older
brother. And then the familiar Murphy grin materialized. "You really want her to stay, don't you?"

There was no such thing as a completely private conversation at the bar. Brett kept his response deliberately
vague in case, despite the ongoing din, he was overheard.

"I want her stay here to be civilized" was all Brett
would commit to. "But for now, you're not working that

bathroom, so get back to tending the bar. Mind that it's the bar that you're tending and not those girls," he pointed out, nodding at the four young women who had just walked in. The women, all in their early twenties, were clustered at the far end of the bar, standing because there were no available stools left.

And they were all looking their way, Brett noted.

"I can do both," Finn assured him, then added with a conspiratorial wink just before he moved down the bar, "Hey, I learned from the best."

Brett merely waved him on, making no comment one way or the other.

"Hey, I'm dying over here. What's a guy gotta do to get a drink around here?" Cameron Lewis asked.

"All you've got to do is just ask, Cameron," Brett responded, picking up a bottle of the man's drink of choice. "Just ask."

"Well, I'm askin'," the man declared.

"And I'm filling," Brett replied, pouring dark, thick liquid into the man's freshly emptied glass.

MISS JOAN'S AMBER eyes slanted toward the front door of her diner. She'd felt rather than heard it opening. There were stories that the older woman and the diner were all but one, and that she could feel every scratch her counter sustained, could literally feel the vibrations of the door each time it was opened or closed.

People who said they knew better laughed the stories off but secretly always felt there was a strong possibility that the stories might contain a kernel of truth.

Her attention shifted to the young woman who had just walked into the diner. Miss Joan still never missed a beat of the conversation she was having with two of her customers as she took down their orders. Those who understood the term knew that Miss Joan had invented multitasking long before it had become a byword for an entire generation. Moreover, the redheaded woman with the sharp eyes and sometimes sharper tongue made it all look easy.

When Miss Joan recognized who had entered her diner, she quickly disengaged herself from the people who had placed their orders. Depositing the slip with their lunch orders on the counter in front of the kitchen, she made her way over to the counter where the diner's newest customer had just seated herself.

"I was wondering when you were going to finally come here on your own. What'll it be, honey?" Miss Joan asked in a welcoming voice.

"A cup of black coffee, please," Alisha requested, never bothering to pick up the menu that lay on the table in front of her.

"And?" Miss Joan asked, waiting for the rest of the order.

"A napkin?" It was more of a question than anything else because Alisha wasn't really sure what the older woman expected to hear.

"No, what'll you have for lunch?" Miss Joan asked patiently. This one needed gentle treatment, Miss Joan had already decided when Dan had brought her around that first day.

"Oh." Alisha paused to think for a minute, doing her best to pull herself together. She'd just left Murphy's and was stalling rather than going on to where she'd been staying these past two weeks.

"Nothing. Just coffee." She was feeling unusually vulnerable right now, trying to center herself and decide just what she *really* wanted to do. She didn't feel as if she belonged anywhere.

"You can't be expected to function on just coffee," Miss Joan chided. "You need something that'll stick to those skinny little bones of yours."

One of the first things Alisha had learned upon coming to this town was that everyone eventually turned up at Miss Joan's, and that the slightly larger-than-life woman seemed to know everyone's business whether or not they told her about it firsthand. Dan had told her that although the woman blustered at times and could bark out instructions like a drill sergeant when the spirit moved her, inside that gruff, gravelly voice was the heart of a woman who could feel other people's pain and had an unending capacity for compassion and empathy.

"I don't—" Alisha began to demur, but her protest never saw the light of day. Miss Joan just took over.

Patting her hand, the older woman said, "Leave it to me, honey. I'll take good care of you." And with that, she told one of her waitresses to bring back "Today's special for the doc here."

As the girl hurried off to give the order to the diner's senior short-order cook, Miss Joan turned to face Forever's newest resident.

"How's it going?" she asked in a tone that indicated she was really interested in finding out just how Alisha was getting along. Tired, drained and trying to find the words she needed in order to tell the doctor she was working with that it was nothing personal, but she'd found new lodging, Alisha didn't have any words left over to spare.

"Okay," she replied, hoping someone would call the

diner owner over so that she could just sit here in relative peace.

"That doesn't sound very convincing," Miss Joan replied. She peered more closely at the new doctor's face as if she was making up her mind about something. "Not sleeping too well, are you?"

Alisha thought of denying the woman's assumption, then decided that there was no point in denying what was probably so obvious. There were circles under her eyes, put there thanks to children who never seemed to sleep for more than ten minutes at a time.

But, in her opinion, complaining about the doctor's children bordered on being a shrew, so she just shrugged and said, "I'm just trying to get accustomed to a new place."

Miss Joan smiled at her as if she knew better. "Tina's kids are a good bunch, but they can be a handful. They're certainly noisy enough to wake the dead when they get going," she testified. She'd babysat the trio on a couple of occasions and could speak from firsthand experience. She had a very soft spot in her heart for the children, but she wasn't blind to their energetic behavior. "But you, coming from New York City—the city that never sleeps and all that—you're probably used to constant noise in the background."

"Yes," Alisha allowed, then added, "but not in the next room."

Miss Joan surprised her by saying, "I've got a spare room at my place. I could just call and tell my husband to get the bed made up if you wanted to crash there for a while—"

She really hadn't expected that. There was more to this woman than she'd thought. "No, that's all right.

Thank you for the offer, but I've already made other arrangements."

Miss Joan looked at her sharply, doing a quick analysis.

"You're not leaving us, are you?" she asked. "I know these folks take some getting used to, probably more than most new places. But if you give them a chance, you might find that you're glad you stayed. These are all good people," Miss Joan assured her, "and they'll be there for you if you need 'em. Living here is like having one big extended family. We've got our share of squabbles, no doubt about it, but deep down, we're all family."

"No, I'm not leaving," she told the woman. *At least, not yet,* she added silently.

Miss Joan nodded, taking the young woman at her word. "Good to hear," she said.

Someone called out to the diner owner, and for a second, Alisha thought her prayers had been answered and the woman would be moving on. But Miss Joan merely waved a hand at the man who'd called out to her, not even turning around. Instead, Miss Joan continued studying her.

"If you're not leaving and you're not staying with Dan and Tina, then—" Miss Joan drew out the word, and suddenly, her face grew more animated as the answer occurred to her. "If you're staying in town, then you got Brett Murphy to rent you his uncle's old room above the bar, didn't you?"

Damn, the woman *was* clairvoyant, Alisha thought. If she'd had that kind of insight herself, she might have been spared the humiliation that she'd gone through because of Pierce.

"Dan said you were very sharp," she told the older woman with a touch of admiration.

"I just pay attention," Miss Joan replied. This might get more interesting at that, the older woman thought. Her waitress returned with that day's special, a whiff of heat swirling above the plate. Miss Joan placed the dinner on the counter before the young woman. "Eat up, Doc. You're gonna need your strength," Miss Joan predicted.

Alisha didn't know if the remark referred to her work—or something else. In either case, she discovered that the scent of the roast turkey, mashed potatoes and even the peas had her appetite suddenly making an unexpected, dramatic appearance.

ALISHA COULD HEAR the noise growing louder before she ever opened the door the next morning and crossed the saloon floor.

Hammering and drilling.

With a vengeance.

The bulk of her worldly possessions were in a storage unit back in New York City. What she'd taken with her was divided up between the two suitcases that she'd hastily packed when she was leaving. She had one in each hand now as she made the significant transition from house guest to renter.

The bar looked empty inside.

"Hello?" she called out.

The door to Murphy's had been unlocked, but once she stepped into the cool darkness, she didn't find a single Murphy around. She thought that was rather strange since she'd told Brett that she was moving in today.

She'd taken a few hours off from the clinic to get settled in. When she'd told Dan and his wife that she was moving to her own quarters—and assured them that it wasn't anything they had done that had her leaving— they had been incredibly understanding and kind about the matter. It had almost made her feel guilty about leaving—but she did want a little peace and quiet in her own space, no matter how small it was.

Except that the words *peace and quiet* really didn't seem to have a place here. Not with all that noise practically making her teeth vibrate.

"Hello?" Alisha called out again, louder this time. Louder or not, she still got the same results. The only thing answering her was the hammering and the drilling.

What was going on here?

As she crossed the floor and went to the rear of the building, the noise, dovetailing and then blocking each other out, grew louder still. It seemed to be coming from upstairs.

Her upstairs, she thought. She'd paid two months' rent; that entitled her to throw out whoever was making all this racket.

Tough talk for a peanut.

That was what her father had always said whenever she would lose her temper about something. The words were always laced with affection, but they did bring her attention to the fact that she was not exactly an imposing figure. It also encouraged her to control her temper whenever possible.

Squaring her shoulders, Alisha began to go up the stairs, a suitcase in each hand.

At this rate, she was just going to toss her suitcases

on the floor and make a hasty retreat, hoping that eventually, whatever was happening up here would stop.

And if the noise didn't subside by tonight, she was going to demand her money back and—

And what? Crawl back to Dan's and ask him if she could move back into the guest room? She couldn't do that. It would be too embarrassing. Sure, Dan and his wife had taken the news well, telling her they understood. But if she came back the same day, they'd think she was a loon. She'd be packing up for good before she knew it.

And going where?

No, for better or worse, right now she needed to stick it out in Forever. But if she couldn't, for whatever reason, settle in upstairs, then where?

Miss Joan's? She could envision the woman working on her, slowly drawing out every shred of information she had within her.

Maybe she could sleep in the clinic, Alisha thought, ruling out Miss Joan's. One of the exam rooms had been converted to a makeshift hospital room where patients who'd had nonthreatening, minor surgery stayed overnight to recover and rest. She could stay there until she figured out her next move, Alisha told herself. All things considered, it couldn't possibly be as noisy there as what she was currently hearing.

Having gone up the stairs far slower than she was happy about, Alisha marched toward what was now her apartment and set the suitcases down on the landing just outside the door. As she entered, she was about to demand to know what the hell was going on here when she suddenly had her answer.

Or at least part of it.

At the far end of the room, where there had once

been a solid wall, there was now a big gaping hole. But instead of daylight coming through, Alisha saw what appeared to be a room or something akin to one beyond the one she was standing in.

Taking a few steps into the noise-drenched area, she could feel the hammering and the drilling all but reverberating within her body.

But the increased noise was nothing in the face of what she found herself looking at. Brett and one of his brothers—Finn, was it?—stripped down to their jeans, their bare chests gleaming with sweat, each manning either a drill or a sledgehammer.

Were they ripping apart her apartment so she couldn't make use of it? After charging her rent? Why would they do something like that?

Determined to get an answer, she marched over to Brett and addressed his back in a raised voice. "What are you doing?" When neither he nor his brother turned around to answer her, she surmised that they hadn't heard her. Small wonder—she could hardly hear herself think, much less talk.

Rather than try again and vainly shout at the two men, she tapped Brett on the shoulder. She nearly regretted it the next moment when he swung around quickly, startled by the unexpected contact.

As he turned to face her, he held the hammer he was wielding aloft so as not to accidentally hit her. "Morning," he said brightly.

Morning? Was that all he had to say while he was destroying the place she was supposed to be staying in? Was he some kind of maniac?

"What are you doing?" she shouted at him. Her voice

all but echoed around the space because Finn had turned off the drill.

"What does it look like?" Brett asked cheerfully.

"Like you're ripping the place apart," she accused, trying very hard not to notice that the man had a very tempting rock-hard body, and that it was hardly *inches* away from hers.

"Close," Brett acknowledged. "We're building you a bathroom."

Chapter Seven

"A bathroom?" she repeated, fairly certain she wasn't hearing Brett correctly.

Alisha had an uneasy feeling that the sight of all those hard ridges along his bare chest and incredibly flat stomach was interfering with her ability to process information properly. Moreover, she was having a great deal of difficulty tearing her eyes away from his torso. It was only with a concentrated surge of effort that she managed to raise her eyes to his face.

For once, Brett wasn't wearing that sexy, cocky grin, she noticed with relief.

"You're building a bathroom up here?" Alisha questioned in disbelief. Just like that? He hadn't mentioned anything last night. Last night, he'd made it sound as if the facilities downstairs were her one and only option.

Brett nodded. If he was aware that he was somewhat underdressed for this conversation, he gave no indication.

"After giving the matter some thought, it didn't seem right charging you that money without throwing in a basic facility." He nodded toward his brother—also underdressed, she couldn't help thinking. "Finn's pretty handy with tools, so I figured we'd give getting this bathroom in place a shot."

That was all well and good, but meanwhile, Alisha thought, she had this gaping hole in her apartment, which negated the whole idea of *having* this apartment in the first place.

"And where am I supposed to stay while this is going on?" she asked. *Look at something else, 'Lish,* she told herself, realizing that her eyes were once more riveted to his gleaming upper body. *Look at anything else.*

Easier said than done.

"Here," Brett told her, answering her question. "Finn's building the bathroom in what used to be the saloon's storage room. It's not going to interfere with your living here."

The hell it won't, she thought. Alisha looked at the gaping hole again. Maybe she could hang a drape or tape newspapers over the opening as a temporary fix.

But seeing as how they were doing all this without forcing her to either bargain for a bathroom or pay for it, she didn't think she had all that much right to complain about the inconvenience or the noise. To do so would seem rather small-minded and petty of her in the face of the Murphy brothers' generous gesture.

Forcing herself to look elsewhere again, she murmured, "That's very nice of you," to Brett. "Of both of you," she amended, realizing that she was leaving out the man Brett had just indicated was in charge of the remodeling. She could only pray he knew what he was doing.

Finn slanted a look in her direction, acknowledging her recognition, then got back to work. Within seconds, the noise as well as the heat was once again enveloping the room—and her.

The noise was coming from the tools. The heat, however, came from another source and was proving to be far more dangerous to her peace of mind. The heat was being generated by Brett's and Finn's bodies as they worked. Muscles tensed and bulged, and their bare chests gleamed with sweat that seemed to be just cascading off their tanned upper torsos.

She needed to leave. To find somewhere with cooler air, somewhere where she could breathe. The air in what was now her apartment was suddenly in dangerous short supply.

"I'd better get to the clinic," she heard herself mumbling.

Brett stopped swinging his hammer, resting it on the floor before him. There were beads of perspiration all along his brow. Alisha found herself curling her fingers into her palms to keep from reaching up and brushing his perspiration away.

"What?" he asked, resting on the shaft of the sledgehammer. "I'm afraid I didn't hear you."

"The clinic," she said, pointing vaguely in the general direction where she assumed the squat, one-story building was situated. "I should be getting to it." *And away from here before I do something incredibly stupid I won't forgive myself for.*

Brett's brow furrowed beneath the damp hair plastered on his forehead. "I thought you said you were moving in this morning."

"I am. I did." She pointed toward the two suitcases in the doorway. She'd intended to put their contents away and make herself at home a little. But she definitely couldn't do that now, not with Brett here like this.

"That's it?" he asked, surprised at how little she'd brought.

Alisha thought of her things, all neatly tucked away in the storage unit halfway across the country.

"I travel light," she said, not bothering to mention the rest.

"Lighter than any woman I've ever met," Brett readily acknowledged.

He hefted the hammer again, ready to resume swinging. The demolition part was very nearly finished. Then came cleanup—but right now, that wasn't his problem. He had to be getting downstairs to get ready for the day's work soon.

"I'll see you later, then," he told her.

"Later," she echoed, nodding her head as she began backing away. Taking a breath, she swung around to face the doorway and quickly vacated the premises, driven away not by the noise but by the spine-melting sight of two half-naked men. Two very impressively built half-naked men. Heaven knew she'd never seen anything in anatomy class that came close to what she had just been privy to. Certainly never anything that had her pulse revving up and launching into double-time the way that it was currently doing.

It felt cooler to her the moment she got to the landing.

Alisha just kept going without a backward glance.

"EVERYTHING ALL RIGHT?" Dan asked when he saw his new associate hurriedly throwing on her white lab coat and then slinging her stethoscope around the back of her neck.

"Fine," Alisha answered a bit too quickly.

Dan gestured for her to come in. He closed the folder

he'd been making notes in and pushed himself back a little from his desk to study his young associate. "I thought you were going to be settling into your new quarters this morning."

"I'm settled."

"That quickly?" he marveled. He looked at her more closely.

"I didn't have much," Alisha reminded him, then added, "And I didn't want to hang around and get in the way."

"In the way?" he echoed, puzzled. "In the way of what?"

She realized that she'd managed to miss a button on the lab coat and began to undo them all. What was wrong with her? She'd seen unclothed patients before. Completely unclothed patients. But none, she was forced to admit, had ever made her spine tingle and her knees threaten to give way.

"The sledgehammer and the drill," she answered, rebuttoning her lab coat.

Dan shook his head. "I don't…" His voice trailed off, leaving his young associate room to jump in with an enlightening explanation—if she could.

"Brett and his brother—" She paused, trying to remember his name.

"Liam?"

Alisha shook her head as she took the seat in front of him. That wasn't it. "The other one."

"Finn."

Her face brightened with recognition. "Yes, that's him. Finn. Brett and Finn are adding a bathroom to the apartment."

Dan absorbed the information and smiled as he nodded. "That just might come in handy," he commented. "Listen, if you want to go back, maybe help out to make the construction go quicker, I can handle the patient load. After all, I've been doing it these last four years. A few more hours won't kill me."

An image of Brett, his chest damp and glistening, flashed through her mind. She could feel herself reacting accordingly just from the memory of him. She definitely couldn't go back to see the real thing. That was just asking for trouble.

"No, that's all right," she assured Dan with feeling. "I'd rather stay here. Besides, I'd probably just be in the way. What I know about construction could probably fit on the head of a pin—with room to spare."

"Well, you're one hell of a good doctor, and that's what really counts," he told her.

She looked at him, slightly bewildered. It wasn't that she didn't welcome the praise, but she hadn't done anything in the past two weeks to merit that sort of thing. What was he referring to?

"How could you know that?" Alisha asked. "I've only been here a few weeks."

Dan smiled. "Well, I could say that I'm a keen judge of character and that I can read things into the way you interact with the patients and what you find significant in their health histories—or I could tell you that I had your file forwarded from the hospital. It makes for interesting reading."

"You had my file forwarded?" she asked incredulously. She'd just assumed, the need for a doctor being what it was, that Davenport would have just been glad she was breathing.

He nodded. "I thought I'd save us both some time if I got to know your work through your previous efforts. That was some call you made in the E.R. with that boy. Considering all the commotion that was going on that night, according to the report, a lot of doctors might have missed that one symptom," he complimented her, referring to the fact that there'd been a telltale pink line forming around the area that had been cut, a sure sign that an infection had set in.

"That's in there?" she asked, surprised. She hadn't made a big deal of it, just made the notation in the chart and treated the young boy—saving his leg in the bargain, she'd thought with quiet pride.

"Every last detail," Dan told her. "You impressed the chief resident, and from what I recall of Gavin Stewart, that's not an easy thing to do."

Alisha stared at him. "You *know* Dr. Gavin Stewart?"

He smiled at her. "Actually, he interned under me," he told her.

"Small world," Alisha marveled. Suddenly, she wasn't quite the outsider she'd been a few minutes ago. They had something in common now beyond their choice of a profession.

"Not as small as Forever," Dan said, seeing the humor in the situation.

"Doctors," Holly Rodriguez said, sticking her head into Dan's cubbyhole of an office. Her expression was serious, but not alarmed. Very little alarmed the steadfast young woman. "Marlene Ryan's here with her son, Zack. I think he's got a broken arm. Marlene said Zack was trying to be a bronco buster like his dad. Apparently, the horse had other ideas."

"Looks like we're on again," Dan said, pushing his chair back even farther and rising to his feet. Alisha was quick to follow suit.

IT WASN'T UNTIL more than ten hours later that the clinic was able to close its doors, allowing Alisha to drag her tired body back to Murphy's.

Too tired for dinner, she'd passed on both Holly's and Dan's separate invitations to join each for dinner with their respective families.

All she wanted to do was fall face-first on her bed— provided she could get it to stay down—and sleep until she had to get up again for work tomorrow.

But as she approached Murphy's, she couldn't help wondering if she was going to be subjected to the construction noise that she'd heard going on this morning. However, at this point, she had her doubts that it would keep her from sleeping. She was *that* tired.

Mercifully, she didn't detect any drilling or hammering when she opened the door to the saloon and walked in. Only the sound of voices, mostly male, raised in boisterous conversation.

A good many of the men were lining the bar. She moved past the patrons like a woman in a semitrance, totally unaware that as she passed, she was garnering looks that varied from mildly interested to borderline lecherous.

The latter was quickly squelched by a glare from Brett, silently putting the offending parties on notice. Brett ran an orderly establishment, which both men and women felt comfortable frequenting.

"Lady Doc," he called to her as she passed him. "How was your day?"

"Long" was all Alisha trusted herself to say as she kept walking.

"Need a little something to help you unwind?" Brett inquired.

From where she was, it sounded more like a suggestion. Dog-tired though she was, Alisha recognized that beneath the exhaustion, she was pretty wound up after the lengthy day she'd had. She didn't remember sitting down after Holly had announced the first patient, which meant that she'd spent more than ten hours straight on her feet.

Retracing her steps back to Brett, she asked, "What would you suggest?"

He had a feeling she didn't realize that she'd just asked him a loaded question. Even tired-looking, Alisha Cordell was a damn gorgeous woman. He had a great many answers to her question that really couldn't be voiced in public, or even really suggested in private, not at this juncture of their acquaintance.

But there was no denying that he did find himself exceedingly attracted to her, and if and when conditions were right, he intended to act on that attraction—but not yet and not now. The town needed another doctor more than he needed to explore tempting new regions, no matter how much he wanted to. He did not want to be responsible for scaring her away.

Brett had to admit, though, that this was the first woman he could recall who had tempted him to this point since Laura Wellington had left Forever—and him—in her rearview mirror.

To date, Laura had been the only woman he'd ever wanted to marry. The only woman who had made him temporarily forget his responsibilities. He found his loyalties torn and his resolve waffling. What had finally made up his mind for him was Laura herself—but not in any way she had intended.

His parents were gone, and his uncle had just died, leaving him to fend for himself and his two younger brothers. Laura couldn't wait to kick Forever's dust off her feet, and she wanted him to come with her. The moment they graduated high school, she'd been hell-bent on taking off. When he hesitated, she had given him an ultimatum. He had to choose: it was either her or his brothers. At fourteen and thirteen, they would have been turned over to become wards of the county.

He couldn't do it, couldn't let that happen. He chose his brothers, and Laura took off, permanently fading out of his life. He'd hurt some, then just shut down that part of him. Pining away was for people who didn't have a living to earn, and he'd had three of them to provide for.

That was in the past now, and in all that time, he hadn't found anyone he'd been willing to give his heart to. While he had dallied with and enjoyed many women since then, none had ever interested him, had ever moved him, the way that Laura had. He'd been fairly convinced that no one ever would.

And then Alisha Cordell had come into town.

Where the hell had all that come from? It wasn't like him to drift off like that. Especially with someone waiting on him. Lady Doc was obviously waiting for him to answer her—after all, he'd been the one to engage her, not vice versa.

"I've got a drink right here," Brett told her, reaching beneath the counter for a bottle he had set aside just for her, in case he could interest her in having a social drink before retreating to her apartment.

The saloon was fairly dim, but there was enough light coming through to filter through the bottle, casting a rainbow of lights.

Alisha eyed the bottle suspiciously. "That's not going to knock me for a loop, is it?" she asked the bartender.

"No loops involved," Brett guaranteed. He crossed his heart for good measure. "It's just going to loosen all those clenched—muscles of yours," he finally concluded with a knowing smile that, despite her best efforts, immediately undulated beneath Alisha's skin and worked its way throughout her entire being in approximately sixty seconds flat. "Ultimately allowing you to relax," he told her.

"Fine, I'll take it to go," she said in all seriousness.

Brett shook his head. They were relatively lax in Forever, but there were some rules they had to follow. "Sorry, it has to stay down here. It won't take you long to finish the drink," he promised. "It's not all that potent."

The drink he served her was pink and foamy, fizzing and sprinkling the skin on her hand as he poured. "What do you call it?" she asked.

"How about the Lady Doc Special?" Brett suggested, trying the name out for size. "Seltzer, strawberry liqueur and a dash of valerian root and chamomile to help you relax. The locals swear by it."

The man had an endless bag of tricks, she thought. "Works for me," she told him. Had she just said that in her head—or out loud? At this point, Alisha really couldn't be all that sure.

Picking up the glass, she tentatively sampled it. It

was fruity and smooth and very light on her tongue. She liked it instantly.

"It's good," she said in surprise.

"I thought you might like it," he said with satisfaction.

The next moment, as he watched, the object of his interest downed the drink he'd concocted rather faster than he'd thought she would. But as he'd just told her, there was nothing harmful in the drink, just some flavored soda water and a few natural herbs.

The herbs were a natural relaxant that would allow her to get the sleep she so desperately needed. He didn't want the noise from the bar, muted though it was by the time it reached the apartment, to keep her awake, even for a little while.

"Thank you," she said, putting the glass down on the bar. As an afterthought, she told him, "Put the drink on my tab."

Then, with measured, deliberate steps, Alisha made her way to the rear of the building, the staircase being her goal.

She counted the stairs as she went up each one, a rather hypnotic alternative, in this case, to counting sheep. Her eyes threatened to shut on her before she reached the landing. Alisha found she had to struggle with them to keep them open.

Finally reaching her door, she unlocked it, went inside and carefully relocked it again. Three steps inside the apartment had her standing in front of the door behind which her bed resided.

With one swift, calculated movement, she pulled open the door, moving quickly to the side in order not to have the bed come down on top of her.

The bed crashed down.

A second later, she crashed down on it.

She was asleep the moment her face touched the squashed pillow.

Chapter Eight

Alisha had always considered herself to be a light sleeper.

She was easily roused by any undue noises, and she had managed to also train her subconscious to wake her if she had to be on call by a certain time. This ability, to wake up within a couple of minutes of the time that she *needed* to be up, came in handy when she'd been an intern, then a resident at Faith Memorial Hospital.

But uncharacteristically, for the first time in a very long time, these past seven hours she'd slept like a dead person. It was a deep sleep where she heard nothing, dreamed nothing, almost as if she had fallen into some sort of suspended animation.

Ultimately what had woken her up was the smell of coffee.

At first, she thought she was finally dreaming. But if that was the case, the aroma would have faded once she was awake.

It didn't. It only grew stronger.

Sitting up and focusing, Alisha half expected to see a coffeepot on that combination appliance thingy that Brett had pointed out to her when he'd initially shown her the apartment.

But there was no pot of coffee on the stove, no coffeemaker going through its paces on the minuscule counter, either.

Was the smell of coffee coming from downstairs? She didn't recall Brett saying anything about coffee brewing at Murphy's.

Still sitting there, now fully awake, Alisha stretched, trying to pull her thoughts together and put them in their proper perspective.

Then it actually hit her. She'd slept through the night. The *entire* night.

Since she never did that, she could only attribute it to the drink that Brett had given her with the natural sedative. But she didn't feel groggy. If anything, she felt refreshed.

And *really* craving that coffee she smelled.

Alisha swung her legs off the bed at the same time that she realized she hadn't changed last night but had fallen asleep still dressed in her clothes.

Glancing down, she saw how wrinkled they all were. "Nice fashion statement, 'Lish," she upbraided herself out loud.

Dragging her hand through her hair, she thought for a minute and actually debated marching downstairs to use the shower. Brett had told her she could do that, but she would have felt a great deal better about showering in the men's room if she had some kind of a lock for the bathroom door, a lock that belonged exclusively to her. She felt very uneasy contemplating using the one that Brett had installed on the door downstairs. What if someone suddenly materialized with a key and walked in on her while she was taking a shower?

The people she'd interacted with at the clinic so far

all seemed rather nice, and she was fairly certain that her privacy was safe with them, but she was a long way from knowing *all* the people in and around Forever, and she had never been one to leave things to chance—especially not when it came to something as personal as taking a shower *privately*.

Alisha was still debating her next move when she heard a knock on the door.

"It's me, Lady Doc. Brett," he said, identifying himself in case she didn't recognize his voice. "You decent?"

"Yes, I'm decent," she told him. "And wrinkled," Alisha murmured under her breath, frowning down at her clothing.

"Can I come in?" he asked.

She glanced over toward the door. Since he wasn't trying the doorknob, that meant he didn't have a copy of the key he'd given her.

Either that, or he was just trying to give her a false sense of security so he could come in on her unannounced when she least expected it. He seemed nice, she admitted, even though he was a great deal sexier than she was comfortable with, but he hadn't fully earned her trust yet. She needed more than just *nice* and certainly a lot more than just *sexy* before she could give someone her trust.

She sighed. She was dressed, so having him come into the room didn't matter to her one way or another. "Sure," she told him. "Come on in."

She waited. Several beats passed, and he still hadn't come in.

"Are you coming in or not?" she asked.

"You're going to have to open the door for me," he

answered. "I had Clarence come in and change the locks the way you requested, remember?"

She remembered talking to Brett about it, but she hadn't realized that he had gone ahead and called in the handyman.

Sliding off the bed, Alisha crossed the half dozen steps it took to reach the door. With each step that brought her closer, the scent of coffee only seemed to get stronger.

When she flipped the lock and finally opened the door to her apartment, she saw why. Brett was carrying a tray in his hands. A tray with a large tumbler of coffee and a bright blue plate with breakfast on it. Eggs, bacon and white toast.

"I thought you might like breakfast to get you started your first morning here," he told her.

Her stomach growled, reminding her that she hadn't eaten for a while, but she refrained from reaching for the tray. Had he made that here?

"Dan told me that you and Miss Joan have this arrangement where she doesn't serve liquor, and you don't serve food."

"I don't serve food," he acknowledged, placing the tray on the small table.

Like the rats enticed by the Pied Piper's flute, she followed the food to the table. "Then what's this?" she asked, gesturing at the contents on the tray.

"That's my *bringing* food to a friend," he pointed out. "There's nothing in that agreement that says I can't cook food for me and mine."

Unable to keep herself in check much longer, Alisha removed the plate from the tray, putting it on the table and the tray on the floor.

"And I fall into that category?" she asked. Alisha didn't know if she found that concept confining—or rather comforting and nice.

"You fall under 'miscellaneous' for now," he corrected. "I live a few doors down from here," he explained as he watched her sit down at the table. "I like to cook breakfast, and I figured you might be hungry since you didn't have any dinner."

"How would you know that?" she asked, surprised—but not as surprised as she would have been two weeks ago. People in this town seemed to know things about one another, things that people in a much larger city didn't bother knowing—or finding out.

Brett took no affront at her tone. He'd probably be spooked, too, coming in from the big city where no one trusted anyone else. "You'd be surprised how fast word gets around in a small town like Forever. Not too many secrets here."

"I wouldn't think whether or not I ate dinner the night before would be something that would fall under the heading of *secrets.* Personally, I just think it's too trivial a fact for anyone to take any note of."

Brett laughed. She probably had a point. "There's also not all that much to do in a town this size. You wouldn't believe what passes for entertainment around here.

"Anyway," he said, changing the subject back to what he was originally saying, "I was making breakfast for myself, Finn and Liam, and I thought maybe you'd like to have some, too."

At this point, her senses all but being assaulted by the tempting smell of the food that Brett had prepared and brought in with him, she was far too hungry to pretend she wasn't.

Murmuring her thanks, she made short work of what was on the plate, and she washed it down with the coffee he'd brought.

The first long sip had her eyes all but widening to their full capacity—and then some.

"Wow, I could have really used your coffee when I was an intern." Eighteen-hour shifts would have been a snap with this black brew running through her veins, she thought.

"Too strong?" he questioned.

She laughed shortly. Boy, was *that* an understatement.

"*Too strong* is too weak a term for what's in here. Who taught you how to make coffee, someone in the asphalt business?" she asked wryly.

"My dad," he told her. "He used to work two jobs, going from one to the other and getting very little sleep at all." He nodded at her coffee. "He'd drink that to keep him going."

"Keep him going?" she echoed. "Drinking this, it's a wonder the man managed to close his eyes. Ever," she emphasized. Even so, she consumed half of its contents before she set the tumbler back on the tray. Alisha sighed, feeling rather full. "What do I owe you for this?" she asked.

His expression was unreadable. He had the ability to turn that off and on at will, she realized, feeling just a touch frustrated because she couldn't tell what was on his mind when he assumed that expression.

"Did I tell you I was charging you for breakfast?" he asked.

"No," Alisha began, but got no further in her response.

"Then you don't owe me anything," he concluded. "By the way, I got you a lock," he told her, placing the item on the corner of her tray, then putting down the accompanying keys. He saw her look up at him quizzically. "The lock's for when you take your shower in the downstairs men's room." She glanced over toward where the hole in the wall had been and discovered that it was covered by a makeshift drape hammered, not hung, into place. "It's going to take Finn a few more days to finish your bathroom," he explained, an unvoiced apology implied in his tone. "After he's done, you won't have to worry at all about someone walking in on you at an inopportune time."

She laughed. He was being thoughtful, and she really wanted to believe it was on the level. But she'd been fooled by a good-looking guy acting thoughtful at the outset of their relationship—big-time. She didn't want to be the fool again.

"With you second-guessing all my needs," she said with a touch of sarcasm in her voice, "you make it hard to leave Forever."

"That is the general idea, Lady Doc," he told her in a moment of honesty.

"Oh?" Did he mean that on a personal level, or was he speaking for the town?

"We don't want you to leave."

Never one to show all his cards, Brett resorted to using the all-inclusive pronoun, but what he was really referring to was himself. He was beginning to realize that *he* didn't want Alisha to leave. At least, he silently insisted, not yet. Not until he decided just how attracted he was to this woman and where that attraction would lead him—if it went anywhere at all.

Picking up the tray from the floor, he slid the plate and tumbler onto it. "Well, I'll let you get to your day. I've got to get to mine," he told her, and then, for no apparent reason he could think of, he added, "I told my brothers I was taking them to inspect my new property this morning."

"You bought some property?" There was obviously more to this man than was evident at first glance. Was he a businessman with his eye on expansion? Or was he referring to a strip of land somewhere, purchased to satisfy the inner cowboy within him, something she was beginning to suspect existed within almost every male in Forever?

"No," he said, wanting to set her straight. "Seems I inherited this chunk of land."

Now that she looked more closely at him, Brett didn't seem to be too happy about coming into the property. That meant that he'd been affected by the passing of whoever had left him the land. Sympathy flooded through her before she could think to stop it.

"Oh, I'm sorry," she said quietly. "Did someone close to you die recently?"

Since her voice was full of sympathy, it caused Brett to wonder just how many times she had dealt with that very same question, or been in a position to offer condolences to a friend or family member of a patient who hadn't been able to survive whatever had brought them to the hospital in the first place. She looked as if she actually was sincerely sorry.

"He died recently," Brett replied, "but he really wasn't close to me."

She watched him, puzzled. His answer didn't make

any sense to her. "Then why did he leave you his property?"

Brett moved his shoulders in a vague, dismissive shrug. "Because I was nice to him and not too many people, it seems, were."

There was more to it than that, Alisha judged. People didn't write wills if the disposal of their possessions didn't matter to them. Whoever had left the property to Brett had a definite connection to the bartender.

"Funny, you don't look like a Boy Scout," she quipped.

The sly curve of his mouth was back. That moment of vulnerability she'd glimpsed was gone. "That's 'cause I'm not."

No, Alisha decided, studying him, Murphy was probably the complete antithesis to a Boy Scout unless she'd totally missed her guess. But there *was* something there, beneath the charm and the smooth talk. He had his walls, and she had hers. Walls came in all sorts of different configurations.

But at bottom, that was his business, not hers, she reminded herself.

"Thanks again for breakfast," she told him as he walked across the threshold.

"Don't mention it."

Brett turned around for a moment to say something else, but she had already closed the door. He heard the lock flip into place. His mouth curved at the corners. It was going to take a lot to win this one over, he mused, going back down the stairs with his tray.

He'd always liked a good challenge.

THE DRIVE TO the property that Earl Robertson had left to him was a relatively short one. The ranch was located just at the edge of Forever. Olivia had come by yesterday to give him the deed, which she'd had transferred to his name.

It was official. The ranch was now his.

Brett brought his car to a stop before the gate. It, like the fence on either side of it, was all but falling apart. Weather and termites had been at it relentlessly over the past few years.

After getting out, he pushed the gate open, then looked over his shoulder at the two occupants still in the car. Finn, as always, rode shotgun. Liam, all but in his own world, most likely writing another song in his head, Brett assumed, was in the back.

"Well, don't just sit there—come on out," he told his brothers.

Finn and Liam got out on either side at the same time. Neither one looked thrilled about being dragged out to view the deserted ranch.

"I thought you wanted me to finish that bathroom," Finn reminded his older brother.

"I do," Brett responded, "but this isn't going to take long."

He took a long look around. It had been a while since he'd been up here. Nothing seemed to have changed, he noted. There was still a cool breeze here, despite the fact that the temperature was climbing.

"I have that practice with the band," Liam spoke up.

"I know. Like I just said," Brett repeated patiently, "this isn't going to take long."

"Don't see why you need us out here anyway. It's not like we know anything about ranching," Finn pointed out. He had his interests and his strengths, neither of which included overseeing a spread or having anything to do with horses.

"Well, neither do I," Brett replied.

He surveyed the field they were in. It was green and lush and perfect for cattle to graze on. In the five years since Robertson had okayed the sale of his herd, the land had had time to recover and flourish—not that he knew very much about ranching beyond that. But he knew potential when he saw it.

"So this is yours, huh?" Liam asked, scanning the area and actually taking it in for the first time. "Not too shabby."

"Ours," Brett corrected. Both brothers looked at him quizzically. "This is *ours,*" he emphasized in case his brothers had somehow missed his meaning.

Finn looked at him uncertainly. "I thought you told us that Olivia said old man Robertson had left this land to you."

"He did," Brett confirmed. Then, before either brother could ask more questions, he said, "What's mine is yours." Brett looked from one brother to the other. "You know that."

Finn flashed him a wide grin. The family resemblance was always strongest when they smiled like that, Brett thought.

"Does that sharing principle apply to that cute lady doc, as well?" Finn asked.

Brett's tone was one of tolerance. It had taken him a while to develop that particular quality, but it had evolved out of necessity. He wouldn't have been able to survive rearing his brothers without it.

"She's not mine," he informed Finn.

Finn, apparently, thought he knew better.

"Yet," Finn corrected. "She's not yours *yet*. But I saw the way you were looking at her the other morning when she came in while we were working on the bathroom—the one you decided she needed," he underscored, his meaning clear: Brett was not as indifferent to the woman as he was pretending. "Hell, brother, it's just a matter of time before that woman is another notch on your belt."

"Or your bedpost," Liam, not to be left out, added.

Brett shook his head. "When are you two going to grow up?" he asked in exasperation.

Finn gave him a knowing look. "Probably around the same time you hang your hat on one bedpost—for good," he replied.

He didn't have the kind of time that a relationship like the one Finn was alluding to required. There were still too many things left for him to do.

"Not going to happen for a long time," Brett promised a shade too quickly, as if he wasn't at ease allowing the suggestion to hang there between them.

Finn exchanged looks with Liam and grinned broadly. "Then I guess little brother and I are going to stay young like this for a long time to come."

Brett snorted as he walked around the field, stopping to check out the soil at random. "Since when does your action depend on what I do or don't do?"

"Since you became our idol and role model, big brother," Finn told him with a very straight face, under the circumstances.

"Maybe I should have come out here alone after all," Brett said. "It's not often that I get the chance to find peace and quiet away from you two lunkheads."

Finn turned to Liam, feigning seriousness. "I think he hurt my feelings."

Liam nodded with feeling, getting into the spirit of the thing. "I know he hurt mine."

"Ha! You two don't have any feelings," Brett countered. "You both have hides like rhinos." He gestured toward his car and began walking back to it. "Now shut up and get back into the car."

Liam appeared all too ready to comply and quickly turned back, picking up his pace, changing it from sluggish to fast. "We're going back?" It was a rhetorical question.

The next moment, Liam was shot down.

"No, not yet," Brett told him. The news was met with less-than-overwhelming enthusiasm. "We're going to drive around for a bit, get the lay of the land the way it is now and then go see how much repair the main house is going to need."

Reaching the car, Finn pulled open the door and got in. "In other words, more work."

"In *any* words, more work—eventually," Brett replied, getting in himself.

Maybe inheriting this property was going to turn out to be a good thing, he mused. It would certainly bring them closer together as a family, the way things used to be when they were younger—as long as he succeeded in getting his brothers in gear.

Chapter Nine

"You're next, Millie," Holly Rodriguez announced through the large rectangular opening that looked out onto the medical clinic's waiting room. "Dr. Davenport will see you now."

Millie Edwards, the woman whose name had just been called, rose from her seat. But rather than head toward the door that would lead her to the rear of the clinic, where the examination rooms were located, the middle-aged homemaker approached the desk where Holly was seated. The nurse was inputting information into the clinic's brand-new computer, purchased just for this very function.

Millie stood there quietly, waiting for Holly to finish what she was typing.

Sensing her presence, Holly paused. Her fingers rested lightly on the keyboard as she looked at the older woman.

"Is something wrong, Millie?" she asked, seeing the somewhat hesitant expression on Millie's almost wrinkle-free, round face.

Millie stood with her back to the rest of the occupants in the waiting room. Lowering her voice to almost a hoarse whisper, she said, "No, but, um, would it be all right if I just wait for the other one? The lady doctor?" Millie asked hopefully.

"Sure," Holly told her, taking care to keep the smile from her lips.

She glanced at the list and called out the name of the next person on it, a big, burly man by the name of Jake Horn, who had just taken over running the local feed store for his uncle.

Jake shuffled past Millie, nodding a general greeting toward her.

"It's not that I don't like Dr. Davenport. I do," Millie said nervously to the doctor's nurse once Jake had gone through the door. "But, um, this is a lady problem and, um…" Embarrassed to even be mentioning what had finally brought the harried mother of three over to the clinic, Millie's voice slowly trailed off on a helpless note.

"It's all right, Millie," Holly assured the woman. "Dr. Dan wants you to be comfortable when you come to the clinic."

"But I don't want to hurt his feelings—or insult him," the woman added, her eyes widening as the last thought suddenly occurred to her.

"Don't worry about it, Millie. Dr. Dan doesn't take offense easily. You're just exercising a patient's right to pick and choose their primary physician," Holly told the woman diplomatically.

Millie still looked unconvinced. "You're sure he won't be insulted?" she asked uncertainly.

"I'm very sure," Holly told her with gentle finality. "Now take a seat, and as soon as Dr. Cordell is ready, I'll send you in to see her," she promised.

Several minutes later, Holly saw Zander Cruz emerge

from exam room 1. After pausing to make a payment on his bill, the man entered the waiting room and then headed for the clinic's front door. That meant that the new doctor could see the next patient.

But rather than send Millie in immediately, Holly rose from her chair and made her way back into the rear of the building.

Alisha looked up as she heard someone coming into the exam room she was currently in. But instead of the anticipated next patient, she saw the clinic's nurse standing in the doorway.

"We can't be out of patients, can we? Or are you my next patient?" Alisha asked, finding the idea mildly amusing.

Holly laughed softly, shaking her head. "Unfortunately, we're definitely not out of patients. It's almost standing room only out there, but I just thought you might want to know something."

"Oh?"

The single word carried a note of leeriness in it. At this point in her life, after her fiancé fiasco, any surprises coming her way were suspect and unwelcome.

"Your next patient is Millie Edwards—and I thought you'd like to know that she specifically asked for you." Holly smiled as she delivered the news. "I believe that makes Millie your first official patient by choice in Forever."

Alisha had been seeing patients for close to three and a half weeks now, but to her knowledge, this was the first one to actually request her—choosing her over the clinic's resident physician.

Alisha's eyes crinkled as she smiled at the nurse,

appreciating the notification. "Thank you for letting me know."

Holly returned the smile. "My pleasure, Doctor. I'll send Millie in now."

Alisha nodded. "Please." She watched Holly leave the room.

She hadn't thought it would matter that much to her, being singled out by a patient and having that patient actually request seeing her, but it did. So much so that Alisha felt as if every fiber of her being was smiling.

Big-time.

The feeling lasted for the rest of the day, weaving its way into the late afternoon and the beginning of the evening—even when fatigue set in.

"Well, you certainly look happy," Brett noted as his one and only tenant walked by the bar later that evening.

The crowd along said bar had thinned out somewhat since the doors had officially opened a little after noon and the "late" shift—people coming in after they'd had their dinner—hadn't begun to pour in yet. Occupied as usual, Brett had still been watching the front door, waiting for Alisha to come through it on her way to her apartment.

He'd found himself keeping an eye out for her every night now, whenever he was on duty—and of late, he was on duty every night, at times sharing the job with one of his brothers, at times going it alone. Liam, devoting himself more and more to nurturing his musical career, played with the band at Murphy's at least two nights a week, if not more.

Finn lent a hand at the bar far more often than Liam did, but the truth of it was, his middle brother was predominantly busy with making renovations to the ranch house that he had insisted belonged to all of them. The upstairs bathroom had been completed, as Finn had promised, within a little more than two days of Alisha's moving in.

His brothers, Brett thought with pride, each had a special talent. His lay in keeping the family together no matter what.

The sound of Brett's voice burrowed into her thoughts, and Alisha looked at her too-good-looking-for-her-own-damn-good landlord for the first time, mildly surprised that she was inside Murphy's. These days, she'd discovered, she came here almost by rote, as if she was on some sort of automatic pilot.

Tonight she'd stopped to have dinner with Holly at the diner where the latter used to work until she'd graduated from online nursing school. Holly had done that just after she'd married Ray Rodriguez, the last of the eligible Rodriguez brothers.

Miss Joan had served them dinner personally, and for once, Alisha noted with relief, the titian-haired woman had been too busy asking Holly questions to grill her—that meant that she'd gotten a pass for the evening.

Alisha had to admit, though, like everyone else in the town, she was growing fond of the eccentric woman. Miss Joan had truly missed her calling. The woman should have been an interrogator for one of the alphabet agencies. She was rather confident that Miss Joan would have worn down just about any suspect who crossed her path.

Not quite ready to pack it in and call it a night just yet, Alisha drew closer to the bar and leaned in. "I'm sorry—I didn't catch that. What did you say?"

For his part, Brett drew in closer, as well. Only a few inches separated their faces. A fact that he had a feeling they *both* noticed.

"I said you looked happy. It's a nice look on you," he commented. "Any particular reason you're currently giving off more light than the sun?" he asked, the corners of his mouth curving not just in humor, but in deep appreciation of the way she looked, as well.

In his opinion, Alisha Cordell was a woman who owned every room she walked into whether she knew it or not, but when she smiled like that, she wasn't just beautiful; she became incredibly stunning.

"In case you haven't noticed, it's nighttime," Alisha pointed out. "The sun's not up anymore."

Brett never missed a beat. "But if it was, it definitely would retreat in the face of the competition it would find itself dealing with, having you beaming like that. Want to tell me what's up?" he asked. And then, just as suddenly, a thought occurred to him as to why she might be looking as happy as she was. "You're not about to go back to New York, are you?"

The question was playfully stated, but he wasn't altogether surprised that the thought of her leaving bothered him. He'd just gotten used to seeing her around, used to looking forward to seeing her walk out each morning and walk in each night. He was reluctant to face that coming to an abrupt end.

"No, not now," she said with feeling. "I'd be leaving Dan in a lurch."

Alisha appeared unaware that her referring to the doctor by his first name had been noted—with a surge of satisfaction—by the man she was speaking with. She was coming around nicely, Brett thought.

"Someday," she interjected, not wanting Brett to think she was in any way contemplating becoming a permanent resident of this one-pickup-truck town, "but not right now."

"Okay, so what *has* you smiling from ear to ear?" he asked, adding, "You might as well tell me, you know. Resistance really is futile. We bartenders are known to be relentless when it comes to extracting information."

Settling in without fully realizing it, Alisha perched on the closest bar stool. "Someone asked for me at the clinic today. Specifically. They wanted me to attend to them, not Dan." She was doing her best not to sound or seem smug, but it really did feel good, she couldn't help thinking.

Brett paused to study her face, and then he laughed, shaking his head.

"Wow, if that was all that it took to get you to smile like that, I would have come into the clinic your first day there and asked for you. Specifically," he underscored, finding himself totally captivated by her dazzling smile.

"That wouldn't have counted," she told him, dismissing his comment with a wave of her hand.

"Why not?" he asked, pretending to take offense at the rejection.

She sighed. Okay, she'd spell it out for him. "Because you wouldn't have meant it. You would have just been doing it to be nice."

Brett paused to get a couple of glasses, then poured her a drink first. Moving the drink in front of her, he dispensed a glass of beer for himself, only half filling it.

"How do you know that?" Brett asked, his eyes locking with hers. "How do you know I wouldn't have meant it? How do you know I wouldn't have actually wanted to see *you* instead of Dan?" he challenged softly.

Alisha had a flippant remark all set and ready to go on the tip of her tongue. It wasn't exactly a put-down so much as a verification that she knew he would have just been trying to build up her confidence—he seemed to have a knack for looking into her soul and supposedly *seeing* things about her she was unaware of. It was something he had referred to as a *good bartender's gift*.

But her remark, well-intentioned or not, never emerged because Brett's liquid green eyes had all but taken her prisoner, seemingly looking deep within the recesses of her soul, and by the same simple action making her very breath temporarily stop and back up within her lungs and throat.

"Because," Alisha finally managed to say, words slowly materializing in a mouth that was bone-dry, "it wouldn't have been genuine. You would have only asked for me so that I wouldn't feel as if I was every patient's second-rate consolation prize. They couldn't get in to see Dan, so they put up with seeing me."

Was that how she really felt about it? Or was she baiting him, seeing how far he'd go to get her to feel confident?

Brett had a feeling it might be a combination of the two.

"Are you a second-rate doctor?" he asked her in a mild, nonjudgmental tone.

"No, of course not," she denied.

Brett heard a little fire in her answer and found it encouraging. She did believe in herself, which was a good thing, but she definitely needed that feeling bolstered.

"Then why the hell would you think that the patients even *think* of you that way?" he quietly demanded.

He would have allowed his voice to become more heated, but he instinctively knew that she guarded her privacy zealously and wanted to keep her conversations that way, as well.

Okay, so they were having an actual serious discussion on the subject, she thought, rather surprised that Brett was capable of being serious. If that was the case, then she might as well level with him.

"Because they all want to see Dan when they come to the clinic," she told Brett.

He shrugged off her reasoning. "It's just easier to go with what you know, with the familiar. There's a sort of unconscious comfort about that—as long as the doctor is competent and doesn't mess up. Give them time, Alisha. The good people of Forever will get used to you, see you for the dedicated doctor that you are."

He'd just called her Alisha, she realized with a sudden inner start. That was the first time he'd used her name instead of calling her Lady Doc.

Had he just done that on purpose? Or was it just a slip of the tongue?

"How would you know I was dedicated?" Alisha challenged.

She wanted him to see that she wasn't going to be taken in by platitudes. If he meant what he said, he was going to have to prove it by convincing her of his reasons.

"For one thing, if you weren't dedicated," Brett said, taking a long drag of his beer, "you wouldn't be out here. And for another, if you weren't good, you wouldn't have all those letters of recommendation to present to Dan at your interview."

Alisha blinked, stunned. The interview had been a private one, conducted between two professionals. "How did you—"

"Small town," Brett reminded her, thinking she really didn't need to be told much more than that to understand what he was saying.

Since he was building his case about her qualifications on her references, she pointed out something she felt was rather obvious. "The letters could have been faked."

How simple-minded did she think the citizens of a small town were? Brett silently marveled, trying not to take offense. Someone like Alisha should have known that brain size had absolutely no real correlation with the town's boundary lines.

"One, Dan's not an idiot. He called some of the doctors whose signatures were on those letters just to make sure everything was legitimate, and two, he's had a chance to observe you in action and he seems to be more than satisfied with you. Dan's not a hard taskmaster, but he's not exactly known as a pushover, either. And he wants the best for his town."

It was growing noisier in the bar again, and Alisha found that she had to raise her voice to be heard, a fact that didn't exactly make her happy.

"Dan told you that?" she asked, torn between being pleased and being less than thrilled that she would be the topic of discussion for the doctor and the bartender, something that sounded like the beginning of a joke recited in a grade-B movie.

"Not exactly," Brett corrected. "Dan told Holly that.

Then she told Ray—her husband," he explained in case Alisha didn't make the connection. "And *Ray* told me when he stopped in for a drink and to catch up. Bottom line, our Dr. Dan is more than satisfied with your efforts, and on top of that, the town's satisfied because they've come to trust Dan's judgment."

It was then that she noticed that Brett had poured her a drink and had eased it in front of her. She gazed down at the glass but refrained from picking it up. "What's this?"

They were back to their customary relationship, and he laughed at her question. "If I have to explain a drink to you, you really do need to get out more, Lady Doc— and to pay attention."

"Yes, I know it's a drink," she replied patiently. "And I know that it's the drink you made for me when we sealed the rental deal for the apartment upstairs. But that doesn't explain why you just made me another one."

Brett's smile was swiftly getting to her. It was almost as if it was actually burrowing under her skin. She explained away the increased heat around her as being the result of the extra bodies that were packed into Murphy's—but if she was being honest with herself, she knew that wasn't really it.

Brett was undoubtedly like that with every woman he served, she reminded herself. The man was a charmer from the word *go,* and she knew all about charmers— they were as shallow as a puddle on a city sidewalk.

"Same reason as the first time," Brett told her easily.

Her eyes narrowed as she looked at the drink, then at him. He hadn't cleared up the situation. "I'm renting another apartment?" she asked drolly.

"No, that drink's yours so we can properly celebrate

your very first patient," he told her. He raised his own glass in a toast—to her. "The first of many who will come through the doors of the clinic, asking for you and seeking out your expertise as well as your delicate touch."

"How would you know if I had a delicate touch or not?" she asked, amused, after she had taken a very long, bracing sip of her drink.

My God, she thought as awareness slipped in. Was she actually flirting with him? Flirting with her landlord? With the bartender? Hadn't she learned her lesson about men like Brett?

She really *was* giddy, wasn't she? Alisha thought in conflicted wonder.

"Now, that's just something I intuitively know," Brett answered, looking down at her hand resting on the bar. He had to tamp down the desire to simply stroke her hand, to run his fingertips over her skin. As he recalled from the all-too-brief contact he'd had with her hand the evening he'd shown her the apartment, it was as smooth as silk to the touch.

"However, if you want to prove me wrong, here I am. Touch me," he invited in a voice that was as seductive as it was gentle.

The look in his eyes was the very definition of *mischievous*—with a very healthy dose of sexiness thrown in to boot.

Had Liam's band just played "Taps"? Or was she hallucinating? Her money, sadly, was on the latter. In either case, she was losing ground, and she knew it.

Chapter Ten

He was daring her. And maybe, just maybe, a part of Brett was laughing at her, as well. Not cruelly—instinct told her that Brett Murphy was not cruel by nature or design—but he was laughing at her in amusement. Amusement that still, no matter how it was sliced, was at her expense.

If only the man didn't look so damn sexy while he was doing it. But even that incensed her, reminding her how vulnerable she'd once been by being attracted to a man's looks.

Now, at least, she knew how to look beneath the veneer.

"Afraid?" Brett asked, his mouth curving.

Her eyes narrowed into small, flashing slits. Brett had inadvertently said just the right thing to galvanize her resolve.

To Alisha, to show fear had always been equal to showing weakness, and to be perceived as weak ripped independence right out of a person's hands. Once lost, independence was incredibly difficult to win back—the same way that trust was difficult to win back once a person was caught in a lie.

She refused to ever be that weak person, and worse, to be perceived as a weak person.

Keeping that thought foremost in her mind, Alisha defiantly placed her hand on top of Brett's, her eyes never leaving his.

"Satisfied?" she fairly bit off.

She watched, her body growing even more heated, as the corners of Brett's firm mouth slowly, seductively, *wickedly* curved upward. She could almost *feel* the impression of his smile within her being. It took her a full second to realize that she'd stopped breathing. Air found its way into her lungs with effort.

"Not by a long shot, Alisha," he whispered, making sure that she was the only one who heard him. Making his response *that* much more intimate.

Alisha.

He'd called her Alisha again. Not the flippant nickname he'd awarded her—Lady Doc—or her title—Dr. Cordell—but her given name. And by using her name the way he did, he made this exchange between them *extremely* intimate despite the fact that there had to be upward of at least fifty-five people milling around the inside of Murphy's.

As if her ability to react was set on some sort of a five-second-delay program, Alisha suddenly pulled back her hand.

"Well, you're going to have to *be* satisfied," she retorted. Pushing her empty glass back toward him on the bar, Alisha rose from the stool. "Thanks for the drink," she told him stiffly.

"My pleasure, darlin'," he said, deliberately incorporating a whimsical Irish brogue into his voice. When she shot him an exasperated look, he winked at her.

He watched as she became flustered, then turned her back to him.

"By the way," he called after her as she started to hurry away, "when's your next day off?"

The question, coming completely out of nowhere, struck her as incredibly odd.

"Why?"

Brett was the picture of nonchalance as he shrugged carelessly. "Thought you might like to get a look at a ranch—or what used to be a ranch," he amended.

Curious, she retraced her steps. Just what was the man up to? "Used to be?" she repeated uncertainly. "What is it now?"

"Deserted," he answered.

He was talking about that property he'd inherited, wasn't he? she suddenly recalled. Exactly what was this charmer's angle? He had to have one because all charmers had an angle.

"You want to take me to a deserted ranch?" she asked incredulously, then came back to the same question she'd already asked. "Why?"

Brett shrugged again as he dried off a section of the bar, his broad shoulders moving like a restless mountain lion surveying the lay of the land before him.

"I thought that maybe you might have some input you'd want to share about the property," he told her. "I'm open to suggestions."

She stared at him. He was kidding, right? "I'm from New York," she reminded him as if that little fact had slipped his mind.

Was she trying to say that since she was a city girl, she had no idea how to view a ranch? "Doesn't mean you can't have a vision, or that you're incapable of ultimately inspiring some good input."

That wasn't why he wanted her to come with him. Alisha looked at him knowingly. "And this has nothing to do with getting me alone on a deserted ranch?" she challenged.

"I'd be lying if I said the thought hadn't crossed my mind," Brett told her, with the appearance of sincerity. "But I'm not looking to put you in a compromising situation," he continued. "And if I do anything to make you pick up and leave, Dan, as well as half the town, will have my head mounted up on a pike as a warning for any other shortsighted Lothario. I just thought you might want to get away from everything for a while, that's all."

Alisha laughed at his flawed reasoning. "Brett, being here in Forever *is* getting away from everything," she emphasized.

"Okay," he allowed, "point taken. *More* away from everything," he amended, this time with a heart-pumping, engaging grin.

Alisha debated back and forth for a few seconds, then told him, "Sunday." With that, she began to walk away from him in earnest.

The noise was once again putting a wall up between them. He knew she'd answered him, but as to what that answer was, he couldn't say for certain. Losing no time, he circumvented the counter, quickly emerging on the other side in order to take a few steps after her and actually *hear* her response.

"What?" he asked, his hand on her shoulder to temporarily stop her in her tracks before she could disappear into the mass of humanity filling up his family's establishment.

Startled, because she hadn't heard him call after her a second time, and she wasn't expecting anyone else to try to get her attention, Alisha attempted to shrug off the masculine hand she felt on her shoulder. She swung around quickly, a confrontational look on her face.

Her features softened the moment she saw who was behind her. "Oh, it's you."

"Me," he agreed, then explained why he'd stopped her. "I didn't hear your answer."

"Sunday," she repeated. "The clinic is closed on Sunday—but I'm on call should anything come up," she deliberately added.

It wasn't just a safety net for her in case she changed her mind about accompanying Brett to this deserted ranch of his; it was also true. When she had become a doctor, she had knowingly agreed to be on call for the rest of her life—or until such time as she was no longer of any useful benefit to the medical community.

For her, becoming a doctor wasn't just a profession; it was also a calling. And, if she was being completely honest, out here she felt there was even more use and need of her skills than in the city where she'd received her training. In New York City, she was a general surgeon. Here, that was still her specialty, but she also got to bandage knees, treat upper respiratory issues and diagnose stomach ailments.

Every day was a challenge the second she crossed the threshold. She had to give 110 percent of herself and apply the same percentage of her skills because she was working in a small town that had no community of physicians for her to fall back on or consult with.

As if reading her mind—the man gave her an eerie feeling that he was capable of doing just that—Brett nodded. "Sure, I understand. If something comes up, that takes precedence. But if there are no medical emergencies, how about I pick you up at nine—or is that too early?" he asked.

Even after being in Forever a month, she was still basically running on New York time, which meant that Brett's nine o'clock was actually more like eleven o'clock for her.

She was accustomed to getting up early and not wasting the morning in bed. "You can make it earlier if you'd like."

She got up early. He liked that. He was an early riser himself. Running Murphy's as well as having had to raise his brothers at one point had trained him to do with a minimum of sleep. His lifestyle encouraged him to get a jump start on each day.

"Eight, then," he said, moving the pickup time up by an hour. Then, with what felt like almost a private smile, he added, "If you change your mind about the time—or about going—you know where to find me."

That Brett had given her an escape clause went a long way in his favor. The next moment, she couldn't help wondering if he was aware of that and had given her a way out for just that purpose.

You're getting way too cynical, 'Lish.

That, too, was due to Pierce, she thought with more than a trace of annoyance. Like the lyric of a song she'd heard on the radio the other morning at Miss Joan's— these people listened to way too much country music, she couldn't help thinking—Pierce had actually *stolen her happy.*

Though she couldn't warm up to country music in general, that lyric, at least, rang very true. Pierce had stolen her happy, her usual sunny way of looking at everything. These days, she weighed everything, took everything apart, searching for the trap, the bad within the good.

She had to do something about that. Otherwise, even though she had broken off her engagement to the philandering surgeon, Pierce had actually won that round—because he had ruined her ability to view things in a positive light when it came to any other man.

And yet, despite everything, there was *something* about Brett...

"So, Sunday at eight is all right?" Brett asked, peering into her face. The look in her eyes told him that at least for a moment, she had gone somewhere far away in her head. He wanted to make sure she hadn't just answered him in the affirmative because she wasn't really listening.

Rousing herself, Alisha said, "It's all right." Then she glanced at his hand, which was still on her shoulder, still anchoring her in place. "Are you planning on releasing my shoulder anytime soon?" she asked, her voice deceptively light.

He hadn't realized that he still had his hand on her shoulder. Probably because he liked making a physical connection with her. He lifted his hand now in a show of compliance.

"Sorry," he told her. Brett took a couple of steps backward, away from her and closer to the bar.

Inclining her head, she silently took his apology and absolved him. The conversation abruptly ended at the same time.

Alisha felt exhausted, just the way she felt every night. The difference being that tonight, along with the exhaustion, there was a host of butterflies, spreading their wings and colliding with each other inside her stomach.

As quickly as she could, she made her way across the crowded room until she finally reached the rear and the staircase. Once there, she paused for a moment, letting out a long breath to steady herself and reclaim her bearings.

She'd agreed to accompany Brett to this so-called property of his. But she could always say no.

At this point, Alisha realized as she took the stairs up to her tiny apartment, she didn't really know if she would go with him on Sunday—or not.

"You and the lady doc an item?"

The sleepy-sounding question came from Nathan McLane, one of Murphy's steadiest regulars. Married for longer than he could honestly remember, Nathan had for years found his way to the saloon's counter every day after his hours as a clerk at the general store were over.

Now that he was retired, Nathan spent even more time seated at Murphy's, nursing a beer—when he wasn't sleeping off the effects of all those beers in the town's jail.

To the random observer, Nathan appeared to be indifferent to the world around him. But closer scrutiny inevitably showed that the exact opposite was actually true. Nathan absorbed everything that happened around him much the way he absorbed the alcohol in his glass. Slowly and completely, usually without comment.

Brett looked at the man who had occupied that same stool when his uncle Patrick had owned and run Murphy's. Nathan was practically a fixture at the saloon. For a moment, he really thought that he had imagined the regular asking the question.

As much a part of Murphy's as the very bar itself, Nathan at times just seemed to blend into the background despite his unique features. Resembling nothing so much as a sun-bleached haystack tossed atop a rumpled man carrying way too much weight around for his five-ten frame, he was a hard man to take seriously.

But Brett had always accorded Nathan the same amount of respect he gave all his patrons. To that end, he took to heart any question or comment that Nathan made.

"No," Brett replied, wiping down the length of the bar directly in front of Nathan—when he became inebriated, he tended to spill his beer a little. "We're not an item, Nathan. I'm just trying to make her feel like she belongs here. Dr. Dan is working too hard. We need a second doctor in Forever."

A few people along the bar mumbled, adding in their two cents and essentially agreeing with the gist of Brett's statement.

Only Nathan spoke up loud enough for Brett to make out what was being said.

"You could try marrying her," Nathan told him, shifting his gaze to take in the bartender. Bloodshot eyes vainly attempted to focus on the younger man. Giving up, Nathan addressed the rest of his statement to his half-empty beer mug. "Just 'cause it turned out so bad for me doesn't mean it will for you."

A hearty laugh greeted the intoxicated advice. "Are you trying to talk the last of Forever's elite bachelors into giving up his title?" Gabriel Rodriguez asked the question as he came around to stand next to Nathan at the bar. "Of course," Miguel Rodriguez's son continued, making eye contact with Brett, "the last couple of men who boasted that they were never going to tie the knot with any female who walked the earth did just that pretty soon afterward."

It sounded to him as if Gabe was putting him on some sort of notice. He could do that all he wanted, Brett thought. He wasn't going to get married for a *long* time to come.

"You talking about your brothers, Gabe?" Finn asked, coming over to join his brother and Gabe at the far end of the bar.

Although Gabe nodded at Nathan, the latter continued communing with his beer, obviously content to let the conversation go on with his supervision, but not necessarily any of his input.

"Yeah, I am. Didn't really know what I was missing until I got married. None of us did," Gabe said honestly. He put one arm around Nathan's exceedingly wide back, practically straining to do so. "Not everyone follows in old Nathan here's footsteps," he testified. "I sure wouldn't trade what I have now for what I had before for all the money in the world."

He sounded sincere, Brett thought. Most likely, he was. You couldn't fake that sort of *happy.*

"That's because you lucked out," Brett told him. For an instant, he found himself thinking of Laura, the one who had gotten away—or more accurately, the one he had sent away with his refusal to choose between leaving Forever with her and staying in the town with his underage brothers. "Your wife never gave you any ultimatums," he added, saying the last sentence more to himself than to anyone else.

And then he thought of the woman he had just asked to see the ranch with him. "And if you're thinking of Lady Doc," he said, looking at Gabe, knowing how the people in this town were quick to try to pair off singles with likely candidates, "that one still hasn't made up her mind whether or not she's staying in Forever. She might take off for that fancy hospital in New York that she came from."

"If anyone can convince her to stay here, it's you," Gabe replied.

But Brett shook his head. "You're giving me way too much credit here," he told Gabe. "That lady's got a mind all her own, and it's not about to be cajoled or coerced by anything that I or anyone else can say," he assured his friend.

Whatever Gabe might have said to contradict Brett's statement never managed to be uttered because another, more pressing matter suddenly took front and center for not just him or Brett, but for just about everyone who was in the saloon.

Nathan had made a strange gurgling sound as he clutched his right side. He attempted to say something to Brett, but nothing coherent came out. The next moment, still clutching his side, Nathan made a guttural sound. His eyes rolled back in his head and then he fell off his bar stool with a resounding thud.

Chapter Eleven

"Is he dead?" a high-pitched voice in the center of the crowd asked as the man the voice belonged to tried to jockey for a better position.

"Naw, probably just dead drunk," the man next to him answered with a dismissive laugh.

A tight knot of people had formed around the heavy-set, unconscious man on the floor, and the participants all seemed to be intent on coming in even closer, despite the lack of space.

The second Nathan keeled over, Brett quickly made his way out from behind the bar. Finn was directly behind him. Moving people aside, Brett reached Nathan's prone body.

Gabe was already crouching on the floor beside the man, feeling for Nathan's pulse. It was obvious by the expression on Gabe's face that he hadn't succeeded in locating it yet. "I can't find his pulse, Brett."

"Ah, don't worry. McLane's pulse is probably just buried under all that fat," another patron volunteered, slurring some of his words a little.

Brett, always more than ready to share a joke, appeared to be deadly serious as he shouted out instructions. "Finn, keep these mindless comedians back.

Nathan needs space. Gabe, you keep trying to rouse Nathan."

"Where are you going?" Finn asked as Brett pushed his way out of the inner circle of curious onlookers.

"To get our own private doctor," Brett tossed over his shoulder, hurrying to the rear of the saloon.

Once there, Brett took the stairs two at a time, reaching Alisha's door in record time. Rather than knocking on it lightly, a sense of urgency had Brett doubling up his fist and pounding. He hadn't liked the way Nathan had looked, and he knew enough about medicine to know that sometimes, every second counted. This might very well be one of those times.

On the other side of the door, Alisha had just finished changing out of the clothes that she'd worn all day and into a baggy T-shirt that had seen far better days and a pair of denim shorts that had long since faded to a shade of nondescript blue. Ready for a quiet hour or two before bedtime, she was startled by the pounding on her door.

Had one of the men downstairs had too much to drink and decided that what he really wanted was some female companionship? They'd looked like a harmless bunch when she'd walked past them, but looks could be deceiving, and it was better to be safe than sorry.

Alisha glanced around for something to drag over to her door to keep whoever was pounding from breaking in. The only thing that presented itself was one of the two chairs at her small table. It was flimsy, but it was all she had.

She was about to grab it when she thought she heard Brett's voice calling to her.

"Are you in there, Doc? I've got a man down, and I need you to look at him for me."

Alisha stared at the door uncertainly, her nerves on edge. Was Brett serious? Or was that just a ploy to get into her room?

"Alisha, please. I don't know if he's breathing."

That did it for her. Alisha flipped the lock and pulled open her door.

Brett appeared worried and far more serious than she had ever seen him.

"What happened?" she asked.

"I'll tell you downstairs," he promised, already heading back to the stairs. But when he turned to look over his shoulder, he saw that Alisha wasn't following behind him. "Doc?" he called out, confused. "Where'd you go?"

The next moment, Alisha came hurrying over to him, her medical bag in tow. "Had to get my bag," she explained.

This almost felt like a stereotypical scenario, she couldn't help thinking. Here she was, dashing down the stairs in the shank of the night, clutching her medical bag, ready to minister to some unfortunate soul who'd been on the wrong end of a bar fight or had tripped and smashed his head.

Or—

At that point, it suddenly occurred to Alisha that she didn't have a clue exactly what was waiting for her.

The noise level was drowning out almost everything else by now. She raised her voice so that Brett could hear her. "What happened?" she cried.

Brett turned his head so that his voice would carry toward her. "Damned if I know. One minute, Nathan is sitting on his usual stool, drinking beer like he does every night. The next, he clutches his side, makes a funny whimpering noise and falls on the floor."

"His side, not his chest?" she asked. The first thing she'd thought of was a heart attack.

At her side now, Brett shook his head. "No, it was definitely his side."

"Which?" she asked as they came into the saloon proper. "Right or left?" She was fairly shouting now.

"His right, I think." Rethinking the incident, Brett confirmed his first answer. "It was definitely his right."

It seemed as if everyone in the saloon had gathered around the fallen man, forming a very large, almost impenetrable ring around Nathan, even with Finn trying to hold the patrons back.

Brett moved protectively in front of the woman he'd gone to fetch and, pushing the throng aside, created a path for Alisha.

"Get back," he ordered. "Everyone, get back. Give the doc some room." It wasn't a request voiced in his usual easygoing manner. This was a command, issued in a no-nonsense tone of voice.

The people in the crowd obediently parted and began to move to either side of the immobile form sprawled on his side on the floor.

Gabe rose to his feet to get out of Alisha's way. "Want us to move him for you?" he asked.

"Not until I know what we're up against," she responded.

Taking out her stethoscope, she sank down to her knees. Putting both ends into her ears, she listened intently as she moved the stethoscope around the man's wide chest. The effort quickly met with success. She could make out the beat of his heart.

The beat was elevated.

Placing her hand to the man's forehead—not the last word in medicine, she knew, but useful just the same—told her that Nathan's temperature was raised, as well.

Not good.

Removing the stethoscope from her ears for a moment, she looked up at Brett. "Could you turn Mr. McLane on his back, please?"

"Finn?" Brett said to his brother, his meaning clear. This effort was going to take two of them.

Brett and his brother moved Nathan so that the unconscious man was flat on the floor, then moved back, out of the doctor's way.

Very gingerly, Alisha passed her small hands slowly and methodically along Nathan's lower right quadrant. She watched his face as she did so. Despite the fact that he was still unconscious, she saw the man wince and heard him cry out in obvious pain. Loudly.

When he did, several of Murphy's patrons, who were angling for a closer position to get a better look at what was going on, jumped back, clearly shaken. The next second, they appeared to be embarrassed because they'd reacted like children around a campfire, listening to ghost stories and jumping when they heard a noise behind them.

The resulting cacophony of explanations and excuses proved to be only just so much more incomprehensible background noise to Alisha.

Unable to hold his curiosity in check any longer, Gabe asked her, "What's the matter with him, Doc? Is he going to make it?"

Brett seconded that concern. "Is he going to be all right?" he asked.

She didn't like to make prognoses until she had all the facts—or as many as were available in a situation. "I can't tell until I open him up—"

Her reply immediately caused a stir amid the bar's clients. She could have sworn she heard someone laying odds on the outcome.

"You're going to operate on him here?" Finn exclaimed in obvious awe and wonder. "Wow!"

"No, not here," she immediately corrected, then turned to look up at Brett. "We need to get Nathan to the clinic," she told him. "No offense, but your floor isn't exactly sterile."

"Yeah, but neither's Brett," someone in the crowd called out, laughing and obviously amusing himself.

Brett ignored the mindless remark as well as the man who'd uttered it. His only concern right now was Nathan. "What's wrong with him?" he asked Alisha pointedly.

She was about to repeat her previous vague comment, but the genuine concern she saw in Brett's eyes had her reconsidering. Instead of saying it was too early to tell, she reviewed the symptoms and gave the man her best guess.

"He's running a fever, he clutched his side when he collapsed and his side is swollen and so tender, he can't bear to be touched even in his unconscious state. It looks pretty much like appendicitis to me." And, she added silently, she was more than 95 percent certain that she was right.

"Can't be that. Nathan had his appendix removed when he was a kid," one of the female patrons volunteered as she made her way to the front of the human circle.

"Sometimes they grow back," Alisha answered. "It's rare, but it is possible. Like I said, I won't know exactly what we're up against until I open him up." Accepting the hand Brett extended to her, she stood. The way she saw it, her immediate problem was one of leverage—and transport. "I'm going to need help getting Nathan to the clinic." That made her think of something else. "And I also need someone to get the doctor."

Finn looked at her, confused. "But *you're* the doctor."

Alisha smiled at that. It looked as though she was finally being accepted here, and not just by one lone female patient.

Still, she wasn't vain enough to think she could do this on her own—unless she absolutely had to. And right now, she didn't. She was perfectly happy just assisting at the surgery, since she surmised that Dan would want to be the primary surgeon.

Nathan was drastically overweight, which meant that there would be abundant layers of tissue and fat to cut through before she could even get at the appendix and remove it. That was better left to a man with experience with this sort of thing.

"The *other* doctor," she stressed. "Dr. Davenport."

"I'll do it," Finn volunteered.

"Okay," Gabe said, coming to stand beside Brett. They both looked down at the moaning, unconscious man on the floor. "That leaves us with the problem of getting Nathan over to the clinic."

"If we had a gurney, we could just wheel him over," Alisha said, thinking out loud. "Except that we don't."

Purchasing a gurney was on her wish list. If she was

going to remain here for any amount of time, it might as well be under better conditions. Or at least the very best conditions she was able to create.

"We can drive him over in my flatbed truck," Gabe offered. "We just have to get him in the back."

Just.

The single word hung in the air, mocking her as she tried to come up with a viable solution that would get her patient into the back of the flatbed without doing him any harm.

"Problem is," she told Gabe and Brett, "if it *is* his appendix, it might be on the verge of rupturing, and if we jostle him too much when we try to get him into the truck, it might just burst."

"In other words, you don't want us to each grab a limb and carry him outside," Brett said, interpreting her words. In a pinch, that would have been what he would have done—get three other men and between them, carry Nathan to the back of the truck that way.

"That wouldn't be wise," she said seriously, trying to think of an alternative. And then a possible solution occurred to her. "If we can get Nathan onto a big blanket and each grabbed a corner of *that,* we might be able to get away with it. That's a little more cushioned than just dragging him by his arms and legs." She turned to Brett. "Do you have a big blanket?"

"Technically, *you* do," he told her. When she looked at him, waiting for an explanation, he said, "There's a folded-up blanket on the top shelf in your closet. For cold winter nights," he added.

"Can you go get it, please?" she requested.

Brett was already hurrying toward the stairs again. "On my way."

Waiting, Alisha bent down and placed her fingers against Nathan's forehead again. It was even hotter than it had been before.

Not a good sign, she thought in frustration.

"Does Nathan have any family?" she asked Gabe as she rose to her feet again.

"He's got a wife," Gabe told her.

It was always good to cover all bases. If her husband was sick, she'd definitely want to be notified. "Maybe someone should go get her," she suggested, looking around the saloon for a volunteer.

"Hell, Henrietta's not going to like having to come down here on account of Nathan," one of the men standing behind her said. There was a murmur of agreement.

"Even if he's really sick?" Alisha asked in disbelief.

"Henrietta'll only say that it serves him right, coming here night after night instead of home to her," another man spoke up, agreeing with his friend.

That just didn't seem right to her.

Ordinarily, she would have just shrugged the matter off. Dealing with all sorts of people in New York had made her somewhat removed from this kind of personal drama. But things were different out here, and she had come to expect a certain level of compassionate behavior from the citizens of Forever.

Consequently, Nathan's wife's behavior seemed horribly insensitive to her. Without fully realizing it, she wasn't going to just stand on the sidelines and let that type of behavior continue. Not when this man needed someone in his corner.

Turning around to face the last man who had spoken up about Nathan's wife, she ordered, "You go and tell that woman to get her butt in gear and bring it over to the clinic. If I'm going to try to save her husband's life, she needs to be there for her man."

Stunned for a moment, the man's thin lips peeled back to display a toothy grin. It was obvious that he liked what he'd heard.

"You got it, Doc," he told her with enthusiasm— and then took off, intent on following her instructions.

Brett reappeared with a blanket in tow and had returned just in time to hear Alisha issue her order in no uncertain terms, dispatching Warren Tate to go get Nathan's wife. There was no question about it. He liked what he had heard.

He grinned, offering the blanket to Alisha. "You can be pretty tough when you want to be," he said. The admiration in his voice would have been impossible to miss.

"Must be all this clean air I've been breathing. Goes straight to my head," she quipped drily.

After shaking out the blanket, Alisha proceeded to spread it out on the floor right next to Nathan's very large form.

She straightened out one end and stepped back. "Okay, I need four very strong men to each grab a limb and, as gently as possible, place Mr. McLane onto that blanket. Then we have to carry him very gingerly to the street and load him onto Gabe's flatbed."

This was *so* not going to be easy, she thought, even as she said the words. The plan sounded simple enough to execute, but her unexpected patient was beyond huge, and they were dealing with a medical emergency that was on the delicate side. If Nathan's appendix ruptured during the transport, she would have only a limited amount of time to clean out the area and keep Nathan from succumbing to peritonitis.

Definitely not ideal conditions.

Crossing her fingers both literally and mentally, Alisha moved completely out of the way and allowed Brett, Gabe and two other men, both huskier than the first two, to lift Nathan and place him as gently as humanly possible onto the blanket.

With Brett taking charge, the four men moved in concert and practically in slow motion. Though unconscious, Nathan still cried out in pain when they finally set him down on the blanket.

The noise shot right through her.

Alisha could have sworn she actually *felt* Nathan McLane's pain.

There was such a thing as being too in sync with her patient.

The silent lecture didn't help. Her empathy continued flowing until her supply of the emotion was all but gone.

When the men each picked up a corner of the blanket, Alisha felt an overwhelming desire to join in and take a corner or a section of blanket herself. She wanted to join the effort to help get Nathan into the flatbed, but she knew that rather than help, she'd undoubtedly just be in the way.

So she held her breath and followed at a decent distance away, watching as Brett gave out orders, reminding everyone to exercise extreme caution when they carefully got the big man into the back of Gabe's truck.

He was a leader, she thought in silent admiration—and, inexplicably, with pride. He wasn't the kind of man who hung back. He only gave that impression at the bar because it suited him.

Gabe drove his flatbed to the clinic.

To her surprise, Brett presented himself at the driver's side of her car just as she was about to get in herself. "I'll drive you to the clinic if you're too tired," he offered.

The offer had that strange, warm feeling materializing again, the one that only he seemed capable of recreating for her.

This wasn't the time, she told herself. She had a patient—possibly a life to save.

"No, I'm fine, thanks."

Adrenaline had taken care of her fatigue, immediately kicking in the moment she saw Nathan on the floor. She suspected, as she put her key into the ignition, that she was going to be running on adrenaline for a good long time.

When Brett rounded the front hood of her car and slid into the shotgun seat beside her, she was certain of it.

"You didn't think I wasn't going to come along, did you?" he asked. "Nathan's a longtime customer—and a friend. Sometimes, it feels like I'm his only friend," he added. "I'm not leaving him alone at a time like this."

"You don't think his wife's going to come?" she asked, starting the car.

"I'm not a betting man," Brett told her. "But if I were…" For a second, his voice trailed off, and then he said, "The odds are less than fifty-fifty that she'll come."

She'd never met the woman, but Alisha decided that she didn't like Henrietta McLane.

And she was finding reasons—even though she wasn't looking for them—to like Brett Murphy more and more.

Chapter Twelve

Parking at an angle in front of the clinic, Alisha quickly jumped out of her vehicle less than ten minutes later.

"Hold up!" she shouted to Gabe. The latter was already out of the cab of his truck and on his way to the back of the flatbed. The men appeared ready to carry Nathan into the darkened clinic.

"Why?" Gabe called back to her.

Alisha didn't waste time with an explanation. Instead, she turned toward Brett and instructed, "Make sure he doesn't move Nathan."

Confused, Brett looked over to the flatbed, where Nathan lay, unconscious, on the blanket. "You're not planning on operating out here, are you?" he asked her incredulously. "Hell, my saloon's cleaner than his flatbed."

But Alisha wasn't heading back to the truck; she was going in the opposite direction. "Just wait," she shouted over her shoulder as she unlocked the door and disappeared into the clinic.

Brett stood where he was, wondering what she was up to. He watched as first one light, then another went on in the clinic, marking her progress through the building. Since there'd been no light in the building when they'd arrived, he assumed that Finn hadn't gotten back with Dan yet and wondered what the holdup was. The fact that Warren Tate, the man Alisha had dispatched to bring Nathan's wife, hadn't returned with the woman was far less of a surprise. Henrietta McLane was not a woman to be coerced into doing anything she didn't want to do.

The next minute, he forgot about Finn and Dan as well as whether anyone could manage to get Nathan's wife to show any concern for her husband. Alisha had returned, and she was pushing the clinic's one hospital bed in front of her. The bed was used primarily for patients who needed to remain under observation overnight at the clinic.

Brett was quick to join her. "Here, let me," he said, taking over. It was obvious to him that she was having some difficulty getting the bed to go where she wanted it to, despite the fact that it had wheels.

Alisha gladly stepped back. "It's not a gurney," she explained, "but at least it's mobile, and I figured it would be easier getting Nathan in on this than trying to carry him in on the blanket."

Brett grinned as he maneuvered the bed until it was parallel to the flatbed opening. "Hell of a lot better than risking dropping Nathan on the ground," he agreed. The others looked relieved not to have to carry the big man into the building.

It was still a tricky proposition, lifting and carrying Nathan from the back of the flatbed onto the hospital bed. Even with the blanket beneath the man and the fact that there were four of them doing the maneuvering, it was still by no means an easy transfer. All four were gasping for air by the time they got the man onto the bed.

Alisha released the breath she'd been holding during the short, taxing ordeal. "Get him into the last exam room."

She was grateful that Liam had elected to come along with them. The youngest of the brothers had walked into Murphy's just in time to see Brett, Gabe and two other men struggling to get Nathan into the flatbed. Wanting to help, he'd gotten into Gabe's truck.

Brett paused for a second before following Alisha's request. Turning toward Liam, he decided that his youngest brother, with his boyish appeal, might just be able to succeed where the previous man sent on the errand had failed. "Why don't you go and see if you can get Mrs. McLane to come here. Lady Doc sent Warren Tate to get her, but he obviously didn't have any luck."

Liam seemed torn for a moment between doing what his older brother asked and wanting to see what happened next. But in the end, he nodded.

"Sure," he agreed. "I'll bring her back." It didn't seem to occur to Liam as he hurried out that Nathan's wife would refuse to come. Liam, Brett knew, still believed that when push came to shove, people always did the right thing, and he approached everything he did in that light.

Let's hope you're right, Liam, Brett thought, getting back to the job at hand.

When Brett and Gabe finally pushed the hospital bed back into the last exam room, he saw that Alisha was already there. She'd donned blue scrubs over her T-shirt and jean shorts and was busy scrubbing her hands.

"Blue's a nice color on you," Brett noted wryly.

"It'll be an even nicer color when Dr. Davenport gets here," she told him. Dan didn't live that far from the clinic; he should have been here by now, she thought. "What do you think is keeping him?"

Brett's shoulders rose and fell in a vague shrug. "Your guess is as good as mine," he replied. "Maybe he thinks that now that you're here, he can ease up a little bit, not hurry as much."

She supposed there was a validity to Brett's thinking, but she wasn't altogether sure if that reasoning really fit the man she'd come to know these past few weeks. He seemed far too dedicated to her to be blasé when one of his patients needed him.

"Still doesn't explain why he's not here," she replied. "He's the most dedicated physician I've ever met."

"I can go see what the holdup is," Gabe volunteered.

Alisha flashed a grateful smile at the rancher. "Would you?"

Gabe was already on his way out. "Sure thing."

As Gabe crossed the threshold, Nathan groaned loudly, seeming to rouse himself. His eyelids fluttered as if he was trying to struggle back to consciousness and having a really hard time of it.

"Where—where am I?" Nathan moaned, slurring his words.

About to dry her hands, Alisha was at her patient's side in a heartbeat. "Mr. McLane, it's Dr. Cordell. Are you in much pain?" she asked, bending over the man so that they could make eye contact.

Nathan attempted to take in a breath and groaned even louder. "It feels...like someone's...ripping...open my...gut with a...rusty can opener!" he cried.

Brett was right beside her, ready to help any way he

could. "I think you can take that as a yes," he told her. There was concern in his eyes as he asked, "Do you think you're going to be able to do what's necessary if Dan doesn't show up?"

Squaring her shoulders as if mentally preparing herself for that eventuality, she answered, "I guess I'll have to." She'd operated before, but not since she'd arrived in Forever and never on a man this size. Nathan's girth presented a unique set of circumstances that added to the seriousness of the operation. The nearest full-service hospital was an hour away.

Bending over Nathan again, she told the man in a calm, soft voice, "It's going to be all right, Nathan. We're going to make you better."

Nathan was clutching the sides of the bed, his knuckles all but white as he twisted in pain. "Just shoot me."

"Can't do that, Nathan. It's against the doctor code," Alisha quipped to cover the nervousness she felt right now. Where *was* the doctor? "I'm only allowed to shoot patients as a very last resort—and then only at the end of the month." She heard the clinic door open and close again, and she exhaled a huge sigh of relief. "Oh, thank God. Dan's here," she declared happily to her patient.

The next moment, as she took one look at Dan when he walked in, her obvious relief turned to confusion and real concern.

"What happened to you?" she cried in palpable distress.

Dan had walked in ahead of Finn. The first thing the other people in the room noticed was the fact that the doctor's right arm was immobilized in a sling.

Forever's first resident physician in thirty years appeared almost sheepish as he answered her question.

"I tripped on a tree root and put my hand out to break my fall—which, as it turned out, was the wrong thing to do in this case."

Alisha glared at the man she'd been counting on to take over in stricken horror. "You broke your arm?" she cried, appalled.

Dan shook his head. "Not exactly. I tore my rotator cuff. Problem is, right now it hurts like hell just to move my hand," he told her. "I'm going to have Tina drive me to the hospital in Pine Ridge tomorrow so I can have this thing x-rayed. Maybe I didn't tear any muscles. Maybe it just feels that way," he said hopefully.

But even as Dan said that to her, they both knew he was just trying to deny the obvious.

There was only one thing that mattered right now. "This means you can't operate," Alisha concluded. She could almost feel the lead weight on her chest.

"Can't hold a scalpel, I take it?" Brett asked the man.

Dan's frustration was evident in his eyes. "Can't even wiggle my fingers right now. Don't worry," he told Alisha when he saw the disheartened look on her face. "It'll get better."

She had no doubt that it would—but that didn't do either of them any good right now. "Not in time to save Nathan," she replied.

Dan made his way to the hospital bed, which was now positioned in the center of the room so that Nathan was accessible from any point. "Finn told me that you think it's appendicitis."

Alisha inclined her head. "That's the most logical conclusion, but we won't know until you open him up. I mean—"

"You're going to have to be the one to open him up," Dan said matter-of-factly. Turning from Nathan, who had once again lapsed into unconsciousness from the sheer pain he was experiencing, Dan faced his new associate. "Ever perform an appendectomy before?"

"Yes, but in a hospital with staff, and this person is particularly...large," she finally said for lack of a better term.

"Don't worry," he told her, sounding extremely confident in her estimation. "You'll do fine. I'll talk you through it." Dan looked around the room. "Holly's not here?"

"I didn't think to get her," Alisha confessed. Her main focus, other than getting Nathan to the clinic, had been getting Dan to take over. Now that wasn't going to happen.

"I can call her for you," Gabe volunteered.

But Dan had taken a closer look at the patient and he now shook his head. "No time." He eyed the two men and then made his choice. "Looks like you're going to have to play nurse, Brett."

Rather than balk at the suggestion, Brett nodded. His life had prepared him for stepping up whenever the occasion demanded it. "Sure. Whatever you need."

"Scrub in, Brett." Dan pointed toward the small sink on the far side of the wall. "You're going to be handing Alisha her instruments."

Brett was game to do whatever they needed him to do. "As long as you point them out," he qualified, "since I can't tell one thing from another."

"No problem," Dan assured him with a smile. "Luckily, I didn't tear anything in my mouth."

IN THE END, the surgery wound up taking longer than any of them had expected.

The operation itself had been going along well—until Alisha, after cutting through the layers of skin, tissue and fat, just barely touched Nathan's swollen appendix with the tip of her scalpel. The small organ immediately ruptured, sending toxic fluid throughout Nathan's abdominal cavity.

Alisha had to go into double time, frantically mopping up the mess inside her patient as quickly as she could in an attempt to contain the infection to the best of her ability.

A one-hour simple procedure, encumbered by Nathan's girth and the state of his appendix, wound up turning into an operation that took upward of two and a half hours to complete.

All of her efforts proved fruitful. The end result was that Nathan had survived and gave every sign of being on the road to recovery. Even so, Dan made a judgment call and decided that the man needed to remain in the clinic overnight.

"Why don't you go home?" he suggested to Alisha as they sat in a room away from where Nathan was recovering. "You've more than proven yourself tonight. My contribution will be to stay and watch over him."

As tempting as that was, she knew she couldn't take Dan up on it. "Because you need your rest," she told the man. "You're going to Pine Ridge in the morning to get that shoulder of yours x-rayed, remember?"

Dan tried to shrug off her words, but the action cost him dearly.

"It can wait," he told her, wincing with pain.

"No," Alisha insisted, "it can't." Hands on her hips,

she leveled a glare at the other doctor. "We're not having this argument, Doctor. The town needs you, and you need to have your shoulder fixed up. You're going home. I'm staying. End of discussion," she declared with finality.

Dan shook his head. It was obvious he was amused at her feistiness.

"You are one very stubborn woman," he told her.

If he thought he was going to flatter her into going along with him, he was in for a surprise. "You have no idea," she warned Dan.

"I'd do as she says if I were you, Dan. And don't worry about her," Brett told his friend. "I'll stick around until morning to make sure everything's all right—with her and with Nathan."

Alisha noted that Dan took the other man at his word and that Brett's taking over the way he proposed all seemed perfectly natural to the other doctor. There was obviously a lot of trust going around, and she found that both unusual—so different from the atmosphere she'd just come from—and incredibly heartening, as well.

"If you're sure," Dan said, already backing out of the room.

"You really don't have to stay here," she told Brett once Dan was out of the room and out of earshot. "I know you said what you did to put Dan's mind at ease, but you really don't have to play babysitter here. I can handle the situation."

"Nobody said you couldn't, but maybe I want to stay," Brett said, surprising her. "Did you stop to consider that?"

She couldn't tell if he was actually serious or just pulling her leg. His expression was entirely unreadable. She still gave him the only answer she could in this case. "No."

"Well, consider it. Because I do," he assured her firmly.

This was a man who thrived in the organized chaos that throbbed through his establishment, Alisha thought. His wanting to remain here with her like this made no sense.

"Why would you want to stay here?" she asked, wanting to understand his reasoning—if that was possible. "It's quiet."

His smile was slow and sexy as it slipped across his lips. "Lady Doc, you might have just answered your own question."

She eyed Brett uncertainly. "You *like* the quiet?"

The smile widened a fraction. "Always have."

Okay, he was messing with her, she decided. He *had* to be. "But you run Murphy's. During work hours, that place is as noisy as the middle of Grand Central station."

"Which is why the quiet is appealing to me," Brett countered.

She was too tired to continue with this and just shook her head, surrendering. "You are a complicated man, Brett Murphy."

The sexy smile softened around the edges as he told her, "Right back at you, Lady Doc."

Exhausted, with her thoughts colliding into one another in her head, she blinked. "You think I'm a complicated man?"

Brett laughed. "No, just complicated. I'm not that simple. I do know the difference between a man and a woman," he assured her with a wink that went straight to her stomach and bored a hole there, making itself right at home.

Alisha laughed then, or maybe it was the exhaustion, stretched to another level and making her giddy. "I'm sure you do."

Brett studied her for a moment, his eyes moving along her so slowly, she could have *sworn* she felt them touching her.

"What's that supposed to mean?" he finally asked good-naturedly.

A sigh escaped her lips as she searched for the right words, words that kept eluding her right now. "Just that you were probably born flirting. Born making women weak in the knees," she added.

His eyes were caressing her, undoing her, she thought nervously, unable to look away.

"How about you, Lady Doc?" he asked in a quiet voice. "Do I make your knees weak?"

She tried to brazen it out, although she knew that she was doomed to failure. "I'm sitting down. My knees are fine."

Brett pretended to give her a long once-over, going from her head to her toes. She had discarded the scrubs and was back to wearing only her shorts and T-shirt. He couldn't help wondering if she knew just how enticing she was in that simple little outfit.

She was a woman who wasn't even aware of her sexuality—which made her all the more sexy to the casual observer.

"Yes, they are, just like the rest of you," he told her.

She laughed softly to herself as she shook her head. "There you go again, flirting."

Instead of denying it, or saying something flippant

in his defense, Brett smiled into her eyes. "How'm I doing?" he asked her, his voice low, stirring, as it seemed to slowly, seductively undulate beneath and along her skin.

Alisha was finding that she was definitely having difficulty breathing. The very way this man was looking at her with his deep green eyes seemed to completely paralyze her.

It took effort for her to finally whisper an answer to his question. "Like someone should pass a law against you."

His eyes still holding hers prisoner, he cocked his head in amusement and asked, "I'm that bad?"

Damn but she wished he'd stop whispering like that and speak up. His whispering was making her blood rush through her veins like a stock car crossing the finish line in the Indy 500.

"No," Alisha finally replied with some effort. "You're that good."

Brett was skimming his fingertips along her face, as if he was attempting to memorize every single feature through them.

"Can't have that," he told her.

The next moment, as his eyes continued to hold hers captive, Brett began to lower his mouth to hers in what felt like slow motion.

It felt as if hours had passed before he finally kissed her.

And made time stop completely.

There was surprise on her part.

Surprise and then pleasure.

Surprise that it had happened at all after her silent promises about never allowing herself to be in a compromising situation again. Pleasure because, well, that was really self-explanatory. His kiss was sheer pleasure. And she couldn't resist it—not even a little.

Alisha gave herself permission, just for this single moment in time, to enjoy what was happening and to kiss this man back. Five minutes from now—if not sooner—she would return to being herself, to being vigilantly on her guard.

But for now, for the next three hundred seconds, she wanted just to feel desirable again. Or at least pretend that she was. And most of all, she wanted to celebrate because she had saved a life. Not assisted in saving a life, but had actually been the instrumental person in saving that life. And that felt absolutely wonderful.

As did being kissed by Brett Murphy.

Chapter Thirteen

You're taking advantage of her.

Brett could almost *hear* the voice in his head taking him to task for what he was doing. For what he was so obviously enjoying.

The voice—his conscience, he supposed—was coming in loud and clear.

He'd also realized at that exact moment that he'd wanted to do this, wanted to kiss this rare woman who had come into their midst, from the very first time he had laid eyes on her.

Granted, Alisha hadn't exactly looked friendly when Dan had initially brought her around, but that didn't matter. The connection he had felt when their eyes first met was on a whole different level than what he figured even she was aware of. For him, it was a little like flipping through a magazine and having his attention suddenly seized by a photograph of a top model. Being so captivated by the woman that he promised himself that, someday, he was going to meet that woman and have a relationship with her, no matter how far-fetched that might have seemed.

For Brett, someday had arrived.

The woman who had returned his kiss was *not* the

doctor who ministered to the patients who came to the clinic seeking help. That woman was professional, skilled and dedicated. This woman, the one he was kissing, was a barely bridled wildcat. He could literally taste it in her kiss.

WHAT IS GOING ON with me? Alisha's brain all but screamed at her.

Have you lost your mind? she upbraided herself.

What in heaven's name was she doing, kissing Brett? He was her landlord, for heaven's sake, and granted, the man *was* sexy as all hell, but she'd promised herself never to let something like that, something so shallow as looks, sway her.

Okay, he seemed kinder and deeper than Pierce had been, but the bottom line remained: Brett was an extremely good-looking man, and good-looking men were true only to themselves and their needs. Hadn't she already experienced that firsthand? How many times did it take for the lesson to be driven home for her? Did she really *need* to go through the anguish of a refresher course where all her plans instantly turned to burned dust?

C'mon, Alisha. You've got more self-control than that, don't you?

Trying to keep her arguments for *why* this couldn't be happening uppermost in her mind, Alisha drew her head back, breaking the delicious contact. Just as she did, she felt Brett drawing away, as well, as if her pulling away could be construed as a time-out.

Or maybe the man had satisfied whatever urge had prompted him to kiss her in the first place.

Whichever way it went down, she was going to find a way to use this to her advantage, Alisha silently promised herself. Popping up to her feet while ignoring the hand that he offered her, she quickly strode to the back of the clinic to look in on her patient.

Recovering from the operation, Nathan was still asleep. Even though she wasn't expecting any surprises at this point, someone, Alisha felt, should remain with the man, and since she'd told Dan to go home, she figured that she was the logical choice.

But when she walked into the room where she had performed the operation, she was surprised to find Dan sitting in a chair by the hospital bed. He looked up when she walked in.

Stunned, she stared at the other doctor. "I thought you went home."

"I changed my mind," he informed her in his quiet, authoritative voice.

"But—" She got no further than that.

"You did a great job, Alisha," he told her. "Now I want you to do me a favor and go home and get some rest. You've earned it."

Didn't anyone in this town listen to reason? she wondered. "You can't stay here with Nathan," she insisted. "You're injured."

From his countenance, Alisha could tell she wasn't going to win this debate. Dan had obviously dug in— and he was the senior doctor here. "My shoulder is injured. The rest of me is doing just fine. Now go," he urged.

"But—"

"That part's fine, too," Dan assured her with as straight a face as he could maintain, under the circumstances.

Just then, Brett came in, drawn by the voices and

wondering if Nathan had woken up. In which case, he thought Alisha might need a helping hand with the man.

"You're back," Brett said to Dan in surprise.

"Never actually left," Dan corrected his friend. He turned toward Brett to enlist his assistance. "Do me a favor, Brett. Get our heroic doctor here back to her place. It seems that she won't leave without an armed escort."

Brett was more than willing to comply. "I'm not armed, but I will escort."

Well, she couldn't make the other doctor leave, but by the same token, he couldn't force her to go, either. Of the three of them, she decided, Brett had the least reason to stay.

"You can go home," she urged Brett.

"And so can you," both Brett and Dan chorused together as if they had been practicing delivering that one line for a long time instead of saying it spontaneously.

Alisha opened her mouth, then shut it again. She couldn't fight both of them, and she knew it. Besides, she really *was* tired. Thinking the matter over, she decided that she was going to need both her sleep *and* her strength tomorrow since Dan was going to Pine Ridge to get that shoulder of his x-rayed. That meant that she would be the only doctor on call at the clinic the whole day.

The very thought of that was exhausting right now.

"Okay," she said, reluctantly giving in. "I'll go," she told Dan, but added a condition to her capitulation. "But only if you promise to call me the second you're feeling weak or tired."

Dan nodded. "Already have you on speed dial," he

told her, holding up the cell phone Tina had gotten him for his last birthday.

Sure he did, Alisha thought, looking at the phone skeptically. Still, she didn't feel up to challenging him and, instead, reminded him that "I can be here in five minutes flat."

Now, there was something she couldn't have ever said in New York, Alisha thought. Not with the way that traffic clogged the streets even in the dead of night. Here she could boast being able to make that sort of time in the middle of the day—as well as all the hours in between.

Dan nodded, not that he had the least inclination to summon her—unless the clinic caught on fire. "Good to know," he said mildly, then turned toward Brett. "Get this woman out of here before she falls asleep on her feet, Brett," he ordered.

"You got it." Brett slipped his hand through his tenant's arm and very gently steered her toward the front of the clinic as well as the front door.

They had almost reached it when there was a commotion on the other side of it. The door had been left unlocked, and the person causing the racket pushed it open and marched right into the clinic, still being loud—and practically breathing fire.

Alisha stopped walking and stared at the large, heavyset woman with the round, angry face. This was the way trouble would look if trouble could take a human form.

"Where is he? Where's that lazy, good-for-nothing faker of a husband of mine?" Henrietta McLane demanded as she took the hallway in less than half the strides that Alisha had made on her initial entrance. Glaring at her, the woman snapped, "Is he back there?"

Accosting her, the woman pointed toward the rear of the clinic. More than twice as large as Alisha and a good foot taller, Henrietta McLane was a force to be reckoned with, and not in a good way. Years ago, her girth accustomed her to ignoring others and always getting her own way.

About to intervene, Brett watched in surprise as Alisha got in front of Nathan's charging wife, physically putting her body in the way to stop the woman from going to the back.

"I'm afraid you can't go in there. Mr. McLane is asleep now," Alisha told the woman.

Henrietta snorted, dismissing the access denial and the woman who had delivered it. "He always sleeps off a drunk, missy—nothing new there. I don't know what's gotten into him, but that man has to know that he can't yank me around like this." Saying that, Nathan's wife began to go around Alisha.

For a second time, Alisha deliberately put herself in the larger woman's path.

As she glared at the woman, Henrietta's complexion began to turn a bright shade of red.

"He's not yanking you around," Alisha told her calmly. Maybe the woman was angry because she was asked to come in so late in the evening. She was quick to direct the focus of Mrs. McLane's anger toward her, putting the blame on herself. "I was the one who asked Liam to fetch you." It had actually been Brett, but as far as she was concerned, that was a mere technicality. She was the one who had wanted the man's wife there.

A number of emotions washed over the pie-shaped face. "Why the hell would you do that?"

Alisha was precise in explaining her thinking. "Because your husband just had an appendicitis attack. I managed to take it out just as it ruptured." Her eyes never wavered from the woman's face. "I thought maybe you'd want to know that."

That her husband had just undergone surgery took some of the wind out of Henrietta's sails—at least for a moment. The woman looked at her uncertainly. "But he's going to be all right?"

Alisha was relieved to be able to give her a positive answer. "Yes."

"Oh." Rather than happiness, the news had indifference registering on Henrietta's wide, sun-lined face. "Tell him to get his butt home as soon as he can walk." And with that, the woman turned on her heel, pushed past Liam, retraced her steps to the front door and marched out of the clinic.

Alisha blew out the breath she hadn't even realized that she'd been holding.

"I'm beginning to understand why Nathan drinks," she commented to the man who had been serving Nathan for the past fourteen years. Anger underlined her words. How could anyone be so callous in regard to a person they were supposed to have loved? "I think if I was married to that impossible woman, I'd spend every evening drinking in order to forget."

Surprised that had just come out of her mouth, Alisha slanted a quick glance toward Brett to see if that had put him off. She was surprised—and maybe just the tiniest bit pleased—to see that her words had made him laugh.

"You're becoming one of us, Lady Doc," he told her, clearly amused by her declaration.

Several weeks ago, she wouldn't have been happy with that kind of a response. But hearing it now created a satisfied, happy feeling that caught her completely off guard. Feeling that way should have made her feel wary—but it didn't.

A FEW OF the regulars had remained at Murphy's, nursing their beers and waiting for news about their drinking buddy. The moment Alisha walked in, they all swarmed around her and Brett, firing overlapping questions.

"Is he gonna be all right?"

"He ain't dead, is he?"

"Did you have to cut into him?"

"Where is he? Did you send him home?"

"Can we go see him?"

Brett took over, raising his hand as well as his voice to quiet the men. "Lady Doc here took care of Nathan. She got him to the clinic just in time. If he'd stayed here with you bozos, he would have been dead."

Rather than question that, the men turned as if one to stare at Alisha. She wasn't sure what to make of it— and then one of the men said, "Let's hear it for Lady Doc!" The next second, a cheer went up. A couple of the men closest to her embraced her, exuding genuine gratitude. Stunned, she looked at Brett.

"Now you're really one of us," he told her with a broad grin, adding, "You did good."

The funny thing was, she really felt that way. For possibly the first time since she had decided to become a doctor, she felt as if her vocation and presence in a situation really mattered.

It was a while before she finally got upstairs to her tiny apartment. Two seconds after she closed the door behind her and opened her closet door, she was facedown on her bed, sound asleep.

THE KNOCK ON her door the following Sunday morning at eight didn't wake her. She had been up for a good hour. Expecting to spend a peaceful morning doing nothing whatsoever, the knock caught her by surprise.

This was supposed to be her day off, but obviously someone hadn't gotten the memo.

The old phrase about there being no rest for the weary ran through her head as she opened the door.

"You ready or do you need a few more minutes?" Brett asked.

He looked even more causal than usual, with faded jeans and a denim work shirt, both of which looked as if they had been through the wash a few too many times and adhered to his body as if they sensed they'd fall apart otherwise.

"You forgot, didn't you?" he guessed from the look on her face. With everything that had been going on these past couple of days, he could see how that had happened.

Rather than answer in the affirmative and admit that it had slipped her mind, she twisted her alibi into a question of her own. "You still want to take me to your ranch?"

"Why wouldn't I?" he asked her, then added, "Unless you don't want to go for some reason." He wasn't about to force her, but at the same time, Brett had to admit that he'd been looking forward to spending a little time with her without the demands of his job—or hers—getting in the way. "Up to you," he told her, leaning one broad shoulder against her doorjamb as he waited for her to think it over.

Instead of turning away or retreating into her apartment, Alisha remained there for a moment, thinking over the option he'd just given her. Since he'd kissed her that night at the clinic, she'd been a little afraid of what she'd felt, as well as somewhat leery of being alone with this man.

But at the same time, in the tradition of a moth moving around a flame, she knew she was more than a little drawn to Brett.

How about a lot drawn?

All the more reason not to be alone with him, 'Lish. You don't want to make the same mistake twice.

The problem with having a little voice that spouted common sense in your head, she'd discovered, was that the voice could easily be either ignored or overridden.

She did both.

"I'm ready," she told him, then glanced down at what she was wearing. Maybe not so ready, she decided. "I just need another minute or so. I'm not really sure what to wear," she confessed.

She looked fine to him just the way she was, he couldn't help thinking. "Any way you're comfortable is all you need to keep in mind," he told her, adding, "You're overthinking this. Forever isn't a formal kind of town. We don't notice outfits so much as we notice the person who's in them."

The way he was looking at her had her fighting a blush—and losing. To cover for herself, Alisha said, "Spoken like a true man. Women notice clothes."

"Well, since you're going to be the only female there, I don't think you have much to worry about." His eyes seemed to caress her as they passed over her again, as if inspecting what he'd just accepted. "You wouldn't have anything to worry about standing in a crowd of women and wearing a burlap sack."

Brett, Alisha couldn't help thinking, seemed to be able to say all the right things at just the right time.

Talk is cheap, remember?

She did remember. Remember that she'd gone this route before, with Pierce. She'd believed his stories, his lies and his initial protestations that he loved her.

This man wasn't Pierce. Pierce had only been in love with what he saw looking back at him in his mirror. He counted first, last and all the spaces in between. So far, she hadn't seen any evidence of that sort of egomania on Brett's part. On the contrary, he seemed to put everyone else first.

But then, Brett might have just been a better actor than Pierce had been.

Give the man a chance. He might surprise you.

"Something wrong?" Brett asked her. "You look like you're having some sort of a mental argument with yourself."

His intuitive assessment startled her—but she managed to recover nicely.

"No mental argument," she assured Brett—okay, she was lying, she admitted to herself, but under the circumstances, she could be forgiven the small white lie. She didn't want to let him in on her vacillation— or the fact that she felt as attracted to him as she did.

Right, like he can't guess.

With effort, she blocked the voice that seemed bent on tripping her up. "I'm just doing a quick mental check to make sure I'm not forgetting something."

Brett decided that she needed a little encouragement. The woman really needed to unwind a little. That was something that Dan had had to learn as well once he'd committed to Forever, he recalled.

"Nathan's recuperating at his friend's house, and the clinic's closed," Brett pointed out. For now, Nathan and his wife were taking a time-out, and Nathan needed his rest. "Looks to me like you're pretty free."

She didn't want to seem too eager. "There are things I have to consider that you don't know about," she told him primly.

He inclined his head. "Fair enough. What's the verdict?" Brett asked, instinctively sensing that if he pushed in any way, she'd push back, dig in and stay home. If nothing else, working at Murphy's had taught him how to read people and act accordingly. Alisha needed to come around on her own.

"That you're right," she answered him after a beat. "I'm free to leave."

There was a stillness in her voice that instantly alerted him. Were those nerves he detected? Was she nervous about spending time alone with him? Was the very thing he was looking forward to frightening her for some reason?

He'd begun to think of her as fearless, especially after he'd witnessed the confrontation between Alisha and Nathan's wife. Maybe at bottom, when it came to personal matters, she wasn't quite so fearless after all.

He did want her to enjoy herself as much as he just wanted to enjoy having her with him today. But he wasn't going to enjoy himself if she was uneasy during the whole time.

"Would you feel better if I had one or both of my brothers come along?"

The offer surprised her. That she was afraid of the feelings she might have for him was one thing. The fact that he *thought* there was fear involved on her part was quite another.

Alisha squared her shoulders like a young prizefighter about to go into the ring. "Why would I want that?"

"So you could feel more at ease," Brett answered simply.

"At ease?" she echoed. "Are you saying you think I'm afraid of you?" she challenged, indignation gleaming in her eyes.

"I'm saying I want you to enjoy the day on the ranch," he told her amicably, avoiding answering the question directly, "and I'll do anything I need to in order to ensure that you do."

He could word it any way he wanted to, but she knew what he was actually saying, and she wanted to make it clear to him that he was wrong—even if he wasn't entirely.

"I am not afraid of you," she emphasized.

He nodded, seemingly accepting her at her word. "Good. Then let's go."

"Absolutely." With that, Alisha walked out of the tiny apartment first.

Brett followed her, waited until she locked her door and then resumed walking behind her as they went down the narrow stairs. He hung back just enough to be able to watch her descent and to enjoy the view of that descent. He especially savored the way her hips moved from side to side.

It was a great deal like watching poetry in motion, he realized, his eyes never straying from the view.

It made him rather sorry that the stairway wasn't twice as long.

Turning around at the base of the stairs, Alisha looked at him, noting the expression on his face. "Why are you smiling like that?"

His sense of self-preservation had him quickly manufacturing a neutral answer. "Just looking forward to spending the day with you, Lady Doc. Just looking forward to spending the day."

Alisha had a feeling there was more to it than that, but she decided that it might be wiser to keep that thought to herself.

Chapter Fourteen

"This is all yours?" Alisha finally asked, breaking the silence.

They had been driving for a while now, and Brett had gone through a parted, partially rotting gate about fifteen minutes ago. She wasn't much when it came to judging distances, but that had to have been at least several miles back.

Accustomed to living in an area comprised of tall buildings with glimmers of grass every so often—usually pushing their way through cracks in the sidewalk—even after five weeks out here, this was a whole new experience for her. Here there was nothing but grass—and the occasional tree—no matter which way she looked. And the sky, she had to admit, was incredible, so blue that it almost hurt to look at it.

"Technically, that's what the will said," Brett answered. The ranch house was coming into view in the distance. He drove toward it. "But I'm sharing it with my brothers."

Somehow, she would have expected nothing less of him. She had come to realize that family was very important to Brett. Alisha caught herself thinking that her father would have liked him. A lot.

Now, where had that come from? she wondered defensively.

"Very generous of you," she told him.

He shrugged off the compliment—if that was the way she had meant it. With Alisha, because of the tone she used so often, he was never quite sure if she was being serious or sarcastic.

"Well, if it's one-third each theirs," he told her, "they'll be more willing to pitch in and help out when I need them."

Because she'd been raised to always strive for goals, to never just sit back and let things be, she assumed he had some sort of a plan for this ranch he'd inherited.

"So what are you going to do with it?" she asked.

He laughed shortly. What he intended to do with all this was still a mystery to him.

"Haven't a clue," he admitted. "Raise cattle on it or maybe horses. Or I could farm it—the soil's pretty rich."

"Are you considering selling it?" she asked.

"Why?" he asked with a grin. "Are you considering buying it?"

She was startled by the question, and it took her a second to answer coherently. "Oh, no, I'm not."

She didn't want to mislead him; it was just that if she'd inherited property like this, the first thing she would have thought of was selling it. But then, she hadn't grown up in these wide-open spaces. Maybe being a landowner appealed to him more than running that saloon of his.

"Right now, this is all just a big question mark to me," he told her, gesturing at the view before them. "About the only thing I do know is that the ranch house on it needs a lot of work."

He glanced at her to see if she was going to make a comment. The glance turned into a gaze. Her profile was even more striking in the morning light than it was inside his saloon with only the artificial light to enhance her features.

Damn, but she was beautiful, he caught himself thinking.

"Aren't you supposed to be looking at the road?" Alisha asked, pointing to the windshield and what lay beyond it.

"I checked the road," he drawled. "Don't worry. It's not going anywhere."

With the road wide open in front of him, there was very little danger of his running into anything as long as he checked periodically that there were no stray animals making a mad dash toward his truck's grillwork.

Alisha could almost feel his eyes studying her. Her adrenaline rose a notch, sending the blood rushing through her veins.

Had she made a mistake, agreeing to come out here like this with him?

"What's the matter?" she asked a little too casually, trying to cover up the fact that having him look at her like that made all sorts of things inside her grow skittish. "Didn't I get all the soap off my face this morning?"

"Your face is perfect," he told her softly. "Just like the rest of you."

Wow, she thought; if she'd been younger and more impressionable, that would have had her dazzled and floating at least five inches off the ground. But no more.

"I'm from New York, Murphy," she told him as crisply as possible. "Nobody sold me a bridge all the years that I lived there."

He knew what she was saying, that she thought he was just flattering her in an attempt to seduce her. It was more complicated than that, although the thought of seducing her was exceedingly appealing.

"Not trying to sell you a bridge, Lady Doc," he told her mildly. "Just telling it like it is."

She did what she could to steel herself off from his golden tongue.

"Where are you taking me, really?" she asked, doing her best to mask the butterflies that were wildly flapping their wings in her stomach.

"To see the ranch house," he answered simply, even though he knew she'd figured that part out for herself. "I thought I'd get your opinion."

She looked at him, confused. He'd mentioned that when he'd first asked her. Was he actually serious? *Her* opinion?

"Hate to break this to you, Murphy, but I know nothing about ranch houses."

"You can still tell if something looks like it's worth saving." It wasn't a question; it was a matter-of-fact statement. "But that's not the only reason I asked you to come out with me."

"Oh?" Here it came, she thought, bracing herself, wondering if this was where a really nice guy suddenly turned into a demanding male.

Brett nodded. "I just wanted to spend a little time alone with you before word started to spread."

What was he talking about? For a second, her mind was blank. Was he referring to the fact that he'd kissed her, and she had willingly kissed back? Did that somehow set her apart? She sincerely doubted it, not in this day and age, not even in a small town like Forever.

Alisha stared at him, not knowing what to make of what he had just said.

"By now," he went on to explain for her benefit, "everyone in town undoubtedly thinks you're a hero—or heroine, if you prefer."

For some reason, his words brought a sense of relief to her. "Why would they think that?"

"Well, you did save Nathan's life," Brett pointed out.

That part was true, but she was a doctor. It was what she was *supposed* to do, what she was trained for. There were no special accolades for that.

"I just did what any other doctor would do. My job," she emphasized.

The fact that she wasn't trying to make what she did come off heroic acted in her favor. He liked her modesty. Hell, he was realizing that he liked everything about her.

"The point is, we don't have any other doctor. Dan's hurt, so he couldn't have operated, and if you weren't here, we would have had to get Nathan over to Pine Ridge pronto. Pine Ridge is roughly fifty miles away. In the condition Nathan was in, the trip there with all its bumps and what have yous would have probably caused that appendix of his to explode on him. The upshot of it is that he would have most likely been dead by the time he arrived at the hospital. So, pure and simple, that makes you the heroine of the tale," he concluded, slowing down his truck.

"No," Alisha contradicted him, "that makes you a very imaginative man. It was no big deal." Although, she had to admit, if only to herself, that she was very satisfied—as well as gratified—with her own performance. Until that night, she had either assisted in the more difficult surgeries or performed a handful of very simple, by-the-book surgeries. Nathan's surgery had been way more complicated and taxing. Performing that appendectomy by herself, even under Dan's watchful eye, made it official. She was a real doctor now, she thought with pride.

"It is to Nathan," Brett was saying. He finally came to a stop, having pulled up in front of a weather-beaten, single-story ranch house that was badly in need of some tender loving care—and *soon*. "We're here," he announced needlessly.

Alisha managed to maintain a straight face as she asked, "How can you tell?"

"A sense of humor," he noted with approval. "Good. You're gonna need one if you decide to stay on in Forever."

Did he think she was still debating that? She'd just assumed that everyone thought she was staying on. The thought had made her feel somewhat trapped when she let it—as well as feel guilty if she decided to take off. The truth of it was, Brett's approach left her more inclined to consider staying in Forever. It wasn't freedom she required as much as the option of freedom.

She caught herself smiling.

"I'll let you in on a little secret," she told Brett as she unbuckled her seat belt. "I'll need a sense of humor no matter where I am." Getting out of the passenger side, she took a closer look at the outside of the ranch house. The paint was curling off in sections. "You weren't kidding, were you?" she marveled. Stepping clear of his truck, she surveyed the house slowly. The view didn't improve. If anything, it grew worse.

Brett shut his door and came around to her side. "About?"

She gestured toward the unhappy building. "The house needing work."

The structure was desperately in need of not just a fresh coat of paint, but it also appeared to be badly in need of structural repair. The sun had baked parts of the exterior, causing it to deteriorate to the point that there were sections that looked as if all she had to do was blow on them, and they would just disintegrate right before her eyes.

"Actually," she decided, "if the inside is as bad as the outside, I think you might be better off starting from scratch."

He'd already toyed with that idea, but he pretended that this was the first time he'd faced that option. "You mean just knocking it all down and building something brand-new?"

She nodded. Hands on her hips, she scrutinized the entire exterior.

"That would be my take on it. But maybe I'm wrong," she allowed, turning toward him. "Maybe the interior is fabulous, making it worthwhile saving the building."

The interior was just as bad as the exterior, but he refrained from saying as much for now. She'd see that for herself soon enough. Instead, he gamely said, "Only one way to find out."

Brett extended his hand to her.

After the briefest of hesitations, Alisha placed her hand in his. She pretended not to notice the flash of electricity that went through her—just as it had the last time. You'd think she would have gotten used to this, she silently lectured.

"Okay," she said, matching his tone, "Let's find out."

There were four steps leading up to the front porch

and the front door. Those, too, were in need of repair. Even more so, it turned out, than some of the rest of the house.

Her shoe went right through the rotting board. With nothing under her foot to support it, her right leg went straight down through the hole that had opened up when she put her weight on the step. Her body thrown off balance, Alisha started to fall.

She had no idea just how far down she might have fallen—the basement was right under the porch—had Brett not been holding her hand. The second the wood cracked and gave way, he instinctively pulled her back, keeping her above the ground. The sudden movement made her stumble backward against him, causing Brett to lose his footing. They both wound up falling backward to the ground.

Through sheer luck, Brett managed to break her fall by giving her something to cushion her body—him.

Flushed, the air momentarily knocked out of her, Alisha found it took her a second to orient herself and another full second to realize that she was lying right on top of him, face-to-face.

Belatedly, she realized that, thanks to him, she wasn't hurt.

The thought that he had taken the impact for both of them quickly followed. Horrified that Brett had gotten hurt because of her, she scrambled to one side while simultaneously apologizing and expressing her concern.

"Oh, my God, Brett, I'm sorry. Are you all right?" she cried, quickly scanning him for any bones that might have been sticking out awkwardly. None were. But that still didn't mean that he hadn't broken anything, she thought.

"I think my chances of running a marathon just diminished," he cracked.

She drew back to look at his expression. "Does that mean you're all right or delirious?" she questioned.

His mouth curved just the slightest bit. "Is there a third choice?"

She continued to scrutinize him as she hovered over him. The fact that Brett wasn't cavalierly getting to his feet worried her. She'd come to know him in the past few weeks, and this wasn't like him.

"You *are* hurt," she cried in dismay. He was hurt, and it was all her fault.

"Not sure yet," he answered honestly. "Taking inventory now."

Really worried at this point, Alisha went into doctor mode. She began pressing first one limb, then the other, working her way along each length slowly, gently and methodically.

When she saw him wince, she asked, "Does this hurt?"

"No." Brett's answer came out in a huff of breath as he exhaled heavily.

She didn't like the sound of that. Was he one of those macho males who refused to admit that he was suffering any pain until it turned out to be too late? Determined to be thorough, she kept on going.

"How about this?" she asked as her fingers kneaded the muscles along his other leg a little harder than before.

When he gave her a negative reply—which still didn't sound all that convincing to her—Alisha slowly examined both his arms. Somehow, she wound up being bracketed by them without fully knowing how that had happened.

It reminded her too much of an embrace that was about to happen. She deliberately moved a little back from him, even as she went on with the examination.

"Stop looking at me like I'm a sandwich, and you're hungry," she instructed, then chided when he didn't seem to be paying attention, "And you're not responding to me."

His smile was sly and managed to get to her at what seemed like the speed of light. "Oh, I'm responding to you, all right," he told her in a low whisper. "Maybe you should stop squeezing like that," he suggested. "You might get more of a response than you bargained for."

She could feel the blush taking over, turning her skin an embarrassing shade of pink. *Stop it. You're a doctor first, a woman second. Act like it!*

"Then you're really not hurt?" she questioned uncertainly. She was eyeing him with more concern than nervousness at this point.

One side of his mouth rose in a devilish half smile that she did her very best to ignore. "At least not where you can see."

On her feet first, Alisha extended her hand to him and waited.

Although Brett could get up on his own power—and did—he took hold of her hand anyway. Once on his feet, he continued holding her hand, his eyes on hers.

The silence grew deafening as it surrounded them. Having her land on top of him like that when his guard was temporarily down had caused havoc to run riot through his entire body, momentarily reducing him to a mass of needs and desires.

Reminding him just how very attracted he was to this woman, not just because of her looks, which he found stunning, but because of the person he had discovered beneath those polished looks. A person worth knowing.

"I'm a doctor," she heard herself saying to him, the words leaving her lips in near-to-slow motion. "Maybe we should step inside the house, and you can show me where it actually hurts."

Brett looked at her for a long moment, wondering if she knew what she was saying. He decided that she did—and not because it was wishful thinking on his part.

With a nod of his head, he released her hand. "Walk behind me so you don't run the risk of falling through another step. I wouldn't want to lose you."

Was that a flippant remark—or something more? *Wishful thinking, idiot,* she upbraided herself. *Get a grip!*

Alisha did as he instructed without comment, listening instead to the sound of her own heart slipping into double time.

She was acutely aware of the fact that she hadn't been with anyone since she'd thrown her engagement ring at Pierce.

Before, actually, since she and Pierce had hit a dry spell before the incident. The dry spell had gone on for almost a month because her schedule didn't mesh with his at the hospital. Each time she was free, he wasn't and vice versa.

It was only after she caught him making love to another woman that she realized their schedules hadn't meshed because Pierce had seen to it that they didn't. He'd told a mutual friend that he wanted to experiment with other women before *having to go through the charade of being faithful to a wife.*

She dwelled on the thought as a last-ditch effort to talk herself out of what she was about to do. After all, she'd sworn off having anything to do with good-looking men because of the disappointment they represented.

But thinking of Pierce didn't make her back away from Brett. Instead, it seemed to have exactly the opposite effect.

It made her feel things, need things, that all centered around this saloon owner/would-be cowboy with the wicked, wicked mouth.

They made it to the porch without further incident. The front door, she discovered, was unlocked. It was apparently in keeping with most of Forever, where people locked their doors only at night—if then. The other, more obvious reason the door was unlocked became apparent on closer scrutiny. Someone had taken the lock out, leaving a hole where metal should have been.

Alisha barely noticed. The beating of her heart, not to mention the fact that her whole being was heating to an almost dangerous degree, had her focused on only one thing: the man who was with her.

The man, she turned around to look at, who was closing the more-than-useless door behind him. The sound of it meeting the door frame echoed inside her chest, signaling a beginning.

"So," she began, her mouth inexplicably dry enough to safely house dust, "do you want to show me where it hurts?"

Brett slipped his hands into her hair, framing her face as he brought his mouth closer to hers. Yes, he ached physically, but that had more to do with her than the fall he had taken.

"Later," he replied. "I'll show you later."

"And now?" she managed to ask, her voice dropping down to a whisper as everything inside her scrambled for a vantage point, silently begging him not to turn away, not to bring her up to this throbbing expectation and then back off.

She'd had so many disappointments, she didn't think she could endure another one, even though this man wasn't the forever kind. He was just someone who had the power to dull the fierce ache, to silence the loud pain now echoing through her entire being. The pain that was bringing her to the edge of her resolve and having her teeter there, turning her into a casualty at any moment.

"And now," he whispered back, his breath feathering along her lips, "we have something else to do, something else to occupy us."

Drawing her in closer to him, he kissed her. At first very lightly, his lips hardly touching hers. All that did was cause the hunger inside both of them to escalate to an almost uncontrollable size.

He kissed her again, longer this time.

The third kiss absorbed them both and sealed their fate—even if neither one of them realized it at that exact moment.

Chapter Fifteen

Looking back later, it was as if a frenzy had seized her. Alisha felt a desire so large, so strong, she wasn't certain just how to approach it, how to begin to contain it, and she was far less certain just how she could appease it.

All she knew was that this desire consumed her, and she instinctively sensed that she would know no peace until she was somehow brought to that final, incredible pinnacle where all these demanding sensations were finally released.

That she was even thinking like this surprised her.

This just wasn't like her.

While, for the most part, she had enjoyed lovemaking with Pierce, the act itself had never been the foremost entity in her life. It certainly was never this all-pervading hunger that threatened to undo her if she didn't feel that exquisite sensation exploding throughout her body.

But this, this urgency, was quite unique. She'd sensed it the moment the lyrical dance between them had begun.

Everywhere Brett touched her, he made her crazy, fueling her need rather than satisfying her desire. Every pass of his lips along her skin, every caress of his warm, gentle hands just heightened her excitement, increased her need. Made her passions grow that much more volatile.

This was different. *She* was different because she felt if she couldn't ascend the summit with Brett, couldn't attain that wondrous fulfillment that each touch of his promised, she would disintegrate into a pile of ashes.

Eagerly, she tugged against his clothing, needing to feel his skin against hers, needing to touch him the way he was touching her.

She knew, *knew* this was insanity, yet she couldn't stop herself, couldn't just regain possession of her sensible side and back away. She *needed* to become one with him, even if it was for only a moment.

This had never been, even remotely, part of her plan for coming to this tiny dot of a place. She hadn't come here looking for love or even acceptance. If anything, the opposite had been true. She came here not to feel anything at all, to purge herself of the ability to *feel* anything at all.

But the exact opposite had happened. She knew that love was far too much to hope for, but some reasonable facsimile would do in its place. At least for now.

Brett made her feel gloriously alive. Somehow, when she hadn't been paying attention, he had managed to open the tomb that she had locked herself into. Opened it and brought her out so that she could see the sunlight. More than that, Brett had somehow succeeded in making her *want* to see the sunlight.

Single-handedly, he had brought light into her darkened world.

Her head was spinning, and she knew that half the thoughts running through her brain could easily be discounted as just so much rambling nonsense once they were dragged out into the light of day. But right now, at this moment, it was all making complete sense to her.

She let the last little tether that was anchoring her to reality go—and became completely his.

ALISHA WAS UNDOING HIM.

Layer by layer, she was stripping him bare, making him want her with an intensity that not only surprised him but downright unnerved him, as well. It did everything but rattle his teeth.

Lord knew he had never wanted for female companionship. Since practically in the cradle, he had been blessed with an easy charm that drew women to him like tiny iron filings to a giant magnet.

As far back as he could remember, he was never alone if he didn't want to be. But the attraction he held for the female of the species neither fed his ego nor gave him an inflated sense of self. It did, however, allow him to perceive the world in a certain light. He'd never once experienced wanting someone and being in doubt as to the outcome.

Here, despite the fact that Alisha was with him, in his arms, igniting him like a torch dipped in kerosene, he wasn't certain of her, wasn't assured that the next time he desired her this way, she would be here.

This match was different for him, and it both frightened him and intrigued him—mainly because what he was feeling gave this woman power over him, and he had never been in that sort of a situation before. He had *always* been the one with the power, the one in charge, and while he had never abused that power, never inflicted himself on a woman or had taken advantage of a situation, even in the most cursory of ways, he didn't know what it felt like not to be the dominant one.

Now he knew.

And yet, rather than run for cover, the way common sense would have dictated that he do, Brett wanted to be exactly where he was. Right here, in this moment, with this woman.

With each article of clothing he peeled away from her, he grew more inflamed, more eager to possess her. More hungry for the feel of her.

He didn't recognize himself.

It didn't matter. All that mattered at this moment was Alisha.

The furniture within the ranch house was large and comfortable and dusty. It was scarcely noticed and, for the most part, ignored. They moved from piece to piece, exploring one another, raising the stakes even as they raised one another's temperatures to dangerous new heights.

Did she realize how crazy she was making him?

Did she begin to understand what all this was doing to him? He doubted it. It was hard for even him to make sense of it.

The feel of her lips, skimming along his skin like the soft, fluttering wings of a butterfly delicately, fleetingly, perching on a flower, had his heart racing at speeds he hadn't thought possible.

He wasn't sure what turned him on more: when she teased him this way or when she allowed the full measure of her intensity to break through.

All he knew was that if he didn't have her soon, didn't completely lose himself within her, he would self-destruct.

Pulling her against him, he possessively stroked the length of her body, bringing both of them to the very brink of an explosive climax, then drawing back. He did it twice—until he wasn't able to hold himself in check a single microsecond longer.

Pushing Alisha back against the overstuffed deep green cushions of the sofa, he raised himself over her.

She was all that existed for him.

Bracketing her face with his hands, his eyes holding hers, Brett began to ease himself into her.

But what had started as an exercise in restraint quickly took on a life of its own. Shifting gears, he began to move his hips more and more swiftly against hers.

Hardly able to catch her breath, Alisha wrapped her legs around his torso, matching his every thrust, going ever faster and mimicking his every movement.

And then she was gasping for air as the euphoria seized her, bringing her up higher still until she finally felt Brett's arms tightening possessively around her. He moaned against her lips as they rushed up together to the very top of the peak. One lone, precarious moment and then they were suddenly free-falling down the steep incline together, clutching each other in an effort to preserve the moment.

To preserve themselves.

WHEN SANITY REAPPEARED, making its way to her on tiptoes, Alisha felt her heart pounding so hard, she was certain that it was going to leap out of her chest and then explode.

Gradually, she became aware of the fact that the weight of Brett's body was pinning her down to the cushions. Not hard enough so that she couldn't move if she wanted to, but just enough to allow her to feel every single ridge, every single muscle of his body as it lay pressed against hers.

The *thought* of his hard, nude body pressed against hers pinned her down more than the actual weight of it did.

With a blazing-hot haze still very firmly wrapped around her, Alisha thought she heard his voice. But for the life of her, she really wasn't sure if she was actually hearing Brett speak to her, or if she was just imagining the whole thing.

She strained to make out the words, if there actually were any.

There were.

He was asking, "Did I hurt you?"

Even now, in such a primal situation, he was being thoughtful. The thought made her heart swell.

She couldn't answer him right away. To do that, she would have had to have been able to breathe, and right now, that was an entirely tricky proposition.

It took her two attempts before she could finally manage one word. "No," and that came out in barely a whisper.

"I'm glad," Brett said, feeling her breath feathering along his chest when she answered him. Felt, too, his immediate response to her. His stomach was tightening into a hard knot even as desire was galvanizing the rest of him at an astounding rate. He wanted her again.

Another first, he thought, stroking her hair. That, too, was a first, he realized. He was actually content just to lie here with her head resting on his chest—somehow their positions had gotten reversed in the past few minutes—and her hair spread out all along his pectorals.

Definitely a picture that Rockwell would have painted

had the era the artist lived in been a bit more flexible, Brett mused as he continued to lightly run his fingertips along her hair.

Alisha raised her head to look at him, curious. "Why would you think you hurt me?" To her recollection, she hadn't done anything to indicate any sort of discomfort in any way. The exact opposite was true.

"I was afraid that I might have been a little too rough in my eagerness to make love with you," he told her honestly. He waited a fraction of a moment, then continued, thinking that if there was anyone he could be completely honest with, it was her—although *why* he felt that way, he really couldn't say. "I never wanted anyone with the intensity that I found myself wanting you," he admitted.

Now, there was a line if she'd ever heard one, Alisha couldn't help thinking.

But even as she raised herself up on her elbow to say as much to him—as well as let him know it wasn't necessary, that she really didn't expect this to lead to anything more meaningful than just perhaps another go-round of lovemaking somewhere down the line—the expression that she saw on his face caused her words to just fade from her tongue. The look in his eyes was so sincere, it stole her breath away.

Still, she forced herself to tell him, "You don't have to say that."

"I know," he told her, softly gliding his fingertips along her face. "I don't have to say anything." He lightly brushed his lips against hers. "But I want to. I want you to understand that I didn't have this in mind when I invited you to come see the ranch."

"You didn't?" she said, just the tiniest bit of mocking in her tone.

"Nope. If anything, I think I wanted to show off a little for you, maybe. Impress you with the cowboy side of me." The admission surprised even him, now that he said it. But he also realized that it was true. When was the last time he had wanted to impress *anyone?* He couldn't remember.

"The cowboy side of you?" she echoed.

Granted, she was aware that she was definitely in Texas, and there were cowboys around in this town, but she had never really applied that description to him. He was just Brett—and that was more than enough.

"Sure," he told her, slipping one arm around her and holding her closer to him. "No woman can resist a cowboy."

Turning toward him, she saw humor in his eyes. He was putting her on. Alisha played along. "Oh? And where's that written?"

He pretended to think for a moment. "I'm pretty sure it's in some rule book somewhere."

"I'm not impressed by cowboys," she told him matter-of-factly.

"Oh? Well, I'm fairly sure you're not impressed by the bartender in me."

Her mouth curved just a hint. "You're right. I'm not."

Brett sighed for effect. "You're a hard woman to impress."

"No, not really," she countered, growing serious for a moment. "I'm impressed by decency, by a man who cares for his friends, who cares for his brothers and doesn't put himself first all the time."

She put her hand on his chest and leaned her head

there for a moment as she studied him. If she didn't know any better, she would have said that she was falling in love with him, but she hadn't given herself permission to do that—not ever again.

But if she *was* to fall in love, it would be with him.

"You didn't tell me that you stayed in Forever to raise your orphaned brothers, even though you had a chance to leave town and follow your dreams."

He didn't like to talk about himself and deftly turned the topic sideways. "You're right. I didn't tell you. How did you find out?" he asked.

The smile she offered was damn near dazzling. He could feel its effects all through his body—a very potent reaction right now.

"You do realize that this is a small town, right?" Alisha asked.

He kept on looking at her, finding it hard to hold himself in check. He could feel himself wanting her as much, if not more, than he had just before they'd made love. Brett forced his mind back on the conversation they were having.

"Miss Joan." It wasn't a guess.

She moved her body into his, giving herself permission to savor this interlude a little longer. "That woman is better than a newspaper or a blog. I have *never* met anyone so full of information before."

"She's the town treasure, all right," he agreed. "Did you actually ask her about me?"

It wasn't a smile on her lips so much as a grin. "I didn't have to. Miss Joan was more than happy to volunteer all that information about you without a single question coming from me. She thought I should *know who I was up against*." Amusement highlighted all of her features as she continued. "Who I was renting a room from. I guess she really believes in that old Girl Scout adage, Be Prepared."

She was making him absolutely crazy again. Every breath she took, every word she uttered, had her body moving against his. Setting his on fire.

"I think that's actually a Boy Scout rule," he told her with effort.

"Whatever," Alisha replied with a careless shrug, a movement that managed to arouse him even more, if that was humanly possible.

Brett framed her face with his hands, lightly testing the waters before surrendering himself to the need that had risen up within him all over again with a fierceness and a fire that refused to be subdued.

"Remind me to send Miss Joan flowers," he murmured against her lips just before he deepened the kiss that swept them back into a world that only the two of them were allowed to inhabit.

"I TAKE IT you had a good day off," Holly said to her cheerfully when she walked into the clinic the next morning.

Alisha realized that she was humming and promptly stopped. Although she had a feeling it was a little late for that. Especially when she saw the expression on the nurse's face. As if Holly knew exactly what she was experiencing at this very moment—and what had caused this feeling.

"It was—interesting," Alisha admitted, deliberately choosing a word that seemed neutral to her.

"I think it was more than that," Holly told her with a knowing smile, then, for good measure, added, "You're glowing."

She was? Alisha couldn't remember being accused of that even when she had first become engaged to Pierce. Looking back, she realized that she hadn't felt this level of happiness, of contentment at that time.

Don't get carried away, 'Lish. This is just temporary, a wonderful, delicious interlude, not forever, remember?

"Must be the lighting," she said out loud with a shrug.

Holly laughed. "I don't think so. The lighting in the clinic isn't *that* good." They were alone in the clinic right now since the doors had just been opened and for once, there was no one waiting to get in. Even so, Holly still lowered her voice when she asked, "So, what did you think of Brett's ranch?"

Stunned, Alisha's mouth dropped open. Denial was the first thing that occurred to her. The second thing that occurred to her was that denial was undoubtedly probably futile.

So instead, she asked, "How did you know I went to see his ranch?"

"One of my brothers-in-law saw you and Brett driving to the old Robertson place. Rafe," she added for good measure, in case Alisha wondered who had spotted them.

Alisha sighed, shaking her head. "There is no privacy in this town, is there?" That still took some getting used to.

"Not so you'd notice," Holly replied matter-of-factly. "But on the plus side, there's always someone to turn to if there's a problem because we take care of our own and are there for each other the way people in the big city aren't."

Holly paused, as if debating whether or not to say

something. As a rule, she was rather quiet and tried not to interfere, but she'd blossomed a bit in the past year, after marrying Ray Rodriguez. "For what it's worth, I think that Brett is way overdue for some happiness of his own."

That was an odd thing to say, Alisha thought. If anyone in the town seemed to be carefree, it was Brett. Was she wrong?

"Oh? Brett Murphy didn't strike me as exactly being a solemn, unhappy man. His female customers seem to all flock to him." Even as she pointed that out, she realized that she was somewhat jealous of those women. Now, there was a new sensation for her.

Holly waved her hand at that. "That's just Brett's surface charm, but that's not who he is. He stepped up when first his parents died in a car accident and then when his uncle Patrick died suddenly. Took over running Murphy's and seeing to it that his brothers stayed in school, had the right work ethic, things like that. That takes a rare kind of man."

"Yes," Alisha quietly murmured. "I know."

Telling herself that she had to be careful and not fall into a trap that would ultimately spell disappointment was getting to be more and more difficult for her.

The door to the clinic opened just then, and she was relieved to see that their first patient of the day had arrived. It was time to get to work.

Chapter Sixteen

If she'd hoped that, despite Holly's inquiry, she could somehow keep the fact that she and Brett were seeing one another apart from the usual public encounters, that idea died a very quick death the first time she walked into the diner after being with Brett.

Miss Joan took one look at her, sidled up to her table with a fresh cup of coffee and happily observed, "Looks like someone had her candle lit."

She had made one vain attempt to discourage Miss Joan's assumption, feigning ignorance. "What does that even mean, Miss Joan?"

"Don't play dumb with me, Doc. You know exactly what that means. Neither one of us was born yesterday," Miss Joan had asserted with a decisive nod of her head before sauntering off with her coffeepot.

After that, Alisha saw no point in making any denials. She and Brett were together for however long *together* would last. Atypically, she made no plans for *tomorrow,* wanting only to enjoy today.

Her todays knit themselves together, and before she knew it, a couple of months had gone by. And then part of another.

It was all good.

EVER SO SLOWLY, Alisha eased the covers off her body and sat up, careful to do it very quietly. She took in a long breath and slowly exhaled it, focusing on nothing more than the moment.

It was hard to believe that over five months had gone by since she had arrived in Forever. The first few days she'd spent in the small town had felt as if they had moved with the speed of a three-footed, injured tortoise. The past month or so had raced by like the tortoise's nemesis, the hare.

That was because she was happy.

Right after she'd performed the appendectomy on Nathan McLane, everything changed. People's somewhat skeptical attitude toward her changed. They accepted her, and she'd found a place for herself, not only in the clinic, but in the general scheme of things in Forever.

Nobody brought up the subject of her possibly moving on anymore, not even Miss Joan. That part she knew was due to the fact that when she wasn't at the clinic, she was with Brett—or he was with her. The bottom line on that was that they were together.

Together. She liked the sound of that, she mused.

She was supposed to be getting dressed, but she lingered just a minute longer, focusing on her contentment. Alisha looked over her shoulder at the object of that contentment—the sleeping man in her bed.

Before she'd arrived in Forever, she would have bet everything she owned that she was never, *ever* going to even *look* at another handsome man, much less place herself in a compromising situation with one. And she certainly would never believe a single word out of that good-looking man's mouth. After all, she considered herself reasonably intelligent. At the very least, she wasn't a village idiot, doomed to be drawn to good-looking men, condemned to making the same mistakes over and over again in a vain hope that this time, the results would be different.

But then, it hadn't been Brett's extremely good looks that had won her over; it'd been his heart. He was a good, decent, kind man who just happened to have a face that could send a woman's heart racing at a hundred miles an hour.

At times, she had to stop, take a breath and allow herself to just be happy because there was still something inside her that was waiting for things to blow up, to go wrong. Waiting for paradise to fold up its tent and disappear into the night, leaving weeds and desolation in its wake.

But that had been her life before, with Pierce, not now. And she planned to enjoy the *hell* out of it until such time that it all ended on her.

Enough with this ruminating—she had hands to hold and medical wisdom to dispense.

Squaring her shoulders, she started to get up from the edge of the bed when she suddenly felt a strong, muscular arm snake itself around her waist, effectively immobilizing her.

"Don't go," Brett mumbled, part of his voice being absorbed by his pillow. "Not time to get up yet," he protested.

Not quite awake, he'd been watching her, or rather her back, and thinking to himself that he'd finally, *finally* lucked out, finally found a woman who he wanted to wake up next to for the rest of his days.

He'd given it time, patiently waiting for that feeling to fade. It only grew stronger with each day that went by.

The feeling was real. And so was she.

"Oh, more than time to get up, sleepyhead," she laughed, shifting on the bed to look at him more directly. "At least for me. You don't open that bar of yours for another few hours, so you can go on getting your beauty sleep. Me, I've got patients probably lining up even as we speak."

Brett didn't loosen his hold on her waist. "They'll wait," he assured her, his voice now devoid of its sleepy state. "It's not like there's another clinic they can take their business to. And Dan's there."

Alisha began to protest only to find herself being pulled back down on the bed. She thought of struggling, but that idea was without appeal.

"Dan's *not* there," she contradicted him. When Brett flashed her a look of confusion, she explained, "Now that his shoulder is better, he's finally getting ready to go on that vacation." That was one of the main reasons Dan had wanted an associate, someone to occasionally take over for him. "I'm supposed to be covering for him. That was the whole point of his getting a second doctor, remember?" Alisha pretended to peer into his face to see if any of this was ringing a bell. "Is any of this coming back to you?" she asked.

Brett shook his head, then said, "Maybe after I have my early-morning pick-me-up."

The gleam in his eyes caused her stomach to flutter. "Which is?" she asked in a hushed voice.

Raising his head for a second, he brushed his lips across hers before allowing his head to fall back against the pillow again. "Guess."

She really, really should start getting ready. Otherwise, she ran the risk of being late, and she prided herself on never being late. "Brett—"

The grin on his lips turned wicked. "You fight me on this, and it's just going to take you that much longer to get to the clinic. If you want my opinion," he said sagely, "you might as well surrender, Lady Doc."

"You'd like that, wouldn't you?" she said, still pretending to resist.

"You have no idea." He caught her earlobe between his teeth and sent a hot shiver down her spine before releasing it.

She could feel a thrill zigzagging all through her, taking her prisoner. Alisha laughed and surrendered. "Might as well," she agreed wholeheartedly, opening up her arms to him.

ALTHOUGH SHE HURRIEDLY threw on her clothes when it was over, Alisha was still late. She didn't get to the clinic until an hour later. The doors had been opened only ten minutes earlier, so she silently lectured herself that she hadn't committed a cardinal sin being ten minutes late. Cardinal sins clocked in at twenty minutes, a voice in her head that sounded oddly like Miss Joan said.

She supposed if she took that sort of a blasé approach, then she didn't feel too bad over having given in to herself—and to Brett. After all, it had been one exquisite, albeit far too short, detour to a haven that was exclusively theirs.

Without realizing it, she was humming as she crossed the threshold. Holly was already in the office, seated at her desk. Alisha was aware that there were several others in the waiting room when she breezed in, but if she stopped to see who, that would only make her that much more late. She could catch up with whoever was out there once she had him or her in her exam room. There was a great deal of merit in Dan's principle of getting to know the whole patient, not just a body part.

"Beautiful day, isn't it, Holly," she stated rather than asked the young woman. "I'll be ready in a couple of minutes," she promised as she crossed to the inner office door. "What's the schedule look like today?" she asked by way of conversation. "Filled to the brim?"

Holly raised her eyes to hers. Alisha caught herself thinking that she had never seen the nurse looking that withdrawn before.

"Not too full yet," Holly replied.

Alisha stopped walking and took a second look at the young woman. She didn't look ill, but she certainly looked uncomfortable. "Something wrong, Holly?"

"There're a lot of things wrong, starting with having to live in a town that could pass itself off as an inkblot."

The voice came from behind her. Alisha froze the second she heard it.

It can't be, her mind cried. It just couldn't be who she thought it was.

Please don't let it be him.

Because she refused to behave like a coward, Alisha squared her shoulders and her resolve as she forced herself to turn around.

Her heart sank.

A second later, her anger kicked in.

"What the hell are you doing here?" she demanded, her eyes narrowing into slits.

Pierce's smile reminded her of the Cheshire cat—it was cold and without an ounce of humanity to it.

"What's the matter, Alisha? Aren't you happy to see me?" he asked her.

Ever the egoist, she thought.

Wearing a freshly pressed three-piece dove-gray suit custom made for him by some trendy designer house, Pierce was far too dapper for his surroundings. She'd never seen anyone so out-of-place-looking in her life, and that included her during her first week here.

Since there were several other people in the waiting room, she didn't want to cause a scene. But neither did she want to sequester herself with him because that would somehow lead to allowing the man to believe he had the upper hand.

So she remained where she was as she bluntly answered his question. "No, I'm not happy to see you."

She saw anger flash across his brow before he said with deliberate, measured cadence, "Even though I've come to rescue you?"

"News flash—I don't need rescuing," she informed him tersely.

His laugh was dismissive, rude and condescending. "Oh, c'mon. You can't mean that. Living out here in this godforsaken place? Are you that far gone that you think you actually *belong* here?" he asked incredulously.

Out of the corner of her eye, she saw Holly picking up the phone and calling someone. The sheriff? she guessed. She wanted to handle this on her own, but it wasn't a bad idea to have a plan B if this turned ugly, she decided.

"The person who doesn't belong here is you," she informed him coldly. "Now, please leave."

Pierce shifted his weight, a sure sign of his growing impatience. "Can we go somewhere and talk privately?" It was more of a demand than a request.

A demand Alisha chose to ignore. "No," she said flatly. "Whatever you came to say, say it and then please leave."

Pierce glared at her, and for a moment, she was certain he was going to turn on his well-heeled shoe and storm out. But then, looking as if he was waging some sort of internal battle with himself, he said, "I came to tell you I was wrong. That I made a mistake and that I'm—I'm sorry." He all but spat out the last words, clearly not happy about having to say them in front of an audience of what he viewed as his inferiors. "If you give me another chance, I promise that I'll more than make it up to you."

She was well aware of the way he *made things up* when he was guilty of transgressions, and she didn't doubt for a moment that there would be more of them.

"I don't need more jewelry, Pierce." Her eyes locked with his. She was not about to back down. "And I certainly don't need more lies."

"I did a lot of soul-searching these last few months," Pierce began again, clearly seeking to wear her down and obviously fully convinced that he could.

She thought she was going to choke. "Soul-searching?" she echoed, stunned. "I wasn't aware that you had one."

His mouth turned ugly, but he caught himself at the last minute. "Okay, I deserve that. I deserve a lot worse," he conceded. "But I've changed, and all I want is a chance to prove it to you."

A pig had more of a chance of changing into a shining Boeing 797, Alisha thought, than he had of changing his ways.

"What's the matter, Pierce? Did you find out your grandmother put in a clause in her will that says you have to be married to someone your parents approve of before you can get the rest of your inheritance?"

She'd meant it as a flippant remark, but she saw something flicker in his eyes before they went completely flat. She stared at him in wonder.

"That's it, isn't it? For some reason, in order to get your hands on the rest of that money, you need a suitable match. Well, I'm sorry, Pierce, but breaking up with you was the second smartest thing I ever did."

"What's the first?" Nathan McLane, in for his post-op checkup, asked. The man, who had the place of honor as her favorite patient since he was responsible for everything else changing for her, leaned forward in his chair in order to hear her answer.

"Coming to Forever," she told Nathan.

"Shut up. This doesn't concern you," Pierce snapped at Nathan, his very stance threatening the man with physical harm if he said another word.

Nathan didn't only because someone else did.

"Wrong. Anything that concerns Alisha concerns not only him, but all of us," the deep male voice declared firmly.

Relieved and surprised, Alisha turned around to see that Brett had walked into the clinic. His very gait challenged the stranger in their midst.

Alisha still had to ask, "What are you doing here?"

He nodded toward the nurse, who finally relaxed now that he was here. "Holly thought you might need reinforcements."

"What she needs," Pierce informed him disdainfully, "is someone her own intellectual equal." His eyes swept over him contemptuously. "Not some dumb cowboy." Turning from Brett, he addressed Alisha. "Look, I messed up and I'm man enough to say it. Now, stop playing hard to get and let's get your things and get out of this two-bit rattrap. You don't belong here."

She took offense at his dismissal of the town. "Where I don't belong is with you," Alisha retorted icily.

Rather than curse at her and withdraw, Pierce grabbed her by the wrist and yanked her to him. "I said, stop playing hard to get, and let's go. You can make me *suffer* for my past sins when I get you home, if that makes you happy."

The next second, Pierce found himself being yanked up by the back of his suit jacket and spun around. "How about *I* make you suffer, instead?" Brett countered. "And Dr. Cordell's not hard to get. For you, buddy, the lady's impossible to get."

Rather than answer him, Pierce doubled up his fist, threw his entire weight behind it and took a swing at Brett.

Brett saw the punch coming a mile away and skillfully sidestepped it. For a split second, he debated his next move—was he going to be magnanimous or was he going to give this pompous ass what he deserved?

The next minute, he made up his mind and muttered, "Oh, the hell with it." He punched Pierce squarely on the jaw, sending the man sprawling down on the floor, howling in pain and cursing a blue streak. Brett grabbed him by his shirtfront and said, "Now, you listen to me and you listen well. If I ever find you coming back and bothering this woman again, if I hear that you're even *thinking* about bothering her again, there will be more things on your body that hurt than just your jaw. And I'm talking permanent pain. Are we clear on that?" he asked, shouting the question into his face.

Still holding his jaw, Pierce pulled away. He looked accusingly at Alisha. "You can't be serious. Him? You're picking *him* over me?" There was no way to measure how completely stunned he was over her choice.

"I'd pick him seven days a week over you," Alisha fired back. "Without even trying, he's ten times the man you will *ever* be. Now, get out of my clinic and out of my town," she ordered. "I have patients to see."

"You'll be sorry for this!" Pierce shouted at her.

"Only if I ever see your smug face again," she replied.

"You heard the lady," Brett said, taking hold of Pierce and *escorting* him out the door. "Leave!"

Brett remained standing there like a sentry, watching as Alisha's former fiancé got into his vehicle and drove away. He stood there for several minutes in case Pierce did a U-turn and came back in.

"He's gone," he told her.

His declaration was met with a smattering of applause that swelled and grew until everyone in the waiting room, as well as Holly, was on their feet, clapping with feeling.

Brett was concerned with only one person in that gathering. He crossed to Alisha, then held his hand up before her first patient of the day, Nathan, rose to follow her into the back of the clinic.

"Before she gets started, I'd like a minute to have a word with Lady Doc here," Brett said.

Nathan sank back down in his chair. "I've waited

this long. I can wait a little longer," he told Brett philosophically.

"Thanks." Brett nodded at him just before he secured Alisha's hand in his and hurried into the back of the clinic with her.

He went into the first exam room he came to and closed the door. While living in Forever was a lot like living in a fishbowl, this he wanted to keep between him and her until such time as he was ready for it to be made public.

"Did you mean what you said out there?" he asked Alisha.

"Probably," she allowed cautiously. "I said a lot of things out there. Which part are you asking about?"

She knew damn well what he was asking her. With a sigh, he spelled it out for her. "The part where you said you'd pick me over him."

He had to ask? she thought, surprised. "Of course I meant it. Pierce is a weasel and you're—not," she concluded, not wanting to flatter him too much and make him feel as if she was crowding him.

"And that's it?" he asked skeptically. "Nothing more?"

She hesitated, then asked, "Such as?"

It took effort for him to curb his impatience. "Such as you were his fiancée."

"Okay..." she replied slowly. She wasn't following him at all. "Brett, where's this going?"

How could he make it clearer than that? he wanted to know. "I'd like to have equal time. I'd like to have *more* than equal time," he emphasized.

The last thing she wanted to do was jump to the wrong conclusion and possibly ruin everything. So she shook her head and said—or began to say, "I don't—"

Okay, okay, he'd put his cards on the table. "I want you to be *my* fiancée— Oh, hell," he cried in frustration. "I want you to be my wife."

She blinked, feeling as though her head was short-circuiting, and she was hearing things. "Wait, you're going too fast," she protested.

"I can say it slower," he offered, then proceeded to do just that, saying the same words except repeating them in slow motion.

"No," she laughed, putting her hand over his mouth to stop him from going on. "I mean *this* is moving too fast. You haven't even said 'I love you'—"

He remedied that immediately. "I love you."

She shot him an impatient glare. "Like you mean it," she stipulated.

"Like I mean it," he parroted obligingly.

She had a distinct urge to punch him but refrained. "Damn it, Brett, this isn't funny."

Before she could say anything further, he caught her in his arms and held her to him. "No, it's not funny. It's very, very serious. Do you think I would have just asked you to be my wife if it wasn't?"

There went her nerves, frog-leaping over one another. "I don't know. Would you?"

"*No,* I wouldn't," he told her firmly. "And for the record, I've never asked another woman to marry me, and I suspect that I never will. So unless you want me to die alone, a shriveled-up old bachelor, you'll tell me you'll marry me."

She wanted to scream her assent, but she held herself in check. She wanted to make sure the man wasn't going to regret this in a few years. "And you're sure you really want to marry me?"

His grin was from ear to ear. "Never been surer of anything in my whole life."

She was quiet for a moment, taking stock of the situation. He held all the cards. And right now, she wouldn't have it any other way.

"I guess if I ever want to get out of this room and practice medicine again," she told him, "I'd better say yes."

It was done, settled, and he couldn't have been happier. She was his. "I guess so."

"Okay, then," she said obligingly, then paused before uttering a heartfelt "Yes."

Brett took her into his arms and said a split second before he kissed her, "Good answer."

And she knew that it was.

* * * * *

MILLS & BOON®

Want to get more from Mills & Boon?

Here's what's available to you if you join the
exclusive **Mills & Boon eBook Club** today:

✦ *Convenience – choose your books each month*
✦ *Exclusive – receive your books a month before
  anywhere else*
✦ *Flexibility – change your subscription at any time*
✦ *Variety – gain access to eBook-only series*
✦ *Value – subscriptions from just £1.99 a month*

So visit **www.millsandboon.co.uk/esubs** today
to be a part of this exclusive eBook Club!

MILLS & BOON®

Maybe This Christmas

Author of *Sleigh Bells in the Snow*

Sarah
Morgan

Maybe this
Christmas

COMING SOON
OCTOBER 2014

* cover in development

Let Sarah Morgan sweep you away to a perfect
winter wonderland with this wonderful Christmas
tale filled with unforgettable characters, wit,
charm and heart-melting romance!
Pick up your copy today!

www.millsandboon.co.uk/xmas

MILLS & BOON®

Why shop at millsandboon.co.uk?

Each year, thousands of romance readers find their perfect read at millsandboon.co.uk. That's because we're passionate about bringing you the very best romantic fiction. Here are some of the advantages of shopping at www.millsandboon.co.uk:

* **Get new books first**—you'll be able to buy your favourite books one month before they hit the shops

* **Get exclusive discounts**—you'll also be able to buy our specially created monthly collections, with up to 50% off the RRP

* **Find your favourite authors**—latest news, interviews and new releases for all your favourite authors and series on our website, plus ideas for what to try next

* **Join in**—once you've bought your favourite books, don't forget to register with us to rate, review and join in the discussions

Visit **www.millsandboon.co.uk**
for all this and more today!